Patricia Adrian always wante͟   e
penned (literally, with a pen)   ͟
fifth grade. Her interests a͟   ͟
women in history), skulking around social media for much
longer than she should, and reading, particularly when she's
on a tight deadline and should be writing instead.

Patricia lives in Germany and can speak a handful of foreign
languages – English is one of them. She has previously been
longlisted for the Women's Prize for Fiction.

 twitter.com/P_Adrian_Writer

THE BLETCHLEY WOMEN

PATRICIA ADRIAN

One More Chapter
a division of HarperCollins*Publishers*
1 London Bridge Street
London SE1 9GF
www.harpercollins.co.uk
HarperCollins*Publishers*
1st Floor, Watermarque Building, Ringsend Road
Dublin 4, Ireland

This paperback edition 2022
1
First published in Great Britain in ebook format
by HarperCollins*Publishers* 2022

Copyright © Patricia Adrian 2022
Patricia Adrian asserts the moral right to
be identified as the author of this work

A catalogue record of this book is available from the British Library

ISBN: 978-0-00-852602-3

This novel is entirely a work of fiction. The names, characters and incidents portrayed in it are the work of the author's imagination. Any resemblance to actual persons, living or dead, events or localities is fictionalised or coincidental.

Printed and bound in the UK using 100% Renewable Electricity
by CPI Group (UK) Ltd

All rights reserved. No part of this publication may be reproduced, stored in a retrieval system, or transmitted, in any form or by any means, electronic, mechanical, photocopying, recording or otherwise, without the prior permission of the publishers.

For my own sisterhood –
everyone who supported me during the
4 years of writing, re-writing and submitting this manuscript.
It would never have become a book without you

Prologue

Rose

July 1940

I f someone had asked me yesterday how I'd feel about riding in the back of an Army lorry, blindfolded, towards an unknown destination, the last thing I would've said would have been 'cold'. And rather annoyed that my carefully concocted plan had been blown to pieces. Even worse, nobody had bothered to tell me where we're heading. They seem to conceal the destination from me on purpose.

If someone had asked me yesterday, I'd have recited the entire range of human emotions tied to the combination of a blindfold and a trip in a military vehicle during a desperate and annihilating war: gut-wrenching, nauseating fear; worry for the future or if, indeed, there is even going to be a tomorrow; paralysing anxiety about what I have said and to whom in the past week or about that incident four days ago when I forgot to pull the blackout curtains at my bedroom window – and what if it has been interpreted as an attempt to send signals to the Nazis. The ARP wardens in my town can be very particular.

As I sit here on the hard metal bench, the feeling that sends my teeth clattering is the cold. I wish my aunt had warned me to put on a pair of stockings, at least, but who would have thought? Heavens, it's the middle of summer and I had left the jacket of my utility suit in the small leather suitcase at my feet. I keep nudging it with the tips of my toes, to make sure it's still here.

I'm tempted, I'll give you that. Tempted to open my luggage and ransack through it until I find that jacket. It wouldn't be hard, I don't think. I'd just have to feel for the three large buttons, for the padded shoulders. That is, if it weren't for this gale flapping the covers of the lorry. How would I know if the wind picks up my knickers or my brassieres? I've burnt though almost all of my coupons for the year, and a pair of knickers would cost me two.

'Is someone there?' It's a woman's voice, trembling. With cold? Fear?

I'm about to reply, *I'm here*, when a man says, 'No talking.'

My aunt didn't warn me about any of this.

The plan was to be closer to David. Closer to London. A job in London, if I'm not mistaken, was what my aunt promised at Christmas when she rambled on about the Ministry of Food. What does the Ministry of Food have to do with a bunch of girls, bundled up in a lorry, going nowhere? Well, we must be going somewhere, though we're probably sliding further and further away from London. From David. Anger bubbles up in my stomach.

'Where are we going?' I ask, shuddering.

'Shut up. We're almost there.'

The lorry takes on a smooth ascent, and in the distance a train whistles. And then, just like that, it stops with a jolt. The same man, I think, helps me get down from the back, as I weave through two sets of legs, presumably from two young ladies like me. There's the sound of a door slamming, and a man calling, 'Oi, what did you tie their eyes for?' he says, and fingers are moving at the back of my head, releasing my blindfold.

'Orders,' says the man who rode with us in the back – an Army officer, from what I can tell. 'It's secret, isn't it?'

But I'm not looking at him anymore. I'm absorbed by the view: barbed wire crowning a sort of concrete wall, its course interrupted by two metal railing gates, in front of which our lorry is parked. There's a hut next to the gates, and two guards flanking them. Behind it, a few hundred feet from us, is the most unusual building I ever saw: it's red brick laced with white marble, with towers and house façades in different styles blended together.

In the corner near me, the tower is plump, has six sides, and it's topped by a roof shaped like a bell. Its ground floor melts into a conservatory, jutting out on one side, all white marble arches. Then there's a façade that makes me think of the houses in Amsterdam I've seen on postcards. Its top is crenellated, but with a round closed balcony at the first floor – blacked out, of course.

Next to it, the mansion changes its appearance again with a length of bay windows extending on the ground and first floor, all lined in gorgeous white marble, that continues to the side in a triple arch, like a covered terrace. The house seems to say 'Tudor mansion' and 'Tuscan villa' at the same time – the most extraordinary combination I ever laid my eyes on.

'Where are we?' I ask the Army officer, while he pushes me towards the guards' hut. I brush by the other two girls I came with, not registering their faces. 'Where are we?'

'More inside,' he barks, hurrying me along. 'You talk a lot, miss.'

'Welcome to Bletchley Park,' says one of the guards, a man about my father's age with a drooping moustache.

Bletchley Park? Hmm.

I am still none the wiser.

I may have no clue about where I am, but I certainly know what brought me here.

It was Aunt Mavis, of course. Last Christmas.

Aunt Mavis doesn't have a family of her own, so my parents always invite her to stay at our house for the winter holidays. One of them invites her full-heartedly (my father) and one of them with mock apprehension and worry about Mavis converting her daughter to a sort of feminist mindset (that would be my mother). And almost every year for Christmas, my aunt refuses them, claiming 'different arrangements', only for us to wake up on Christmas morning with the buzz and hum of her Austin 7, settling into a spot right in front of our farmhouse.

Of course, this happened last year, too. I woke up to the sight of her elegant car, with its square cabin for driver and passengers, like a carriage box, the long snout ending in a triangular grille, the two headlights that resembled a funny pair of spectacles. My aunt was so elegant, too, with her tailored coat and buttoned leather ankle boots and silk stockings. I'm twenty years younger and she made me feel old and dusty in my flowery dresses.

By the time I descended from my bedroom and into the dark corridor, my aunt hadn't finished fussing with her suitcase – which always contained a box of beautifully wrapped chocolate pralines from Selfridge's – and my mother was tying up the laced-trimmed apron she always wore when we had guests, rolling her eyes, and murmuring something about 'modern arrangements'. For years I hadn't known why there was so much fuss about the arrangements, not until the winter holidays of 1934, when certain discussions made my mother's mouth much looser around all the sharp edges. The famed 'arrangements' had, in fact, to do with the birds and the bees, and, in my aunt's case, often involved a set of broken promises and a man with a family he had to be with for Christmas.

These are the sorts of arrangements that are much frowned upon in the small town in Norfolk where I come from. The mothers would have none of that. But my father and Aunt Mavis's own mother was long gone by then so there was no one to tell my aunt off.

And nor was there anyone to tell her that even if a set of people invite one for Christmas dinner, some *opinions* remain uninvited.

The dinner felt like a bad omen from beginning to end. My mother was piling up my aunt's plate with mashed potatoes, green beans, and her famous gravy, right on top of the roasted leg of lamb that was the crown jewel of the dinner she prepared to impress. 'You don't get that in London, do you, with all the rationing?' my mother asked.

'One learns to get by,' said Aunt Mavis.

'Sure, if you work for the Foreign Office,' said my father with a smile. By that point, I was barely seeing my father smile.

Not since that day in September, when Prime Minister Chamberlain announced that we were at war with Germany. Since then, he had forgotten how to smile, how to laugh, and how to do many, many things around the house and the farm. My father seemed to have lost himself in his own murky stare, a swamp of memories from the Great War that gushed out from where they'd stayed hidden for so many years.

'Yes, of course,' said my mother. 'Other rules apply for government officials than for the rest of us.'

Aunt Mavis raised her hallmark thin, arched eyebrows. Aunt Mavis wasn't a beautiful woman – her features were too sharp. But there was something in the way she carried herself that must have made men stop in their tracks. Married men, apparently, more often than not. 'It is certainly not like that. I only referred to the fact that one comes to know people from all walks of life. This happens when a woman works in a position like mine.'

By the way my mother narrowed her eyes, I could tell where this conversation was heading, like a train at full speed.

'Rose could also learn to network in the same way, of course, if she were in a similar position,' continued my aunt, directing her stare at me.

I busied myself with my plate, dragging a chunk of meat through the gravy. The entire conversation was uncannily similar to the one we'd had five years before. Except that, since then, I had changed sides. I was on my mother's side now.

'And are there any positions for a girl like Rose?' asked my father too quickly, in a way that made me suspect this entire conversation was choreographed.

This was all the confirmation I needed – it was my fate they would go on about. And like five years ago, I'd be no more than a spectator. I wasn't expected to have an opinion about what was best to do with my own life. I could just as well have been watching a cricket match – that's the sort of influence I'd have on the final result.

'Well, since you ask, Albert, there are,' said my aunt. 'I've heard about so many positions with the Ministry of Food, for instance.' I still stared at the plate, feeling the drill of Aunt Mavis's eyes. 'Clerical work. There's so much to be done now, with all the food rationing.'

'In London?' asked my mother.

'Yes, in London, mostly,' replied my aunt. 'But I could make some enquiries.'

'Did you hear that, Rose?' said my father, with so much hope in his voice that it broke my heart. Because I knew that if he asked me, I would break his.

Five years ago, the conversation had revolved around whether I should go to grammar school or not. My father had been losing to my mother's arguments of: 'She doesn't need so much learning to make a good wife', or 'Too much school does something to girls' heads; look at your sister,' (that would be Aunt Mavis). No amount of 'times are changing' or 'four more years of school won't do any harm. You don't want to marry her off at fourteen, do you?' could persuade my mother that too much school wasn't the shortest path to a life of spinsterhood.

So, back then, my father had brought out his most powerful weapon, which was Aunt Mavis. She was the one who managed to pierce through my mother's armour, and off I went to four more years of school. Which I didn't mind at the time: it was certainly an exciting prospect at that point and I did, even then, prefer reading to actual farmwork. And, as always, there was a lot of farmwork at home. But, of course, that was before David. So, last year my views about continuing my education and self-improvement and so on were quite different from what they had been four years previously.

'Yes, Father,' was all I managed to say.

'Did you hear that Rose is engaged?' said my mother, at which point I risked a glare at her pursed lips.

'Yes, I have,' said Aunt Mavis. 'I've even brought a bottle of champagne to celebrate.'

'Posh,' I said, trying to smile.

'You can meet David tomorrow, when we go to the Fosters's house for Boxing Day lunch,' said my mother. 'You know, it will be just us, the extended family.'

'Isn't she a bit too young to marry? She's only nineteen.' Determination faded into concern on my aunt's face and I couldn't resent her, even if she planned to take me away from my darling David. If she'd known how it would break my heart to a million pieces if I had to part with him, she'd never have insisted. Butterflies started waltzing in my stomach at the thought of the dance we were going to together that evening.

'Why wouldn't she marry if she's found a good man?' said my mother. That was what had saved her from a bleak life spent in service, all those years ago. A good man at the right time, when men were in such high demand after the Great War. A man with a farm she could call her own.

'But they don't need to hurry, do they, Betty?' said my father. 'The lease on the flat doesn't expire for another year.'

'David and Rose will take over his father's shop in town once they're married,' my mother explained. 'But they don't have a place to live because the rooms above the shop are rented to a RAF officer's wife and their two children. He's stationed somewhere in Africa.'

'Cairo,' I said in unison with my father. What I didn't say was that we could have stayed with our parents, in theory. David was having none of that. And nor would I. Imagine the two of us, frolicking in a bedroom next to my parents. Or us having to live with his mother. Not that I have anything against his mother – but every minute of every day?

'The officer is coming back at the end of next year, and then David and Rose can move in,' continued my mother.

'I wouldn't plan anything beyond tomorrow,' said Aunt Mavis. 'We are at war.'

'It isn't much of a war,' said my mother.

And it was true. After Germany had invaded Poland, nothing had happened. Only waiting and rationing and more waiting and trench-digging. Not even an errant German aeroplane came to bother us. So we all carried on waiting.

'Not for the Polish,' said Aunt Mavis. 'And I wouldn't count on this quiet lasting. The war has just begun.' She then turned to me. 'It will be like the last war. The war will bring women out of their homes and into men's jobs.'

'Why would Rose want a man's job?' asked my mother, and, indeed, I couldn't help agreeing with her.

My father, also reduced to a quiet onlooker, began stuffing

his pipe in a way that made me think he wanted to murder that tobacco, not smoke it.

'Rose could do so much more,' said my aunt. 'She's such a clever girl. There are so many opportunities for young women out there.'

'She could go to university,' said my father.

'Yes, she could,' said my aunt, nodding.

My mother pursed her lips. 'Why on earth would Rose need a university degree to run a shop?'

'But maybe Rose wants to do more than that,' said my aunt, flicking an imaginary dust mote off her silk shirt. And then it struck me. My aunt had her elegant car and her elegant clothes and her perfectly applied lipstick because there was nothing else in her life she could spend her money on.

She had her pristine red nails, and her lovely ankle boots, and no one else in her London flat for Christmas. I thought, *she isn't trying to persuade me that she lives the perfect life. She's trying to persuade herself of that*. And I didn't want her life. I wanted David.

As if she could hear what I was thinking in the remotest corner of my mind, she turned her green eyes towards me. Icy-green, like my father's. 'Rose, really, is this what you want?'

I got to my feet, the question surprising me like a slap. My parents rarely bothered to ask me what I wanted – my mother poked me towards marriage, while my father sulked or brooded.

And all the while, I kept my steady course, doing my best to jump from moment to moment when I could be alone with David. But all of a sudden, my own eyes, something between the dreamy green of my father's and the earthly brown of my mother's, were open wide. I took in the dim interior of the parlour and the windows that my mother had painted black to spare money for the blackout curtains; we barely used this room – only for occasions like this. I took in the heavy table that my father had inherited from his father, the deep scratches within the wood hidden under a white tablecloth, starched to crispness. I took in the dusty fabric of the very chairs we sat on, the heavy-set glass-doored cabinet in a corner of the room, with its porcelain figurines; among them reigned a Royal Doulton of a shepherdess that my parents received at their wedding. That was where I was heading: to the cabinet to pick up the finest glasses that my mother owned.

I fingered the etchings on the glass which was as wide as half my palm at the bottom and which opened upwards even more, like a fan. I grabbed two glasses at a time by the thin legs that supported their entire weight, wondering whether they were suitable to drink champagne from or not. Whether they were elegant enough.

'Rose?' asked my aunt as I placed the first glass in front of her. 'Did you hear me?'

And for a moment it all lay in front of me, clear like the crystal glasses. My entire life with David. Our home, our parlour, our shop. 'Oh, yes,' I told my aunt, 'I'm precisely where I want to be.'

And I was. Back then, I was. Now, I have no idea where I am, and where or what we are all heading towards.

Part One

THE GIRLS

June 1940

One month earlier

Chapter One

Rose

As the Germans roll into France, my aunt's warnings ring louder and louder in my ears. But that's the last thing I want to hear. I much prefer David's voice. We meet at the toolshed, and I sink into his arms. He undoes my colourful headband, releasing a tangle of dark-blonde curls onto my back. These days, I don't think much about going to the hairdresser's. All I can focus on is the feel of David's warm hands, insinuating themselves between my shirt and my skin, caressing my back. His palms are callused and roughened, and I want to keep kissing them for all that they'd become while he helped us. Instead, I close my eyes and he leans his head onto mine.

'I'll have to go, you know,' David says in a thick voice.

'Where to?'

'The RAF, I think.'

I jolt back, catching his hand between my collar and my neck. He releases it without looking at me.

'What are you talking about?' I say, though I know very well the answer to my own question.

My aunt told me all about the war, and how we won't be able to escape it. I hadn't been inclined to believe her. For a while, nothing happened – just waiting. For me and for David, and really it was more about waiting for the rooms above the shop to be free than for anything else. The war lost itself in the tall grasses of daily worries, and of farmwork.

There was so much to be done that I couldn't help but miss the grammar school and its quiet ways: classes followed by some reading in the evening, compared to the never-ending work at the farmhouse. No matter how hard I tried, the list of things to do never seemed to end. My arms remembered why I had been so eager to leave for school four years before, while the history books that I received as a prize at the end of my third year lay forgotten in a corner of my bedroom.

There were sheep to be milked, and the chicken pen needed mucking and fixing. I went about the job with a hammer I found in the toolshed and some old wooden planks, kept from when my father had redone the stables. There was no more of that, as he found it more and more difficult to rise from his bed. He barely did so when spring blossomed and there was work to do in the fields. We spoke about hiring a farmhand, but then David offered to help us.

His soft hands bled and hardened into farmer's ones, while I taught myself to drive the tractor. We could only dream of getting away from it all in a few months' time, with nothing else to worry about except the shop.

And then events started hurtling towards us, channelled

through the speakers of the wireless set. German tanks rolled through half of Europe in the blink of an eye, striking closer and closer to home. Norway, Belgium, the Netherlands.

We entrenched ourselves on our little island, and I started perusing my history books again, as if trying to find reassurance in wars past that we couldn't possibly lose this one. The calls for digging for victory became louder and louder and there was talk of commissions roaming through the country's fields, looking to fine lazy farmers. So, when the RAF built a hangar partly on our outlying fields, relief coursed through my veins like molten chocolate, of which I hardly saw the likes any longer.

The RAF, so close to my home now. I can't say that I'm surprised by David's decision. But I can't find the words to agree with him, either.

David has a lot of words for me, it seems, though. 'It's better if I sign up for myself, Rose. I can pick the service I want to be in. It's no good to stay around and wait to be called up by the Army. I don't want to be in the Army. So I thought—'

'This is nonsense. You don't know if you're going to be called up. Why serve yourself up on a silver platter?' I ask, knowing already it's as good as battling the wind. I can't stop David from going any more than I can stop the war. My aunt was right. We shouldn't have trusted the quiet. It couldn't possibly have lasted. The war is here, bending our lives. I want to ask, *what about me? What about our dreams? What about the life we were meant to start? Together.*

'Rose,' he says, 'don't be unreasonable. Do you think I want to go?' A strand of his dark hair falls onto his forehead, making him look heartbreakingly boyish. The smell of oil from the tractor becomes so pungent that I begin feeling nauseous.

'No, I suppose not,' I say, my heart in my throat. 'It doesn't suit me, does it?' I gulp. 'I suppose the RAF is a choice as good as any. My father says pilots were much safer during the Great War than the soldiers.'

My father told me a great lot of things that I'm not keen to hear. He gave me detailed and horrifying descriptions of life in the trenches, gangrene, dozens of soldiers caught in barbed wire while the aeroplanes were diving and dropping bombs. He must have seen my terrified face, because he returned from that faraway place, where all of these memories were coming from, and rushed to add that all he meant to say was that the RAF was probably safer than the Army.

There are no answers for this in my history books, considering the speed with which warfare is changing. The world has never seen the likes of it.

David catches me in his arms, squeezing me tight, leaning his chin in the place between my neck and my shoulder. 'Yes,' he says. 'Yes. You must be right. You know so many things.'

The next day, while David registers for the RAF, I take a shovel and a spade to our flower garden. Yellow marigolds, rosebushes with red silken buds bleeding into bloom, daisies, lavender, foxgloves, shy pink peonies, tart mauve geraniums. A dance of shapes and colours. Lovely and useless in a time of war. What did the wireless say? Digging for victory. I stab the earth right underneath the peonies with the tip of the spade, driving the tool entirely into the mud, then put my entire weight into it. The peonies come out, root and stem. I roll them onto the side. The velvety pink, the soft opening of the blossom stained with earth. I pick it up and toss it to the side, into the empty wheelbarrow. I think, *this is a time when beauty will go wasted. Who knows what else will go wasted, lying dead on its side long before its time should have come.*

I grip the handle of the spade, biting again into the earth, pressing on and on, ruining flower after flower after flower. I catch my mother's shadow moving behind the kitchen window, but not once does she come outside. She's so proud of her flower garden. She used to put out a chair in the midst of the fragrant bushes on summer evenings to do some knitting and mending outside.

I think, *this will be the least of the sacrifices we'll have to make.*

I turn towards the daisies, my back to the kitchen.

By evening, my arms ache so much that I can't lift the spade anymore, and the garden has been reduced to gaping gashes where the flowers once were. The plants lie in a heap, corpses covered in mud and bleeding dust.

Chapter Two

Evie

My bloody father is as much of a bloody dictator as bloody Hitler. No, this isn't friendly banter or the kind of benign exaggeration so popular amongst boys around my age, like my brother, Will. Papa is a sadistic, cold-blooded tyrant. What kind of man sends his driver to fetch his daughter from her secretarial school in London while she's in the middle of her class, claiming a family emergency, and rushing her home to Kent only for her to find an empty house?

Well, relatively empty: the smattering of servants that stayed with us are going about their business in distant corners of their manor. If I didn't know better, I'd say that they're purposely staying out of my way, but with our footmen gone into military service and two of our maids deserting us at the beginning of the year – not yet replaced – and as much work as ever, who knows? My mother, by the way, isn't at home either; she's attending another of her WVS committees. She has had trouble enough replacing the nanny, so don't get me started on staff these days.

I'm not like my family, you see. I don't understand why I need to have an army of servants around me, catering for my needs. This is why I went off to the secretarial school, even though Mother pretended she fainted when she heard what I wanted to do. But I was about to go mad if I spent the war presiding over housewives who didn't need to be told what to do for the evacuated children.

Oh. The children. My head might explode if I have to wait for Papa to come back from fox-hunting (I kid you not) and tell me about this family emergency. I could always ask the children – my little brothers – about what's happening, about what sort of tragedy has befallen us. I certainly hope this isn't about Will. Even if the scoundrel refuses to write to any of us, to a single member of this family, I can't stop worrying about him. He joined the Royal Navy last year, you see. A few weeks before he sent me that baffling letter where he announced that he never wants to have anything to do with me ever again.

I still don't understand what I have to do with Papa throwing Will's lover into the street – the children's former nanny, the now-infamous Elinor, about whom we never speak. I've done nothing wrong.

That's Will for you, always keeping his cards close to his chest. If I remember correctly, none of his mates from Oxford wanted to play poker with him anymore. Which isn't necessarily to say that he's a cheater, only that he's so good at bluffing, but who knows? Will has always done the strangest things for the strangest reasons.

Once he went to Oxford, he started being on friendly terms with the servants. I caught him more than once chatting in the library with the nanny (ha ha) and one of the maids – I'm not so sure which one anymore – and often when his Oxford set was visiting. My father said they were all communists (Will's friends, I mean). In hindsight, after it was revealed that Elinor was his lover, I'm not so sure exactly what my brother was, nor what he is at this moment.

And nor can I ask anyone. Except – oh, the shame – my little brothers.

I pull the cord in the great library and stop pacing for a few moments. Around me, the walls are cushioned from bottom to top with books that nobody reads, bound in leather covers. Papa is too busy hunting for influence, and I've never seen my mother with a book in her hands. Her social engagements don't leave her any time for that. The only person in our house who reads has disappeared from our lives.

Through the open bay windows I can hear the snip of the gardener's scissors. I look over the hedges in the maze, towards the woods. Nothing. No one but the trees. I sink into one of the armchairs in the reading corner, which is actually the don't-bother-me-corner in our house – three fauteuils gathered around a massive teak table imported from France in the time of one of the Louis. I always forget which. The forced softness of the velvet grates on me and I gather my hands in my lap, just in time to appear composed for our butler, who wastes no time in materialising into the room. 'Yes, Miss Milton?' he says with a slight bow. I adore his reliability, but he's so bloody officious – even more so than Papa himself, which is quite a feat.

'I was wondering if my little brothers were in?' I say, trying not to appear too keen.

'I'm afraid that Master John and Master Edward went for a ride this afternoon.'

'Ah,' I say. 'Brilliant. Do you by any chance know where they've gone?' I get up from my seat. 'No matter. I'll ask directly at the stables.' If anything, the fresh air might help me clear my head.

He stares at a point behind me with such intensity that I turn to see what he's looking at. There's nothing there except a shelf of books. He clears his throat. 'I'm sorry, Miss Milton, your father instructed that you are to wait for him at home.'

'Oh? Is that so?' There's little that I like less than to be told what to do. There's nothing that I like less than being told what to do by Papa.

'I think Lord Milton was simply suggesting that you might want to freshen up a bit after your journey.' He gives me a tiny shake of the head. It's barely there, but enough for it to tell me that I should know better than cross him.

And I do know better than to cross Papa when he doesn't want to be crossed. It pushes him into a stony stubbornness where he's even less likely to do what I'd like him to do and he's more likely to do his best to be as disagreeable as he possibly can.

I need to find out what happened, though. I'm sure this is one of his cruel mind games, where he keeps me waiting on purpose.

I study our butler for the length of several batters of my eyelashes, wondering if he knows anything about this family emergency.

'Is there anything else, Miss Milton?'

Humph. Well, yes. But even if our butler knows what the

emergency is about, I'm not entirely sure he would tell me if he had been instructed by Papa to be discreet.

And in this house, there are other ways to come by information. 'Yes. Will you please tell Brown that I want her? I do think I need freshening up a bit. I'll be waiting for her in my room.'

———————————

In my room, where no one else would be listening, of course. I pull the lid off one of the boxes of powder – silver, engraved with flowers that flow into spirals – and then set it down again. I pull at the corners of my eyes, as if they could erase the black rings underneath. Young men called me 'pretty' a few years ago, during my first season in London, but I don't think I am.

All they ever saw was the mask, all that rouge and lipstick and dark-blue eyeshadow. Underneath, I'm a tall girl with strong thighs (from all the riding, I reckon) and rather washed-up features: discoloured grey eyes, a pale complexion, wispy, limp blonde hair. Brown can do wonders with some skilfully applied makeup. She does make me feel like a Hollywood star. But how many people ever saw the true Evie under all that?

Well, Jasper did. And my brother. Definitely my brother; he could always see me, and through me. Yes, and Brown, who slips into my bedroom carrying the polished wooden case with her tools.

'Miss Milton!' she says, giving me a coy smile. Brown is by far the best gossip in this house and if she doesn't know what's happening, then I can't imagine that anyone else does. 'What a pleasure to see you.'

'I imagine it's a surprise,' I say, while she moves to stand behind me. She sticks her hands in my hair and starts manoeuvring my tangled curls gently. Jasper and I had been to a sort of dancing club last night, right off Leicester Square, with a real live band. Suffice to say that I was in quite a hurry this morning to arrive at class. Not the first class of the day, of course – that had been a bit of a miss.

'How would you like it?' she asks.

I shrug. 'I don't know.'

Brown lays out a selection of hairpins. 'Why would it be a surprise?' she asks, while her hands move with quick, precise movements in my hair.

'Well, I didn't quite plan to come home today, if you get my meaning.' Through the years, I've come to learn that the best way to talk to Brown is to give her snippets of honest information she can use later to make small talk in the kitchen. I like to notice these things about people: find their buttons and then press them.

'We've been expecting you for a couple of days now.'

'How so?' I ask, unable to repress a twitch of my brow.

She combs my curls to the back of my head, her eyes lowered in a pose so untypical of her. Brown is the sort to look people in the face, to check if they're telling the truth or not.

'Since we heard about Master Will,' she says in a soft voice.

I turn. 'What is it about Will?'

'You don't know?' she says, still not looking at me.

'Well, no, I bloody don't know, or why else would I be asking?' I wipe the palms of my hands on my slacks.

Brown picks up a strand of hair from the front, loops it around her finger to form a roll, and pins it on top of my head in a victory curl.

'I'm so sorry,' I say, 'but nobody tells me anything. My

father isn't here and I'm going completely mad. What is it with Will?'

'Dunkirk,' she says in a small voice. 'Your brother has been missing since Dunkirk.'

It's evening and my father still hasn't returned. Nor have I left my room. I don't want to leave my room. I don't want to see the servants' pity that my own family didn't tell me my brother had been missing for days and days. I'll never forgive Mother for this. I've learned to expect anything from Papa – but that Mother couldn't be bothered to send a telegram or to give me a call. God forbid that she should have taken the trouble herself, yet she could have asked one of the staff to do it for her.

And my darling Will, with his coppery hair and freckled nose, that he should have vanished after Dunkirk. Brown tried to cheer me up when I started crying by parroting what Mother must have been telling herself since the news came out: that there are a lot of people unaccounted for since Dunkirk. People who haven't necessarily died. Who may be wounded or who are waiting to be reassigned after their ship was sunk.

Because that's what happened; my brother's ship was sunk and while he's not quite missing yet, nobody in his unit can tell Papa where he is.

That's the irony of it, Will wanted to cut his ties with us, but Papa's ties to everyone in this bloody country are too good to allow my brother to disappear without a trace.

And the worst of it is that I haven't seen my brother in a year. I sit in my room and stare at the discoloured canopy of my bed, wondering why I didn't urge him to tell me what I'd done wrong, why he was so upset with me. Why I didn't drive to wherever he was doing his training for the Royal Navy and insisted I see him and ask him what was going on. I know he wouldn't have been able to ignore me in person the way he ignored my letters.

He'd never ignored me before, not even when everyone else did. And there's another thing about Will which I realised in this year of not speaking to each other: he was one of the two people in the world with whom I could never wear a mask, who loved me for who I am. Not even dear Brown, who is possibly my single ally in this house, knows all about me. Now there's only Jasper, and I reckon I would have gone positively mad without him.

Imagine this: a little girl who has no idea who she is, no concept of it whatsoever, but everyone else has a rather clear idea about who this girl should be. Mainly, the impeccably educated young lady. My mother and father have been striving towards creating that perfect version of me ever since I was in the crib, without getting their hands dirty.

For that, they'd have had to be hands-on. My entire childhood, I barely saw my mother, except if there was some sort of function where the children's presence was required, which hardly ever happened. The governesses were the ones who carried out the instructions and handled the less-palatable sides of child-rearing, which, I have been told, is most of it.

They must have done their jobs well, because the mask-wearing had come effortlessly to me for more than twenty years. I imagine I must have cut a fine figure when I first came out as a debutante, and throughout my first two London seasons. I've been told, much later, that everyone was shocked that I didn't secure a husband. That was the thing about my mask. I looked the part of the rich, spoiled, mannered, not overly educated – in any case, without any academic pretensions – elegant sort of girl. But behind the mask, not even I knew what was hiding. I knew I longed for something else, but I couldn't put my finger on quite what. There was an absence in the way I always tried to find the right, but not overly opinionated words, in the way I swirled around a crowded room. Looking for something that wasn't yet there.

And then, one day, the future ninth Earl of Something tried to fumble in the décolleté of my white silk dress and covered my lips in slobber in a cloakroom at a banker's house. I should have been out of my mind with excitement – if I'd had a penny each time the other debs had mentioned him with a broad smile on their faces. But I didn't know how to get away faster from him. Perhaps I was being too picky, as my mother had said. Perhaps I was waiting for the right man to come along – and he did, but in what my parents would describe as 'the wrong place.' What they've been describing as such ever since.

It was a completely different story with Will. He tried to rescue me from the endless cocktail parties and dances in private houses long before that incident. He started taking me to the opera with his set. And behind the scenes at the opera. And to private dancing clubs.

This was why, when he said he never wanted to speak to me again, I thought that was an angry tantrum after Papa dismissed Elinor. As if, of all people, I'd had anything to do with it. I didn't understand why Will would quarrel with *me*, because I'd never, ever done anything to mistreat Elinor. If anything, I was on friendlier terms with her than was proper.

In fact, seeing as she's always been such an odd bird, I

think I treated her exceedingly nicely. She never spoke much. I can hardly remember an exchange with her that comprised more than four lines. So I could never understand my little brothers' abnormal attachment to her, and I could never understand what persuaded Mother to keep her once she found someone suitable to replace her. She'd never cared if *I* grew attached to any of my nannies or governesses (to be fair, I didn't).

Mother must have mellowed with age – I've spotted her more than once in the boys' company and I could swear she actually inquired after their wellbeing. This is why she didn't let Elinor go. At least, that is, until she tried to sneak into our family.

When one of the maids invites me to finally 'join my father', I'm so angry that my head is whizzing. I shove the door open and storm into Papa's study. He's sitting at his desk, leaning back into his carved chair. He's even had the gall to change from his hunting gear before summoning me. The way he pats his grey moustache, he's the very image of composure itself.

'How could you?' I wheeze, barely stopping myself from staying, *How dare you?* I have to remind myself to stay calm. To feel the terrain bit by bit.

'Good evening to you, too, Evelyn. Have you had a nice journey?' He gestures for me to take a seat.

I walk up to his desk and lean my hands onto it. 'How could you not tell me about my brother? Didn't you think I'd want to know?'

'I'm already making enquiries into what is happening to

your brother. Now, could you please take a seat? And spare me the cheap theatrics. You do have a flair for the opera, don't you?'

A chill shivers down my spine. He couldn't know. He doesn't. Then anger twists and turns in my stomach. And *if* he knows, then what? What does he care?

It was rather insidious when it began, half-baked allusions to my reputation and potentially ruining my future by appearing so often at Jasper's side. That my brother should know better than that. Papa, trying to appear genuinely concerned. For me.

As if.

And at some point after Will left us, Papa told me to my face that Jasper was aiming for our fortune and that I should steer clear of him. That all he sees in me is the family's money. And then, when that didn't work either, he threatened to disinherit me. Told me that I wouldn't be able to live low-maintenance; that I'm simply not built that way.

But, lately, since I led him to believe that I dropped Jasper, I've been saving more and more from the money he gives me, to show myself that I can live frugally. Dining out no more than two or three times per week. And if I have to, I could go without the restaurant sorties entirely if he refuses to support me. He might think I'm too spoiled to give up this sort of life, but oh, how wrong he is. 'What theatrics? How can you fetch me from London like I'm a naughty dog and leave me to wait for an entire day? How could you?' I'm so angry now that I'm almost crying.

'Please start behaving like a well-bred young woman and not like a fishwife.' A blush creeps up his throat and he raises his tone. 'I shouldn't wonder, considering the company you keep. How dare you speak to me like this?'

I sit down, breathing hard. This isn't the first time Papa and I aren't agreeing about his conduct or mine. 'Of course,' I say, trying to keep my voice from trembling. 'One can get away with any sort of perversity as long as one remains bloody mannered throughout.'

'Young lady, you will mind your language, or—'

'Or what?'

He throws a sheet of paper in front of me with certainly much less composure than he intended to. *Good, good, good.* When I pull him out of his perfect manners, it means I'm beginning to win.

'What is this?' I glance at the sheet, which seems to be a sort of inventory of the opera's props and a list of names next to them. I recognise most of the names. I am, let's say, quite intimate with at least one of them. Jasper's name pops out so much for me, it could be written in red ink.

'I allowed you to go to London only because you agreed to something,' he says, leaning back again in his chair. The scoundrel is ripping the rug beneath my feet. I'm slipping and I don't know why yet. 'You broke our agreement.'

'I—' Our agreement. Our. Agreement.

After threatening to disinherit me, Papa turned a leaf again. He spoke to me in this very office about secretarial training and a sort of agreement, which I didn't quite understand at the time. There was a confused conversation that felt like a bad dream, in which he told me about status and about a magnifying lens being directed towards him and his entire family, a man of his calibre, and he went on to tell me about conduct. I'd assumed he meant

Jasper again. I suppose I could have gotten away with choosing him as a husband if Jasper had proceeded to rebuild the family's fortunes after what had happened with his father. Or paid his father's debts. But there's no chance of that. Jasper loves what he does, and it allows him to make a living, and that's about it.

Nothing like his father, who was a banker and very much an English gentleman, from what I've heard – half-whispered gossips, rumours twisted by the passing of time – who had gambled on a losing card and lost it at. There was talk about embezzlement and running off with the money of more than a few influential people.

While much isn't certain – Jasper never likes to discuss the details – some things are. That Papa had entrusted the man with his money, too. And that he went on to recommend him to a handful of his friends, which made the entire business impossibly embarrassing for Papa when Jasper's father disappeared. It would be the Shame of Shames to have his daughter associated with 'that man's' son – what if *people* came to believe that, in the end, Papa had indeed had a hand in the business? Why, he could never show his face in society again. And saving face is, in the end, all that matters. At least, according to him. So when Papa offered to allow me to pursue the secretarial course in London, I decided to snatch my new freedom and be as discreet as possible about my own doings. Without asking too many questions.

In full knowledge of all that, I tell my father, 'I'm not sure what you mean.'

'Don't you dare lie to me. Don't you dare.' His voice is more of a growl.

'I'm not lying,' I say. 'I never understood the terms of our agreement, because you didn't bother to properly explain what you wanted.'

'You believed what you chose to believe, Evelyn. I think I've been quite clear.' He cracks his knuckles. 'Your course with the secretarial school has come to an end. Since you seem so intent upon casting shame on your family, you will spend your time from now on at Milton Hall. Remembering our values. Looking for a suitable husband.'

I want to say something, but all the blood has drained from my lips. 'You can't do that. I won't stand for it.' The moment Jasper and I have been dreading has arrived and, in spite of all our preparations, the ground is slipping from beneath my feet. If Papa cuts off all support, how would I be able to make a living? Jasper has to earn for an entire family, as it is. His mother, his little sister; they all depend on him. It was only last night that we last spoke of it. *But I don't know how to do anything,* I told him. *There are so many opportunities for women right now,* he told me. *Especially for educated young women.* I snorted in the most uneducated way. *If you think that knowing how to use two dozen pieces of cutlery and in what order counts as an education.*

And yet.

Opportunities.

I lean back in my chair. It's now or never. This is the moment. And then I can't help thinking about Will. If Will were here, things would be so different. Once Papa has cut me off from the family, I know Will would help, at least with advice. Will was the one who pushed me towards the secretarial school. He said nothing about his gloomy predictions: how the immensely wealthy would fall and a new world order would ensue. His way of preparing me for the future was pushing me to acquire a skill. A skill for a life he and his communist set at Oxford dreamed of (and discussed at great length).

Yes, Will always tried to care for me. But Will isn't here. So I have to stand up for myself.

'There will be no husband, Papa. You either accept this is who I am and how I choose to live or I—'

'Oh, Evelyn. Evelyn. You still don't know what that sheet of paper is. Of course you don't.' He pushes a finger into Jasper's name. 'This is proof against a thief.'

'What? He's not. He'd never do that.' Jasper may be many things, but a thief, he is not. Certainly not.

Papa cocks his head. 'Perhaps. What matters is who sees this piece of paper – and in what context.'

I'm not sure what he means by this, but I'm holding my breath. All the courage is draining from my heart.

'It would be so unfortunate if this paper were to be shown to the police, let's say. Or to the press.' He draws a sharp breath through his teeth, like a whistle. 'What a scandal. A very unfortunate spot for whoever is delivering justice, also. The public would be expecting it. Justice, that is. And the public loves nothing more than a scandal, don't they, Evelyn? Especially when it comes to a family like ours.'

Tears are filling my eyes and all I want is to make them go away. To disappear. To be more like Papa – cold and unfeeling. Unemotional. I've never been like everyone else in my family. I have what they call a 'nasty temper'. And even I know when I have to hold it back. 'Please,' is all I say. 'Please.' If Jasper comes into a spot of trouble, what will happen to his family? There's no one else there to support them, not since their father died. Papa doesn't even have to put him behind bars. A scandal would be enough for him to lose his reputation – and his job as a tenor with his company. And if something is certain, it is that there will be a scandal. Considering what everyone knows – or think they know – about his family.

Papa gingerly takes the sheet of paper from my hand. After a moment of numbness, I scrabble to get it back. This sheet could destroy Jasper, and he knows it.

'Hush, hush, little kitty,' he says. 'No need to try and tear this. I have the originals somewhere else.'

'Please, don't do this to him.' Jasper doesn't deserve to go to prison and I shudder to think what would happen then to the rest of his family.

'It's all up to you,' says Papa. 'Be a good little kitty. Stay put at Milton Hall. Maybe even find a husband. He'll be safe.'

I think I'd rather not, but even I know better than to tell him this. What I need now is time. Time to think. Time to find a way out of this situation. For me. For Jasper.

'You can trust me,' he says, perhaps sensing my doubt. 'Cross me, and you'll see what happens.'

There's nothing between us after this. Silence. I have nothing more to say to him. He must have known that I was ready to cut all the strings that were attaching me to him, and he found the one way of preventing me from doing so. Like always, he's one step ahead. Never in my life have I felt so small, so unimportant. What I want is nothing to him. I am nothing to him. All he cares about is himself, his name, his reputation.

And I hate him.

But I don't need to tell Papa any of this. 'If you would please excuse me.'

In lieu of a response – which I wasn't expecting, anyway –

he shows me the door. His eyes have taken on that satisfied gleam that they have when he's very, very pleased with the way things have turned out. By the way he has arranged them.

And then, I just know he has planned all this. He revels in the way he has laid out the trap, how we've all fallen into it. This was never about my brother: he never cared whether I found out or not. I turn to him from the threshold. 'You didn't bring me back to tell me about Will. You never cared if I knew about Will. You brought me back to keep me in your grip. Your only daughter.'

There is no trace, none whatsoever, of compassion in any of the strained features of his face. 'You're no daughter of mine. You're a catastrophe that has to be contained for the good of the rest of the Milton family. And you're dismissed now. You'd do well to stay out of my sight.'

Chapter Three

Rose

The day when David leaves comes too soon. I promised myself – and not only myself – that I won't cry, and yet tears stream down my face. Aside from that, I lose the remaining shreds of my dignity when I blow my nose. David places his palm on my cheek as if his touch could prevent my tears from spilling.

'You promised you wouldn't do this,' he says, a crooked smile on his lips. 'It's why I agreed to let you accompany me to the station in the first place.'

'As if you could have stopped me,' I blurt. 'It's just that I'll miss you so much.'

He coils his arm around my neck and pulls me close. The smell of his aftershave, tobacco woven into the cloth of his RAF uniform, is intoxicating. 'I'll see you soon,' he says. 'They'll probably let me come home after the training is done.'

I inhale the scent of him for the last time in weeks, maybe

months to come. And then a voice inside my head says, *maybe the last time ever*. I try to stop a sob, but it explodes like a hiccup. There's no more room for pleading and appealing as the country fills with the exhausted soldiers streaming in from Dunkirk. The tales that are being told: hundreds and hundreds struck down on the beaches while they waited for the ships to carry them home. The brave push of the Royal Navy and of thousands of men with their little boats, who had come to help. The fierce battle going on above their heads, as the Luftwaffe's aeroplanes tried to decimate our soldiers, and the RAF fighting to protect them.

There's no denying it: David has to go. He has to.

'Besides, don't you think I look rather striking in my uniform?' David distances himself from me to demonstrate. I have to admit that the dark blue suits him. A spring spent on the farm broadened his shoulders and thickened his arms. Underneath that uniform is the shape of a real man.

I rub my nose with my crumpled handkerchief. The whistle of the locomotive calls the passengers to board. 'I bet you'll be a roving success with the ladies.'

He smiles and gives me a short kiss on my lips. 'But there is only one I'll think about.'

And what will I do? I want to say. What will I think about?

Then David breaks away from me, jumping on the train. 'I have to go, Rose,' he says, disappearing inside without waiting for me reply.

'David!' I call in a voice that didn't sound at all like my own.

Next to me, another girl wraps her arms around her beau's neck and refuses to let go. I think, *we're too small, we can't stop the music, so we all have to dance along to the tune.*

David's head appears at one of the windows, further to the right. In the rush of soldiers, airmen, and sailors on the train, he's the only one I see, his cap tossed a bit to the side on top of his tussle of light-brown hair. The smile on his lips tries to erase the sadness in his shining eyes. 'I love you,' he says, stretching his hand through the window.

'I love you, too.' I leap towards him. It's too late; the train is already moving and as I'm about to brush the tips of his fingers, he drifts further and further away from me.

My arms fall to my sides and I stay there, in the train station, for a long time, not quite sure what I should do with myself.

Chapter Four

Evie

It would be appalling to complain about being confined to a gorgeous mansion, yet here I am, complaining. The library is full of books, I can go out for a ride anytime I want, or I can help with the WVS as much as I like – courtesy of Mother, who barely speaks to me since The Transgression. Yet I want to do none of those things. I want out, out, out. To London. To Jasper. To be free to enquire about Will.

To be able to ask around would be to hope.

The housekeeper's nephew was at Dunkirk, too, I've heard, and he was granted a few days' leave. He came to Milton Hall one afternoon and told the servants what he lived through during those horrible days, but I don't know the specifics; to make matters even worse for me, I've been deprived of a good gossip. Brown was taken ill the very day of my sudden arrival and has been in hospital ever since. She had her appendix removed and her recovery didn't quite go as smoothly as expected, so we've all had to do without her for much longer than anyone had thought.

The day when I'm allowed to drive to the hospital and pick her up is the event of the week. I'm chaperoned, of course – I'm allowed to leave the mansion only to accompany a handful of sick villagers to the hospital, and Brown back to the Hall. The WVS is organising carpools because of the petrol rationing. The WVS has a hand in everything these days.

I might not be good at many things, but, goodness, I can drive. Petrol rationing has struck me hard. I push my foot down onto the pedal and feel the car jolt from underneath me, my head whipping back for a fraction of a second. I swivel into the curves of country lanes and touch a sliver of the grass with my front wheel. I roll the window down and let the wind tousle my hair. We used to be as free as this, Jasper and I, driving round and round Piccadilly Circus. We used to take another woman in the car with us, as a precaution – one of the other singers from the opera, for instance. Like Claire.

It seems, though, that we haven't taken *enough* precautions.

My tousled hair is the first thing that Brown sees when she gets into the car. 'Goodness, Miss Milton, I see that I'm urgently needed at the Hall,' she says, pointing at my mishmash of tangled curls.

I snigger and gesture for her to sit down. She's so pale and her face is drawn, the wrinkles in the corners of her eyes like crinkled paper. The skin on her cheeks hangs a bit, like a balloon that is starting to deflate. For the first time in my life I wonder how old Brown is. She must be well into her forties, a faithful companion of Mother since she became Lady Milton. Brown was always a given to me, as much as Mother, Papa, my grandparents, aunts and uncles, even more of a given than my younger brothers, who came much later.

'You have no idea,' I say.

'What news of your brother?' she says, wrapping herself in her cardigan, though it's still warm outside.

'None.' I switch into a lower gear to help the car climb a hill.

My brother. How I've missed him during these past weeks, twisting and turning, looking for a way out of my golden cage. I wrote to all his friends at Oxford, but the letters were returned, unanswered. The men have gone to war.

How I could have used his advice. Will is clever, unlike me. Will has seen more of life than the inside of great houses and dancing halls. If there's a way out of Milton Hall without harming Jasper, he'd find it.

'None at all,' I say. 'And I think he doesn't want to be found by us. I wouldn't even know where to start.' I think about the housekeeper's nephew and how he came home. 'I think everyone who was at Dunkirk was allowed a few days' leave. I thought about this. A lot. This might explain why no one has heard from Will for days and days. If he's not with his unit, I mean.' I sigh. 'He would never consider coming home if he were on leave, not after what happened with Elinor last year.'

'Of course not,' says Brown, staring through the windscreen. 'But this gives you a place to start the search, doesn't it?'

'What do you mean?'

'Do you think your father might have tried to find Miss Thompson?'

Elinor. I lean back into my car seat. I considered Elinor, too. I have a lot of time now to consider how things are playing out. 'I don't think so. I think he might be too proud. And I think Papa is bright enough to realise that even if she knew where he was, she wouldn't tell him.'

Brown stretches her legs and says nothing for a few moments.

'We should try to find Elinor, this is what you're trying to suggest.' I don't phrase this as a question.

'We?' says Brown.

Out of the corner of my eye, I see that she's smiling. It's an exhausted smile that almost makes me want to pull over and do something inappropriate like take her hand. Or maybe even hold her.

'Brown, you're so clever,' I say, slowing down the car. No need whatsoever to reach the Hall too quickly. I might even have to take a small detour. There's a road that bypasses the village and slithers around the hills, around the farms.

'Too clever for my own good – that's what your mother always says.'

'She says that?' This doesn't sound at all like something that my mother would say. 'It's very true, though.'

Brown makes a sound similar to a muffled giggle. I've rarely seen Brown laugh – she's so serious and guarded at the Hall. And anyone who knows what's in their best interest should always be guarded around Papa. And I reckon Brown mostly knows what's in her best interest.

'You're so good at talking to people and piecing things together. If you were a man, you could be a detective. Like Sherlock Holmes.'

'Sherlock Holmes?'

'Yes, exactly.'

'Don't be daft, Miss Milton. Women can't be detectives.

And certainly not women like me. Maybe if I were a foreign heiress or such, I could be a detective. But not me.'

'I suppose you're right.' I think being with Jasper – or maybe being at secretarial school – taught me a few things. It taught me to look differently at people. Today, I see Brown for the first time. I never thought about her life before.

Girls like her, from families who have been in service for generations, they didn't have any choice, except going into service themselves. But I suppose there are a few more options nowadays than there used to be in my grandmother's day. 'You could open a ladies' hairdresser's,' I tell Brown. 'You would be startlingly successful, I reckon.'

Brown wraps the cardigan tight around herself again. Once I started, I can't seem to be able to stop myself. 'You didn't go into service because you wanted to, did you?'

'When?'

'When you first went into service.'

Brown frowns. 'Why are you asking, Miss Milton?'

'I was wondering.'

'About me.'

'Yes, about you.'

Our eyes meet and she stares at me as if trying to guess my motives. Again, I'm frightened by how tired she looks. 'You'd better look to the road, Miss Milton.'

My thoughts hop back to my brother. With nothing else to do around the Hall, I never quite cease to think about it. Where did everything go wrong? What happened? Nearly two years ago, he was the one who saved me from my life of ceaseless cocktail parties and dances where I was meant to meet that perfect rich man whom I wasn't keen on meeting at all. That was the problem itself: I knew this wasn't the life I wanted, but

I didn't know what to wish for instead. I was never taught what else was out there.

Will came in with his fizzy communist Oxford set, like George, and darling absent Edmund who spoke of the equality of women in the workforce (while I suspect Edmund has never been close to a woman in his life). Will coaxed me into starting at the secretarial school, and I had a roaring laugh when I saw how shocked Mother and Papa were to hear that I wanted a qualification. And then Will took me to the opera, which didn't feel like a very communist thing to do, but Will's set was always full of amusing contradictions. And then he introduced me to Jasper.

And the moment I met Jasper, I knew what I wanted – or, at least, who I wanted to be with. But being with Jasper isn't a possibility anymore, not even a remote one, so finding my brother is all I have left.

'Where do you think Elinor went after Papa dismissed her?' Where would a nanny go? Probably to find a new job. 'Do you think she might have found a position at a short notice?'

'With no references from your parents? I rather think not. And these things go around so quickly. I think it would be next to impossible for Elinor to find a position in any house.'

She's right. 'Her mother,' I say. 'Her mother helped out in the kitchens? I think she went back to their village long before Papa found out about her and Will.'

'Bletchley. Her mother was from Bletchley.'

'That would be a good place to start.'

'I reckon,' she says, her face turned away from me.

'I don't think I know anyone in Bletchley,' I say and then realise a moment later that this isn't true. I know Alastair and he's Papa's friend and the loveliest man in the world, but the last person I'd send in search of a missing person. Even if he works for the Foreign Office or some kind of Naval Cipher School or something similar.

'I don't know anyone either.'

'Do you think one of the maids might still be in touch with her? With Elinor, I mean?'

'I don't think so. No, I don't think any of the girls who are still at the Hall ever were on friendly terms with her. Elinor was always a bit cold to all of us, even though she was the one who came from the factory.' *Ah, yes*, I think. *The old story with the factory.* And her Cockney accent, which she ironed out by the end of her stay with us. 'She never knew her place, that one. I'm not surprised that things turned out the way they did.'

'Well, I was certainly surprised. I never expected this from Elinor, quiet as she was.'

Brown shrugs. 'It's always the still waters. And she barely spoke to any of us downstairs, and who does that? Of course she had something to hide.'

'But are *you* happy with your lot? With the place you have?'

Brown becomes quiet for such a long time that I don't think she's going to answer my question. I'm not expecting her to – she always shrinks when I interrogate her too openly.

We pass by three or four girls about my age, walking together on the side of the road, probably looking for some downtime in the pub. So radiant in their powder-blue, belted jackets. These must be the WAAFS from the airfield that's been built close to the Hall. The country is full of girls and women doing war work.

That's it. 'The WVS is everywhere these days,' I say. 'I think there must be a WVS in Bletchley, too.'

'I reckon.'

'Mother could write to them, don't you think? If she wanted to find out something.'

Brown smooths her dark-grey skirt. 'Like a woman's address?'

'Precisely.'

'That's certainly a good idea.'

'Mother would think it was a good idea if it came from you.' Mother must be the most desperate of us all to find Will. Her eyes are always red and swollen these days, and I'm in complete shock, since I always assumed that she only cared about her children as far as they cut a good picture in the world. But both Will and I proved to be disappointments by refusing to do what we were expected to. 'I think she's missed you terribly,' I add, exaggerating just a little bit. 'If I gave her the idea, she'd say it's no good.'

'Aha, I see,' she says, the tired smile reappearing on her face.

'Do you think it's a good idea?'

'I think it's a great idea.'

'Might you tell Mother so?'

'I think I might.'

'Good,' I say, more pleased with myself than I've been in days. Something, at least, will be done. Something is inching forward. 'Good.'

The stout, U-shaped silhouette of Milton Hall profiles itself against the horizon. Brown shifts in her seat. 'It's not about being happy with one's lot. It's about making the most of it. I didn't have a choice, Miss Milton. I had to go into service. My parents were poor, you see, so what choice was there for me? The key is always, always to make the best of what you have.'

She gives me a sidelong glance and I can read the slightest hint of reproach in it. Of course. She must have heard everything about me and Jasper – and she plainly doesn't agree with me. But why would she? I'm rich, spoiled, and educated. Why would I want to throw away all of this?

For love, I think. I'd throw away all of this for love.

Chapter Five

Rose

I still don't quite know what to do with myself after days and days. They're all the same: work, work, work, yet not enough to fill the void that David's departure left behind. My time is senseless without him as I carry on, limping on the inside. My mother sends me every now and then on a half-useless trip to the grocer's – since we have almost all that we need on the farm – which instead of cheering me up, makes me feel the stab of David's absence even harder. I can't meet him anymore at the back door of the shop once I've made my purchases, where he used to pop for a quick cigarette and a kiss. I'm only met by the concerned looks of David's father, and I don't want to share my misery. It would make it all the more real.

All the while, my own father sinks deeper and deeper into the lonely place he went to when the war began. One sunny day, my mother makes him his favourite food – peas, stewed with a juicy bit of smoked ham. He still pushes the plate away from him.

'You can have my portion, too, Rose,' he says and knocks down half of his cider in one gulp, looking out of the window.

I want to say, *don't look out there. Look at me. Look at Mum.* I know what he sees outside: the edge of the airfield. Every time an aeroplane buzzes – and that's often enough these days – I can see his fingers curling, trying perhaps to grip onto the last shreds of his sense of safety.

I want to say, you can't change the fate of the war if this is all you think about. All we can do is sit around and wait for news.

News.

'Do you mind if I turn on the wireless?' I say.

My mother cocks her head, waiting for my father's reply, but I've already sprung from my seat.

'Rose,' he says. 'Not while we're eating.'

My hand hovers above the polished wood button of our wireless set. 'I'm so sorry. I thought you were done with your lunch.'

'I wouldn't mind a bit of music,' says my mother, in an utterly surprising move of siding with me.

My father looks out of the window again and I take this as all the approval I need. I turn the volume up. The room doesn't fill with either music or a newscaster's soothing voice. It's Prime Minister Churchill's nasal voice that booms from the wooden box.

France is lost. It seems we're on the brink of the Battle of Britain.

I reel from the intensity of the blow, feeling for the back of my chair. I often came across maps of France in my history books – the square-ish shape with the laced contour of its borders. Now the Nazis with their red armbands are seeping through it like blood, the swastikas spinning, spinning, spinning, the mass of invaders overflowing, pressing against each other, towards the Channel. That they should have infected so much of the Continent in just a few weeks, teetering on the edges of Normandy, Calais, and Bretagne, ready to spring into the narrow waters and beyond at the lightest push is terrifying.

Next to me, my mother lays a hand on my father's arm.

And my David? He's also gone to battle.

Fear clenches my stomach and I can barely still hear the Prime Minister's words.

At the table, my father shifts uncomfortably in his seat. My mother steps towards the wireless and turns it off in a decisive move. She doesn't even look at me. 'I think this is quite enough, Rose,' she says.

'May I be excused,' I say – not really asking – and go to my room.

That an entire country should be lost, while we were having our quiet lunch...I sink onto my bed, staring at the dark beam above my head. That beam has been here all my life, watching over me as I go to sleep, ever since I can remember. I think, this beam will be here for a long time to come. So many times I've fallen asleep in this bed, a bed that served me all my life. I'm ready for another bed, another life, but who knows if I'm ever meant to see it? How many French or Polish girls like me died while the Germans advanced? Bombed? Ripped from their beds? Running from the invader? And what did they do to them when they found them?

I twist, wrapping the covers tighter around my body, as if

they can hide me from the worst possible futures. There's no telling what will come. A much more gullible version of me still thought at Christmas that the life that included my marriage to David by the end of the year was still a possibility. Even more than that, a certainty.

And my aunt warned me. I can't say that my aunt didn't warn me.

In the fields, I dig harder than ever. I muck out the chicken pen with such fury that two of the rotten planks at the bottom of the first floor crack. Hot tears drift down my cheeks, as I shovel and shovel amongst the smell of chicken shit with a whiff of mould, feathers, and dust floating through the air. I cry because no matter how hard I work, there's always something that needs cropping, chopping, milking, or fixing and no amount of work will make it better, or give me any peace, and no amount of work in the world, no matter how hard I try, will ever change the outcome of the war.

All of this while I seek to keep busy, busy, busy. With David gone, I dread the moment my days melt into evenings, and I become too tired to stir. I try to fiddle with my schoolbooks, but nothing sticks, not one of the names of great men who changed the course of history – and how many women were amongst them? Never in my life had I felt so small, so powerless.

The evening when all my friends are up at the village dance, I stack the books in a neat pile next to my bed and go down to the kitchen, where my father is smoking a cigarette he rolled himself.

'Where's Mum?' I ask.

'Around here,' he says, looking at me, yet not quite seeing me. 'Churning butter, I think.'

Outside, the darkness rolls in, melting into the day like wisps of fog. I have serious reason to doubt that my mother is churning butter at this hour.

'There's a dance tonight, with a real live band,' I say. 'They're supposed to have a very good lead singer. A man from Blackpool, I think.'

'Ah. Yes. Interesting.'

'But I can't go, you know. It would feel disloyal to David if I were to dance with other boys. Even if it were with his friends. It would be odd, I guess. And who knows what people will think. People like to talk.'

My father nods. 'Ah, yes, the gossip.'

'Exactly,' I say. I can't imagine anything more chilling than cold glares and the sound of whispered conversations behind my back.

The matter of the dance having been settled, I turn my attention to the kitchen. The metal stove has been wiped spotless; the dishes – white with a pattern of coloured flowers – are resting in their drying rack above the stone basin. Even the heavy, scratched table has been wiped clean of crumbs. A single plate with a few slices of bread pudding is in the middle. My mother has wiped out every source of possible fidgeting I'd have in this room. There's nothing else to be done.

'I was reading about Hannibal's campaign,' I say, trying to lure my father into a conversation. Any conversation.

My father used to love to hear me talk about the military campaigns of Napoleon, the Roman Empire, Eleanor of Aquitaine. I used to be so eager to gulp historical facts, to look up the dustiest, most forgotten history books in Miss Northon's School for Girls, so that I could report back at home with novelties.

'You know, what fascinates me the most,' I continue, 'isn't necessarily the fact that he managed to threaten the existence of Rome itself – Hannibal *ante portas* – but the before and after. Did you know that as he marched on from Spain, he lost more than half of the Army he left with from Carthage? I always thought about those poor men of Carthage, bundled up and sent out to fight, dying so far away from their families.'

My father's eyes clear of the mists. 'Rose. I'm sorry, but war isn't something I want to talk about right now.'

'Yes, sure,' I say, rising from the table.

'Mind how you go, Rose,' he says, as I exit the kitchen.

After leaving my father with his brooding, I thump up the stairs, smarting. All my friends are out having a fantastic time at the dance, for all I know, and David is who knows where, in training; my mother is nowhere to be found, and I've never felt so alone in my life. I miss the scurrying and the whispering of my grammar school, the constant presence of someone I could talk to whenever I needed to, whether it was to complain about a teacher or about the fare they presented us with at lunchtime. Nothing, but nothing like the dark, quiet first floor of my parents' farmhouse.

And then, halfway up the creaking stairs, I remember. There is someone else like me. Someone else who won't go to the dance tonight; someone else who is also waiting for her sweetheart. I turn on my heels and shout in the direction of the kitchen that I'm going out, then make for Maud's house.

Maud is in the kitchen, boiling nappies for her sister's baby. Maud's sister stopped being a nice girl in the winter of last year, and the loss of niceness began to show. Unfortunately for her, the footman who had robbed her of her innocence preferred taking the high road rather than making an honest woman out of her, so Maud's sister had had no other option than to leave her employment at the time, entrust the baby to her mother's care, and look for a new job in an aeroplane factory. Maud's sister is certainly pleased about the new job opportunities that the war is creating – she would have been shunned all the way to Norfolk without it. News travels fast around these places and nothing travels faster than a good piece of gossip.

'Rose, take a seat,' says Maud, stirring the cauldron again.

I plop myself into one of the wobbly chairs. The kitchen is much more crowded than ours with hardly any place to move between the assorted chairs and the cupboards lining the walls. A smell of wet dog permeates the air.

'These bloody nappies,' says Maud. 'I swear, all day long I do nothing but boil nappies. You'd think my sister could pop in every once in a while and contribute to clear up all this mess she made.' She looks up at me, her long, dark hair caught in a net at the back of her head, combed and curled up away from her temples. Maud's family struggled after her father was hit by a car years ago – scraped up off the road he was walking along – yet she always took great pains with her appearance. 'I'm sorry. You know I love the bloody rascal, but he makes so much work. You wouldn't believe it.'

'It never ends, does it?'

'What?'

'The work.'

'Ah, yes, that.' Maud sighs. 'You know, I was thinking of taking up a job at the factory, too. My sister won't shut up about it. And the money. You should see the dress she bought herself last month. You'd think she'd give something towards feeding this little mouth,' she says, lifting a nappy with the tip of a spoon and smiling.

'The factory. That would be nice, doing something for the war and all. I can't stop thinking about what Mr Churchill said. With the Battle of Britain starting...'

'There you go. The aeroplane factory. You should think about it.'

'You mean me?' The restlessness slushes and shatters within me. 'The aeroplane factory. Why not? I assume this would mean that we'd do our bit. Though I was rather thinking about the Women's Royal Naval Service.'

'The Wrens?'

'Yes, I mean...' The thought begins shifting and taking shape as I speak. 'Why not? I'd get to see the world. And then, there's that lovely uniform. The crisp shirt, that beautiful tailored jacket, the golden buttons.'

'Yes, I reckon you're fancy enough for them.'

'What do you mean?'

'Oh, come on.' Maud tucks back a slip of hair that has escaped her flowery headband. 'You know what I mean. The Wrens are looking for the posh sort of girls. Grammar school and all that. I wager you'll fit right in.'

'Hmm. Do you think they might send me around the world? Ceylon and all? I don't think David would like that. I don't think I'd like that.'

Maud's face falls. 'Why would they send you all the way to Ceylon? A girl? Why would they need girls on the other side of the world?' She rubs her temple with the back of her hand. 'I still haven't heard about Frank, you know.'

'Ah.' I don't quite know what to say. There hasn't been any news from Frank, her sweetheart, since Dunkirk. 'I gather not all men have been accounted for. It's been mad. I'm sure... I think... Maybe poor Frank is lying wounded somewhere in a hospital. Maybe he's with his unit...'

'Maybe he's lying dead on a beach, Rose, and there's no one to tell us, because there isn't a single bloody living breathing person around him who cares.'

I open my mouth and close it, all thoughts vanishing, cowering, and trembling. She spoke aloud my greatest fear, my worst nightmare. David being struck down from the sky, while I go mindlessly about my own business; not worrying about a thing. Though it seems to me that I hardly do anything lately except worry.

'And what do we do about that? What do we do to change this?'

'What? You're suggesting I should go on foot to France and find him myself?' says Maud.

'No, not on foot,' I say. 'You couldn't cross the Channel on foot. But a boat – yes, a boat might just do.'

Hands in the pockets of my working breeches, I take the long way back home, through the centre of town. So what if anyone sees me dressed like this, when the world is burning. And besides, everyone I know must be at the dance, anyway. I drag my feet across the pavement, slowing in front of the café that used to belong to Luigi's father, before his entire family were branded 'aliens' and they were packed up and sent to the Isle of Man, from what I heard. Or across the seas to Canada, but that seems too ludicrous for any government to do, so I don't believe everything that's whispered around in town. Why would someone send Luigi and his family packing? They've done nothing wrong.

That evening, I'm not drawn to the broken windows of the café, staring at me like so many damaged teeth. To the upturned chairs and stained walls. That evening, I march up to the next door, which is painted a faded green. To it, a poster has been glued of a stylish young woman, her hand raised to her fancy blue beret in salute. Her uniform is so posh, like Maud said, with the tailored jacket, the white shirt, and the dark-blue tie. *Join the Wrens!* says the poster, *and free a man for the fleet!*

Free. What a word. Might we be free this time next year? Free to travel the world? Or will we be confined to our homes, or even worse?

But I don't dare. I can't. What if David comes home on leave and I'm not here, but halfway across the world? Wouldn't that be the worst thing that could happen to me?

Close. I want to be close to him. To see him every day, to touch him, knowing he would still be there. Biggin Hill, he said. After his training in Yorkshire is done, he said he'll be up at Biggin Hill.

Chapter Six

Evie

I may live in a golden cage, but a cage is still a cage. For two weeks my parents ignore my presence at the dinner table, so I make it a habit to excuse myself before the meal starts, professing a headache. No one asks questions. They just ask me to be there when they receive guests. They ask if they can 'trust me to be a gracious host'. I nod with a strained smile.

I have to conceal my delight at actually seeing other people or my parents might change their minds, dismiss it as a bad idea after all. Not that I have friends I could tell about my miserable fate.

No one tells me anything: if I want to know if there's any news about Will, I have to question my little brothers. If I want to know how the war is truly going, I can't ask Papa anymore. According to the wireless, everything is splendid. Except that we're in the middle of a bloody war and we're bloody losing it and I'm bloody wasting myself away. But you wouldn't know all that after listening to the news.

After two weeks of this, it's a relief when Papa summons me to his office. I should certainly know better. He lays in my hands a letter from Jasper.

So he's been censoring all my correspondence. What a surprise.

Not really.

Before I start reading, for the briefest moment, I wonder if he's been keeping to himself any correspondence that might have arrived from Will's friends.

He probably has.

Jasper asks what is happening. Why I haven't written. If we can meet in the village – he can come up from London for an evening to see me. My stomach twists and knots together at the thought of seeing him. How I long for a few hours together. To see him, to have a proper laugh for the first time in weeks. How he enjoys to tease me.

But that isn't meant to be.

I make an inventory of all the honest answers I can give him.

Dear Papa has taken control over my life, that is what's happening. I haven't written because the truth wouldn't go past my father and the truth is that I think of him every night when I stare at the dusty canopy of my bed and I miss him so much that I feel a hole opening in my chest and that hole deepens even more when I realise that I can never, ever see him again if I want him to be safe. And no, I don't want to meet him in the village, but not for the reasons he thinks might be true.

None of those answers will be laid down on the piece of

paper that my father places in front of me. 'I think you have a letter to write,' he says with his smug smile.

I'd very much like to take the ink pot from his polished desk and spill it on his head. See what that would do to his smug smile.

I know I won't do that. I pick up his fountain pen, the one that has a golden tip and is encrusted with rubies. 'Please don't tell me what to write. I know. And I'll show you.' I roll the pen between my fingers. How much is it worth? I have no idea. Probably enough to feed an entire family for many months. Maybe a year. Jasper's family, for instance. 'You do want the letter to sound as if it's written by me, don't you? And not by you.'

The lies drip from this golden tip more easily than I would have thought. I blame it on the pen. It's probably used to lying. I tell him I've returned to my family home. That secretarial school isn't for me. That I'm certain I won't work a single day in my life, and why would I when I don't have to. I'm painting a smeared image of myself on this fine sheet of paper and there's a sort of pleasure I take in this. What I really think of is Jasper's face lighting up when telling me about America, about all the possibilities. I remember how struck I felt and what a lonely place I thought it would be. I remember saying, *silly, who would we know there? It would just be us.*

What a dream that would be now. So many futures, turned to shambles.

The pain drips into the sheet of paper. Every sentence I write hurts physically, but I cannot stop. My father moves closer, looking over my shoulder and I can literally feel his breath on the back of my neck.

My scrawling becomes pointier, rushing into itself. I grit my teeth so I don't have to cry. 'Done,' I say, promising myself that he won't have my tears.

Papa bends down and rips up my letter. 'Evie, you never learn. Never write anything down that can be used against you.' He shakes his head, then hands me a fresh sheet of paper. 'Again.'

I bite my lip and bite down on a few words. 'I know what to tell him to keep him away.'

'It will come back and bite you in the arse, dear girl. You have no idea. No wonder women make such awful politicians. Actually, they make no politicians at all.'

I open my mouth to protest.

'Again, please,' he interrupts. 'This time, without compromising yourself and this entire family.'

My pen hovers in mid-air. I have to be fast, or he'll start telling me what to do, because that's what he usually does. And the anger that's biting at my chest will come loose and I'll tear the other sheet of paper I've fully scribbled and we'll get nowhere.

So I have to write something. And fast.

I thank him for everything.

My signature at the bottom of the page is an ugly, pointy thing. I take more time with my last name.

Milton.

Milton is supposed to be a thing of beauty.

At least, that's what Papa always says.

———————

I try to distract myself, but I am failing. I spend conspicuously large amounts of time getting my hair dressed by Brown. There is nothing else to do. There isn't even a proper war going on: no parachutists dropping from the skies, no German soldiers swarming on the beaches. The beaches that are full of barbed wire in this mid-June instead of tourists.

'Your mother has heard from the WVS in Bletchley,' Brown tells me one day, while she's curling my hair.

'Did she?' I say, not even daring to hope. With so little else to do, I think so much of Will and Elinor these days. If not, I have to think about Jasper and how he hasn't written to me. How I could tell him the truth and try and send the letter through Brown, eluding Papa's control.

Brown purses her lips. 'The lady there confirmed that Mrs Thompson lives in Bletchley and that she doesn't want to make contact with anyone at Milton Hall.'

'Oh,' I say. 'And what is Mother going to do about it?'

'Nothing at all. She was appalled by the blunt refusal. She felt so ashamed that she should have even asked in the first place, and that a bunch of women in Bletchley would gossip about her, the lady of Milton Hall, being turned away by a cook.'

'Goodness.' I roll my eyes so hard that I literally feel them turning in my head.

'You know how she is.'

'So she'd rather stop any enquiries about her son, so as not to cover herself in shame. I'm speechless.'

Brown shrugs.

'What do *you* think about it?' I ask.

Our gazes meet in the mirror. She blinks, obviously trying to clear any trace of expression from her face. 'I don't think anything.' Sometimes, Brown is terribly odd about Will's disappearance.

I look down, toying with my golden watch, rubbing the tiny diamonds on the bracelet. 'What do we do next?' I tap my fingers on the shiny surface of my beauty table. 'Is there anyone else downstairs who might have Elinor's address? Who might write to her?'

''Fraid not. She wasn't the friendliest, that one.'

I try to remember the times I caught my brother speaking to her, in the library. The times I caught him and his set with her, on the lawn, inviting her to play rounders with them. How I once saw her going down into the village with them. She wasn't the only young woman in the group. There was someone else with them. 'There was a maid. Esther. She left last year, too.' Without giving any sort of notice, for that matter. Appalling manners. I hope Mother used strong words in her reference, but I suppose not. That's not the sort of thing she would do.

'Yes, that was her name,' says Brown.

'Do you have any inkling where she might be?'

Brown stares at me again, through the mirror. 'No, I don't,' she finally says.

'My, my. Something even you don't know.' I pick up a brush with a silver handle, an inheritance from my grandmother. 'I'm not surprised. She was cheeky, that one. Can you imagine? Last summer she came and asked me, of all people, to help her find a new position. I've never heard anything like it.'

Behind me, Brown stands still.

'I was coming back from a ride, and she waited for me by the stable door. She asked me if she could have a quiet word with me while I handed Starlight over to the stable boy. I thought she must have been waiting for me for a long time.' I remember her narrow face. She had a full lower lip she kept biting into, and a thinner, well-contoured upper lip and high cheekbones. She must have had wonderful dark hair underneath her cap, yet I never saw it. I remember thinking that she was such a pretty girl. 'She'd been waiting for me, I think, and I wondered then how nobody had noticed. I mean, can chambermaids go about the house and do as they please, unchecked?'

'I suppose they find ways, miss. Where there's a will, there's a way. She did find a way out of Austria.'

'Ah, yes, that was it. I knew there was more to it. She had an accent I could never quite place.' I put the brush down on the glossy surface of the vanity table. 'Austria. Yes.' The need for domestic help is dire here – Mother does nothing but complain about the quality of the young women in service. So many are streaming in from Germany and Austria, I've heard from our guests. Esther was the only foreigner we've ever hired. I think we never had any reason to complain about her; she was the sort to keep her head down. Well, at least until she left us. And I never did mention to Mother the incident at the stables. I shudder. 'And yet, what kind of girl asks her own employer to find her a new position?'

'A desperate one,' says Brown, combing the hair at the front of my head into a pompadour.

'Why would she be desperate? What did we ever do to her? Do we beat people? Do we starve them?'

'It's unthinkable, isn't it, what people in this house do to other people.' Brown pulls the hair at the back of my head a bit too hard, then rolls it onto itself to form a long, loose bun. I can't make up my mind if she means Papa in general, or the spot of presumed shame that he's so intent upon averting.

Chapter Seven

Rose

The day after France falls, I receive a letter from David. He says flying is the most fantastic thing he's ever done, and that in a few days he'll be embarking on his first solo flight. He says that when the war is over, he'd like to take me on an aeroplane, too, so I can see the world from above.

That's my David, always flying high, always thinking about taking me with him.

I believe I'm not really thinking about it, but, a few days later, while I'm washing the dishes with my mother, I blurt it out. 'He said this is our finest hour.'

'Who said that?' says my mother, scrubbing furiously at an old mug.

'Didn't you hear? Mr Churchill, on the wireless.'

'Ah,' says my mother. 'He said a great deal. I don't remember it all. Though I will say this: he has a wonderful way with words, that man.'

I think, *and you have such a way of trying to make me change course when you don't like where I'm going*. 'So this is it? Scrubbing pots and pans? Waiting?'

The wait is perhaps the worst of this all. Waking up every day, hoping that something extraordinary will happen. The way the day crawls into evening, the same as the day before, the same as tomorrow will be. The way I look onto the street every few minutes, hoping that the postman will deliver me a letter that will be the cue for me to start living again.

'I hope this isn't about joining some sort of women's service,' she says, passing me the mug. I focus on wiping it dry with a tea towel, hoping she won't notice the heat in my cheeks.

It's uncanny how she often presses her finger where it hurts most. 'No, no women's services for me.'

'Good, because you know what I think. A woman's place is at home. This is why they call it the "home front". We fight our battles at home, Rose. The Army isn't a place for girls.' She attacks the dried crust on the straw pot as though it's been stained through some ingenious plot of the Germans, just to vex her.

'That remains to be seen. The last war got the women out of their homes and onto the factory floors.'

My mother wipes the surface of the stone basin as if giving the stewing pot a respite to gather its forces. 'You're talking like your aunt now. And do you reckon that was a good thing?' She lets go of her scourer. 'What the Great War did was to leave a lot of widows and spinsters in the world. Think about poor Mavis. She was such a pretty girl – why, all the boys wanted to dance with her. Do you know what she did wrong, as opposed to me, who ended up marrying and having a beautiful daughter?' She looks at me pointedly.

I shrug. I know where this conversation is going and I refuse to play along.

'Nothing. Nothing at all. Like me, she had a fiancé when the war started. But he never came back home. So next time you think about rushing into something, think again. Think of Aunt Mavis.'

Aunt Mavis. Yes, Aunt Mavis. Of course. I stare at the kitchen table, its zigzag of scratches blurring before my eyes. My mother means that I should feel sorry for Aunt Mavis, who, of course, has no family to look after, just her humble top job with the Foreign Office. In the heart of London. Aunt Mavis, who has offered before to help me.

'There, there, don't be upset,' says my mother.

I'm not upset. Perhaps with myself a bit, for not thinking earlier of Aunt Mavis.

My mother goes on. 'Now, I was young and eager once, too. I know how it is. You want to help. I'll ask the WVS what we can do, all right? Maybe we can take up some knitting. That will surely cheer us up in the evenings.'

Knitting isn't at all what I'm thinking about, but there's no need to tell my mother everything. Lesson learned quite a while ago.

She nods and attacks the stew pot with renewed force. 'There you go. I knew there would be a way. Imagine joining one of those women's services and not being at home when David is on leave. Wouldn't that be the worst thing in the world?'

'The worst,' I say, already thinking about something else entirely.

The next day, I pick up the wicker basket and the rationing coupons and wave my mother goodbye with undisguised cheerfulness. My mother rubs my shoulder. 'There, I knew you'd come around. Don't forget lard. We're running low on lard.'

'I'll certainly remember,' I say, and hurry to town.

Because I have a plan. For the first time since this terrible upending of my life has started, I have a plan. One that will perhaps bring me back to the helm of my own fate. I weave around the grocery store and make a beeline for the Post Office, congratulating myself on my idea.

When I pick up the receiver in the telephone box, my hand is trembling. It's the biggest decision I've ever made in my life, and there's no one to advise me. I can't tell Maud, or my father, and by no means can I tell Mum. I wish David were here. Even as I tell the operator from the Foreign Office my aunt's name and her section, I don't know if this is the right decision.

For a long, long time, there's no one on the other end. I'm tempted to put the receiver down and run away. Do I really want to return to the farmhouse, though? Return to the loop of my ever-repeating days? Stretching like a wasteland full of sand and scorch in between the times my David will be home. The days full of waiting.

'Mavis Wiley speaking.' My aunt's obsidian voice cuts through wire and air, all the way from London.

'Aunt Mavis!' I say. 'How are you?'

'How are *you*, Rose? To what do I owe the pleasure?'

'I don't know. I was wondering…' The moment has come

and words are teetering on the tip of my tongue, unwilling to come out.

'Is your father all right?' she asks, lowering her voice.

'As well as he can be. Considering the circumstances.'

'Terrifying, isn't it?'

'Are you worried about it at the Foreign Office?'

My aunt clears her throat.

'Right,' I say. 'Right. You can't talk about it.'

'Rose, if you want to catch up, you can call me tonight.'

'No, not tonight. I…I was wondering…' I tug at the cord of the telephone, hard. 'I remember you mentioned a while ago a job in London? I was wondering if that was still a possibility?'

And it's that simple enquiry, one single question, that starts a storm. A telegram summons me to London, to an interview. Panic is written all over my mother's face. 'You are summoned? Why so?'

I tell her what Aunt Mavis taught me to say: 'They must have found out that I speak German. They need German speakers these days.'

'Yes, but how would they know that?' She wipes her hands on her apron again and again and again.

'From the school records, probably.'

'Right,' she says, not completely satisfied and rushes to the oven, where her pie is burning.

Later, she asks, 'But why you and not your former classmates, too?'

I shrug, trying to appear as impressed as a boiled turnip.

'Maybe they are yet to be summoned. Maybe they began at the end of the alphabet.'

'Odd,' my mother says. 'The Foreign Office, out of all the places in Britain. I expect your aunt had a hand in this.'

I don't reply, leaving all the fretting and worrying to her. It never occurs to me to ask Aunt Mavis a few more questions. For instance, where this interview is. And if the whirlwind will set me down in London, in the end.

———————

The storm uproots me and places me firmly in front of the gates of this spectacular place. The guard leads me through them to one of the huts by the entrance. He opens the door and gestures me into a humble room. The hut is made of wood, lit by a single bulb literally hanging from the ceiling. There's a battered table and three chairs with metallic frames dotted with rust. The contrast to the appearance of the house couldn't be more violent.

The guard says, 'You can't come in if you don't have a pass. I'll have to fetch someone. Wait here.'

After my eyes adjust to the sickly looking light – there is one window, to be fair, but it has been obstructed according to the blackout regulations – I plonk myself in the least battered chair. One leg proves to be shorter than the others, so it wobbles when I shift in my seat. I'm about to move to another chair when the door blasts open and an RAF officer strides into the hut. He gives me a hand (which I shake), his name (which I forget instantly, but he mumbles something about Group Captain) and a document printed on yellow paper.

'I'll need you to sign that,' he says, laying the document and a pen on the table.

I grab the pen. 'Where?' I ask.

'Not so fast,' he says. 'Read it first.'

'Sure.' I pull it closer, ready to read. 'Are you my superior?' I ask.

Aunt Mavis hadn't been waiting for me in London, at the address mentioned in the telegram. Just the two Army officers and their lorry, who had asked me my name and then proceeded to bundle me into the back. On reflection, perhaps I should have asked more questions. But Army officers wouldn't kidnap girls like me, would they? Especially not to bring them to a splendid house with dubious furniture. 'Are you conducting the interview?'

The RAF Officer says, 'I'm afraid I can't tell you anything until you sign the document.'

'Right-o. The document, then.'

The document is, apparently, the Official Secrets Act. As I read on, butterfly wings flap in my stomach and my palms grow moist. I'll be involved in secret activities, it seems. So secret that I won't be able to speak to anyone about them, or else I'd make myself guilty of high treason.

The butterflies in my belly flutter from fear to excitement. How I'd like to be able to tell David about this, to share the thrill.

My, my. Little Rose Wiley, involved in secret activities. I wager this is what my aunt must feel like. No wonder she loves her job so much. A job it seems I don't know very much about at all.

As I reach the end, the RAF officer taps the yellow

document. 'Just to be clear about the activities you're going to be engaged in, Miss Wiley.'

I want to ask what activities, but he moves on too quickly.

'Any information about your own activities will be provided on a need-to-know basis. You do not ask questions about what happens at Bletchley Park. Not to persons outside of Bletchley Park, not even to persons outside your own section. In fact, speaking to anyone about any activity you might be undertaking at Bletchley Park, even to persons within Bletchley Park, is strictly forbidden.'

This word again, *activity*. I've been in this room for half an hour now or half an eternity and I'm none the wiser.

'Any breach of the Official Secrets Act is considered treason, punishable by prison or worse,' he goes on.

'Pardon me? What does "worse" mean?'

'I always forget what the punishment for treason is. I think it's death by hanging. Or by firing squad.'

So much for telling David.

'But, my family. What will I tell my family? Does this mean I am to remain here?'

How do I explain to my fiancé that I'm in a place called Bletchley Park if I'm not allowed to speak about my work? Pardon me, my 'activities'.

'Yes, you are to remain here for the duration. And it's rather standard procedure for the girls to be hired as clerks for the Foreign Office. Tell your family you're a typist.'

'A typist. I've never been near a typewriter in my life. My family will know that.'

The RAF officer clears his voice. 'I'm sorry, Miss Wiley, you'll have to clarify this with your direct superior. Now, if you don't mind.' He points at the bottom of the paper. 'If there aren't any more questions…'

I have plenty of questions, but not of them refers to the Official Secrets Act. It's rather clear to me to keep mum, like the posters tell us.

I pick up the pen and scrawl my signature at the bottom of the document. This makes me think about Goethe's Faust and his pact. I seem to have no idea what I'm getting myself into. What I'm really signing up for.

'Welcome to Bletchley Park, Miss Wiley.'

If things have been happening fast since I received the telegram, they're happening even faster now. The RAF officer leads me through the park, towards the mansion. Our short walk passes by a pond with swishing reeds, two swans rippling its murky surface. On one of the sides, there's a wooden dock and a boat. But there's no time to admire the landscape of lawns and trees and the small lake. An invisible rope tying me to the RAF officer's quick pace drags me through the arched entrance, between the two marble griffins, and into the house.

The interiors are as startling as the façade of the mansion: walls clad in polished oak, pink marble arches dancing in front of the stairs. To my right, instead of a door, the wall is punctured by three rounded arches. Behind them, there's an enclosed hallway, with a stained-glass ceiling above which vaults upwards. The hallway opens to three or more rooms – there isn't time for me to look. I take a peek to my left, where a door opens to a small antechamber that leads to the vastest library I've ever seen in my life. But this is far from a place of peace and serenity: while the walls are lined with books, the floor has been taken over by desks and chairs and men and women and piles and piles of papers.

'Don't dawdle, Miss Wiley,' calls the RAF officer, and I have to hurry after him up the stairs.

My hand lingers on the carved wooden banister that stretches between the six-sided pillars on the landings. The gridded panels are framed by carved flowers giving way to lustrous oak on top. The lower parts of the panels cover the bottom of the stairs, so it seems that the staircase is afloat. I've never seen anything so extravagant, but then again, how many manors have I visited in my life?

The RAF officer is already on the first floor, opening a door and signalling me to hurry. I rush behind him, dragging my suitcase.

'Professor Walton, Miss Wiley for you,' says the RAF officer and gives me a push inside. The room is a strange mixture of old and new, sumptuous and clerical – thick rugs (probably an inheritance from the mansion's glorious past) and the same walls panelled in wood, all framing a few shabby pieces of furniture, even more scratched than the ones in the guard's hut: an L-shaped desk with two chairs and another massive rectangular desk that looks like a huge box with a pile of papers thrown on top.

Behind it sits a tall, lanky man with a pair of tortoiseshell spectacles that magnify his eyes. They're blue, and both end in a set of smiling wrinkles. He must be in his late thirties or early forties. If it weren't for those wrinkles, he would have looked like an overgrown boy who can't even take proper care of his own clothing, with his creased shirt and his tweed jacket that's missing two buttons at the cuffs. He invites me to take a seat and extends his hand. 'Edmund Walton, Miss Wiley. Thrilled to welcome you to Bletchley Park.'

Behind me, the RAF officer closes the door, to my huge relief. This man looks friendlier and like he might actually answer a few questions. I depose the suitcase at my feet. 'Where are we exactly, Professor?'

'Well, if you're asking about the nature of the organisation, Bletchley Park is a mix of the Navy's old Room—'

'I don't want to be rude, but where are we? I mean, geographically?'

'I think about halfway between London and Coventry.'

The map unravels in my mind. So we are north of London – not catastrophically far from Biggin Hill, where David will be soon. And there must be a railway station close to here – I heard the whistle of a train as I arrived. 'Ah, thank you. This is good to know.'

I'm itching to ask what Bletchley Park is, but I know better than that.

The professor ruffles a few sheets that are spread in front of him. 'Miss Wiley, is it true that you speak German?'

'I've taken German in grammar school.'

'Italian?' The professor ticks something on his sheets.

'No, I'm not Italian.' I'd have thought that the Foreign Office would have checked my background before inviting me onto the premises. And what about my aunt? 'Nor are either of my parents. My father's sister, Mavis Wiley, she also works for the Foreign Office. In London.'

'Erm, no, Miss Wiley, that much was clear. I was only wondering if you can also speak Italian.'

'No, no, my second foreign language was French.'

'All right,' he says and ruffles through his papers. 'There's a very special place where we send people who know German.'

I have no idea if he realises what he seemed to say, especially considering what has been happening to the British 'aliens' since last year, but the giddiness is like laughing gas and it has clouded my head. I almost – almost! – snigger.

'First, we give them a little test.' The professor places the piece of paper in front of me and passes me a pencil. 'Please try to fill in as many words as you can. It's German.'

On the sheet there are three sentences with incomplete words. The blank spaces have been marked with dashes. Some of the dashes have a number from one to five scribbled underneath in tiny writing. It's a sophisticated game of hangman.

Riddles. It's so nice to stretch my fingers, to make them ready for something other than housework. It's so nice to close them around a pen. I feel like I'm in school again – I didn't even know how much I've missed it. Being good at something, flexing my brain muscles.

The professor asks me if I want some tea.

'No, thank you,' I say without thinking. I tap the pen against the sheet. 'Professor, everyone is allowed a sort of clue at the beginning of the game. That's how it's usually played.'

The professor pushes his spectacles up his nose. 'What game, Miss Wiley? I'm afraid I'm confused.'

'Hangman.'

'Hangman?' He half turns the sheet towards him. 'Right, right. I never looked at it that way. Interesting example of lateral thinking.'

'Lateral thinking?'

'Yes, yes. A clue, you said. Very well, then. These are

military terms. German military terms. Ah, yes, I should mention this, perhaps: the tiny numbers underneath some of the blank spaces are to be associated with the same letter. For instance, if you identify "one" as "A", you can place "A" above every space marked with "one".' He rotates the sheet towards me again. 'Have I made myself clear enough? I'm sometimes in the habit of speaking to all kinds of people as if they were my students.'

Perhaps he's trying to be nice, but I do wonder if he assumes that I'm simple-minded because I come from a farm. Yet so did my aunt. I shift in my seat, uncomfortable. I know how it must look, Aunt Mavis intervening with the Foreign Office for a job for her niece. And what if I fail the test? Would they still give me a job then? 'No, it's all crystal clear.' I have to do my best not to embarrass her.

'Well then.' He glances at his pocket watch. 'Miss Wiley, you have ten minutes.'

I frown at the piece of paper and chew the end of my pencil. The first thing that stands out for me is a U connected by a dash to a four-lettered word: *U-Boot. Submarine*. The two Os each have a tiny 3 scribbled underneath. I scrawl Os above all the threes on my sheet. I guess another word: *Formation*. I now have the As, two Ns and one S. Words begin emerging, like the shiny tiles of a fireplace when you clean the soot. *Africa*. C is 4. I fill in the Cs, then realise something is amiss. The German spelling is *Afrika*. I erase and fill in the blanks with Ks. I have a new word: *Geschwindigkeit. Speed*.

I write and erase, rewrite, pause and think. Professor Walton fidgets. He crosses and uncrosses his legs. I look up – a mistake. He leans over the desk and grabs the sheet.

'Let's see what we have here,' he says.

'No, no, I'm not done!' I say, grasping at my piece of paper.

I've only found thirteen or fourteen of the twenty words. The rest are sorry incomplete bits, splintered by blank spaces. I'm sure I can do better. At least, I could try.

Professor Walton clicks his tongue. 'This should be enough, I believe. Speed is of utmost importance for this—' He glances at the sheet and shakes his head. 'I daresay!'

'I know. If you could give me two more minutes. Not to be disrespectful, but I'm quite certain the ten minutes you promised me weren't up.'

Professor Walton leans across the desk. I can smell tobacco on his breath. 'Miss Wiley, do you know what that was?'

I shake my head. The butterflies in my stomach are going so mad that I'm almost nauseous.

'That little game of hangman, as you called it. Miss Wiley, you just managed to crack more than half of an ultra-secret message of the Luftwaffe.'

Secret messages. The Luftwaffe. I'm so excited that I could cry.

'Miss Wiley. Do you know what we do with people who know German?'

Chapter Eight

Evie

I'm on top of Starlight, my gorgeous bay mare, heading for the woods. Two weeks since my letter to Jasper and not a word. It's as if time itself is standing still. I dig my heels into the mare's soft belly and she jolts forward into a gallop. There's no news from Will either, and not a soul who cares that my life is wasting away. Even if I were allowed to leave Milton Hall, I don't know what I would do. It's tempting to think that I could find a husband and a sort of freedom – I suppose, as arrangements go, Mother and Papa don't bother one another too much – but what then? The same endless dinners when we don't have to speak to each other as long as we cut a good figure in public?

On days like this, with nothing else other than the rustling leaves of trees to keep me company, I do miss the doom-and-gloom talk of Will's set. The way they predicted the fall of our corrupt civilisation, concentrating so much power and so many riches in the hands of so few, while millions lived on the brink of starvation. Pushing women forward to more active roles in society; the real, working society, as they said, and not the one revolving around tea-o'clock. I do think this is why Will and his friends deliberately conversed with Elinor and Esther in sight of everyone at Milton Hall: as much a provocation to Papa as it was a statement about their values.

But they were outsiders, Elinor and Esther, as Brown had said, so this is why they were the only ones the boys had been able to recruit to their cause. I can't imagine Brown or our butler having tea with Will's set; they would have been too mindful of breaching etiquette. I'd caught them once having tea. Will, Esther, and Elinor, that is. Will himself was handing a cup and saucer to Esther; it must have been Esther, with her striking eyes, I come to think of it now. Mother's finest porcelain, the white one with blue flowers. They were both smiling and they stopped doing so when they became aware of me. Elinor had stared at her hands, as if my presence in the room suddenly put her in the wrong place.

A tree trunk fallen in the middle of the path snatches me back to my present. For a split second I wonder if I should pull the reins and lead the mare around it. Instead, I dig my heels into her belly, spurring her on. The knock of her hooves on the beaten earth drums faster, faster, faster. And just like that, mere feet before we both reach the trunk, she stops. I hit the ground with a thud. The pain reverberates from my lower back to my hips. 'Stupid horse,' I mutter.

She snorts.

I push myself up onto my feet, pulling hard at her reins, harder, perhaps, than necessary. Her nostrils flutter and I read fear in her wide eyes, in the way she shies her head away from me.

'It's not your fault,' I say, gentler this time, more to remind myself. 'It's not your fault.'

She still pulls her head away from me and, in between her snorts, I start hearing it, too. A distant buzz, rising.

'Shush, stupid. It's aeroplanes.' There's an airfield not far from the village and since it was built the buzz has become as much a sound of these parts as the neigh of horses or the birds singing in the forest. For the people, at least.

Starlight takes a few steps back, throwing her head from side to side. It's almost as if she's trying to shake me off. The buzz increases as the planes come closer and closer. Through the foliage, I can see patches of sky.

'Shush. Let's go home, shall we?' I say, moving to her side.

My instinct tells me we should go home. My instinct, as someone who has been riding for so many years, also tells me that I shouldn't try to mount her. I take her by the reins and lead her towards the house.

'All right, then.'

As we approach a clearing, there's a whistle that makes me cover my ears. After that, a thud so loud that the ground beneath my feet shakes. Starlight rears and neighs and her eyes dart wildly in all directions. It takes all my strength not to let go of the reins.

Bollocks.

These aren't RAF pilots flying out.

When I think I've calmed her enough to continue home – at a brisk pace – there's another thud. And another. The buzzing is so loud that it makes my teeth clatter. I can't hold the mare any longer, but I can't let her go, either. I try to remember what has been said to me over and over and over again. I should take cover, but where? We must be two or three miles away from Milton Hall. I pull Starlight with all my strength towards a tree, tugging hard. I try to bind her reins around the trunk. There's another thud and she shies so suddenly that she nearly breaks my wrist. I pull again, so hard that the froth around her mouth is pink with blood. I have to bind her, or who knows where she'll run to? I manage to lash the reins to a tree and then jump into a patch of nearby bushes.

How stupid it would be to be caught riding out in the woods. By a bomb, I mean. I was never the rustic sort of girl; to be forever in communion with nature wouldn't suit me well. I assume they wouldn't find my body, or what would be left of it if I were struck, because they wouldn't even know where to look.

This hits me harder than any of the Nazi attacks. If they never find me, will Papa think I ran away? And what will he do to Jasper because of it?

Inside, I'm screaming.

Starlight strains against the tree and her calls are more than I can bear. I cover my ears, but even my palms can't muffle the searing buzz above me. The planes must be right overhead.

Is this how Will felt at Dunkirk? Scared out of his mind? He wouldn't even have had the shelter of trees above him. *Oh, Will.*

The evening after the incident in the cloakroom, when the earl presumptive covered my face in slobber, I was supposed to have met him again at a private ball, where I was to be chaperoned by Will. When I told him about the slight feeling of nausea I experienced when thinking I'd have to meet him again, my brother laughed and told me to follow his lead.

To my surprise, he took me to the ball and paraded me around the room, shaking hands and smiling at other young gentlemen in evening suits with their hair combed back, like him, and at other young ladies in white evening dresses, like me. And after the round was done, after everyone had seen us, and the dance had begun, we slipped into a taxi, and from there into a Lyons Corner House. We marched into the thick fog of the restaurant, to the thrilling accords of a live band, weaving our way through the dancers.

I'll never forget what I was wearing that night: a white silk dress with short lace sleeves, the top covered in silvery beads, reminding me of a debutante, but not quite. I'll always remember that dress because that was one of the most important evenings of my life. When we arrived at a table in the corner, Will's friends were waiting for us. They weren't alone – they had company from the opera that evening. Edmund and man next to him moved aside to make room for us between them.

I slipped into the space they'd created, watching the man to my right in the corner of my eye. It hadn't been his frame that had drawn my attention – Jasper is neither particularly tall, nor short – nor his features. He's not necessarily handsome, with his oval-shaped face, too-long chin. But there was the glint of mischief in his eyes that caught my attention. And what had stricken me most then, and what had fascinated me to no end ever since, was the very way he was sitting.

He didn't try to take up more space, like many men do, in that boisterous way of elbows-on-the-table-legs-spread-apart, when they want to show off how big they are. He didn't try to make himself smaller either, like Edmund did, to my left. Jasper was perfectly contained to the exact amount of space he was taking, like a man who knew precisely where he belonged and what he wanted to do with himself.

And that is Jasper in a nutshell.

'I don't think we've met each other,' he said, shaking my hand as if I was a man. 'I'd have remembered.'

'Am I so memorable?' I teased, slipping on my sociable mask again, even though I hoped I wouldn't have to, after Will had rescued me from the ball. The Evie that everyone expected made her appearance again, though the real Evie was rolling her eyes.

'I don't know,' he said. 'I don't know you that well. All that I can say is that I have an excellent memory, especially when it comes to faces.'

His bluntness was a shock of cold water in my face. So much so, that I kept my mask on. 'I believe etiquette demands of a gentleman to be at least slightly flirtatious. If not for anything else, to preserve the self-esteem of the lady in question.'

'Is that so?' he said, his eyes shimmering in that way again. 'I'm sorry to say that, in this case, you don't know me at all, either. The compulsory society dance makes me dizzy, so I prefer to sit and not dance at all.'

'Ah. So you're one of them,' I said, pointing at the rest of Will's set.

'Oh, no, I leave changing the world and all that to the people in this room who know better,' he said, lowering his voice. 'In my opinion, there's no significant change without a significant spill of blood beforehand, and I'm not clever enough to tell if it's worth it or not. No, I can't change the world. I just want to live my life, do you know what I mean?'

I didn't at the time, but oh, how I know now. That slipping through the crevices, that ability to make the best of everything. How I miss him. How I miss the feeling that he brought life into a room when he was in it. How I miss the certainty with which he always took the next step. I'm sure Jasper would know what to do in this situation.

My legs are numb, so I change my position and the bushes rustle. I realise what a monumental idiot I am. How could I ever believe that twigs and leaves would protect me from a bomb?

I can't cower and hide between leaves hoping that if I don't see the Germans, they won't see me either. As if they'd aim at me, a girl, alone in the middle of the woods. And if there's danger, if there's a bomb heading towards me, I'd rather see it coming. With shaking legs, I head towards the clearing, hoping to catch a glimpse of the sky. Of what's happening.

And there they are. In a mist of smoke, not far to my right, I make out the shapes of six or seven aeroplanes, darting so quickly about that it's impossible to tell friend from foe. My teeth keep chattering and I literally feel the hairs on my arms standing on end. I should get back into the woods. Or run home and return for Starlight later. Instead, I stand at the edge of the clearing, transfixed. One of the aeroplanes breaks free from the group and lunges towards me. I scream, but I don't move. He can't see me. And if he does, maybe it's one of our boys.

The aeroplane drops altitude. As it whooshes above me, it's close enough for me to see the swastika on its wings. Right now, I wish nothing more than to have listened to Jasper. He also used to say that we are doomed, but in a different way to Will's set. Not long before Dunkirk, he'd received an offer from America. I avoided the conversations about this, diverted them with jokes. Could he really not see? If I broke the ties with my family and left for another continent, what would there have been for me to do? An eternal pendant, hanging around Jasper's neck?

Will had told me to be brave. *Don't be such a snob. You can be Evie, even without the Milton in your name.*

I should have been brave. Perhaps then I wouldn't have found myself here, heading for a direct collision with my own end. For the first time in many years, I say a prayer in my mind. *Please, God, don't let it end like this. Don't let this be the end.*

As if on cue, the aeroplane plunges one more time, then changes direction, to the left and back skywards.

Still holding my breath, I loosen Starlight's reins and mount her. The mare darts into a gallop and, no matter how hard I tug and pull, I can't control her. I can't think about Jasper or Will or the aeroplane anymore. I focus on staying in the saddle, trying to trust that she'll bring me back to safety.

Chapter Nine

Rose

No, I have no idea what they do at Bletchley Park with people who speak German. I try to persuade myself that nothing bad would come of it, since this has been arranged by my aunt, but then again, when did I see my aunt today? Not even a glimpse of her in London, or here.

'No, Professor, I'm afraid I don't know,' I say, clenching my fists. I can only think that I never asked any questions, not in London, not when I was asked to climb into the lorry. I trusted those men dressed as Army officers.

'We give them a job.' Professor Walton gives me his hand again. 'Welcome to the German Air Section. Miss Wiley, you're our newest decodist.'

'German Air Section?' I give my hand to the professor as if in a dream.

He gives it a brief squeeze, then rises to his feet, still

holding my fingers. 'No time to waste now. Let's introduce you to your new colleagues.'

As I scramble to follow him, I have a million questions. What does this section do? What is expected of me? And where am I to sleep tonight?

I pick up my leather suitcase again and rush after the professor who stops a dozen steps along the same corridor I came down and opens a door. 'Through here,' he says, and ushers me into the room. On the floor, there's the same dusty green carpet with a red and yellow pattern as in the other office, and the walls are also panelled in wood.

On the wall to the right, there's a bookcase and a narrow desk; papers of all shapes and sizes spread across it. The back of the room isn't quite a back: there are huge bay windows, reaching from floor to ceiling and I wager they would once have offered a splendid view, had they not been covered in blackout cloth. Directly in front of the window there's a trestle table that seems unsteady on its legs, and dissonant chairs with scratched metal frames.

Two of them are occupied. The professor points at a man about my age with a loose pilling jumper that hangs on his bony frame as if it's draped on a clothes hanger. The man has watery blue eyes and straw-blonde hair. 'Miss Wiley, this is Dr Ralph Milner. He's a lecturer at Oxford and an expert in German Romantics.'

Ralph grins and shakes my hand with fervour. 'Welcome to our section.'

The professor then points me to the other man in the room who is somewhat shorter, with a neatly trimmed moustache, his dark hair combed back and oiled. Not a single strand looks amiss. He's dressed in a crisp suit with a white shirt and a tie knotted so tightly that the movement of his neck seems restricted. 'And this is Mr Henry Thornton.'

'A pleasure,' he says, pursing his lips. His eyes take me in from head to toe and I doubt I'm making a good impression: my dark-green utility skirt is creased at the hem, where it flares a bit, there might be moist spots in the armpits of my ivory shirt, and my curls must be sticking out in all directions after the wind has toyed and tossed them as it pleased. 'And you are?'

'This is Miss Rose Wiley,' says the professor. 'Your new colleague, as anticipated.'

'Ah,' says stiff Mr Thornton. 'And what are your qualifications, Miss Wiley? What are you reading at university?'

I'm hungry, tired, and I have no idea what I'm doing in this room or where I will sleep tonight – if something has even been arranged. And I don't have the slightest clue what I'll tell David about what is shaping up to be a minor debacle. 'The newspaper,' I say.

Ralph giggles.

'Miss Wiley wasn't attending university,' says Professor Walton.

'Oh,' says Mr Thornton. 'Well.'

The professor pulls at his rather loose bow tie. 'Her German is excellent. Her test results were impressive. She was recommended by a relative.'

'A relative,' says Mr Thornton.

For a moment, I'm wondering why the head of section didn't conduct the interview himself, but then something mischievous awakes within me and taps me on my shoulder.

'Do you also teach at Oxford, Mr Thornton? Or is it Doctor Thornton? Or Professor?'

'No, Mr Thornton is, I mean *was*, a German teacher at a secondary school,' says Professor Walton and draws towards me one of the three empty chairs.

'Oh. Well,' I say, trying to mirror Mr Thornton's dismay.

'You might be wondering why there are so many free seats,' says the professor. 'We're hoping to expand soon – the amount of traffic we receive is absolutely appalling. Goodness, I don't mean to frighten you.' He chuckles.

'Traffic?' My mind pulses with what Professor Walton said in the office. Luftwaffe messages. Decodist. German Air Section.

My colleagues turn to the long sheets in front of them, gridded sheets with countless rows and columns. Around them are scattered piles and piles of papers, written in neat rows of three-lettered…strings? Of gibberish? Going on and on and on.

Professor Walton slides a lined sheet of paper under my nose and pushes a pencil towards me. 'Miss Wiley, no use in wasting time. We might just as well get on with it.'

I peer over the stack of papers on the table. The 'I beg your pardon' is stuck in my throat. My colleagues glance at me from the corners of their eyes. At least, Ralph is. Henry stares at me as if I'm a sort of curiosity at the zoo.

My mind turns into a piece of paper, identical to the one my colleagues and I have before us. I'm not sure what the professor means by getting on with it, but he certainly does. 'This is for you. Please write your initials here, at the top.' He indicates the upper left corner. 'You can copy down your traffic here first. Try and sort it by call signs and location in chronological order.' He moves swiftly to pick up one of the pieces of paper written in the three-letter strings and put it on top of my lined sheet of paper. 'Ralph can show you the call signs later. This is the groundwork.'

I nod, hoping that the terror I feel within isn't written on my face. Groundwork? I hardly understand a word he is saying. Now would be the time to ask him to be more explicit, and stop talking to me as if I were one of his students. But he moves along too fast. 'You have to leave a free row under each message you copy.'

'Aha.'

'Ralph, could you please give me your key sheet?' says the professor.

Ralph, sitting next to me, passes him a piece of paper.

'Miss Wiley can copy one for herself later,' says the professor. 'It will also help her become a bit more familiar with the terms, don't you think?'

'Certainly,' says Ralph, giving me one more of his wide smiles.

'This is the key sheet,' says the professor, tilting the page towards me. I spot the three-letter clusters again, but in the same row there's a corresponding word for it. In German. 'You use it to decode the message you have transcribed onto the lined sheet of paper.' He pushes his spectacles up the bridge of his nose, then stops. 'I think there isn't much more to it.' He chews the inside of his cheek. 'No, I think this is the work. It's not very complicated, you see, Miss Wiley. I think you'll be brilliantly suited to it.' The professor glares at me. 'Do you have any questions?'

'No?' I say. I'd probably have a million questions, if I knew where to start. I am in such a pickle that all I can smell is the vinegar.

The professor pushes the pencil closer to my fingers. 'If you do have questions, don't be afraid to ask.'

I can give him nothing but silence – I can't even start to wrap my head around everything he's told me. Messages, key sheet. Notions floating around my head, colliding with each other.

And yet, for an odd reason, this man in front of me thinks that I'm suitable for this kind of work. Secret work.

'Go on, then,' he urges me. 'Don't be shy.'

I straighten my back. I haven't let this war toss me out of my orbit of becoming the proud owner of the grocery store in my town, out of a life of becoming David's little wife, to make myself ridiculous in front of three men. This position in such a secret organisation, doing something that I don't fully yet comprehend, this is a hand stretched out to me by fate. Did I not complain about my life at home, scrubbing chicken shit and stains off kitchen aprons?

So I reach out and grab the pencil, my fingers coiling themselves around it. I missed this, even the simple gesture of holding a pencil, getting ready to jump onto a task, a piece of homework. I've done this before, in school. Every lesson a journey further into the unknown, every small step trampling it into the familiar. It always starts in the same place: with what I know. With what I can do. 'If you don't mind, Professor, I'd like to start by copying the key sheet?'

'No, no, why don't you start with the messages first?' says the professor. 'We could assign you a batch from the Atlantic – northern French bases. They're quite new, you know.' He scans the table, rustling corners of sheets, here and there. 'The bases, I mean. There weren't any until this month.' A painful reminder that the last of our great allies on the Continent has fallen.

Henry springs to his feet and beats a mound of sheets into shape, before passing them on. 'There you are, Professor. I took the liberty of arranging them according to frequency. This should be the right pile.'

'Excellent, Mr Thornton,' says the professor, dropping the stack in front of me with a thud. 'Excuse me, Miss Wiley, they slipped. I don't know what we'd do here without Mr Thornton's organisational skills.'

'I do hope Miss Wiley will help us on that account,' says Henry. He toys with the buttons of his shirt cuff. 'Perhaps she could start there? It could give her a sense of what we do.'

There's something opaque in the way he says these words, in this suggestion. There's a certain sting to it, though I can't work out why.

The professor gives him a puzzled look. 'There's no need for that, Mr Thornton. Miss Wiley can bite into the work straight away and we can explain as we go along.'

'But I'm sure that if the messages were organised and logged in a more efficient manner, that would do wonders for the speed with which we can decode.' Henry points at the crumbling stacks of papers on the table.

'Certainly, Mr Thornton,' says the professor. 'The speed with which we decode would also be greatly increased by hiring another decodist, and this is what I have just done. We will be thirty-three per cent faster, to be specific. So best we allow Miss Wiley to get on with it.'

Though I'm not quite sure what this is about, an uneasy feeling grows in the pit of my stomach. Henry knits his eyebrows and the urge to look away from him makes me start scribbling.

According to the sheet, PMD corresponds with *Bewölkt*. Cloudy? PMF is A. PMM is 33. PMO is *Kreuzer*. What's a *crosser?* I turn the sheet to Professor Walton. He did say I should ask, but all that meets me is Henry's icy glare. 'That is, if we assume that Miss Wiley can decode at the same speed as us,' he says.

'I beg your pardon?' says the professor.

'We can be quicker by a third if Miss Wiley can decode as fast as us,' says Henry. 'If not, it will be much less.'

'I'm not sure what you're trying to imply, Mr Thornton.'

I'm starting to have an inkling about what the illustrious Mr Thornton is implying. Doubt gnaws at me – what if he's right? I don't have any fancy studies like any of the gentlemen in this room. Just the German I learned in my grammar school.

'Professor Walton,' says Ralph, tugging at the sleeves of his ancient jumper, 'Hugh Carter from the naval section wanted to speak to you. My apologies. I forgot to mention this.'

Henry's eyes widen.

'Ah,' says the professor.

'Apologies again, I was caught in my own traffic and forgot,' says Ralph.

'Better get on, then,' says the professor and gets up from his seat.

Barely has the professor exited than Ralph pulls his chair closer to mine. 'He's such a gifted linguist, but sometimes he makes things seem more complicated than they truly are. You're not the only one who struggles with this.' He sifts through the sheets with the three-letter strings and pulls one out. 'So let's simplify, eh?'

I give Ralph a wobbly smile. I'd like to tell him that I'd like nothing more than for him to make things simple for me, but a cursory glance at Henry ties my tongue. Who knows what he'll tell Professor Walton.

'These, Miss Wiley…May I call you Rose?'

'Please do.'

'Rose.' He arranges the sheet with the letters next to my lined sheet of paper. 'These are intercepted messages from the Luftwaffe.'

My breath catches in my throat. 'Luftwaffe?' As I had suspected and as the professor mentioned during our interview.

'Yes, these are messages that go between aeroplanes and their bases, for the most part.'

'These are actual Luftwaffe messages?'

Ralph chuckles. 'Don't expect highly sensitive plans of attack sent between Hitler and his minions. These are the more mundane kinds of messages. Weather reports. Statuses on fuel or intended trajectory. Sometimes, if we're really lucky, reconnaissance flights that have stumbled upon British convoys.'

I fail to see how a Luftwaffe aeroplane finding a British convoy is a stroke of luck. While the Germans haven't yet set a single foot on our British Isles, blood has been flowing in the water aplenty. And not only are our battleships endangered, but also the precious transports of food that keep us alive.

'The German aeroplanes will stumble upon the convoys, no matter what we do,' says Ralph, probably having seen something on my face. Dismay? 'It's better if we know about it. It's even better if we know about it in good time, so we can warn the convoy.'

'I see.' It dawns on me that issuing such a warning could save lives. Many lives. Not only for those men out at sea. I've read enough military history to know what people under siege might turn to eating once their supplies are exhausted.

'Moving on,' he says. He brushes with his hands a strand of hair that keeps falling into his eyes. 'You can see why the Germans would encode this information using low-grade codes, not machine-generated ones.' He stops himself, clears his throat. 'No need to bother ourselves with those. All you need to know, for now, is that the Germans use a key sheet that changes at the beginning of each month. So once we crack the meaning of a three-letter code, it will stay that way until the end of each month. It's the second now, and we were lucky this month. A key sheet dropped out of the sky yesterday. Though the bottom was a bit...um...burnt.' Ralph rummages at the bottom of a pile of papers. 'We're missing just a few more cracks. The messages are double encoded, really, using the Luftwaffe booklet. It's less relevant, though, in these circumstances. No need to double-decode the message.'

'I'm not quite sure—'

'This may be, perhaps, too much information for now. All you need to know is that you can use this little book to search for potential meanings of three-letter groups which haven't been cracked yet.' He passes the slim booklet into my hands. The paper is yellow, rough and bloated. I leaf through it. German words are associated with clusters of three numbers. 648 for *Quadrat*, for instance. Square. Some of the pages are soaked through with brown stains.

'I'd really wash my hands after touching that, though,' says Ralph.

'What do you mean?'

Henry snorts. I'd been so absorbed by Ralph's explanations, that I'd completely forgotten all about his presence in the room. Blissfully forgotten, may I say. There's something about the way he looks at me that makes me fidget. *It's not my fault*, I want to tell him. I didn't ask to be handed a lined sheet of paper. I would have been more than happy to sort the messages, like he said.

'Let's say that…these booklets *fell* into our hands with the help of a few well-placed bombs,' says Ralph.

I put it down, the blood draining from my cheeks. Blood. 'I'll go and wash my hands, then.'

Ralph glances at the door. 'In a minute.' He explains to me about frequencies, about looking out for the ones that have been assigned to me, about ordering the messages, so I can look for patterns. 'In principle, the job is simple. You copy down the messages on your lined sheet of paper, leaving a few rows for the translation in plain German. You decode by looking at the key sheet. If you stumble across something that might seem time sensitive or important, you show it to the professor. The faster we decode, the higher the odds that when we find something that's important out there, we can convey the information to the Air Ministry in good time. We have an excellent working relationship with the Air Ministry, unlike—'

'Ralph,' says Henry, pursing his lips.

'Yes. No need to go into that, do we?' says Ralph. 'It's not hard, Rose. Even if you know only basic German, you can learn the technical terms in a jiffy.' He snaps his fingers to demonstrate. 'I'm sure you'll do perfectly fine.'

'Until the beginning of next month, at least,' says Henry, without stopping his scribbling.

I stare at my hands, and at the lined sheet of paper beyond

them. I've never met anyone quite like Henry in my life, but there have been enough blokes whistling at me on the street and calling after me. I do what I always do in these cases: ignore these voices; focus on the task at hand.

Never in my life have I dreamed of doing such exciting work. Is this how Aunt Mavis feels every day, when she goes into the Foreign Office? Decoding enemy messages. Trying to find that particular piece of information that might save lives. Me. Who only yesterday carried out her tasks at the farm. And this had been a telephone call away, all this time.

'Come, I'll show you to the lavatories, Rose, all right?' says Ralph, pulling out the chair for me.

Once we're in the corridor, he whispers to me, 'He doesn't mean it that way. Henry. It's just that we're all terribly tired and overworked. I'm sure you'll soon get along. He's trying to do his best. We all are.'

I can't help but wonder, *how good will my best be?*

Chapter Ten

Evie

I n the evening, I tell Mother that I'm popping out to look for Starlight. Horses in the woods at night and all that. I know bloody well that I have no chance of finding her – as far as I know, she could be on her way to London or to Scotland.

I'm not looking for the mare. Of course, if I do happen to find her, that would be great.

But what animal in its right mind would dart towards a fire? It must still be raging on the airfield that has been bombed today. The columns of smoke guide me towards the site.

I tried. I tried to stay astride the mare, and I couldn't keep her reined in for long. It would have been kinder, perhaps, to have left her tied to the tree. But what if a bomb came crashing towards her and she couldn't get out of its way? She might have died of fear or cut her mouth open from prancing about. On the whole, though, it might not have been the cleverest idea to mount her. When I finally reached the wine cellar that serves as our air-raid shelter at the Hall, I was quite the sight. Dusty from head to toe, rotten leaves in my hair, a cut knee.

All for the best, though. Not only that Mother has come within inches of me – which she hasn't done since I've been ordered back home – but she actually gave me an embrace so tight that it knocked the breath out of me. Lucky us that Papa was in London today.

'Evie, where have you been?' she demanded.

Behind her, Brown had risen to her feet, her eyes shining with tears. 'We've been worried.'

I told them about the aeroplanes, the swastika. My little brothers were kind enough to tell me that the Germans could have shot at me with their machine guns, if they'd wanted to. My knees trembled for a moment, but I tried to smile. 'They were welcome to try.'

Mother's face tightened in an expression of pain. 'Don't you say that. Never. Never.'

In spite of my own fear, I smelled it then. The opportunity. I leaned in closer to her. 'I couldn't stop thinking about Will.'

There had been more than one reason that I'd thought about Will, in fact, though I kept quiet about Dunkirk. Instead, I told her how final his break from us had seemed. How it was long past the time to start mending things. She stared at me intensely for long minutes and then squeezed my hand. 'We'll talk about this later.'

And we did.

At least something good has come out of this day.

Which probably isn't what the poor people who work for the RAF could say.

As I near the airfield, my eyes sting because of the smoke. The burnt smells make my throat itchy and I have to cough. So this is what war feels like. The endless days of waiting for something to happen seem like bliss today. But then again, we know what we're facing from this day forward.

Fires. Craters in the once-smooth asphalt runway. Twisted wrecks that were once aeroplanes, still burning. The bits of buildings that are still standing, covered in earth. Tiny hills that have sprouted where there was once flat land. Next to one of these mounds, firemen, ARP wardens and villagers with spades are gathered, digging. Stretchers and two ambulances, waiting.

And except for the rustle of fire and the whoosh of water, there's silence. Even the children who have gathered to watch are quiet.

I move nearer to one of the women hovering around the site. 'Why are they digging?'

'Digging out,' she says. 'The airwomen. All buried.'

I remember WAAFS with a jolt. A cluster of girls about my age.

'A dozen of them, I reckon,' says the woman, leaning in closer to me. She wipes her hands on her dusty apron.

'A dozen?' I gasp.

She nods. 'Folks say they were supposed to hide in the trenches when the alarms sounded, but they all refused. Stayed up to guide the boys through the air.'

Heroes. These women are heroes.

I inch my way closer to the place where all the digging is taking place, just in time to see the men pull out one of the girls. Two ARP wardens are holding her by the shoulders, while a fireman helps guide the legs. The beautiful blue jacket is now a muddy brown and all her hair has come loose. Her head wobbles back as they move her along. Bouts of nausea surge in my belly. They gently put her down her a few feet away, but not on one of the stretchers, not even close to one of the ambulances.

A young nurse breaks into a run and touches the airwoman's face, her chest. I move closer, on wobbly feet, close enough to see the airwoman's open eyes. A blue as icy as the sky they're turned towards, but sightless.

The nurse shakes her head.

This isn't an airwoman; this is a young girl in a fancy uniform, probably barely out of school. She's dead now and she has a mother and a father who will find this out today. I could have been dead, too, if the gunner of the German aeroplane had fired. Today, I could have *not* been anymore; I could have lain, bleeding, in the depths of the woods.

And what do I have to show for it, for the joy of being alive? I stand here, like a useless statue, because not a single part of my bloody 'education', like languages or riding or playing the piano or drawing, ever taught me to do something useful. By far the most helpful people here are the farmers and the dayworkers in the village, the very same people at whom dear Papa looks down his nose.

One of the firemen shouts, directing the villagers where to dig. I stand there, meaning to help, but not knowing where to begin. I stand. I stand, my useless hands hanging limply at my sides, watching as they pull dead girl after dead girl out of their early graves.

Chapter Eleven

Rose

As I reach the door to my billet, a wave of dizziness comes over me. I lean against the painted wood and try to remember the last time I'd eaten. My mind is a darkness as deep as the blackout outside.

For a few days, my work went well, the stacks dwindling as I grew into my job. Ralph had been correct. I'd cried that first night when I arrived 'home' to my billet, for many reasons. But then, on the next day, the language of Messerschmitts ceased to be so foreign. And I delivered on the promised increase of thirty-three percent of decoded traffic in our section.

Until yesterday afternoon.

I give my billet's door a hard push, trying to signal my arrival, hoping I won't stumble upon anyone in the kitchen. I march down the dim hallway as if I'm a collection of aeroplane parts and worry.

The presence of my two landlords is like a stream of cold water in my face. Tom is sitting before a cleared table, reading this morning's newspaper. He does that often – he works for the railways and his timetable is rather irregular. 'Rose.' He appraises me from head to toe, stopping on my buttoned shirt and on the bit of skin on my legs visible between my ankle and the skirt's hem. 'You found your way to our house today, I see,' he says with a lewd wink. He passes his cigarette from one skeletal hand to the other and takes a deep drag.

'It's not what you think,' I say. 'I had to work.'

'Work,' he says, his thin eyebrows jutting upwards.

'Yes, work,' I say, wondering if he's implying what I think he's implying and not liking it a single bit. After I've spent last night partly decoding the endless stream of messages that landed in our room, partly sleeping on the dusty – but thank heavens – soft carpet covering the floor, I won't stand for bawdy jokes and this sort of innuendo. 'There was so much work to do for us typists. So much to type.' *Decode*, my whole battered body wants to scream, but I know I can't. Not for anything in the world. 'And you won't find that there,' I say. 'You'll have to wait for tomorrow's newspaper.'

Anger – or hunger? – churns in my stomach. Good. Better than worried sick, like I've been all day. Today has been the darkest day for us in the history of this war. Luftwaffe bombers and fighters have been streaming overhead all day, destroying airfields. Fires have been burning in the skies, and I didn't have to listen to the wireless to find that out. I only had to listen. Or to look at my lined sheets of paper and what they said.

I should be proud, considering all odds. Pleased. The German Air Section has issued so many warnings today for the

Air Ministry, naming destinations of raids, helping raise the barrage balloon before the bombers reached their targets. But all I felt was fear, its metallic taste in my mouth, even though none of the airfields that had been targeted today was in Yorkshire, where David is still completing his training. *Would he be safer on the ground?* I didn't necessarily want to know the true answer.

Nell, my landlady, dries her hands on her clean but crumpled apron, then smooths her already perfectly even chignon. She can't be more than thirty, I think, but with her tightly buttoned chemises and stiff hairdos, from a distance she looks as old as my mother. 'I wasn't quite expecting you at dinner today,' she says, and I wonder if this is a reproach. 'Would you care for something to eat?' she says, motioning towards the cleared table.

Judging by her tone, it's a polite request I should by all means refuse.

Sod it.

I'm too hungry, too tired.

'Yes, please,' I say.

Tom pretends to check the clock on the wall. 'A bit late for tea, innit?'

'I agree,' I say. 'I wager you know how it is with these unusual working hours.'

'Working hours,' he says, and puffs his cheeks.

I turn away to avoid seeing him. It's always like this with these people. He makes me feel like an intruder in their home, like someone whose only purpose is to disturb their cosy intimacy. And Nell never says anything, just watches me with her cold, deep-set eyes, quiet like a fish.

Why did they even bother to take me in?

Nell picks up a plate from a cupboard and heads towards the pantry, while Tom says, 'Was this the same in your mother's house? You had tea when it suited you? The Foreign Office isn't paying us to be your servants.'

Nell stiffens.

And so do I. 'Nor do I give you my ration books so you can keep them to yourselves.' In two strides, I'm in the pantry, taking the plate from Nell's hands. 'Thank you, Mrs Pike, I can take over from here. I thought I was being polite by allowing you to decide which share of the ration was due to me, but I see you and your husband think the opposite.' I cut myself two large slices of cheese and one of ham. I slap a large chunk of bread on the plate, an apple, and turn on my heel. 'Good night,' I tell them and stomp to my room.

It had been a bit of a debacle explaining to David what I'm doing in Buckinghamshire. He's still up in Yorkshire, finishing his training. *A typist?* he'd said. *Do you even know how to type?* I told him that I had engaged my aunt's help to find a job closer to Biggin Hill, and he'd been mollified. *Well, if we're going to be so close to each other.* There was no need to explain to him that Bletchley was on the other side of London, and then a bit. Not yet. *I miss you so much, Rose. Are you sure you can't come down here for a few days?*

I couldn't and I can't – leave is, for now, out of the question. I only have to think of the undecoded messages amassing in our room. I was itching to talk to him about my work, about all the messages we read. Messages that are intercepted from the

Luftwaffe itself. But the needle of secrecy was stinging, and I kept my mouth tightly shut.

I slap my plate down on the small table in my room. Small table, small room. A bit larger than a broom closet – just enough to fit in a narrow bed, the table and the chair at its foot. If the chair is drawn, I have to climb over the bed to get to the other side of the room, where I keep my suitcase and all my clothes. There isn't enough space for a chest of drawers, so I have to keep some of my trinkets in the gas mask box. And I can't imagine how this room is meant to be kept warm in winter – I shudder at the very thought.

There's a knock on my door. 'Come in,' I say, without thinking.

Nell appears, and before I can say anything else, she puts a steaming mug on the table in a single move. 'A chamomile tisane,' she says. 'You looked… I thought it might be nice.'

I melt at the nice gesture. This chilliness has been seeping into my bones for days. Never in my life have I been unwanted somewhere, not until I met Henry Thornton and the Pikes. Professor Walton and Ralph are nice to me, and kind, but they keep a certain distance. I'm not sure they know, either, what to make of a young woman working in their room. As their equal. Henry certainly doesn't. And home is so far, far away. Half a world, not just a hundred miles. No, an entire world away, a world where I was David's fiancée, eagerly waiting for him; not a young woman wrestling with intercepts of Luftwaffe messages.

I cradle the mug in my hands and let the warmth drip into my fingers. 'Thank you. It was precisely what I needed.'

Nell hovers in the threshold. 'You're welcome.'

I beckon her to my bed. 'Would you care to sit?' I ask,

though I wonder what I could possibly talk about with her. She reminds me so much of my school teachers, and I can't imagine a chit-chat with them. What would make a suitable conversation? The raising death toll? The impending German invasion? The weather?

'No, thank you,' she says. She pats her chignon again. 'There was... I don't quite know how to...' She stares at her clipped bare fingernails. 'Tom wanted me to ask you if you could pay us for next week's lodgings in advance? Only this once.'

Of course, I think. This explains the tea. My first impulse is to refuse them. If it starts here, there's no telling where these people might stop. Money in advance, for now. Curling noses when I ask for my fair share of the ration. What might come next? Where my imagination fails me, theirs might not.

'Please,' she insists. 'Just this once. It's for... I don't quite know how to put this. It's a private matter, of course, and rather embarrassing for us.'

Why should your embarrassments give you the right to ask something from me?

As I prepare to refuse Nell, an expression of pain contorts her features. For a moment, there's a crack. Through it, I can read emotion. Shame? Something else? It's gone sooner than I can identify it, but it's enough for me to change my mind. I've managed to set some money aside from my wages. I could pay them in advance. Only once. 'Next week?' I ask carefully. 'And there will be no more talk of money needed in advance the week after that?'

Nell shakes her head. 'No, no, I promise you. By no means.'

'All right. You'll have your money tomorrow afternoon,' I say, though I could easily reach for my savings from the box under the bed. But I don't want this woman to see where I keep my money. The waves of exhaustion wash over me again.

I have to remember to speak to the Bletchley billeting office in the morning. Perhaps there is something that can be done.

———————

Professor Walton stops chewing the end of his pencil and looks up at me from across the scratched table. He doesn't stare at me in that indecent way men do when they try to assess the size of my brassiere. For the love of me, I can't possibly imagine him ever looking at any woman in that way.

No, he has that absent gaze that looks right through me while his wonderful brain lifts up in the air a hundred different notions and starts connecting links between them that nobody but him can sense. I wonder what his wonderful brain sees before he surprises us with conclusions about the trajectory of a pack of U-boats or the routes of Luftwaffe aeroplanes by analysing traffic, without even looking at the content of messages. But, in the same miraculous way, his brain never seems to notice the crumpled state of his own shirts, stains of food that survive for days on his tweed jacket, and missing buttons. It's the kind of thing that any woman would notice. My mother would be appalled to think that there is a Mrs Walton waiting for the professor at his billet. She doesn't take care of him as a woman should. But then again, maybe there is no Mrs Walton and if the professor's landlady is anything like the family I'm with myself—

'Are you tired, Miss Wiley? Do you need a break?'

I flex my fingers and rub at the pencil blister on my middle finger. I wouldn't mind a break. It's enough to stare at the crumbling piles of messages on the table to change my mind, though. If I thought there were lots of sheets on the table when I first arrived in the German Air Section, now there are twice as many.

Too many. When I hear the squeak of the door opening, my heart beats faster, fearing it's another messenger who wants to empty his haversack onto our table. We'll never catch up, at this pace. We'll be buried in messages and the worst part, the very worst part, is that the need to decode quickly is more desperate than ever.

Not a day goes by when I don't think about David, about the danger that is maybe flying towards him at full speed, a belly full of bombs.

Not a day goes by when I don't wonder if I'll ever be able to burrow my face in the nook of his neck and wrap my arms around him again.

'Miss Wiley?' says the professor.

'No, thank you, I'm fine. I don't need a break.' In fact, I do, but the professor never asks my other two colleagues if they need a break. I was also the only one he asked yesterday evening if I wanted to go home. Of course I refused. I wanted to work – I truly did. Even if the stream of messages had waned to a trickle, if we didn't catch up, as much as we could, we stood no chance of keeping up with the messages today.

And if I had gone home, wouldn't that have meant that I can do less work than a man?

Henry twists the cuffs of his shirt. 'I could certainly use a cuppa,' he says, looking at me.

'Wouldn't that be nice,' I say.

If Ralph or the professor asked me for tea, I wouldn't mind. But the insidious way Henry asks me to fetch tea... Like this is something I should have thought about, without him telling me. Something that's self-evident, a law of nature. Just like my kind father, God bless his soul, who wouldn't even consider lifting a single dirty dish from the table as long as my mother and I lived under the same roof with him.

'Henry, Miss Wiley has her own work to mind; she doesn't have time to fetch you tea,' says Ralph, as always, picking up on every nuance. Ralph is a milkman's son, his feet still planted firmly on the ground while he worked himself up from scholarship to scholarship to Oxford.

I smile in the way that makes my cheeks ache. Surely it would be all right to bring everyone a cup of tea, every now and then? Perhaps we could all take turns instead of lingering in this state where we could all use a cup of tea which nobody fetches? I'd like to tell them we should all behave 'normally', but I don't even know what 'normal' would be. Equal, perhaps? I'm not sure. And I don't know how to say this without offending sweet Ralph. Perhaps I should ask him to treat me like he treats either of the two other men in this room? But this doesn't sound quite right. I'm not a man and I don't want to pretend to be one.

So I sigh and wrap my fingers around my pencil again, still thinking about a lovely warm cup of the increasingly discoloured tea.

'Professor, could you please take a look at this?' Henry slides his lined sheet of paper towards our chief of section. His eyes are wide, almost all whites.

Professor Walton blinks. 'When was this sent?' Not waiting for an answer, he checks his pocket watch. 'Less than two hours ago. There might still be time.' The professor rises from his seat so quickly that he nearly topples his wobbly chair over.

He grabs Henry's sheet with messages and hurries to the door, stopping mid-way, stretching his hand back towards the table. 'Mr Thornton, the original message, please.' Henry hands it to him in less time than I need to blink. With a whoosh, the professor is gone into the corridor, the echoes of his steps reverberating into our quiet room.

'What happened?' I ask, my hair standing on end. 'What's wrong?'

'Nothing is wrong.' Henry smirks. 'I've stumbled across two possible destinations for the Luftwaffe's raids today.'

Ralph whoops and whistles. 'At times like this, I wish we had a dozen or so people in our section, to be able to make some proper noise.' He shakes Henry's hand. 'Congratulations, mate. Bloody well done.'

'How extraordinary,' I say. There's the sting of tears in my eyes, but by looking at Henry's pleased face, I remember I mustn't be overly emotional or he might find a way to say something petty about this. So I also shake his hand, like a man. 'Congratulations.'

Henry hands Ralph and me a slip of paper with two names written across them. 'These airfields.'

I draw air in, and then forget to breathe at all. A name pops out. The airfield in Yorkshire where David is training.

'Rose?' asks Ralph.

The prickling in my eyes is here again and there's nothing I can do against my eyes becoming moist.

'Rose, what's wrong?' says Ralph.

Henry snorts and slips back into his seat, drawing out a clean lined sheet of paper.

'This,' I say, pointing to one of the names on the piece of paper. 'That's where David is training to be a pilot.' My mind races back and forth, faster than a Spitfire. *Run*, I think. *Telephone. Call and let them know. Call and find out.*

'Rose, you must be thrilled,' says Ralph. 'The RAF will be warned that an attack is coming and they will have enough time to mount their defences. Or our boys will meet them in the sky long before the bombers reach their targets.'

A murkiness surrounds Ralph's words, lifts them in the air and twists them. 'Meet them? Do you think they'll send him, too? But he's still in training.' Though being on the ground would hardly make him safer. *Perhaps Professor Walton hasn't managed to alert the Air Ministry in time. Perhaps David's airfield is a smoking ruin.* I try not to think about what might have already happened.

'Rose?' asks Ralph.

'Do you think I might be able to make a quick telephone call?' I say, holding onto my last shred of calm.

'You can't possibly…' says Henry.

'Rose,' says Ralph, placing a hand on my shoulder. A heavy hand, the hand of a man who is used to reining in draught horses, and not just holding a pencil. 'I don't think that would be wise. Remember the Official Secrets Act?'

I wrest myself free. 'I didn't intend to warn them. I wanted to check if David was safe.'

Ralph bites his lip. 'Do you think that would be wise? They might have other more important matters to concern themselves with right now.'

'I did insist that women would be rather unsuitable for this kind of work,' says Henry. 'They allow their own emotions to govern them. You'd never see that in a man.'

My head is too busy with David to curl itself around the meaning of Henry's words. But Ralph's nose twists itself into something halfway between anger and disgust. 'Of course men are governed by emotions too. Rage rather than concern or sadness. Does this help them make better decision? I doubt it.' He turns to me again. 'This is good, Rose. Professor Walton is issuing the warning. You have to trust the Air Ministry now that they'll do their job. Like they trust you to do your own job.' He points at the stack of papers. 'Our work here makes this possible. I mean, finding information that would help our boys out there.'

I twist a handkerchief in my hands. I don't remember bringing it out of my purse, but I must have, since it's smudged black from my eyeliner.

'I'll tell you what, my throat is parched,' says Ralph. 'How about a nice cup of tea? How about I fetch us all a mug each, and then we try to get on with it?'

And get on with it we do. There is no alternative here, except for getting up and carrying on, even if we're running on three hours' sleep and an orange-coloured tea that tastes like chewed tobacco. And exhilaration. This must be what keeps us going, in the end. Professor Walton returns to our room to say that he managed to alert the Air Ministry in time. I tell him about David. I don't tell him I don't know yet what to hope for him, exactly. Safety, in any case. I don't tell him that I'm distracted, but so is he, distracted by his own work, not seeing the way I revolve around the same basic sentence for minutes at a time.

At around seven, Ralph gets up in a hurry and runs to the professor's side of the table. Excitement is written on their faces. 'When was this sent?' asks the professor, wiping his spectacles with an old piece of cloth. His eyes are red, the lids swollen.

'Oh,' says Ralph.

'That's circa...' – the professor checks his pocket watch in what is to all of us a familiar gesture – 'five hours ago.'

Ralph's face drops.

'We all do what we can. And in this room, we all do more than is humanly possible,' says the professor, in an uncharacteristic surge of empathy. The professor doesn't lack kindness, no, no. What he lacks, I think, sometimes, is...a certain ability to gauge people's reactions.

I think the professor is someone who has lived alone a lot. Who certainly works alone. But who am I to judge an Oxford professor?

And I shouldn't forget why I came to Bletchley in the first place. My breath catches in my throat to think that I might have come all this way to be closer to David, and that he might not even reach Biggin Hill. The thought that he might not even survive his training makes me nauseous. Even if we issue the warnings, there will still be damage. People will die. And as hard as I try to push this thought to the back of my head, it's here, floating on the edges of everything I do today. That fear of not knowing for sure.

'I'm sorry,' says Ralph.

'Don't be. I repeat, we do what we can and we can't do more. We need staff. Did I tell you about the idea I'm trying to implement? Two shifts at least, maybe three?' The professor checks his watch again. 'I'd best be on my way.'

Henry leans over. 'Is that for the Air Ministry? It's certainly too late. The Germans never attack at night.'

'We might as well give it a try.' The professor collects his tweed coat from the back of his chair where he'd set it hours before and slips it on top of his shirt's rolled up sleeves. 'Miss Wiley, what was the name of your fiancé, again?'

'David,' I say, setting down my pen.

'Last name, I mean.'

'Foster. David Foster.'

'All right, then,' he says, stumbling out through the door.

We're tired and aching from all the hours we've been sitting down, but I don't feel exhaustion anymore as I wonder why the professor asked about David. I collect another heap of messages from the North Sea and set them in front of my lined sheet of paper, sorting through them. My pencil flies across the page, copying, decoding, translating. Weather reports from earlier in the day. A speller – a name that doesn't have a corresponding three-letter code, that has to be spelled letter by letter when mentioned in the Luftwaffe's secret messages. *Scharnhorst*. I remember this one. It's a battleship. This is something I wouldn't have known last week. Decoding the enemy's communications, using them to help our boys out there, this is something I wouldn't have even dreamed about a month ago.

I'm hungry, my bottom feels like a hundred pins have been stuck through its bones, and I'm so tired that I'd fall asleep if I laid my head on the table, but this doesn't matter. What matters, what truly matters, is what I do. *They trust you to do your job.* Goodness, I wish, I so wish I could tell David about my job. He'd be so proud of me. So incredibly proud.

'Two to three shifts?' says Henry, startling me.

'That would be terrific, don't you think?' says Ralph, erasing something from his sheet. 'Rose, is there anything I can assist you with?'

I force a smile. 'No, thank you.' He never asks Henry if he needs any help. Why does Ralph assume that I can't find my way around the work as well as he does? In the end, it's copying terms from a sheet and translating them into English. It's not too difficult for my delicate woman's brain, in any case.

'Where would he find the staff?' says Henry.

'I gather there's also a problem with the costs,' says Ralph.

'It's rather hard to ask for more money when you're a top-secret organisation, don't you think?' says Henry, arching his eyebrow. 'They'll probably hire more women; they're cheaper.'

'Yes, that would be a smart decision, don't you think?' I say. I have an inkling of understanding about what my father once said about not hearing his own thoughts. And between worrying about David and trying to get any work done at all, this conversation is too much for me. 'More work for the same money. Hire four women for the price of three men.'

Henry rolls his eyes.

'I'm so sorry,' says the professor, striding back into the room. 'It was too late. But I think this is all the more reason to ask for more staff.' He picks at a piece of paper. 'And a larger room.'

I try to put the force of all my expectations into my glare. The professor sits down.

Ralph makes a discreet gesture of pointing at me. 'Ah, yes, Miss Wiley. Apologies.' The professor rubs his eyes. 'I have good news. I have made some discreet enquiries. The attack was diverted earlier today. And your fiancé is reported to have landed back safely.'

'Landed back?' I say. 'He flew out today?' I can't suppress a shudder, even though relief courses through my veins like molten lava. He is alive. He is alive.

Henry's glare burns me in the side of my head, as I'm still facing the professor. I pretend to concentrate on my work again, allowing my thoughts to settle. *He's fine. He's fine. He's fine.*

The letters on the sheet of paper in front of me arrange themselves again as if a fog is clearing. The worry had held me tightly in its grip today, tighter than I'd thought. It's my turn to go to the professor. It had been my turn for minutes, perhaps half an hour, if only I had seen it. I tuck my swollen feet into my shoes and rush to the other side of the table. 'Could you please take a look at this?' I indicate to him a certain row.

The professor frowns. 'What am I looking at specifically, Miss Wiley?'

'A sighting.' I tap, pointing to him the communication from the reconnaissance flight. 'Here. The Luftwaffe spotted a convoy of the Royal Navy speeding towards Orkney. But this isn't everything.' I show him the rows above and underneath, the radio frequencies. 'This is the same base. And this... This here...' I show him a message at the top of the page. 'This specific aeroplane was communicating with none other than the *Scharnhorst*.'

'The *Scharnhorst*?' The professor leans in closer to the page. 'Are you quite sure, Miss Wiley?'

'Positive. I've been tracking its movements for a few days now.' I fetch the lined sheets of paper I've filled in over the past few days. I point to him the batches of messages I've decoded, grouped by the radio frequency. 'Here. And here. And here.' In my mind, the snake-like trajectory of the *Scharnhorst* comes to life, sneaking out of the Baltic to catch our sailors unawares. It's not always easy to follow the route of various warships or packs of U-Boats, since they might make their way into Ralph's pile of messages to decode today and into mine tomorrow.

There's an Indexing Section, I've heard, where the ships' movements are tracked down and noted as they appear in the messages of various sections, but I've never been there. Only Professor Walton and Henry have access to their archives. Ralph and I are too junior. What that RAF officer told me before he asked me to sign the Official Secrets Act is true: we are only told what we need to know, and not a word more.

Professor Walton examines the sheets for a few more minutes. 'I'm just... Perhaps you're familiar with the intricacies of our relationship with the Admiralty, Miss Wiley?'

I shake my head.

'Let's just say I need to be prepared the battle ahead.' The professor gathers all the papers I'd handed him and he makes his way to the corridor again.

I return to my seat, unease growing in my chest. Ralph pats my arm. 'Rose, mighty well done. Tracking the *Scharnhorst*'s movements! That's clever intelligence analysis. I'm so proud of you.'

Henry says nothing. Not that I would have expected him to.

The professor is oddly quiet as he returns and hands me back my papers. 'Thank you, Miss Wiley,' is all he says.

I'd like to ask what happened, but the words are stuck in my throat. Henry jumps much faster at the smell of blood. But whose blood? 'Is something the matter, Professor Walton?'

The professor sighs. 'Mr Thornton, you know how it is with the Admiralty.'

'Indeed,' says Henry, nodding. 'Was it particularly difficult this time?' he prods.

'Well,' says the professor. 'Let's say my task would have been easier if I'd stumbled upon one of the people we usually speak with.'

Ralph turns to me. 'It's quite hard to explain to someone who hardly knows of our existence and who is completely in the dark when it comes to our methods that they should definitely trust the intelligence we feed them,' he whispers.

'Ralph!' hisses Henry. 'The Official Secrets Act!'

Professor Walton lifts his hand. 'It's quite all right, Henry. I think Miss Wiley needs to understand a few of the intricacies of our position.' He takes out his handkerchief and wipes his forehead. 'The Admiralty doesn't trust information that is being fed to them by civilians.'

'So what does it mean for us?' I ask. 'All these convoy sighting, everything...'

'It's quite a struggle to be taken seriously,' says Professor Walton. 'Especially when their own intelligence specialists have reached different conclusions.'

An explanation for my colleagues' long faces starts to take shape. 'What are you trying to say, Professor? Does it have to do with the *Scharnhorst*?'

'I'm sorry, Miss Wiley. Their own specialists disagree,' says the professor.

'So...' This can't be. 'Do they choose not to believe us? Does this mean...does this mean they will do nothing about it? The *Scharnhorst* and at least another battleship are speeding towards a British convoy and the Admiralty will do nothing about it?'

'I'm sorry, Miss Wiley. The Admiralty refuses to issue a warning.' The professor lays his hands on the table. 'They said this is a mistake, that the *Scharnhorst* can't possibly be where we believe it to be.' He clears his throat and looks downwards. 'How certain are you, Miss Wiley, that the *Scharnhorst* is in that position?'

My fingers grow cold. 'Positive. Absolutely certain,' I say, though now I doubt everything. I glance down at my papers, checking everything. But it was all there. The name, the radio frequency, the reconnaissance flights that had been mounted from the coast. From across the table, Henry cranes his neck, as if trying to check if my work is in order.

'What I'm trying to say, Miss Wiley,' says the professor in a small voice, 'is that we all understand that you're still fairly new. And the work may seem straightforward, though it can be quite overwhelming at times. Especially when it comes to the more complicated issues that arise from intelligence analysis.'

'We're not judging you, Rose,' Ralph says in a low voice. 'It happens.'

I'm so stricken by the fact that my colleagues think I made a mistake, that I can't even begin to defend myself. At the same time, my eyes check the rows of my lined sheets of paper, trying to glean all the facts that led me towards my analysis of the *Scharnhorst's* movements, not seeing anything.

The professor stares at his pocket watch again, but this time he slams the lid shut in a forceful gesture that seems out of step with his kind nature. This, more than anything, makes me want to sink into the dusty carpet. 'I do believe, my cherished colleagues, that it might be time to call it a night,' he says.

His words feel like a dismissal. Ralph stretches and yawns.

Henry says, 'If you don't mind, I'd like to continue for a little while, or we have no chance of catching up.'

'I do believe that we're all tired and therefore prone to mistakes,' says the professor, not looking at me.

My eyes sting. It seems I've made a mistake that has brought shame on our entire section and shattered our credibility. I want to disappear altogether, and the thing closest to it would be to disappear out of the room. I get my bearings in a heartbeat and rise to my feet. 'I bid you a good night, gentlemen,' I say, doing my best not to explode in a warm gush of despair while I'm still in the room.

The last thing I want to be called, on top of it all, is overly emotional.

Outside, in the starless blackout, my companions on the way to my billet are the bitter taste in my mouth and the wet saltiness on my cheeks.

Chapter Twelve

Evie

Mother has gone into full Lady Milton mode. She's holding a great reception at the Hall tonight and she's done well to do so. Not only was it clever to hide our special visitor in a sea of guests so Papa couldn't smell what we were up to (this was Brown's idea), but I also salute the fact that we're looking for some normalcy in the midst of all this sorrow. It's been more than a week since the attack on our airfield and what happened here has happened dozens of times across Britain. The Luftwaffe comes day after day after day and tries to wreck our country. Let them try. The wireless says that we take down so many more aeroplanes of theirs for every plane of ours. I don't want to be defeatist, but the Germans can do quite a lot of damage – I've seen it with my own eyes.

No more of all that tonight. Let the champagne, the quails' eggs, the salmon roe, and the venison in wine sauce flow. Let the hum of conversation and laughter cover my manoeuvring tonight.

Because Mother and I have conspired. This has been my little beacon of light. There's nothing like a dinner party to look forward to, especially when the Germans have raided the airfield twice. We're getting better at digging ourselves out – there are a few bulldozers waiting to shovel earth aside and make the airfield functional within a few hours. Nobody else has died and the airwomen have been replaced. 'I know all this because I pass by the airfield every day,' I tell the man who sits next to me.

The man who Mother purposely seated next to me. Mr Alastair Denniston, a small man with clear blue eyes, perfect manners, and a kind smile. The sort of man who would never be mistaken for a spy. Our dear Alastair.

'This is extraordinary,' says Alastair, his eyes sliding to the young woman seated next to him. 'We never have this kind of action. An aeroplane buzzing by, at most.'

'Oh?' I say. 'I wouldn't have thought that you have no action in the war, considering your…position within the Foreign Office.' I smile coyly. Alastair used to work for the Cipher School or something like that – Mother filled me in on all I needed to know before the dinner party. He's now been transferred. To Bletchley.

'We do have action, but of an entirely different sort,' he says, while toying with his white napkin.

This doesn't help me. I always like to go into an operation like this with a battle plan. But I have none. I have no idea how to ask this mild-mannered man to go and hunt down a woman for me.

'Has Bletchley been spared from raids, then?'

'There is the occasional alarm, you see. And we have to take shelter. But the town has been spared, indeed.'

'Is it a nice town? I can't recall ever being there.'

'It isn't memorable.' He smiles again.

'So are you acquainted with the...the townspeople?' I down half a glass of champagne to hide my smirk. Or to toast in advance, hoping for a miraculous answer.

'Not quite.' He gives the young woman seated to his right another darting look. 'We've been so horribly busy since the Germans started attacking. So much traffic to handle. And we could make such a huge difference for our fight. For our boys. If we weren't so monstrously understaffed, we could make such a difference.'

'How interesting,' I say, though this is certainly not the answer I'd been hoping for. 'I have an old friend who moved to Bletchley last year. A Miss Elinor Thompson. Does the name mean anything to you?'

He presses his lips into a thin line. 'I'm afraid not.'

'I hoped that you might have turned to the town to recruit people for your venture. I can imagine the distance doesn't reasonably allow a commute from London.'

'Indeed, it doesn't. This is why most of our staff are billeted with local people – we have men and women pouring in from all parts of Britain.' He leans in closer to me. 'You see, the people we hire, they need to have a certain set of...of skills. And education. Not the sort I'd randomly find in a town like Bletchley.'

I allow him to lead the conversation down this blind alley for a single moment while I regroup, while I try to find a way to guide it back in the direction of Miss Thompson. 'Is that so? I must admit I'm intrigued. What sort of people?'

Alastair throws Papa, who sits close to the end of the table, a cursory glance. There was a time when they were quite close, the two of them. God only knows why. I can't imagine two people more different than these two. But we haven't seen quite so much of Alastair lately. Perhaps he might know how dear Papa really is? 'We have all sorts of people,' says Alastair, 'depending on the kind of work we need them for. I'm afraid I can't tell you more without compromising the operation. However, I can tell you this much: I'm sure you'll stumble upon familiar faces. I remember once meeting Professor Walton at your house? Or perhaps I'm mistaken.'

I clap my hands. 'Edmund Walton! That's extraordinary!' I tone my voice down. I don't want to attract more attention than necessary, now that I've found out the whereabouts of someone from Will's set. No wonder the letter I sent him never received a reply. That is, unless Edmund sent a reply that was confiscated by Papa.

'You know the professor?' asks Alastair.

'Quite well. Though I haven't seen him in some time.' Darling Edmund Walton, with all his beautiful notions going quiet when someone new was around. Someone like Jasper. That evening when I first met him, I can't remember if he said a single word.

'You wouldn't have.' He chuckles. 'I'm afraid I've been keeping him all to myself since the war started.'

'Ah. It would be so nice to come down and see him,' I say, knowing that there is no way in this world that Papa would allow me to take a little trip so close to London. Even though there was no chance that I'd even think about meeting Jasper.

'Would you?' Alastair pauses and softly rubs his chin.

I make use of the small lull in the conversation. 'You

mentioned something about billeting your staff with local people. I assume you keep records of this?'

'Of what?'

'Of the people whose houses serve as billets?'

'Certainly. In an operation such as ours, we must keep track of everything.'

There's a small commotion as the maids bring in the main course – venison braised in red wine. I've heard talk about the terrible rationing on the wireless, but there isn't much trace of it at the Hall. We can hunt on our land and we raise every sort of farm animal one can think of: pigs, hordes of chickens, cows, sheep. We have milk, ham, cheese, and meat aplenty. We grow our own vegetables. I'm sure if people had taken precautions and started raising a few farm animals of their own, rationing wouldn't be so keenly felt everywhere. We are Britons. In the course of history, we never looked to the Continent to save us before, so why should we do this now? Why shouldn't we be able to feed ourselves?

I must move quickly with my questions, before the eating resumes and the buzz of conversation around the table stops covering my manoeuvring. 'I was wondering if you could see whether there's any record of a Miss Elinor Thompson? Or her mother, Mrs Thompson?' If Elinor can't be found, I could maybe ask Alastair to try and reach her mother with a query. A message for her daughter that doesn't appear to be sent from Milton Hall.

Alastair frowns. 'I suppose so…'

'You see, Miss Thompson was a nanny here, at the Hall. We lost her forwarding address, unfortunately and…' The expression on Alastair's face tells me that the warmth and the fuzzy friendliness between us is dissipating. 'My little brothers miss her so much,' I hasten to add. 'It would be wonderful if we could find a way to get in touch with her.'

'I can see why,' he says. He glares at the silver fork.

Goodness. I've made him uncomfortable. How disappointing. He's quite like Papa, who is all cosiness and lovely manners until someone asks something of him. Beware of needing something from Lord Milton of Milton Hall.

'Perhaps…' says Alastair. 'Maybe… Have you considered…? Of course you haven't. I was wondering…' He clears his voice again. 'I was wondering, Evie, do you know any German?'

I nod. 'Yes, I… Yes.'

This must be the least subtle way to change the course of a conversation I've encountered in years. Such a lack of delicacy. And Alastair won't even look at me.

'May I ask, then, how well you know German?'

'Well enough, I suppose. I've had a German tutor since I was eight or nine. And two years ago I spent an entire summer in Germany.'

With the von Hitlersteins, as I used to call them in my correspondence to Will. It was all Hitler this, Hitler that. The Nazi salute as we sat down for lunch. What their tall, blonde, hollow-brained son did in Hitler Youth. I wonder if Papa knew about his old friends' sympathies. I suppose he did. I still wonder what he was thinking, packing me up and sending me to that barrel of gunpowder that was Germany in 1938. They invaded Czechoslovakia weeks after I came back.

Alastair's face brightens up as if he's won the grand prize at a draw. 'This is all I hoped for.' His voice drops to a whisper, which suits me, since the murmur around us is quieting. 'Tell you what, Evie, how about— I have a proposition for you.' He toys with the silver cufflinks of his shirt and I can tell he's nervous again. At least, I think so. This man has proven to be full of surprises tonight. 'I've told you that since the Battle of Britain began, we have to do a mad amount of work. My staff work from early morning well into the night. And sometimes they sleep on the floor.' He stops, his eyes widening a bit. 'I don't mean to frighten you. I'd better be honest, though, I suppose. We need more staff, but I can't find enough Oxford professors and young women I can trust. Young women who know German don't grow on trees. So I wanted to ask you if you'd be interested in joining our little enterprise? Not quite so little, really. And I can promise you exciting, top-secret work.'

For the first time tonight, I don't quite know what to say. I had been grasping at straws, and this kind man wants to pack me up and whisk me off to Bletchley with him. I can't possibly think of a single counter-argument. I'd be able to try and find Elinor myself. I'd reach Edmund, in any case. And it would be a miraculous escape from the unbelievable tedium. It's such a wonderful proposition that it seems too good to be true.

'Are you sure I can be of use to you?' I can't possibly think of a single thing that I might be able to do.

'Oh, yes. I have just the job for you. It's quite the steep learning curve, but I think you might like it. And if you don't, there's always room in the indexing section.' He does that thing again where his eyes dart from side to side. 'I might be getting ahead of myself.'

'I don't know what to say.' And I honestly don't. My gaze slides towards Papa, watching the maids intently as they bring out the *saucières*. He doesn't trust the maids to do the job as well as the footmen when it comes to serving, but the footmen have gone to fight and Papa doesn't trust anyone anyway.

'Is this about the amount of work? Or the fact that young girls work alongside men? Provisions for propriety will be made, I can assure you, especially at night.'

I smirk. Alastair is such a decent, well-mannered man. What kind of sector of the Foreign Office is he in charge of, that he'd be so secretive? And that involves work at night? 'No, no. Working with men certainly isn't a problem for me.'

'And as for the billet… Well… I'm sure that some special arrangements could be made. Are you familiar with Lord and Lady Waters of Gloryoak Manor?'

Papa looks up, watching me watching him. *Checkmate, Papa.* 'I tell you what, Alastair,' I say. 'I'd be more than happy to join your little venture. That is, if you can convince Papa he can do without me for the duration of the war.'

Chapter Thirteen

Rose

When I wake up, the blunder from the night before still weighs heavy on my shoulders. Sleep hasn't kept its promise to make me forget, and in the mist of waking, the shame threatens to cloud my eyes with tears.

A single word reverberates, making the edges of my skull ache.

Home.

Home.

Home.

I think, *I'm not made for this*. My mother was right. Jobs aren't for women. Either I made a mistake, or I can't persuade my colleagues that I didn't make a mistake, which amounts to the same thing.

I should have probably stayed home.

As I pull on my skirt and button up my shirt, I wonder how I'll be able to face my colleagues today. How I'll be able to face this day without hearing David's voice. And then the shadow of my worst fear becomes as solid as a piece of lead in my stomach: what if I have to face every day from now on without David?

No, I think, if I do as little as showing up for my work at Bletchley, I'm helping keep David safe.

The lead moves to my feet as I march towards the kitchen – perhaps the day might seem less daunting with a full stomach. The only thing I hear is the sound of my steps; no quiet murmur of conversation, though to be fair the Pikes don't seem to be the chatty kind, not even among each other.

And yet, one seat at the kitchen table is taken. Nell is sitting with her back to the entrance, her chignon immovable while her fingers dance, smoothing some sheets. I stop at the threshold, considering whether I should veer into town and try picking up some beans on toast from somewhere instead.

Too late.

'Good morning, Rose,' she says in a voice that sounds like sandpaper. She's clutching a sheet covered in small handwriting. More, a dozen or so, are strewn on the table, alongside torn envelopes. 'If you'd like breakfast...' She clears her throat. 'Help yourself.' She turns again to her letters, smoothing them out with her hands.

I think, *I don't need this.*

I think, *so this is how it's going to be.*

I've had quite about enough of these people.

I say, 'I will,' and head towards the pantry. I make myself a few sandwiches and wrap them in a clean linen napkin. I will have to talk to the billeting office and see if there are any alternatives. If they could find me some nice people I can live with it would make my life so much easier.

But first of all, I need to speak to David.

The only way I can get through this day is to hear his voice.

This isn't a day to sit around and wait for the bus. This is a day to walk to work and make a stop at the Post Office on the way.

———————

I head for the red telephone box nested against the Bletchley Post Office.

'Rose, lovely, how are you doing?' The sound of him is clear as bells in the morning, like a blue sky after a storm.

'David!' I say. 'Is it too early?'

He gives me his gargled laugh. 'Not at all! I've been up since five. I was just getting ready to take off.'

'Already?' I say, glancing at my watch. I've come such a long way and yet it's barely quarter to eight.

'Rose, lovely, listen, do you have spies here at the airfield? I meant to call you today. I have news!'

Spies, I think. *Heavens.* If he knew how close to the bone he's striking. 'Wonderful,' I say, all the things I meant to tell him falling like a stone in the pit of my stomach. There's a heaviness touching everything around here, and compared to it, David is pure light. But hasn't he always been my sun?

He takes a deep breath. 'You're now engaged to an RAF Pilot!'

A fist tightens in my chest. I know what this means. He'll be out there, in the heat of it all. He'll be the one waiting for the Luftwaffe to strike, ready to bear the brunt of the attack. I can't even begin to tell him how much I know, because he'd never believe me. As far as he's concerned, I'm a typist at the Foreign Office.

'Rose?' There's so much expectation in his tone, so much unbridled joy. I can't bear to disappoint him.

'How amazing,' I say. 'A pilot! I'll be the envy of all the girls at home.'

'Yes, you will, for more than one reason! And stop stealing all my cues.'

'Oh? What cue?'

'Didn't you guess already?'

'I don't like to play the guessing game, and you know that.' If he knew about the guessing games I play each day at work, and how I fail sometimes, and what that means…

He chuckles.

I think, *work*, and check my watch again. I certainly don't want to be late today, especially not after last night's debacle. Not while my head of shift, Henry, is watching me. It seems that not even my beloved David can pull me from the clutches of Bletchley Park. I think of my work, no matter what I do. This is my life now, and I need to hurry. 'Tell me. Please.'

'Fine, fine. You're no fun when you're like this. Are you ready, Rose?'

'Uh huh.'

'I'm coming home.'

'What do you mean, home?' I can't quite wrap my head around it. He has barely finished his training as a pilot and he's being sent home? Surely that isn't how things work in the RAF, not when the skies are swarming with Luftwaffe bomber and fighter planes every day?

I don't even dare to hope.

'Not *home* home,' he says. 'I've been assigned to an airfield near our town. Isn't that fantastic, Rose? We could see each other every few days, when I'm not flying out. It's much better than going to Biggin Hill. You can come back home now.'

My knees turn to jelly. Utter absolute molten jelly.

I'd like nothing more than to be able to see him every few days.

I don't know if, in my new position, that is even remotely possible.

And then, for the first time since I came here, it strikes me. I don't know if I could leave my job. What would the German Air Section do without me? And what would my days look like? The same endless drudgery, plodding along as I wait for news from David? A thought sneaks up on me, clouds my judgement.

I'd rather wait here.

Here, I can make a difference.

And yet. There's David.

'What do you say, Rose?' There's so much expectation in his voice that it breaks me to bits.

'That's the most wonderful piece of news in the world,' I say, though my voice is fading.

One month ago, nothing would have made me happier than hearing that I'd be able to see my fiancé every few days. Nothing in the world.

You'd think a month wouldn't be enough to turn things on their head.

You'd be wrong.

That's the trouble with wars.

They change things.

Chapter Fourteen

Evie

I wager that if the Foreign Office were looking for a conspicuous and utterly hideous headquarters in which to locate their top-secret operations, they couldn't have found a mansion more suitable to this purpose than Bletchley Park. It's as if the house can't make its mind up if it wants to be a Swiss chalet or an Italian villa or a Victorian manor.

And don't even get me started on the people and the airs they give themselves. There was an incredibly brash RAF officer in the little guard hut who absolutely refused to grant me access to the place before I signed one of his ridiculous documents. The Secrets Act or something like that. I told him that I was here at Commander Denniston's personal invitation and wondered, rather loudly, what he'd make of it if he knew I was being barred access. The RAF officer shrugged and told me that the commander would ask me to sign anyway, so I might as well do it now. And to give his words more effect, he mumbled something about a firing squad.

As if.

The very idea that darling Alastair could be in charge of something so terribly secret verges on absurd for anyone who knows Alastair even a bit. But I know these military types; they take themselves very seriously. So I abstained from laughing in the officer's face, signed his yellow piece of paper, and he finally waved me through. The day has been tiring. I didn't have time for a proper breakfast, so I asked the officer where a girl could get a cup of tea and a cigarette. He tsked and waved me through to Edmund's office.

Thank goodness for Edmund Walton. He jumps up the moment he sees me, almost knocking over the table, and shakes my hand so hard I might think he wants to rip it off at the shoulder.

'Evie, what a pleasure to see you!' he says, positively beaming. 'Have a seat. Would you like some tea?' he says, gesturing towards a rather shabby set of mugs.

'Edmund, darling, you are a blessing.' I rummage in my purse for my cigarette case and offer one to him.

'No, thank you.'

'Still the good boy?' I say, and take a deep drag. No more hiding in the corners of Milton Hall. The sting of the smoke fills my lungs. Edmund pours an orangey liquid into one of the tin cups.

'Commander Denniston told me that you'd like to support us,' says Edmund.

'Alastair spoke to you? How kind of him. I might have mentioned that I know you.' Darling Alastair, smoothing the way for me. Not only that he managed to rip me out of Papa's claws – I have no clue what he might have told him about this prospective 'work' to make the old bat let me out of his clutches – but he also put me directly in the way of the man I wanted to find.

This is too easy.

Edmund nods. 'I told him you're just the sort of girl we're looking for. Clever, educated, someone who can keep a secret.'

'Stop, or you'll make me blush.' The burnt ash at the top of my cigarette threatens to topple over, scattering all over Edmund's desk, which is already full of papers. 'An ashtray?'

Edmund obligingly places a saucer in front of me. 'So you agree to work in my section? I can promise you it won't be dull. And it will be rather important.'

Aren't they all rather important in this place? 'Sure, darling,' I say, my mind already on other things. I take a sip of the so-called tea in my mug. It tastes like soapy water.

'I wager you'll like the work. And the other people in our section. You won't even be the first woman – there's another girl, Miss Wiley. But, of course, we'll have to see how that goes once we can alter the working schedule to shifts. It's simply too much to handle in normal working hours. I am so glad that you're joining us, so glad.'

'Me too. You know how fond of you I always was.'

He shifts his papers and pushes back the spectacles up the bridge of his nose. 'There's a test we usually give to prospective candidates, but I don't think it's necessary here. I know from Will that you speak impeccable German.'

'Right,' I say, jumping at my cue. I can't ask him if he knows anything about Will because I don't know what my brother has told him about our falling-out. I don't even know if he received my letter and simply refused to reply to me. So I have to tread carefully. 'I don't know when you last spoke to Will?' I don't have to pretend to have tears in my eyes. They're real. 'Do you know we haven't heard from him since Dunkirk?'

From the way he leans back in his seat, I can tell the blow catches darling Edmund completely by surprise. 'No, I didn't know that.'

I take a deep breath. Here I am, finally, face to face with one of my brother's friends. After all this time. And he hasn't heard from him either. Will's absence is a shadow darkening the room. 'When did you last see him?'

'Three months ago, I think? He was here.'

'In Bletchley?' I take a deep, deep drag from my cigarette.

'He popped over to see me,' he says. My piece of news caught him so unawares that I think he'd tell me anything now. A small consolation.

'Perhaps not only you,' I mumble. 'Of course he would. I think Elinor came back to Bletchley, too.'

'Elinor?'

'Yes, Elinor Thompson. The nanny?'

'Elinor is here, in Bletchley?'

From the way Edmund blinks, I can tell he doesn't know much about Will's affair, about his falling-out with Papa. I can't tell if he's disappointed that Will didn't come all this way just to see him. All the better. If my brother does write to him – or come back to Bletchley, for that matter – it's more likely Edmund would tell me.

'Anyhow, if you hear anything, would you please let me know?' I say. 'His unit has reported him missing since Dunkirk, but everything has been so chaotic ever since. We've all been worried sick.'

'I'm sure you have,' says Edmund, looking as if he's fallen

from the moon. 'Of course I'd tell you right away. Though I can't imagine why he wouldn't have written to you... If...' He stops and I can almost see how the very thought dawns on him, seeping like a blood stain. 'Do you think he might...'

There's a knot in my throat and I can barely speak. 'I don't even want to think about it.'

Edmund nods. 'No. No, we won't.' He brings out his handkerchief from his breast pocket and crumples it. 'Right. Right. Let's introduce you to your new colleagues, shall we?'

The room he leads me to is down the hallway, but just as stuffy as his own office. It's large enough to accommodate one table with six chairs and, today, all of them are taken. 'Evie, welcome to the German Air Section. Allow me to present your colleagues. They are Mr Thornton, Dr Milner, Miss Wiley and you are...' He squints at a petite redhead who sits at the top of the table.

'Lucy Stevens,' she says, lighting herself a cigarette.

I like Lucy already. The other girl sits next to the man with the old jumper and has a look on her face like she might burst into tears at any moment.

'Ah, yes,' says Edmund. 'Excellent. As you can see, reinforcements have arrived for our team. Our protests haven't been in vain.' I can almost giggle at how ceremonious Edmund has become. Is he also like this around his students?

'This means we can soon swap to a shift system, more appropriate to meet the needs of our section and the Air Ministry,' he continues. 'But first, we have to train our new colleagues!'

Edmund looks at everyone in the room, as if, once again, weighing all the possibilities. 'Dr Milner, could you please show the basics to Miss Stevens? And I'll train Evie – that is, Miss Milton, personally.'

The man with the old jumper elbows the girl standing next to him. 'No disrespect, Professor Walton, but I was wondering…since Rose is the newest here, perhaps she might do a better job of explaining the more elementary notions to the new recruits? And then Henry and I could take over?'

'Erm…' says Edmund.

The man widens his watery blue eyes, making a very strange face. 'And, of course, I would be supervising the more delicate matters. If the girls have any questions.'

'All right, Dr Milner,' says Edmund, clearly not aware of what he's agreeing to, or why.

The other man, the one called Henry, twists his moustache, opens his mouth to say something, but then seems to think the better of it. Dr Milner moves a chair to make room for me next to the girl I now know is called Rose. She smiles at both of us, ruffles a stack of papers, and brings out two lined sheets of paper, handing one to Lucy and one to me.

'The first thing you need to know is what we do here,' she says. 'No, wait. First, welcome to the German Air Section. I speak for everyone when I say that we're very pleased to see you. I hope you'll enjoy the work as much as we do. Because what we do…' The sadness clears from her eyes. 'What we do is break the Luftwaffe low-grade codes.'

On the other side of Rose, Lucy raises her eyebrows.

'Break codes?' I say, not sure if I understood her correctly. How could darling, harmless Edmund be involved in something as secretive as breaking German codes? And Alastair, too.

'Yes.' Rose's face is transformed, brightening. She has long hair, perhaps reaching the tips of her shoulder blades, but except for being combed back from her face, it's rather plainly styled. She has a small nose and a small mouth, and the kind of wide face with flat cheekbones that isn't pretty until she smiles. I can tell she isn't from the deb lot – she's wearing a plain, dark-green utility suit that doesn't flatter her waist at all. 'Do you see all of this?' she says, pointing at the stacks of papers littering the table. 'These are messages sent between Luftwaffe aeroplanes or between aeroplanes and their bases that have been intercepted by our wireless listeners. They include everything from weather reports to hints of planned attacks.' Rose pauses and her words begin to sink in. I look to Edmund and he smiles at me.

'Don't worry, it's not complicated,' says Rose. 'You'll start decoding in no time at all. I've only been here for a few weeks myself.'

Decoding? Me? Who does Edmund think I am and what does he think I can do? I am in no way qualified to decode enemy messages. I have no idea what sort of picture he has of me, or what Will has told him, but it's to be expected of darling Edmund – I don't think he has the faintest idea about women and their occupations.

'It's arguable whether the *quantity* of decryptions isn't as important as their *quality*,' says Henry. 'And, of course, it's important to stay focused on the task. Not to allow yourself to be distracted.'

Rose looks at the papers on the table and pushes back her dark-blonde curls. The tips of her ears are red.

'Wouldn't you like to ask Professor Walton what you wanted to ask him, Miss Wiley?' asks Henry, pursing his lips.

'I don't think this is the right time,' says Rose, lowering her voice.

'I think this is as good a time as any,' says Henry.

'You're certainly a man of strong opinions,' I say.

Henry ignores me. 'Miss Wiley here wanted to see her fiancé.'

'Is that a crime in this place?' I say, feeling my back straightening. I bloody loathe the sort of bloody officious prick that Henry clearly is. So full of his own self-importance, so ready to prey on shy girls.

Rose shoots me a thankful look. 'I really don't think this is the right time.'

Edmund fidgets with a stack of papers. From the feverish movements of his fingers, I can tell he's completely overwhelmed by the situation. I can't help feeling sorry for him. Edmund is the sort of man who doesn't lift his nose from his books, not the kind to sort argly-bargy in an office.

'It is a crime, if Miss Wiley intends to go back home,' says Henry. 'I took pains to explain to Miss Wiley that there is no going back home. That she's bound to Bletchley Park as long as there's a war.'

I try to catch Edmund's eye, and I succeed. 'That's true,' he says, and, for a moment, I can't help feel that I've exchanged one sort of prison for another.

Well, at least the people here are a bit more interesting than the ones at Milton Hall. And the prospect of filling my days is fascinating, to say the least.

I'd have to speak to Edmund later, in private. Goodness

knows, I'm not cut out for codebreaking. Where did that idea come from?

'I didn't want to *leave* leave,' says Rose. 'Professor, you must know how much I appreciate this opportunity and how much I love my work. I was hoping for a few days off, so I could go back home and see my fiancé? He's about to move from Yorkshire back to my hometown.'

'I'll see what can be done,' says Edmund, still not looking at any of us.

'I do believe this is out of the question, Miss Wiley,' says Henry, 'as long as Britain fights for its survival. I hope thoughts of your fiancé haven't made you miss the pile of undecrypted messages on the table. Messages that can save lives.'

'I only needed a day or two,' says Rose, pleading.

'We need all hands on deck, especially since we're about to change to a shift system, isn't that so, Professor?' says Henry officiously. 'It's awful how young women need to be consistently reminded of their duty.'

'There, there, Mr Thornton,' says Edmund.

'I don't need to be reminded of my duty,' says Rose, her cheeks now burning. 'That is why I said this wasn't the time to speak to the professor.'

'I think you also mentioned you needed leave,' says Henry. 'And last night, at the first mention the professor made of withdrawing, you jumped at the opportunity faster than he could finish his sentence.'

The man with the old jumper, Dr Milner, shifts his chair closer to the table. 'She was doing nothing of the sort, Henry. And I'm under the impression that you pushed her to speak to the professor today.'

Henry says, 'I wouldn't have if she hadn't told us before the professor came in.'

Lucy puts out her cigarette with a twisting move.

'And I think you're keeping Rose from doing her work, Henry,' says Dr Milner. 'I think she was trying to explain to the new recruits how the Luftwaffe low-grade codes work.'

'Yes,' says Rose, taking up another piece of paper. 'These are the cracks we found for the month. I think the best way to move forward would be to allow you to copy your own sheets. This is what helped me most when I started a few weeks ago.'

I take the sheet absently from her hand, and can't help thinking what an odd bunch I've been thrown in with. I wager Jasper would think Rose is a bit of a wet rag and Henry is a total lump. I wonder what she'd make of Edmund, though. I wonder what she'd think of me, thrown in with the lot of them. And then I almost laugh when I think of Will, and what he'd say if I told him that I'm about to break German codes side by side with darling Edmund, of all the people in this world.

Chapter Fifteen

Rose

My mother has sent me a telegram asking me to call her at a neighbour's house this evening, and it can't be a good sign that she decided to go through all this trouble just to speak to me. So for the second time in two days, I find myself in the telephone box next to the Bletchley Post Office.

'Rose, dear, how are you?' Her voice is crackling with good cheer.

'Great. Absolutely great,' I say, knowing there is no point going into detail. I'm dreading it, in fact.

'We are both so happy, your father and I.'

'Oh,' I say, fearing why that might be.

'I called to ask when to expect you. So we can make arrangements.'

'Arrangements?'

'Yes, for your arrival. When are we to expect you?'

I have no answer to that, except for silence. I have cried

about it. I have fretted. I have chided myself for being so impulsive and asking Aunt Mavis to find me this job, but what could I have done? I couldn't have known David would be coming back home. And I don't know if I would have wanted to miss this opportunity at Bletchley Park, all difficulties aside.

This is my chance to do something that matters.

'Rose?' says my mother, impatience trembling in her tone.

'I don't know. I don't.'

'Hmm,' she says. 'But— Hmm. How long is your notice period, then?'

'I don't know.'

'You could ask Aunt Mavis. Should I ask your aunt Mavis? She should know.'

I remember the Official Secrets Act, and the RAF officer's words. 'There is no notice period.'

'There you go,' she says. 'So when are we expecting you?' It's not really a question.

'You don't understand. I can't leave this place.' The RAF officer had said "for the duration". *Of the war.* And the war is far from over. And I can't possibly forget what was said today in the German Air Section room, about the piles of messages and the impossibility of a few days' leave.

There is no way I can explain to my mother that even though it's only been a few weeks, I've become an essential part of the team. That I've grown roots in this town – or, at least, in one of the rooms of the Bletchley mansion.

'What do you mean you can't?' says my mother, her anger bubbling. 'You're a typist. Since when are typists chained to their desks? Aren't there enough girls like you out there?'

I think, *no, there aren't enough girls like me, not by a long shot.*

Yet I can't explain to my mother the intricacies of my position. 'I can't leave Bletchley, not as long as the war's on.'

'This must be a joke.'

'I assure you it is not.'

'What has your Aunt Mavis got you into? I should have known better.' There's another silence on the other end. I can hear my own heart racing. I can tell she's not happy with me. But what can I do?

'Rose. Do you know how crazy the girls around here are for pilots? Do you know how sought after they are, especially with so many of our local boys gone?'

'Yes,' I say, suspecting that I don't even know half of it. Bletchley Park doesn't allow me much time to spend in pubs and at dances, to have my finger on the pulse of how sought after pilots are.

'And men...' She sighs again, which definitely isn't a good sign. 'You're too young to know the ways of men, Rose, but with so much on offer around these parts... So many young girls in search of good company. And your David certainly is good company.'

I can't think of a single response to that. It's because of what my mother ventured to say about men, and how she said it. 'David loves me,' I say, more to persuade myself. 'He'd never.'

'Of course he does, dear. I never claimed anything else. It's hard, though. It will be hard. What will he think if he hears that you don't want to come back home?'

'I want to come back home,' I hiss, though it's not entirely true. 'I just can't.'

'What will he think? And if he thinks you don't love him...'

'He won't think that. He'll understand.'

'But do *you* understand, Rose? Do you? I don't think you understand the dangers of your position. There's a war on. Do you know what happened in the last war? How many young men didn't come back home?'

My fingers grow cold. 'I hope you're not—'

'I'm not. I'm saying young men like David will be at a premium. Think of Aunt Mavis.'

'Please leave Aunt Mavis out of this,' I say. 'I've had enough of Aunt Mavis for one day.'

There's that all-freezing silence again. And at the end of it: 'How about a few days' leave? Perhaps to remind David how much he loves you, indeed? If you're not quite ready to give up your job…?'

'Yes,' I say, eager to end the conversation. 'Yes.'

'Good,' she says in an even tone. 'At least that. And when can we expect you?'

'I don't know yet,' I mumble. 'That's still to be settled with my head of section.'

'All right. I trust you know what to do.'

'Sure, Mum,' I say. 'You can count on that. Is there anything else? Any news from home?'

'Not quite,' says my mother, in a tone that makes me think the opposite.

'Did something happen? Did somebody die?' There's a whirlwind of faces spinning before my eyes, all young men from our town, gone to fight. On any given day, it could be any of them. I think, *Frank, Maud's sweetheart.*

'I don't know.' She sighs. 'We've heard about Luigi. The ship he and his father were travelling on to Canada has been sunk.'

'Sunk?' I parrot.

'In the Atlantic. It was travelling without a convoy apparently, though I'm not sure what that means.'

But I do. It means they had been left to the mercy of fate and German U-boats.

'Is he all right?' I ask. I can't even bring myself to ask her if he's alive. 'And why were they on their way to Canada anyway?'

'They were being deported,' she says in a small voice.

There's a knot in my throat, and for a long time I can't even speak. 'Why? Why would they be deported? What have they done?'

'I don't know, Rose, it's all gossip. It's not that...Well, he was Italian.'

'And is this a crime in this country now?'

'Rose, there's no need to get yourself worked up like this,' she says in her most motherly voice. 'I'm sure the government are doing what is right.'

'Yes, right. I'd love to be as sure as you are.'

'He might still be alive,' she says. 'Some of the documents they were carrying were thrown overboard—'

I think, *this is too much*, and put down the receiver without saying goodbye.

———

I sway on my feet as I go back to my billet, my thoughts oscillating between the hollow promise I made my mother and how I will pay for it, and whatever is happening to Luigi. My own troubles seem so small compared to his. How does it feel, I wonder, to be torn from the place you think is your home, from the people you think are your people, everything taken away from you, imprisoned, sent away?

My mind can't wrap itself around all the reasons someone would have to do this. I almost stumble into the kitchen of the Pikes' house. The sight of my two landlords arrests me on site. Nell is standing next to the table, while Tom examines a piece of bread. 'What is this?' he says, oblivious to my presence.

'There wasn't enough for more,' says Nell in a low voice.

'What? The coupons? Did you take Rose's?' growls Tom.

'I have coupons,' says Nell. 'I need money. I don't have money.'

Tom pushes the bread aside. 'Then ask her for some more.'

'I can't,' she says in an almost whisper.

'You can't do anything properly, can you?' says Tom. 'I'll handle this, then.'

I don't stay around long enough to listen to Nell's answer. I make for the stairs, slipping out of my shoes and thanking providence for the lock ensuring that I have at least a sliver of privacy.

Today's events have swept me away from the billeting office; the importance of finding another place to sleep has faded, in comparison to everything else. But tomorrow, maybe, I'll start looking for a way out of this house.

Chapter Sixteen

Evie

It's not so hard to come by information, in the end, if you ask the right people and if you are in the right place. All it takes is one visit to Alastair's office, one little piece of praise about how impressive the operations are. 'I didn't even think the existence of such a place was remotely possible, and the sheer tenacity to bring together people of such different backgrounds! The ability to make them work as a team on top-secret operations! This is a feat that could move mountains! Or win wars!'

Alastair beams in a way that tells me he's so touched that he can't even find the words to say so. I push on. 'I can't believe you thought of me. I'm both flattered and honoured. It's such a pleasure to come to work every day.'

The very best of it all is that I'm telling the truth. There's a light to this place that can penetrate even through my thick skin. I wish I could see Jasper's face when I tell him about my work. My. Work. Even when I went to the secretarial school, I never thought that I'd actually work one day, that I'd earn money through my own toil and exertion. It's hardly enough to pay for my meals at the Bletchley Hotel, but it's my own.

And yes, thank goodness for my billet. If I had to thank anyone for that, it would have to be Papa, and I don't want to open that door yet.

'So many interesting people,' I say. 'Edmund is a treasure. And did you know, I even caught wind that one of the former employees of Milton Hall is working here.' This is the first lie I have to tell today and I already feel a bit more like myself. 'I'd certainly love to see her. I was away in Germany when she left, and I'm afraid that we never had the chance to say goodbye. She's such a darling; she was such a good nanny to my brothers.' This last bit isn't a lie – my little brothers realised when Elinor left that something hadn't been quite in order and an air of quiet resentment had floated around the place for a while. Well, not quite quiet. My brothers can't be quiet. Unspoken resentment, let's say. 'The one whose forwarding address we lost, if you recall? It would be wonderful if I could trace her.'

'What's her name?' says Alastair, his pencil poised.

'Thompson,' I say. 'Elinor Thompson.'

'All right,' he says. 'I'll see what can be done.'

No later than the same afternoon, Alastair visits me in my section. Darling Edmund is out to speak to the Admiralty or

Air Ministry or whoever he has to speak to, but Stiff Henry is here to wag his tail respectfully when Alastair arrives. The others probably don't even know who he is, considering how we're all meant to wear horse blinders in this place. I don't even know who works in the adjoining room, for instance.

So my colleagues are blissfully unaware who has graced us with his presence until Henry bows so deeply that I think he might mean to kiss Alastair's feet. 'Commander Denniston.'

Rose frowns, Lucy swirls her pen, and Ralph jumps out of his seat and shakes Alastair's hand. 'Commander, what an honour.'

'The professor is out, but I'm his deputy, if you need to communicate anything to our section,' says Henry. 'Thornton is my name.'

Alastair makes a pacifying gesture. 'Please, don't let me bother you. I just wanted to speak to the Hon. Miss Milton here, if you don't mind.'

'Honourable?' says Henry, his moustache drooping to yet-unseen lows. I can see the mean calculations taking place behind his too-carefully combed hair.

I move over, making room for Alastair at the table. He passes me a scrap of paper. My fingers tingle with giddiness. 'I found a Thompson,' he whispers, 'though I'm afraid this isn't who you were looking for.'

I glance at the name and address inscribed on the piece of paper, at the woman's job. Perfect. Just perfect. 'I do think you've helped me a very great deal.'

Rose

After the commander leaves, Ralph sets down his pen. 'I'll say.'

'Who is that?' Lucy asks, in her usual straightforward manner, speaking out loud my silent question.

I wish I could be more like Lucy, some days. Most days. No one ever taught me how to be more Lucy. Red curls and green or orange stockings, the words on her mind always on the tip of her tongue. All I was ever taught was how to keep my mouth shut. To listen. To please. To be a nice girl.

No one taught me how to be fearless – I wonder where Lucy learned not to be afraid of anything and, most of all, to speak her own mind. Nor is Evie afraid to do the same, for that matter, but Evie is made of an entirely different mould. She doesn't even exist in the same plane as the rest of us.

'That was the man in charge of Bletchley Park,' says Ralph. 'Am I right, Miss Milton?'

'Uh-huh,' says Evie, fingering the piece of paper the man in charge of Bletchley Park has given her. Her hand moves to the pearl necklace hanging about her neck. 'And please, ignore the whole Honourable nonsense. In case you didn't know, I don't like to be constantly reminded that I am my father's daughter.'

I think, *your father must be a lord in order to be able say something like that*. I think, *yes, she's made from an entirely different mould*. She was sought out by the very man in charge of Bletchley Park. And I can't even get two days' leave to go home. I thought this place was supposed to make us all equal in matters of gender, of background and education. Yet, I earn much less than any of my male counterparts for the same work, and Evie has her own secrets with the man in charge whom I didn't even know until he came into our room to call on her.

I think, *there is no such thing as equality in this world*. But then, I hadn't even thought it was possible for me to have the same job as a man. And it's not as if I do my job just as well as Ralph and Henry – I only have to remember the most recent hiccup with the Admiralty that had probably cost us some face.

I'm about to bury my nose into my messages again when the professor comes back into the room. 'Miss Wiley, I'd like to have a word with you.' His eyes are avoiding mine, yet again.

What have I done this time? After the incident, I've steered clear of any attempts at 'intelligence analysis'. In fact, I've steered clear of anything except the hard, solid facts that I've been taught. Use the key to decode the messages. Transcribe the messages and translate them. Show the others how it's done, melt to nothing the pile of messages put in front of me. Ever since, I've managed to detect two possible raids, a 'spotting' in the Atlantic, and managed to stay away from further misunderstandings.

Having said that, I have to admit that there are a few habits that I haven't been willing to shake off. Like the one of grouping on my lined sheets the messages according to base, and within the same base according to frequency. Just by observing how many messages a base sends, and to whom, there are quite a few conclusions that can be drawn regarding possible plans. Or flurries of activity. Not that I hurry to share my presumptions with anyone in my section. No, no, I know better than that.

'A few days ago, you reported on possible activity of the *Scharnhorst*,' says the professor.

'Yes,' I say, a cold shudder running down the length of my back. Not this again. How long will the *Scharnhorst* haunt me?

'I'm sorry to report that the *Scharnhorst* was involved in sinking a few of our ships around Orkney,' says the Professor. 'Hundreds of sailors are dead or waiting to be saved from the sea.' He rubs his forehead.

'I'm sorry, have I understood you correctly?' I say.

'Are you saying that the *Scharnhorst* was where Rose predicted it would be?' says Ralph.

'Yes,' says the professor. 'The Admiralty's analysts were wrong. They rejected our intelligence on the basis of their own estimates and, well... What happened is regrettable. I wanted to say... I meant...' The professor wipes his spectacles. 'I think I'm speaking on behalf of the entire section when I say how much we cherish your work, Miss Wiley.'

I look straight at Henry and he grunts. I throw him a grin. *Ha. What do you say about that?*

'I think you've established yourself as a very valuable member of our team in a very short time,' says the professor. 'I've asked for your promotion to clerk, Miss Wiley. Congratulations,' he says, and shakes my hand.

Henry's eyes turn as round as a pair of coins.

Well, well, I think. *Well, Well.*

Evie

The day has been eventful, to say the least. By the time I finish work, it's too late to seek anyone in their own home. So I leave visiting the name on my piece of paper for the next day, though most of me wants to hurry and knock on their door, knock it down, if needs be, and look for answers.

I'm used to being rejected. I never properly learned to make friends. I grew up with my tutors and governesses, and they provided me with an excellent education, except on one point: I never had to find common ground with other children in a classroom. That didn't particularly improve in my times as a debutante. I met a lot of girls and I've seen some of them around since I arrived at Bletchley, but we never go beyond a polite *Hello* and enquiries about each other's families.

It was the same when we had teas together, before the war. The same discussions about who they danced with, who invited them to dine at the Ritz, and making predictions about whether he was going to pop the question or not, about the latest fashions and designer dresses. And while I do absolutely love a nice dress, there was this nagging feeling of emptiness after the first half hour of being with them, that question bouncing about my head. *Is this it? Is this all there is to my life?* It's odd. I'm perfectly capable of steering a conversation wherever I want to steer it, but I'm unable to make any friends who stick.

And all this while, everyone was looking at me through a magnifying glass, wondering year after year if this season would be my season, the season when I finally found a husband. I started doubting even more that I'd ever find anyone. I never even had a true friend. Except my brother.

When he abandoned me, the cut was even deeper than the drifting away of friends. Papa used to be our common enemy, but now I don't know where we stand. And I have to find out.

But today, I have to rein myself in. The woman I plan on visiting is less likely to give me the answers I want if I go to her home late at night. So back to my billet it is.

Billet is rather a demeaning word for where I live now, I

have to say. Papa, as always, has stretched his tentacles about the place before even allowing me to take the first step out of Milton Hall. As soon as Alastair asked me if I would join his operation at Bletchley Park, Papa started to enquire after a place for me to stay. I assume he wanted someone to keep an eye on me, make sure I'm not up to no good. If this means living in another country manor, bypassing the restrictions of rationing — including that of petrol — and enjoying the fine company of Lord and Lady Waters, that's fine by me. I won't take to the streets in protest.

The maid takes my jacket when I arrive home. 'Someone is waiting for you in the Yellow Room, Miss Milton,' she says.

'Oh?'

My first thought goes to you-know-who. It would be so like him, to track me down and come all the way here to talk to me face to face. Maybe not just talk. But then my heart starts to race, and for entirely different reasons.

Papa would throw a fit if he found out. Who knows what else he might do? By the time I've reached the Yellow Room, I've almost broken into a run. I throw the door open and see Brown's lean silhouette, standing in front of the window.

'Miss Milton, there you are,' she says, stretching her hands.

I grab the tips of her fingers. How I've missed the feel of them in my hair in the mornings. How I've missed someone who touched me lightly, so as not to hurt me. 'Brown, what a lovely surprise.'

'Are you quite all right, Miss Milton? You look rather dishevelled.'

'Yes, what?' I pull my hair back. 'I've had quite a long day.'

'Then perhaps you'll be glad to hear the news I bring.' She rummages in her plain purse, pulls out an envelope, then folds it back inside. 'Your mother sent me. There's news of Will.'

'Is there?' My knees wobble and I grip the back of the nearest chair – heavy sculpted wood and yellow silk, to match the walls of the room. The one thing standing between me and slipping to the floor.

'Your brother is alive and well, just with a different company, or whatever they're called in the Royal Navy. He's on a different ship.'

'That's brilliant news indeed.' Relief surges through my bones, and then something else. I've gone through all this trouble, I've come all the way to Bletchley, because he can't bloody be bothered to reply to my letters. This has to end and it has to end soon. I think about the name written on the slip of paper, and I think how I must go and see that woman. And how she must provide me with some answers. She must.

I ask, 'How did you find out?'

'Your father never stopped making enquiries,' says Brown.

'Oh, yes, I assume Mother would never have allowed that.'

'Of course she wouldn't have stood for it.' She sits down in the armchair opposite me, brushing my arm. 'Are you really quite all right, Miss Milton? You don't look well.'

I force a smile. Brown is one of the few people in this world who would notice when I'm not all right. 'It's all been quite a lot. For all of us.'

'It has, hasn't it?'

'Air-raid alarms, hiding in holes under the ground, then doing our best to fight these people off. My job is quite interesting, by the way.' I dig in my purse for a cigarette and then turn it between my fingers, unlit. 'I don't mind being here.'

'Are they treating you well, Miss Milton?'

'Goodness, I'm the Honourable Miss Milton. Who would dare to treat me badly? From my lovely landlords to my charming colleagues.' Even Stiff Henry. 'And yes, there are some nice people in our...erm...office. Quite lovely.' I think of young Rose, with her wide green-brown eyes, sometimes ferocious like a little cat, sometimes shy like a doe and eager to please. I haven't quite figured her out, but she's been so kind to me. Though rather bossy. I think of red-haired Lucy, with her permanently lit cigarette, battering her eyelashes and throwing out dry remarks.

'You've come all this way and now Will has reappeared,' says Brown.

'No matter. I'm close to finding some answers.' I place back the cigarette in its box. 'I'm so sorry, Brown, you must be exhausted. Are you thirsty? Should I call for tea?'

'No, no,' she says, getting up. 'I should be on my way.' She stops in front of me, swaying a bit on her legs. I can read indecision on her face, then she holds out the folded envelope to me. 'I've received some post that was meant for you, Miss Milton.'

I pick up the letter with trembling hands. I know who it is from even before I tear the envelope. We've done this before, Jasper and I, sending letters through Brown to avoid detection from Papa.

The message is only a few sentences long. Jasper must be seething.

Evie,

What is this nonsense?

I know you love me.

Has he found your price?

Is this who you are, Evelyn Milton?

Jasper

I crumple the letter in my hand. I was expecting this, and yet I can't even begin to explain how much it hurts. It hurts so much that I'm almost numb. 'He's wrong,' I tell Brown. 'He's wrong.'

I smooth the bit of paper out and read it again. 'He's wrong. He thinks I'm staying away because I'm afraid Papa will disinherit me. He has no idea. I'm doing all this for him,' I whisper to Brown.

'I know,' says Brown and I realise how much Brown is risking, too. How much is at stake for her if Papa ever finds out how she has been helping me.

What have I ever done in this world to deserve this woman's affection? And how much does it cost her to support me, even if she doesn't necessarily agree?

I lose a moment in quiet appreciation of this woman, who knows much more about me than I could ever explain to anyone. And who certainly knows more about this situation than even Jasper himself.

'He has no idea. No idea.' I don't know how he came up with this, but Jasper's assumption hurts physically. He can't possibly think I gave him up for Papa's money. He knows, he must know how little I care about all of it. How much he means to me.

I have to set things right.

I call for a pencil and paper. I have to write to him, immediately, and explain this isn't the truth.

As soon as the maid arrives with my utensils, I sit down at the coffee table.

I have no idea how to start telling him what he needs to know. Should I tell him that I love him? That I'm doing all this to protect him? That it has nothing to do with Papa and his money?

Though, come and think of it, everything has to do with Papa and his money. Or else, he wouldn't have the means to blackmail me. I never found out whom he bribed at the opera, so that lying piece of proof would find its way into his hands. It's nauseating how money can buy anything. Even someone's guilt.

'What do I say?' I ask myself.

Brown looms above me, a concerned expression on her drawn face. 'Think about your father.'

'All I do is bloody think about my father,' I snap. 'No. I have a different problem.'

I could tell him everything. I could tell him that Papa has proof against him, proof that would at least cost him his job, the ability to support his family. I could tell him that if he cares about them, he will keep his distance.

Knowing Jasper, he'll run into the trap, headfirst. Maybe he'd tell me Papa can try, though I don't know for sure. *Stop being so obsessed with your family. Stop trying to live the way they want you to live*, he told me while I still went to the occasional private ball, to keep up the appearance that my life was going on as usual.

Maybe he'd understand, but I don't know that for sure

either. What will we do if Papa ruins his reputation and throws me out? How would we live? I can imagine he'd find a way to cast me out of my position at Bletchley, too, and no more wages for me, no more posh billet.

There are some people who can survive any kind of difficulties in life, and I do know this: I am not one of them.

So for his sake, I must keep Jasper where he is – far, far away from me.

I push the golden tip of the pen hard into the piece of paper. Nobody understands; there's no one I can talk to. No one to advise me.

Will understood. Will would know what to tell me now.

Yet Will isn't here, even if he's bloody alive, and whose fault is that?

So I have to do what I think best, even though it will hurt. Both me and Jasper. But it will hurt less than if I cross Papa and he keeps his word.

And the bloody bastard is usually as good as his word.

Jasper,

It's over. Please accept this. Never write to me again.

'An envelope,' I say, trying to force myself to be cheerful. Not quite. Trying not to cry. But holding back my own feelings has never been something I was very good at.

Brown lays her hand on my shoulder. 'I'll take care of that. Your father mustn't suspect, remember?'

'Of course. Isn't it all, always, about my father?'

'If this matters at all, Miss Milton, I think you're doing the right thing. I think you're being very brave.'

I wipe the tear rolling down my cheek and glare at the yellow silk wallpaper that has given its name to the manor's Yellow Room. 'Nothing matters, in the end,' I say, a claw tightening in my chest. 'Only money. Money and power. And woe betide anyone who has yet to learn this lesson.'

Chapter Seventeen

Rose

L ucy is the one who stops us in the corridor after we finish work and suggests we should have tea. Evie checks her wristwatch, something that looks more like a gold bracelet with diamonds. 'Tea at half past six? I'd say a drink, rather.'

Our other two colleagues file past us and Lucy grabs Ralph's arm. 'A drink? The Bletchley Hotel?'

'Sorry, dove, I have plans for tonight,' he says and winks.

'Dr Milner,' she says, swatting his shoulder. 'I wouldn't have presumed...'

'It's always the quiet ones, dove,' he says and Evie shudders.

'All right,' says Lucy. 'Wait for me downstairs. I need to freshen up a bit.'

I think about refusing. After all, I'm so very tired, and the prospect of sitting down for another hour or two fills the bones in my bottom with dread. But then, sleep won't come to me until much later, and a few hours with my terrific set of landlords or closed in my room would send anyone screaming.

'Come on, Rose,' says Evie. 'I've had enough of this house for today.'

We're loitering at the edge of the pond when Lucy reappears, her makeup polished to brilliance. Her lips shine even redder, her face an unreal white against her dash of fiery hair which she tames with the help of a simple green silk band that matches her stockings.

'You've overdone the powder a bit, darling,' says Evie, opening her purse. 'You look like a ghost.' She brings out a little jar with a red lid. 'Here.'

'Rouge, excellent,' says Lucy, extracting a small pocket mirror and handing it to me. 'Can you hold this for me, please?' She applies the smear in two quick moves along her cheekbones.

'Much better,' says Evie.

'Just my colour,' says Lucy. 'I use a bit of lipstick, sometimes, when it can't be helped.'

'Keep it,' says Evie. 'I'm rather hopeless with it, when Brown isn't here to apply it.'

Lucy frowns, the jar of rouge a dash of colour in her extended, open palm.

'My lady's maid,' says Evie. 'Actually, she's my mother's.'

One has to be so posh to say this with ease. This makes me more uncomfortable – I never know how to behave around Evie without being a total numpty. She doesn't even have to open her mouth. It's the way she dresses, the way she carries herself.

For instance, today she wears a pair of dark-blue slacks

with a high waist, flaring to cover her white sandals with tiny heels. Her shirt is also white, with ruffled sleeves that cover half her arms, a collar of pearls on top. The fabrics are simple, yet there's something in the way they embrace her body, in the way they don't crease, that has 'expensive' written all over them. If I wore slacks, I think I'd look like I was wearing a sack. She isn't thin, Evie, but she's tall, and clothes drape well on her.

'No, thank you, really,' says Lucy as Evie closes her palm.

'I insist.' Evie picks up the mirror I'm still holding, rubs at the inner corners of her eyes, then applies lipstick. Her golden tub looks like a Helena Rubinstein – the stuff of dreams for girls like me. The pinkish-red colour makes her face come alive. 'It will do,' she says. 'It's not like anyone can see us.'

Lucy puffs and rolls her eyes.

At the Bletchley Hotel, we find a quiet table at the back of the bar. Lucy swivels her eyes around. 'Are you looking for someone?' I ask.

'Yes. Men,' she says.

'At the bar?' I ask, nodding towards three middle-aged men on high stools, nursing a pint each.

'Not interested in the type with a ring on their finger,' says Lucy. 'I don't plan to pay for more than one drink myself.'

'I love your dress,' says Evie.

'Oh, this?' says Lucy. The dress she's wearing has a green floral pattern, with short sleeves and a bit of cleavage. The way it's cut is remarkable – there's a sort of knot shaped like a flower under her breasts, and folds of fabric start there: two upwards, ending in the sleeves, and two downwards, flaring the skirt to the sides, but just the right amount to show off Lucy's shape. 'I made it myself.'

'Did you now?' says Evie, touching it. 'Remarkable.'

'My mother and my sisters, we all sew.'

'Did you ever consider making a living out of it?' I ask. 'The seamstress in my town is impossibly busy since rationing began. There are never enough coupons to go around for clothing.'

'There's only room for so many seamstresses under one roof,' says Lucy.

Evie points at the green stockings. 'And these?'

A waiter in a white shirt and dark trousers turns up at our table. 'What will you have, ladies?'

'A gin and tonic,' says Lucy.

'A sidecar, please,' says Evie.

'I'm sorry, we don't have that,' says the waiter.

Evie smiles. 'Of course, I forget we're not in London.'

'We know how to mix a sidecar, even this far from London,' says the waiter. 'The problem is with the Cointreau. You may imagine, miss, it isn't so easy to come by anymore.'

I expect Evie to blush or to look embarrassed, but she just laughs. 'Fair point. A gin and tonic for me too.'

'For me, as well,' I add. I examine the hem of my utility skirt. I feel so plain compared to the other girls. 'I don't dare to wear anything else at work.'

'What's wrong with a pretty dress?' says Lucy.

'I didn't want to look unprofessional,' I say, imagining the face Henry would make if I wore a colourful dress like Lucy's.

'As if what you wear has anything to do with how you decrypt,' says Evie.

Lucy taps the table with her red fingernails, while the waiter sets down our drinks. 'You'd still be better than Henry at what we do even if you came to work in a bathing suit and swimming goggles.'

'I'm not better than Henry,' I say.

'You're a clerk now,' says Evie. 'And you've only been here a few weeks, as I've heard.'

'Clerk or no clerk, they still won't let her have a few days off to see her sweetheart,' says Lucy.

'Oh, do tell,' says Evie.

'Let's say that I came all the way from Norfolk for him, and now he's going back to Norfolk.' My improving spirits clear away as I remember David. I still haven't found a way to get back home, and my mother's words reverberate in my head. What if he thinks I don't want to see him? What if he thinks I'm doing this on purpose? I make a mental note to call my aunt soon – perhaps there's something that can be done after all.

'Ouch,' says Evie.

'See? This is why I'd never bother for a man. It's not worth it.' Lucy eyes the two RAF officers who are walking into the room. She gives them a smile, then looks down in coy shyness. 'Is there anyone special for you, Honourable?'

'Let's just say that the family doesn't approve.' Evie fidgets with her glass, then takes a small sip.

'What do they hold against him?' says Lucy.

Evie's gaze shifts from her glass to her nails as if she's uncomfortable.

'Status was a problem, I presume?' asks Lucy.

'You could say so. My parents would never be keen on the working types, who have to support their families.'

I think, *this really is a different world altogether*. Another Britain, invisible to people like me, like my family.

'I bet you're from them deb lot. I bet you met the Queen.' Lucy's green eyes gleam, and the thrill is written all over her face.

'You make it sound more exciting than it really is. The season is an unending string of pointless cocktail parties and dances, where you eat and drink and dance until your feet fall off and you're so tired that you see no reason whatsoever to get out of bed in the morning just to repeat what you've already done the night before.'

Lucy remembers the RAF officers at the table next to us and gives them a cursory glance. One of them winks. 'You make it sound so glamorous,' she says.

'But the dresses,' I say. 'All the wonderful jewellery you must own. The aristocrats,' I say. One has to be exceedingly posh to speak like her, and have such a blatant disrespect for all the beautiful things in one's life. I could never speak like Evie about dresses that cost, probably, as much as our food fare for a year.

'Do you think they're any better than your mother's friends because they have money?' says Evie.

'Work on a farm for one year, day in, day out, and then tell me that balls and receptions are such a chore,' I say.

Lucy is too busy leaning towards the table next to us, so that one of the RAF officers can whisper in her ear. She giggles, then turns around to us. 'The gentlemen are asking if they may join us.'

'All right,' says Evie.

I collect my purse. This is simply too much for me. What would David think if he saw me here, sitting at a table with two strangers, looking for entertainment for the night? What would I think of myself? And what if he's doing the same in a different bar, on the other side of England? Staying in the bar with the girls tonight seems to invite that very outcome.

It would break my heart.

So I tell the girls, 'Of course they're more than welcome to. I'm tired – I'm afraid I'll withdraw for the night.'

'What a shame,' says Lucy, her attention diverted more by the gentlemen who are collecting their pints to bring them over.

'Please, Rose, don't, I didn't mean to—' says Evie, and for a moment, she looks like she's genuinely sorry.

'No harm done. I'll see you both tomorrow,' I say, and hurry to the Post Office, hoping to catch Aunt Mavis at home tonight.

Evie

Even though I woke up with a pounding headache after staying much too late with Lucy last night, I must have my answers today. I don't care how I find them. I have had enough of people failing me, or judging me, or not giving a fig. Of pretending. I don't care if she doesn't want to give me the answers I need, she *will* give them to me, all the same.

After I've come all this way, there must be something to make it worth it. I will find that rascal and apologise to him for something I don't even know I've done and we will make our peace. I think last night made this even clearer to me, as I was lying, concealing, pretending to be someone else again, to have a blast with two young gentlemen looking for some fun. I thought Lucy would like me more for it. But this made Rose like me less.

I want someone again in my life who likes me for who I am, not for who I pretend to be.

The entire bloody universe conspires against me. First of all, there are so many messages coming in today that in spite of the fact that all of us are working to our full capacity, the piles of papers on the table are rising at alarming speeds. Rose throws a cursory glance over my lined sheets of paper. 'Aha,' she says, tracing with her finger a cluster of messages. She then pulls closer her own sheet, comparing. 'Look at this,' she says, pointing at the call signs. 'Do you see the contingencies in these signals? And these are all bases in northern France.' She goes on to study the coordinates. Her face lights up and her eyes move rapidly, while she traces clusters from one sheet to the other. 'There. Do you see it?'

'Sure,' I say. I don't have the faintest clue what she's talking about. I thought I had the hang of the job after a few days – it doesn't require advanced knowledge of physics to copy down messages, look for the meaning of the codes, and translate them into English – but Rose sometimes sees things in the lists that only the professor and Ralph see.

'May I have this?' she says, holding up my sheet by the corner.

'Go ahead.'

She moves on to whisper something to Edmund at his little desk. There's a fair amount of whispering going on with Edmund. I wager they'll miss each other as of tomorrow, when we start working in shifts. Rose and I will work under Henry's supervision (Hurrah! Nope. Not really.) and Ralph will be the head of another shift, working with two young men sent to us by the RAF.

I genuinely wondered at Edmund not picking Rose for his own shift, but this would be so typical of Edmund; running away screaming from a girl, if he likes her.

Though Rose seems so wrapped up in her own fiancé. It is a bit romantic and tragic, to travel so far, to go to such lengths for the person she loves. Didn't I do the same to try and find my brother?

I drag my seat closer to them, listening. Though I should probably be on my way to the kitchens, taking care of the matter, taking it into my own hands. Rose hasn't picked the best of times to distract Edmund, really.

'So you see, Professor,' says Rose, 'everything indicates a possible coordinated action by the Luftwaffe in the region of northern France.'

'When were these messages intercepted?'

'A little more than two hours ago,' says Rose.

'Any indication of where they might be headed?'

'Yes,' says Rose, louder. 'Here and here.' She rustles the papers. 'I was wondering, Professor, might there be a way to give feedback to the listening stations so they could focus on certain frequencies?'

Edmund leans back in his seat. 'I daresay.'

'I'm sorry if I'm overstepping myself.' Rose picks up her lined sheets of paper.

'No, no, that's an excellent idea,' Edmund rushes to add.

'We could increase our chances of obtaining relevant intercepts.'

My eyes roll so hard in my head that it hurts. How do the two of them manage to speak like people in a book? I knew that Edmund was officious by the nature of his job, but what's Rose's excuse? She always, always strives too hard, never lets her hair down for a moment. At least she's wearing something nicer today – a white dress with red and yellow flowers that embraces her waistline and flares all the way down to her knee. I can see why Edmund would be taken with her: she's rather sweet under all that officiousness and serious talk.

He takes the pieces of paper from Rose's hands as if he doesn't want to hurt them. 'So what would be the relevant frequencies?'

The wail of the air-raid alarm makes me jump from my seat. It goes on and on and on. My head pounds.

'To the air-raid shelter,' says Ralph, already holding the door open for us. 'Follow me.'

Edmund pushes his spectacles up the bridge of his nose. 'I'm sure there's no call for panic.'

Rose sways indecisively. 'Should we stay and finish up? It could make a world of difference today.'

On my way to the door, I grab her by the elbow. 'Nonsense.' I remember the swastika on the Messerschmitt's wings and what my little brothers had said; how the pilot could have shot me if he'd wanted to. 'We're leaving.'

And sure enough, by the time we reach the ground floor there's the unmistakable buzz of aeroplanes above us. I've heard this before. I know what they leave behind. I'll never forget the sight of the burning carcasses of our own aeroplanes, the limp body of that girl. 'Hurry,' I tell Rose, holding her tight. 'Hurry.'

———

Rose doesn't let me go even once we're in the air-raid shelter. We're pressed shoulder to shoulder in a corner of what appears to have been the wine cellar in the mansion's times of glory. People clustered in groups as they filed in, grabbing whatever they could to sit on. Rose and I found a sack full of sand. We seem to have lost darling Edmund and Ralph as we rushed here. The light is so dim that I can't make out the faces more than three feet away from us, so they are lost to us, for now.

I don't mind the dark. Rose moves closer to me. 'Have you done this before?'

'Hiding? No. Not quite. But one flew right above me when I was in the woods.' I shudder at the memory.

'This is much more frightening that I thought it would be.' Rose fidgets again, which rather annoys me. I'm too busy remembering how to breathe. 'It's one thing to see their moves on paper, and another to have them right above your head.' She stops, straining to listen. 'I wonder if David is afraid when he faces them up there.'

'Oh?'

'David. My David. My fiancé. He's a pilot.' Her voice trembles. 'I like to think that what we do helps them.'

'It does,' I say, staring at her hand, not quite daring to touch it. 'It really does.'

She nods. 'We once issued a warning for their airfield.' In the distance, there's a boom, but Rose doesn't seem to hear it. 'But, of course, he isn't with that unit anymore. He finished his training and now he's been assigned to an airfield a few miles from my home.'

Above us, the buzz intensifies. 'What are the odds?' I ask, though she's already told me as much last night. I can completely understand what it is to think of nothing other than your special someone.

'I know. I know.' She shifts again.

'You must miss him,' I say, thinking about Jasper.

'You have no idea. I wish I could see him. Just for a few days.'

I remember that discussion I interrupted when I arrived. The injustice of Henry's words. 'What a weasel,' I say, not caring if he's within earshot or not.

Rose gives me a startled look.

'Henry, for saying that you have to be reminded of your duty. The day I first arrived? I know no one who's more aware of her duty. Perhaps our butler.'

'I'm not sure if that's a compliment.'

I snort in an unladylike manner that would appal our butler. And Papa. 'I'm not sure either. But you have to learn to let your hair down more, Rose. Have you even been to London since you first arrived?'

'London? Yes, I was thinking of going to London once David was assigned—'

'How about doing something, for once, that doesn't involve your darling fiancé? I should probably take you to London.' But then, there are Papa's warnings. 'Though I can't. I really can't. Humph. How about going to the pictures?'

'The pictures?'

'Yes, you should probably learn that there's more to life than one's fiancé and work.'

'I am finding out that there's more to life than my fiancé. Though I do miss him an awful lot.'

I'd like to tell her that I'd like to help her, when an explosion rattles us to the core. Masonry dust flies all around us, making us cough. My teeth chatter. Rose creeps even closer to me.

'What was that?'

Around us, there's only silence that goes on and on and on. I'm dizzy before I realise that I'm holding my breath more than actually breathing.

'Are you thinking about your sweetheart, too? I wager you must miss him.' whispers Rose.

'I really do,' I say, in all honesty. 'But I also miss my brother, Will.'

And here it is again, that brush with death, the way it floats above our heads while I have been avoiding doing what I wanted to do all day because I thought I had time. I have no more time, not if I want to fix things with my brother. Because the time is now.

As we file out of the air-raid shelter, I strike in the opposite direction from the rest of my section. Rose runs up to me. 'Where are you going?'

'The kitchens,' I say. She frowns in a dazzled kind of way. 'I'll be back directly. I promise I won't need long.'

'All right,' she says. 'I'll tell everyone you need to freshen up a bit, so don't be long.'

I know what she must think, that there's so much work to be done. Always the work. And her fiancé. I could almost laugh if I wasn't worrying so much about how to gain access to the kitchens.

But I needn't have. Bletchley once used to be a great mansion and they all look the same to a certain extent: kitchens at the back, a small corridor leading towards them. As I weave my way through the hallways, there's so much commotion after the raid, with people returning to their stations, that nobody even thinks to ask what I'm doing here. Who I am to be sniffing around.

And today, the kitchens smell like burnt food. Kitchen workers are setting aside pans while a chef, a proper chef, is shouting orders. I can imagine not all fires had been extinguished before everyone rushed to the air-raid shelter.

No one cares what I'm doing here, nor who I'm looking for. Suits me well enough. It's, also, nobody else's business.

I find the woman quickly, by a chopping board. I recognise her by the old-fashioned embroidered bonnet she always used to wear when she worked at the Hall.

'Mrs Thompson.'

Elinor's mother looks up, squinting, then wipes her eyes with her forearm. 'Miss Milton. Aye. How can I help?'

Her tone tells me that she isn't thrilled by this opportunity to be of service. But Mrs Thompson never impressed through excess warmth, though Mother warmed up to her, for some reason, and agreed to take Elinor in when the boys' first nanny ran off with the second footman without so much as a day's notice.

Elinor had happened to be visiting her mother and Mrs Thompson suggested she take charge of the boys until Mother found someone more suitable. It took quite a while until that more-suitable person was found and, by then, the boys were quite fond of Elinor (goodness knows why) and she was never replaced. Until the Will debacle last year.

'It's not a matter of how you can help,' I say. 'I think I owe Elinor an apology.'

'Do you now, Miss Milton?' She resumes the quick chopping of the peppers on the board. 'And what would that be for?'

I have no idea. But to say that I'm looking to deliver an apology seemed a better idea than to say that I was looking for a person. I pretend to look around. 'I'm sorry, this isn't quite the time or the place.'

'You're right, Miss Milton. This isn't the time. I'm working.' She pauses. 'So you *think* you owe her an apology or you owe her an apology?'

I put on my nicest smile. 'I would certainly love to discuss the matter personally with Elinor. Apologise face to face. If it isn't too much to ask, could you please tell me where I could find her?'

Mrs Thompson rubs her face again with her forearm. 'Miss Milton, it is too much to ask. 'Fraid Elinor wants nothing to do with you lot.'

'I mean no harm.'

'She wants to be left alone.'

'You don't understand.' I feel the smile fading quickly from my face. My grip on this woman is slipping. And so is the chance to find Will. 'It's about my brother. I have to find my brother.'

'And what does Elinor have to do with that?'

'Everything.' Is she pretending to know nothing or are the two lovers keeping her in the dark too? I can't possibly imagine Mrs Thompson hasn't heard from other employees at Milton Hall about what happened. Though Papa would have tried to keep the entire matter very hush-hush.

'You're wrong,' says Mrs Thompson, looking me square in

the face for the first time since I came to the kitchens. 'My daughter has nothing to do with this. Please leave her alone.'

'I mean her no harm,' I say.

'Miss Milton!' Mrs Thompson raises her voice. 'My daughter has quite enough on her mind right now, thank you very much! So please understand when I say that you should leave her alone, and leave me alone too.'

The buzz in the kitchens stops. Everyone is watching us. Mrs Thompson sets her jaw in a way that tells me that no threats, no tears in this world will persuade her to tell me where her daughter is. I retreat with my back to the door, keeping my opponent in sight.

Fine. You might have won this battle, but you won't win the war. I'll track down your daughter. I'll make her tell, in the end.

Yet that last word she used reverberates in my ears.

Alone.

Alone.

Alone.

Chapter Eighteen

Rose

We pick a picture to go to together. Lucy suggests *Gone with the Wind*. Evie rolls her eyes and proposes *Sherlock Holmes*. It's Lucy's turn to roll her eyes, so I ask why don't we see *The Wizard of Oz*. Lucy says, 'Fair enough,' and Evie shrugs.

We choose the day right before our first night shift. Mine and Evie's, I mean, because Lucy works on a different schedule, with the professor.

The lights go dark and I huddle in my seat, waiting for the picture to begin. It doesn't. There's a collective rustle of disappointment as a government newsreel starts.

Heavens. Didn't we have enough of the propaganda?

But within a few minutes, I'm in tears. The short film shows pilots having a cigarette then rushing to their aeroplanes. Fighter planes. Spitfires? In the picture, they seem so small. They look so much like wasps, even with their propellers and landing wheels and their unmistakable buzz. It strikes me to my core. Is that machinery meant to keep my David safe? That's it, all of it?

Evie notices. 'Rose, what's the matter?'

'Nothing,' I say.

'Is this because of David?' says Evie.

Lucy whispers. 'Who's David?'

'Her fiancé,' says Evie across me, as if I weren't even there.

'Yes,' I say. 'I just want… Is it too much to ask to see him for a few days?' I know the answer myself. We're besieged with messages while Britain is being besieged by the Luftwaffe. And every single clue that we find matters. Saves lives. I wipe my tears with the back of my hand. 'Never mind. I'm only throwing a little tantrum.' *If I do my job, I will see him again. Soon.* I wish I could explain this to him, that what I do helps keep him alive.

We spoke on the telephone the other day. He told me that he'd shot down two German aeroplanes and that's he's on his way to becoming an ace. And then he asked me when I'm coming home. The explanations knotted in my throat and I didn't manage to say much. 'But why?' he kept asking. 'Why?'

I told him, 'I love you'.

And then he said that since he'd been transferred from Yorkshire to Norfolk, he'd changed roommates three times.

'Why?' I asked.

He said, 'Because they never came back.'

He said, 'Someone comes and picks up their belongings – a few changes of clothes, a book, the photographs. Takes down their posters. That's all a man leaves behind. There's nothing more to it. And then, the next one comes in.'

After that, I found nothing to say. Except that I wanted to hold him.

I repeat to Evie, 'Never mind.' I can't find the proper words to explain to her any of this – because there probably aren't any.

Evie brushes her perfect curls to the back of her head and frowns. Evie has been frowning a lot these past few days. 'Never mind? I do mind a lot.' She bites her lips, smearing her deep-red lipstick on her teeth. 'Is there somewhere quiet where we can go? We need to talk. All of us.'

I think how Tom isn't expected until later tonight. How Nell is having tea with her mother today. 'Sure,' I say. 'We can go to my billet.'

As I put the kettle on for my guests, I almost forget that my billet isn't my home. That I deeply dislike this house and that the billeting office is looking for alternatives. As I raid the pantry, I remember Tom's scoffs and Nell's pursed lips. And when I reach for the tea leaves, I pick up a proper portion for a proper tea.

Let them strike that off my ration allowance.

The smell of tea is a rush seeping into all corners of my mind and, in the fever, I pick up a tin with Nell's rock buns. They taste like chalk and they break into crumbs when I touch them, but the thought that she'll look for them and find them missing makes me giddy.

I'll dare her to come and ask me what happened to her rock buns.

'So the professor said he can't spare you?' says Evie.

I lay down the teapot. 'Rather, Henry suggested it to him.'

'Ah, yes, I remember,' says Lucy. 'Might you have a light?' she twists a lacquered wood cigarette holder between her fingers.

'But I'm not... I think I wouldn't be comfortable leaving, not now, when there's so much at stake.'

Lucy rummages in her purse for the cigarette, while Evie lays a silver lighter in front of her.

'Nonsense. Life's too short,' says Evie.

'Hear, hear,' says Lucy.

'Yes, but—'

'Stop it, Rose. You should go. You need to go,' says Evie.

Lucy fiddles with the lighter. 'I agree. You should go.'

I want to go, I want to see him, I want to hold him once again, more than anything in the world. 'I can't. Who will handle my messages?'

'We will,' says Evie, shooting Lucy a look. Lucy nods.

I stop for a moment, considering, twisting the hot mug of tea in my hands. 'I can't imagine how all the messages could be handled by two people instead of three, if I'm away.' And I'm almost too afraid to try. A few days with David. Wouldn't that be bliss.

Lucy stretches her package to Evie, who gets her own cigarettes out. 'Then it won't be handled by three people. I don't mind doing an extra shift or two.'

'Nor do I,' says Lucy.

I'm so touched that I don't even know what to say. 'But why would you go through all that trouble for me?'

'Bletchley Park, as everything else, is a man's world,' says Evie. 'If girls don't stick together, who is there to stick up for us?'

'Exactly,' says Lucy. 'We have to help each other.'

A feeling of warmth starts in my chest, spreads through my limbs, my face, and brings me close to tears. It's so wonderful I can't believe it. Surely if there is someone covering my shifts, neither the professor nor Henry would have anything to object to?

This would be too beautiful to be true.

'And we have to keep helping each other,' says Evie.

'Of course. Like a secret society or something,' says Lucy.

Evie grins. 'I like that. A girls' club. *The* Girls' Club.'

'I hate that name,' says Lucy. 'We have to come up with a proper name.'

'The Girls' Club of Bletchley Park?'

'No, we need something catchier,' says Lucy, puffing on her cigarette.

Evie says, 'Sisterhood, then? The Bletchley Park Sisterhood?'

While they bounce ideas between them, other aspects dart through my mind. The logistics of it all. 'Girls,' I say. 'I can't let you do all those double shifts for me. You'll be exhausted.'

'It's just for a few days,' says Evie.

'You'll owe me a favour, then. Who knows when I'll want to be off to London for the night, on short notice?' Lucy winks.

'But we can swap shifts,' I say. 'Of course. I can take over a few shifts from you, and then you'll do my shifts while I'm away.'

Evie tsks. 'Rose. Really. We don't need to.'

I think of those gruelling days when I barely left Bletchley Park, before the girls came. The night I spent on the floor, the way my bones ached, how my head was spinning when I got back to my billet. 'No, no. I insist.'

'All right,' says Lucy. 'If you insist.'

'Great!' I say. 'Wait a moment. I'll fetch all we need, and then we can start making plans.'

'What do we need?' says Evie.

'A calendar, pen and paper, for instance,' I say.

Evie waves me off with her hand. 'Fine. Fine. I'll leave all the logistics to you.'

I dash up to my room. I find pen and paper in a jiffy, but the pocket calendar is proving to be harder to track down. I stumble upon it in the gas mask box. Just as I prepare to return to the girls, the key turns in the lock of the front door. For a moment, I freeze. All I can think is, *not Tom. Please not Tom.* I move carefully to the top of the stairs, and from above I see Nell's chignon bobbing. She's heading towards the kitchen, and fast.

'Tom?' she calls in a quiet tone.

I rush downstairs and the noise catches her attention. She stops on the threshold of the kitchen and turns to me. 'Rose?'

'I'm sorry,' I say, out of breath. 'I invited some friends for tea. It was rather short notice.' I'm seven again and I broke my mother's porcelain cups by playing with them. I want nothing else but to hide.

Nell looks into the kitchen. And then, to my surprise, she recoils. I dash by her. 'Evie, Lucy, meet my landlady, Mrs Nell Pike.'

Evie jerks her head to look at her. Her blue eyes widen and, for a moment, she stops breathing.

Nell hovers, shifting her weight from one foot to the other. Then she takes a decisive step towards us. 'Miss Milton. The last person I expected to see in my kitchen.'

'Elinor,' says Evie. 'Elinor Thompson.'

Chapter Nineteen

Evie

The name is wrong, all wrong. *Mrs Pike*. But it's her, unmistakably her. The eyes, the way she pats her hair. The chignon. I've found Elinor in Rose's kitchen. This is so absurd that I almost want to laugh.

If I weren't on the verge of crying. 'I'm so glad to see you, Elinor.'

Her jaw squares in a way that says she isn't pleased to see me. 'Miss Milton. How are the boys?' She draws herself up straight, and even so the top of her head barely reaches under my chin.

'They miss you so much. They've been livid with Papa after what happened.'

Rose stands in the middle of the room, as if she can't quite decide what to do with herself. She probably doesn't understand a single thing about what is happening, but Lucy is ahead of her. Lucy is always ahead of us. 'So you two know each other?'

I smile, calculating. I've found Elinor. Now all I have to do is not startle her. Let her think I will go wherever she leads me. I tell myself I can do this. I've been lying for as long as I can remember; can't I find a string of little lies to pick her brains? Anything so I can have my answers. Anything to make her put in a good word with Will, though who knows where she might be with Will now? Maybe they parted ways. Maybe she met someone else. And married so soon? It can't be. It's been a year. She wouldn't have had time for it all.

Will must be hiding her from us under a false name. That's it. That must be it.

The silence stretches, and then Lucy, again, is the girl who presses on. This girl has no shame, and perhaps there's a thing or two I can yet learn from her. 'So?'

'I used to work for Lord Milton,' says Elinor. 'I assume you can say we know each other, Miss…?'

'Stevens.' Lucy stretches out her hand as if she's been waiting for this cue ever since Nell came into the room. 'Lucy Stevens.'

'I'd offer you some tea,' says Elinor, 'but I see Rose has taken care of it.'

'We work together,' says Rose in a small voice. 'The girls wanted to help me find a way to see my fiancé.'

At this point I want to scream, will you stop going on about your bloody fiancé?

'Don't let me keep you,' says Elinor. 'Have a lovely evening.'

'Elinor, wait,' I say. 'Since you're here…' I scour feverishly for the right thing to say. I finally decide there is no such thing.

No time for elaborate lies. No time to beat around the bush. So here it goes. 'Would you please tell Will that I'm sorry? And that I've been worried sick about him?'

'I can certainly pass that on, but...why would you...?' Elinor frowns, but all I can hear is that she could pass it on. So she's in touch with him. He speaks to *her*. 'You do know that I'm not the person you have to speak to? That I'm not the one you have to apologise to?' There's a tinge of anger in her even voice.

Lucy, again the undefeated champion in assessing a situation, picks up her purse. 'I'm sorry, ladies, I should be on my way home now. I wish you all a lovely evening.'

'I don't quite understand,' I say, still stuck on my previous exchange with Elinor. And by the time I realise I should probably say something nice to Lucy, the front door slams shut. What a clever girl.

Just in time for my greatest hiccup of all time. 'I'm afraid... I'm not sure where...' For once, I don't know where to begin. I don't know what to say not to offend her. This woman is the first person I've found in months who actually *speaks* to my brother. 'You mentioned you were in touch with Will? Please be frank with me. Honestly, I don't know what I'm stepping into. I don't even know what the situation is.'

Her eyes dart from side to side, but her expression barely changes. She's the same Elinor: the same pretty nose and beautiful lips, always hidden underneath an immovable mask of coldness; those rounded female shapes concealed by clothes that make her look like a grandmother. 'What situation?'

'I mean...the *situation*.' I look to Rose, hoping that she would take the hint that perhaps this is a conversation best carried on between Elinor and me, but she's seemingly rooted to the floor. 'With you and my brother.'

'Oh, my, Miss Milton. Do have a seat,' says Elinor, and I realise that I've been standing all this time. 'And speak plainly to me. I have no idea what you're talking about.'

I don't know how to start the conversation without offending this woman. 'I want to tell you that I wasn't upset. At all. Not for a moment. You know how fond I was of you, always, and I was truly glad to hear about you and Will. I have no idea what my father might have told you...'

The composure disappears entirely from Elinor's face. Her eyes widen in sheer panic. What did I say? I thought I was rather tactful.

'Merciful Lord, what are you on about, Miss Milton? What has your father told you?'

Uh-oh. What in the name—?

'That you and Will were having an affair. That the moment he found out, he dismissed you.'

'Your father never dismissed me. I handed him my notice and he told me to pack my bags and go. That man. That man! He's even worse than I imagined he could be.'

'You didn't have an affair with my brother.'

'Miss Milton,' says Elinor, twisting the ring on her finger. For the first time, I see the ring. On her finger. 'Never. Never. I never had an affair with your brother.'

I'm so mortified that I can't even begin to grasp what's happening. In no way. My mouth has a life of its own now. 'What happened? I don't understand. Why did you hand in your notice? Why does my brother refuse to speak to me? What did I ever do to *him*?'

Elinor sighs, then seems to consider for a long time. I look to Rose, as if she might be the one with the answers, as if she could tell me what I've done wrong in this situation. Finally she says, 'I'll leave you to it.'

Elinor sighs again, then gets up and opens one of the cupboards. It's a cheap metal cupboard with scratched white paint that rather looks as old as her. All this time, I've been suspecting that she eloped with my brother, that she somehow seduced him with her cold ways for his money. But now I've caught Elinor in a stuffy poorly lit and scarcely furnished kitchen in Bletchley. Not at all the glamorous life I'd accused her of. She picks up a cup and a saucer, then lays them on the table. 'You don't have to go anywhere, Rose. Not on account of me. I have nothing to hide.' She fills all our cups and mugs. 'I need tea for this. Plenty of it.'

'Rose, you can stay. You might as well have a seat.' For one odd reason, I'm nervous about what Elinor might have to say. I'm sorry, *Mrs Nell Pike*.

'Miss Milton, do you remember Esther?'

'Yes, of course.' The Austrian maid. 'Your friend, if I'm correct?' The girl who asked for my help to find a new position, just before she left. The girl I caught with Will and his friends more than once. With Will serving her from Mother's china set.

'Yes, my friend,' says Elinor. 'When she first arrived, she hardly spoke any English. And I couldn't speak German. We taught each other how to speak one another's language.' Elinor's face is briefly lit up by a smile.

'You speak German?' says Rose.

'Yes, quite a bit,' says Elinor. 'In any case, did you know that Esther is an Austrian Jew?'

'No,' I say. 'I had no idea.'

'Yes, she used to live in Vienna before she escaped. Her family was quite well-off. They used to have a box at the opera. That's how she became friends, at first, with Will. They spoke a lot about the opera.'

Oh.

The most important things in my life, they all seem to revolve around Will and the opera.

'She still had a number of nice dresses,' says Elinor. 'I asked her, "Why did you bring all those nice dresses with you when you came here? What did you need them for?" I mean, you should have seen them. Silks and velvets and silver threads. Esther said, "So I can remember who I am." Esther had never scrubbed a pot in her life before she came here.'

'Then why would she seek employment as a maid?'

'Why? What do you mean, why? Because of the Nazis. It was the only way out of Austria.'

'Goodness,' I say. 'I never knew that.'

'Will did.' Elinor's expression darkens. 'And so did your father.'

'I'm not sure I understand.'

'Miss Milton, do you truly have no idea what your father did?'

I shake my head so hard that I'm dizzy. 'Why would you think I do? Why would I lie to you and come to you looking for answers?'

'Your father, Miss Milton, denounced Esther as a dangerous alien. Last summer she was taken away from Milton Hall and imprisoned in a camp on the Isle of Man. A camp where she's being held to this day.' The anger makes Elinor's voice tremble. She opens the kitchen drawers, extracts a pile of crumpled pieces of paper and lays them down before me. Letters. In German.

'A friend of ours was in the camps on the Isle of Man,' says Rose.

'I'm sorry to hear that,' says Elinor. 'What happened to him? Was he released?'

'No,' says Rose. 'We don't know what happened to him. I mean, we know, but...' Rose fiddles with the cup of tea in her hands as if she wants to strangle it. 'He was being deported to Canada when his ship was sunk.'

'Good merciful Lord,' says Elinor. 'This is what our government does, isn't it? Imprisons these people, holds them in a camp surrounded by barbed wire. For months and months no letter from Esther came through. For months and months I had no idea if she was all right. If she was still here, or in Canada or Australia.'

A pit opens in my stomach and I hold onto the table, as if trying not to fall off my chair. I scan the letters, written in a mixture of German and English, as I now see. 'Goodness. I had no idea. That's beyond despicable, even for Papa's standards.' And I thought that what he was ready to do to Jasper was beyond imagining.

'Your father,' says Elinor. 'Your father has no conscience. None whatsoever. Your father is no better than the Nazis. He can make people disappear with the snap of his fingers, and he never hesitates to do so.'

This must be the best description of my father I've ever heard in my life. It seems that behind her silence, Elinor had been hiding an insightful and observant mind.

'I had no idea.' And then, it strikes me. 'But what does all of this have to do with me? I never knew. Why did Will refuse to speak to me? What have I ever done to him?'

'You didn't help her.'

'Who?'

'Esther.'

'What? I don't know what you're talking about,' I say half-heartedly, because I know perfectly well what Elinor is talking about. The day she met me at the stables.

'When your brother left for his training, he told Esther to ask you for help, if she were ever in need.' Elinor looks straight at me, as if she can see the truth written somewhere on my face. And the truth is that she's right. Not so long ago, I wondered what kind of woman asks her employer for help to find a new position. I remember what Brown said. *A desperate one.* 'But I didn't know. I never knew. Was Papa onto them? Why didn't they tell me?'

'She sensed something was amiss. She asked you to help her.'

Help her. Help her find a new position.

I never helped her.

Chapter Twenty

Evie

Someone has a lot to answer for. And, as usual, that person is Papa.

But what Elinor – Nell – said is that I had my part to play in all of this. That I could have prevented it all from happening, if only I had helped Esther when she'd needed me.

I wish there was a way to make it right.

I wish there was a way to make amends.

I search for another cigarette in my purse. I'm so nervous that I drop the package out of the open window of the Bentley and into the street. It flies far behind me, its clatter hidden in a mix of exhaust gas and engine purrs. I'd rather not think about the fact that the car itself – and that I have only as much petrol as I need for my short runs to Bletchley and back to my billet – is all due to the person I loathe most in this world. I make myself take a deep breath and look at my watch. Four hours until my night shift begins.

I need to find a place to spend the remaining hours until I have to work, after I ran out of Elinor's house. A quiet place, where I can put my thoughts together.

Maybe a bar. Maybe the bar of The Bletchley Hotel.

I need to find a way to calm down.

I need to find a way to make amends.

I need to find the way back to my brother.

And I will find it.

Rose

After the girls leave, I'm a statue, rooted in the hallway. From the kitchen I hear the clatter of porcelain, the splash of water. Sounds washing over me. Thoughts whirl in my head like storms after the exchange between Evie and Nell. Elinor.

I think, *I should have followed the girls outside.* I want to follow the girls outside. Anything not to have to face Nell now.

It's my fault. I brought Evie here.

And then, every fibre in my being rises against the urge to run away. I did this. I can't allow Nell to do the washing-up after I invited guests who weren't welcome into her house.

I make myself return to the kitchen. Nell is bent over the stone basin, but her hands are propped against its edges. Her neck is arched downwards. I touch her shoulder, a hint to make her notice me. 'I'm sorry. Do you need help?'

I point to the dishes collected in the basin. Nell glares at them with blank eyes. 'What? Yes. I mean, no. No need. I'll take care of it.'

I tell her, 'You don't have to. I should do the washing-up.'

She pats the back of her chignon, as if checking everything is in place.

'Why don't you sit down for a moment?' I turn my back. I busy myself with the dishes while the chair screeches on the stone floor. It's easier to say what I have to say if I don't look at her. 'I'm sorry. If I'd known about Evie, I would never have invited her. And I'm sorry for pinching your tea.'

'Hm,' she says. 'I don't know if I'm sorry. Maybe some things do belong out there, in the open.'

There's the same steady rhythm to her voice, bar the coldness. There's something encouraging me to go on. 'So you know I asked the billeting office to find a new home for me. It's not because of you. Sometimes… It's odd. It's as if…as if your husband doesn't want me to be here.'

There's silence on the other end, stretching from one corner of the room to the other. I want to turn around and see her face, to see if I've gone too far, but I don't. 'I'm sorry if I offended you,' I say under my breath.

'Tom will be livid,' she says.

I remember the scene I caught between them, the small piece of bread, her composure, the barely sensed fear behind it. 'If you could not mention this to him, at first,' I say, taking a step back. 'Nothing is decided.'

'I tried to be fair to you.' There's the screech of the chair behind me, the sound of steps. I wonder if she's coming to confront me. Then a window is opened and into the kitchen drifts a breath of fresh air.

'I'm sorry. I've been so far away from home. It's not easy.' I rub the mug I drank from with a tea towel. 'You haven't been the most welcoming. But you shouldn't have to be. It was selfish and silly to expect it.' I watch her from the corner of my eye. Nell is glaring outside, into the falling evening. She tilts her head from one side to the other. I wonder what thoughts course behind her dark-brown eyes. Nothing had rippled the surface, nothing of what had been going through her mind, nothing of the pain for the lost friend, of the wail of injustice. Maybe she's been as lonely as I am all this time, unable to reach out to me, across our differences in temperament and position in this house.

Nell shivers. 'No, I can imagine. You're right. We haven't been welcoming. And yes, Tom didn't want lodgers, but we needed the money. We need it desperately.'

'I'm sorry to hear that.'

'Why do you keep apologising? It's not your fault.'

What is it about this woman that makes me feel like a little girl? I set the dishes aside and turn to face her. I'm not a little girl anymore. I'm not someone who only does what her mother and what her teacher tell her. I'm someone whose work is of national importance, because I'm the sort of girl who, when confronted with a problem, finds solutions.

I'm very, very good at finding solutions. 'You said that you can speak German. People like you are at a premium at Bletchley Park. You could find a great job.'

'A job?'

'Yes, a job. A job like mine. A job that pays quite well, in fact, enough to pay for lodgings.' I grin.

She reaches for her apron, forgotten on the back of a chair hours ago, and ties it around her waist. 'Tom would never allow it. This is why he married me, first of all. To take me out of service.'

'This isn't service.' I cross my arms, taking my most martial stance. 'Except the most honourable kind of service, for your country. Don't you want to do important war work?'

'Isn't it awfully late?' She winds the clock on the wall.

I refuse to give up. 'It's very exciting. I'm afraid I can't say more, since it's top secret.'

'I assumed it must be very exciting, since the Honourable Evelyn Milton is your colleague. But no, please, let it be. Please. And if I can ask for one more favour... Could you please stay with us for a few more weeks? I promise I'll be on my best behaviour.' And with this, Nell smiles at me, and it's a smile so sweet and kind that it breaks my heart.

'All right,' I mumble. 'But only if you agree to speak to me at breakfast.'

Part Two

THE SISTERHOOD

August 1940

Chapter Twenty-One

Rose

Of course things couldn't have been easy for me. This is the last shift I have to do before I leave to see my David. It's also a night shift. It's also the second shift I have to do today. It's also the third double shift I have to do in a row. I would like nothing more than to set my head down on the trestle table and sleep. And did I mention that at midnight begins a new month?

'You have to be extra-careful today,' I tell Evie as she arrives.

'Why?'

'The key sheets change in an hour.'

Evie brushes her blonde curls back with her fingers. 'Why in an hour?'

I point at my watch. 'For the Nazis, it was midnight an hour ago. First midnight of the month means a new key sheet. Calculate about two hours for interception and how long it takes for the messengers to arrive. So, new key sheet, new codes. We start at zero.'

Her lips form a silent O.

'You'll need to make two stacks of your traffic,' I tell her. 'One for messages intercepted before one o'clock on the 1st of August and one for messages intercepted after one o'clock. Or you'll mix the codes with one another. The code we know,' I say, tapping my sheet with decrypts, 'and the code we have yet to break. As I said, we start at zero. Our decrypts will be worthless. New key sheet means an entirely new code.'

Evie whistles. 'Nobody bothered to tell me that when I first started. It was all, *Oh, you'll get the hang of this in a jiffy.*' She rolls her eyes. Evie is one of the laziest people I know – but she's mostly well-meaning, I suppose. I think she isn't used to working for anything.

'It's fine. We'll find our way through them,' I say. 'Like we have until now. A few days of hard work and we're back into the codes.' I wish everything wasn't wrapped in such a foggy murk, though, after having worked already for a full eight hours. I've heard the first days of the month are always a struggle to wrench the meaning out of the three-letter strings. It's a time for coaxing, comparing, confronting, inferring.

Today I'm not chomping at the bit to crack new codes. As if Henry can hear my thoughts, he says, 'Your timing, Miss Wiley, is impeccable. If you've decided to run back to your fiancé after all, couldn't it have waited a few more days?'

Timing is everything. The more Luftwaffe aeroplanes attack us, the more our boys are shot down from the sky, to be replaced by younger boys with less training and it goes on and on and on. Most of the time, even though I try not to, I wonder, how much longer will David manage to elude it?

Not a day goes by when I don't approach my billet with a claw in my chest, dreading the worst news when I arrive. How absurd would that be, going through all this in order to go home and then never being able to be with him again.

But going home and actually seeing David, that might prove to be a completely different matter. All the explanations, all the lies I'd have to tell... No need to worry myself sick now. No need to fret. I'll handle this as soon as I'm there. In spite of it all, in spite of our last conversation, he told me he'd be there to pick me up at the train station. But his tone had said it all. I have to be there when he comes for me, or... 'No, it can't wait,' I tell Henry. 'I'm already late as it is.'

'And yet, we need all hands on deck,' he says.

I bury my nose in my decrypts. There's no point in answering. He knows perfectly well that Bletchley won't crumble and fall in my absence. Though he does manage to make me feel guilty about leaving the section to frolic about with my fiancé.

Next to me, Evie tries to appear calm, but by the way she checks her watch every few minutes I can tell she's as nervous as I am about the codes changing. 'Don't worry,' I whisper. 'We'll know when we know.'

And, as expected, shortly after one o'clock in the morning, the messages that come in don't yield anymore to the ciphers on our sheets. As precisely timed as any German raid that we ever stumbled upon in our decrypts. I stare at the pile of messages, an opaque mass of three-letter strings that refuse to reveal their purpose. I rifle through the raw intercepts, unsure where to begin. There are so many separate groups of three letters, each with their own meaning. How do we know which is an incoming air raid? How do we recognise a 'spotting' in the Atlantic? How do we identify a reconnaissance flight that's signalling a pack of U-boats to pound a British convoy?

'What now?' says Evie in a whisper, while Henry spreads at least half a dozen pieces of paper with messages in front of him.

What now?

Obviously, Evie is expecting me to tell her what to do, just like I have ever since she joined us. 'We do what we always do,' I say. I pull out one of the sheets of paper I filled in yesterday at around the same time and scan the frequencies. Then I bring out a sheet from two days before. 'Look here. Some bases are bound to send the same messages around the same time. Do you see these weather reports?' I point at two corresponding rows on two sheets. 'They're almost identical. The reconnaissance aeroplanes report every single day from the same squares. See? Otherwise, they can't compare like with like.'

Evie frowns. 'So they send the same message two days in a row?'

'Sometimes they do. Like this one here. "Today, nothing to report." If you look carefully for messages of the right length that crop up in the messages sent by a few of the bases, you could find the meaning of four clusters at once.'

I pick up two of Evie's completed sheets. 'You could try and group the intercepted messages on the page, the ones from the same bases always in the same position. Even if you have to leave some blanks, then it's easier to compare.' At this point, even Henry has ceased to pretend he isn't listening. The urge to ask whether he has anything to do flutters on the tip of my tongue. I also wanted to ask, *what was that about timing, Henry?*

But, in the end, I stop myself. It's enough that I'm leaving in the morning when I know that I'm needed here.

'So what do I do first?' says Evie, her pencil poised.

'First, you copy your messages, arranging them as always by frequency and by call sign. You can see now why we always do so; I thought it might help in the first few days of the month. And then I'll highlight the possible weather reports so you can check them against the coordinates from yesterday.'

Evie nods and, for the first time since I started working here, for the first time since I started working at all, I realise that none of the girls can replace me tomorrow. And, of course, that in his own mean way, Henry is right.

Thank heavens that by tomorrow night some of the codes will have been broken, which will give Henry and Evie some headway.

Which means it's high time for me to give them that headway. I put my head down, comparing, trying, erasing. I call every decrypt I make and write it on the blackboard. Henry makes his own calls. But his trips to the blackboard, which we use, as I was told, until we fill our key sheets, are barely half as often as my own. Evie checks with me every time before she calls out her own.

And then, just as we near the five o'clock mark, I stumble upon it. A reconnaissance aeroplane feeding back coordinates to its base. Coordinates of a Royal Navy convoy, perhaps, or a battleship.

Heavens, this is it. The urge to keep impressing the Admiralty is a fist in my stomach, twisting. We need to prove to them how valuable we are. I draw out all the messages in my sector of traffic, highlighting the three-letter clusters that crop up in the 'spotting'.

'Henry, Evie, I'm onto something. Could you please look out for these codes, see if you have anything in your messages? It's urgent to crack them.'

Henry comes over to my side of the table and examines the message.

'There's still time,' I tell him. 'It was only sent an hour ago.'

When my search doesn't yield more than one coordinate, I extend it to the other uncracked messages on my pile, looking out for the codes I still need. Evie shouts out another one of the numbers and we're closer.

'May I?' I say to Evie. We start rummaging through her pile of undecrypted messages, looking for the missing codes. My vision clouds, the numbers dance, and I have to rub my eyes. This makes the matter worse – black spots twirl and twirl.

The door opens and a chilly gust breathes under our papers. I hold onto a message I was examining. A pat on my shoulder startles me out of my knickers. Next to me stands Lucy, her red hair pulled back in wide curls, her rouge spotless, her calves clad in bright-orange nylons. I don't know where she finds them, or how she comes up with these colours, but she always brings a spot of cheerfulness to our room. Even though Henry says she looks like a schoolgirl, and never misses a chance to roll his eyes when he sees her. 'Come on, dove, it's time,' says Lucy.

'Time for what?'

'Time to go.'

'Just a moment,' I tell Lucy. 'I need half an hour, at most, and I'll be done with this.' The idea of being able to send the coordinates in due time gives my stomach a jolt.

Evie places her hand on top of mine. 'No, Rose, she's right. It's time to allow Lucy to take over.'

Lucy says, 'Do you want to miss—'

Henry interferes. 'Miss what?'

Evie's grip around my hand becomes firmer. 'You've been working for sixteen hours,' she says. 'I think that's quite enough. Why don't you let Lucy finish the job for you?'

'I think you're running out of time,' says Lucy, passing me a rectangular flat package, wrapped in brown paper.

'What is this?'

Evie collects my purse. 'I'll escort you outside. To the train. Oh, pardon me, the bus,' she says with a pointed look.

'What is the matter with you?' says Henry. 'Let the girl finish. You're worse than geese.'

David. I can't miss the train.

The girls are so clever not to mention this is front of Henry and start another endless and purposeless conversation that will eventually make me miss the train.

But what about the Admiralty?

Lucy says, 'It's time to let someone else take over, eh?'

I have a decision to make and I made it hours ago. I promised. I promised. *Be there at the appointed time or I shouldn't bother at all*, he said.

I tell myself they'll manage without me. I jump to my feet. 'Well, that's it then, I reckon. Wish you all a lovely day.'

'Just so you know, I'm not going anywhere until I finish the job,' sneers Henry.

Thank providence he hasn't realised yet where I plan to go and that today is the day. I clutch the package Lucy has given me, not sure what to do with it. I shoot her a questioning look. She leans in and whispers. 'A little something for you. Knock him dead. Knock them all dead.' I almost laugh. Lucy has been watching too many Hollywood movies lately, unlike me. But with so many blokes ready to take her out, she's spoiled for a choice.

Evie wraps her arm around mine. 'Shall we?'

Outside, while Evie drags me through the gates of the park, I tear the wrapping paper, too curious to wait until I'm somewhere more private. It's a pair of stockings, it turns out. Pasture-green stockings. I remember Lucy's words. *Knock him dead.*

Chapter Twenty-Two

Rose

When things start well, sometimes they turn sour at the end. I race to the train station, to the appointed meeting place to rendezvous with my landlady, who had promised to bring me my packed suitcase, so I didn't have to parade it under Henry's nose.

The train isn't even here yet, and after I pick up my luggage, all three of us are cocooned in an uncomfortable silence, spiked by curious looks between Evie and Nell. There's a flutter in the pit of my stomach, and I don't think it's hunger. I can't believe I'm leaving; I can't believe that by this afternoon, I'll be home, touching my David's face, picking up the pieces of what is left between us.

I make Evie promise she'll let me know if matters are quite under control at Bletchley, and that she'll take care of what I asked her to. After she says yes, I send them both on their way, clearing the path for a few hours alone with my thoughts.

Trying to pin down those magic words that I will tell David, the magic words that will make him understand the importance of my work, and why he has to forgive me.

Evie

What an odd little creature Rose is, I think as I gently spur on my Bentley on the way to my billet. The mists are clearing, leaving room for a bright morning. I swear if she'd asked one more time whether I'd let her know if we needed her, I was going to run out of the train station, screaming.

I wanted to tell her that the place won't go to pieces without her. And really, if I was about to see Jasper, Bletchley Park would be the last thing on my mind. I ease the beast into its place in the Gloryoak Manor's garages and wink at the chauffeur, tossing the keys to him. 'Could you take care of petrol?' I ask, rushing towards the main house. Lord and Lady Waters never go out, so their petrol ration is fair game for me. I'm such a lucky girl. On some accounts.

Goodness, I do hope I'm not too late for breakfast.

'Miss Milton,' says the maid. 'There's a letter for you.'

'Thank you,' I say, peering at the silver tray in the main corridor, in the corner destined for my correspondence.

When I spot my brother's sloppy writing, I can't help thinking it's about bloody time. After I spoke to Elinor, I wrote to him again, telling him how sorry I am and that I'm ready to make amends. That I'd do things differently if I had the chance to do them again. This letter is proof that he, at least, reads my messages. 'This day is about to become even better,' I tell the maid and pick up the envelope. At the foot of the marble staircase, I stop. No point in drawing this out; he's tortured me long enough. And then there are all the things I have to tell him. Where will I even begin?

The slip of paper inside is so small that I almost drop it to the polished floor. Just five words are written on it.

Being sorry is not enough.

Rose

By the time I arrive at the train station in my home town, it's the middle of the night. Well, not quite; the sun is setting and no one is waiting for me. Not my parents, and not my darling David.

No wonder, since I was meant to arrive six hours ago and I can't even blame the war and the train schedule for this debacle.

This morning, when I boarded the train to London, I thought it was a miracle that I found a seat in one of the carriages and that I didn't have to stand in the corridor for the duration of my journey. In fact, it was less of a miracle and more the gentleness of a soldier, who stood up and made room for me. 'Sit down,' he said with a coy smile. 'You seem like you had a…erm…quite a night.'

I thanked him, setting the sting aside because I knew that standing for an hour wasn't worth proving him wrong. In the end, it had been quite a night. But the blessing bent into a curse when I snuggled into my seat, putting my feet up on my suitcase. Heavens, they felt swollen. Before me lay several quiet hours of not having to think about anything. Anything at all.

My eyes closed unnoticed, even by me. They opened to

someone shaking my shoulder – the conductor himself. Through the gap in the train's window that hadn't been blacked out, I read the station's name. Exeter.

The unannounced changes of direction are meant to confuse the enemy, but often we get lost ourselves. And it's so challenging to find a way back, in all sense.

I waited on platforms for hours, changed trains more times that I could count, always verging on tears. In Norfolk, the overcrowded train stopped in the middle of a field, and we were asked to walk to the next station. I dragged my suitcase through the mud, slipping on my knees. Yet, I carried on.

And here I am. But 'home' looks as deserted as no-man's land. Across the street, the wind whistles through the broken glass of Luigi's café. Before I can think about what to do next, I hurry in my mud-caked shoes to David's house.

Evie

The shift system is so disconcerting that sometimes I have no idea where I am. I used to think I was a night owl, but one thing I've found out since I started working at Bletchley is that doing the foxtrot in the middle of the night and doing some casual codebreaking in the middle of the night don't quite amount to one and the same thing. And if you're good at one, you're not necessarily good at the other.

Nor is darling Edmund keen on either. His eyes look red and swollen even behind his tortoiseshell spectacles after a night of work. Not quite the bright and sunny welcome we'd expect as we come into the room for the morning shift.

'I have some rather unfortunate news, I'm afraid,' he says as Henry and I barely have the chance to take our seats.

What is it this time? Did they cut our rations of tea again? Are we going to drink, for the rest of the war, hot water, hope, and a dash of sugar?

'I'm afraid the Germans have changed the encoding,' he says.

'I thought that happened yesterday already?' I say, turning to the blackboard. Yesterday, as I left my night shift, half of it was already full of decrypts.

Today, it's much less than that. Across the table, Lucy shakes her head, dark-blue circles around her green eyes.

'Unfortunately, it happened again today,' says Edmund. 'We are precisely where we were yesterday at the same time.'

I'm itching to correct him, to say that yesterday, at the same time, we were better off, but I know better than that. 'No point in fretting, then,' I say. 'Better get on with it.'

I draw up my papers and make room in front of me to spread them out properly. It's not that bad. I'll do whatever Rose taught me to do yesterday – track down my bases, the usual reconnaissance flights, their squares. Just look at me, the good, hard-working girl I've become. I wish Jasper could see this; he'd never believe it, not in a million years. I wish Will could see this. He always, always said that I was far too lazy.

'Could this be a mistake, Professor?' asks Henry.

'What precisely?' Edmund stops scribbling.

'That the Germans changed their codes again.'

'Oh, yes, indeed!' I find myself exclaiming. 'Could it?' Then I remember the von Hitlersteins, the sheer brainless persistence in following every single day the same patterns, from the questions they asked the children at breakfast to the way the napkins were folded at the table. *Um, yes, slim prospect.*

'I certainly hope so,' says Edmund. 'Though I don't know if

I believe this to be the case.' He pushes up his spectacles again, by which action I can tell he's not only tired but also nervous. 'No point in wondering. We should carry on.'

And carry on we do. It's nice to have received some pointers from Rose. I copy a few coordinates from the day before, a few form greetings. All by way of trying to find messages of the right length and comparing them to each other. This, on the whole, proves to be a little fun. Even if only for the face that Henry makes every time I call a decrypt, the way he furtively looks down at his sheet to see if it matches. Or if he can demolish my decode, the bloody imp.

The truth is that I'm doing well enough to attract Edmund's attention. He pulls up a chair next to me. 'How do you do this? How did you find so many decrypts so quickly?'

I explain to him Rose's system and how, frankly, I'm nearing the end of what I can do with her tips. He examines my sheets and then his own. 'Miss Wiley checks messages of the same length, coming from the same bases against each other?'

'Yes?'

Darling Edmund rubs his temples, closing his eyes. I lean in closer to him. 'Edmund, dear, how long have you been working? Don't you think it might be time to head home?'

He smiles, though he's so tired that the corners of his mouth seem to be looking downwards. 'I wish I could, but look what we have to show for' – he checks his watch – 'nearly eleven hours of codebreaking today. Weather reports.'

I click my tongue. 'Oh, really, dear, we're all doing our best.'

'I'm not saying you're not.' He's awake, sheer panic written on all his face. I think nothing scares Edmund more than offending a woman. Not even the Nazis. 'I think Miss Wiley's system is brilliant, following a trajectory on the same coordinates. What a beautiful mind she has; a pity she wasn't born a man. I mean— No, you know what I mean.'

I arch my eyebrow in that way only I can arch my eyebrow.

'Evie, you *know* what I mean.'

I'd be the first to make him pay for his little remark but, sadly, I know what he means. If Rose had been born a Robert, he wouldn't have been expected to rush to his fiancée, waiting for him at home. Our friend Robert would have told his family that he's doing essential war work, that he can't be replaced, and his family would have believed him.

Our Robert would have been here today.

I shake this feeling off. 'But we'll leave Rose alone for now, won't we?' I say, patting Edmund's hand.

———

By two o'clock in the afternoon, we're all cross-eyed, seeing three-letter codes even when we blink. Lucy is still here because she's covering Rose's shift and Edmund can't go home because he's Edmund. And bloody Henry has found something. 'Professor, may I have a moment of your time?'

'Why, yes, of course,' says Edmund, in a way that means, *just wait, I need to fall for a moment under my chair.*

Henry comes to our side of the table with a small stack of messages and his own lined sheet. 'Look at this, Professor. The Nazis, they're transmitting coordinates for the planned raids.'

It's like a burst of electricity goes through us all. Edmund ruffles the sheets. 'Everyone, pay attention.' He wobbles to the blackboard and quickly writes down a set of three-letter clusters. 'These codes are high priority. These are the coordinates of where the attacks will strike today. Coordinates or spellers, we don't know yet. Comb through your messages, see if you have anything like this, and try to focus on them.'

Across from me, Lucy yawns, but dutifully starts checking her messages. Edmund sends me to her to explain Rose's system, so she can work more quickly. Lucy fixes me with an intense stare, then asks me to repeat the part about the recurring coordinates of the weather reports. 'Bollocks,' she whispers, 'I never write them in order.'

'Oh, turd!' I say.

Lucy's green eyes gleam with disappointment.

'It's fine,' I say. 'You can start doing this today.' Lucy bites her lip. 'Better not mention this to anyone, all right?'

Henry calls for the first airfield name that will be targeted by the Nazis today. 'Bramcote! Bramcote!' he says. 'The Luftwaffe gave out the coordinates for Bramcote!' His usually neatly combed moustache is frizzy and shivering.

Darling Edmund pulls up his long, skinny legs and collects the messages from Henry. 'Excellent,' he says. 'So it is possible, after all.'

While he's out phoning in the new information with the Air Ministry, there isn't a peep from any of us. We work hard, looking for coordinates, for clues.

We can do this. We can manage. No matter how many traps the Luftwaffe sets for us, no matter how hard they try to elude us, we will defeat them.

Rose

Mrs Foster, David's mother, told me, 'He was mighty upset with you, Rose.'

Her words ring in my ears as I hurry down the empty street. Night is falling fast while I drag my suitcase all the way to the pub, feeling my way across the cobbles with the tip of my foot. Soon there will only be the stars to guide me through this darkness punctured by my heavy breaths, the sound of my heart thumping in my ears, and the clack of my heels. My feet are so swollen that they're spilling around the edges of my shoes and every step sends jabs of pain, yet I keep on. Mrs Foster said David waited for me for hours at the train station before giving me up for good. She fixed me with a pitiful stare and said, 'I'm sorry, Rose, but it's too late now.'

It will never be too late, not as long as both of us are alive and breathing.

I made it here after all that has happened; this is not the time to lose my way. And that particular way leads to the wooden door of the pub. I lean my forehead against it, grasping the metal, hard. Judging by the voices inside, you wouldn't think there's a war going on. The shouts and the clamour. The clink of glasses and laughter. The sort of male banter that always makes me want to hurry out of the room.

There's no hurrying out of anywhere now. There's only hurrying *into* something. Sweat has dried on my clothes and the dust has caked to mud on my feet. I don't even want to think about the state of my face after sixteen hours of work and an entire day spent travelling. It's a far cry from the rouged, neatly coiffed Rose with her bright, restful smile who should have been waiting for David on the outskirts of the airfield.

This is what I have to offer and all of it is David's. Then I remember the stockings that Lucy gave me earlier today. *It would be like painting over a glob of mud.* Nonetheless, it's better than the state of me right now.

With a racing heart, I draw back into the shadows and slip out of my nylons in the middle of the darkened street. Well, not quite in the middle, on the side of a building. The pub's door creaks and opens as I pull the stockings around my hips. No, no, no. Not now. Not now. A sliver of light pools at my feet, missing me by inches. There's a man on the threshold, staring out into the night. From behind him, the sounds of the pub cleave into the darkness, filling it. Too loud, too many. How can I step in there as a young woman, alone? And imagine the humiliation if David were to reject me in front of the entire male population of the town.

The horror. And what if – what if – my own father is watching?

I clutch my suitcase. Maybe now isn't the best time to handle this. Maybe it would be wiser to go home, have a decent night's sleep, and make myself pretty for tomorrow. Pick up the pieces in broad daylight, not risking cutting myself on the shards of darkness.

I take a deep breath.

And yet...

On the other side of this door, there's David.

David is there.

On the other side of the door.

I push against the handle so hard that I almost topple onto the floor of the pub. The clamour and the buzz dies away. I look around at so many faces, brushing over the surprise, the amusement caused by my presence here. There are too many men and I can't find my David.

'Rose, girl, what is it?' says one of my neighbours. 'Are you lost?'

I stare down at my calves, clad in pasture-green stockings. All of this is so absurd that I want to burst into laughter and into tears at the same time.

And yes, probably I am lost.

But then there's a rustle, and from the back of the pub, a man in RAF uniform is coming towards me. My heart stops altogether. It's David. David! He walks with his legs spread apart, as if he knows the entire pub is watching him and he doesn't care. I want to squeal, to jump into his arms, to tousle that insane tuft of golden-brown hair. I want to say that I'm sorry. Instead, I'm rooted to the spot, barely holding back my tears of relief.

So long. So close. I didn't think we'd ever get to this moment.

He stops a few inches from me and the pub quietens even more, waiting to see what we'll do. His friends laugh at him, Mrs Foster told me. They say I have him wrapped around my little finger.

I look into his face, into his eyes. How long have I dreamed of this moment? How handsome he is, in truth.

He looks down at his watch, the flicker of a smile on his lips. 'Ah, right on time, Rose.' He snatches the suitcase from my hands. 'Let's get you home, shall we?'

Evie

When darling Edmund comes back, he looks like he's been struck by lightning. Literally. His shirt is unbuttoned at the neck and two buttons from his cuffs are missing, but it's possible they were missing before and I might not have noticed it. What do I see these days, my nose constantly buried in these papers? If anyone had told me that I was going to work, and work this hard, I would never, ever have believed them. What has my life come to, without a single dance or an outing to the cinema or theatre? Or the opera, for that matter.

'Too late,' says Edmund, without waiting for our questions.

And with this, the lightning strikes us too. Edmund points at the pocket watch. 'It's three o'clock in the afternoon. The Luftwaffe has been rampaging for most of the day. Bramcote is a burning ruin. Not my words – those of the Air Ministry.' Darling Edmund's capacity to reassure us by continuing to float in his own world is gone. Wrecked to pieces.

The trestle table itself looks as if it's been bombed. Our piles of intercepts have vanished in a mess of sheets, mixing messages communicated in three different codes. And how much will it still grow from day to day, if so many messages will prove to be uncrackable? Around me, everyone moves as if we're in a bad dream: the first of the month over and over again, for the entire duration of the war. It's sheer madness. Nobody can manage such an influx of messages, not even a team ten times our size.

It's not that it hasn't happened before, this discovering of bits and pieces of information when it's already too late. It's that we probably all know – and won't say – that it will go on and on and on, no matter what we do.

'So now what?' I say.

Edmund looks listlessly at his sheets. 'I don't know,' he says.

'What's the point?' says Lucy.

Humph. Exactly. What *is* the point?

Henry draws himself up. 'The point is, Miss Stevens, that we don't give up. That we don't declare ourselves beaten. So now the Luftwaffe pushes harder. We push back. Every moment we spend on the decodes allows us to find new ways of codebreaking. We are forging new paths now, and we have to forge them, if we want to succeed.' Henry's lip trembles and it isn't just determination. There's also a sort of blind desperation.

'As much as I don't like to concede it, Henry is right.' I realise that I've spoken out loud when Lucy turns to look at me, her long face changing into a grin. 'He is. I mean, if we don't try to crack these codes, there's no one who can do it for us. No one will hand us a quick key. But who knows, maybe the RAF can be of some assistance.'

Edmund guffaws. Henry fixes me with a curious stare and then, finally, when he gets the joke, he laughs.

'Right-o,' says Edmund. A pang goes through my heart. *Right-o.* Something Will always used to say. My eyes meet Edmund's – I think he must have realised this.

'Well then,' I say, sharpening my pencil. 'Better get on with it, hey?'

We work hard. We push against exhaustion, against the Germans' scheme. By the time the afternoon shift starts streaming in, there are neat rows of code cracks, shining bright white on the blackboard. Edmund has gone to issue some warnings and I have no words to describe how thrilled I am to see Ralph's friendly smile, though it melts by the time I explain to him that the codes keep changing. And judging by Lucy's face, she's ready to put her head on the table and have a nap as soon as our colleagues take over.

Edmund stumbles into the room. 'Dr Milner, what a pleasure to see you. Right-o.' My heart gives a little jolt again.

Will.

You bloody, little, stinky bastard.

Not enough? I'll show you not enough.

Rose

We lie in a field of rye, staring at the clouds rushing above us. There was so much I wanted to explain to him. I had a plan – all gone now, molten in this silence. I stretch out a hand and the tips of my fingers touch his. The thrill. The shock of the feel of him. Something deep within me responds, and after that my entire body wants more, more of him, more of his skin. I grasp his entire hand with a hunger I'd been hiding from for a long time, then roll over until my chest is level with his. He turns his face enough for his lips to brush against my cheek. The tingle pulls deep, through my whole face and down my chest.

I start kissing him softly, my touch gentle like a breeze. He puts his hand on the side of my face and pulls me towards him, closer, closer, and we melt in a long kiss. His hand wanders to my nape, sending shudders down my spine. My hand slips through the buttons of his shirt. The skin on his chest is burning. He rolls me, pulling me on top of him, his hand finding its way up my thigh. There's a tug around my female parts and I realise this is behaviour far, far from the nice girl I was meant to be.

Nice girls don't neck with boys in fields. Nice girls don't do things like this before marriage.

Well, nice girls don't go to work a hundred miles away from their homes, while their fiancés are risking their lives every day, while every day their fiancés fly might be their last.

Each time David takes off in his Spitfire, he might never come back.

The truth of it punches me in the stomach and I reel back. Seeing him, being with him, makes it even more real. Before I can stop myself, tears are streaming down my face. David rolls me back onto the ground. 'Rose.'

He sits up and puts his head between his hands. 'You know what? Last night, when you came into the pub, I didn't even want to look at you. And then I did, and you looked like you were about to cry. My mother raised me better than that. That is, not to make girls cry. But with you, I don't know. I never know. First I'm here, and then you're not. And then you don't come when you say you'll come. And then you come, all the same.' He runs his hands through his hair in frustration. 'I'm tired. You're making a laughing stock of me.'

I sneak up on him from behind and lace my hands around his neck, leaning my head on his shoulder. There's that smell of tobacco and aftershave again, *his* smell. I inhale as if I want to fill my entire being with him. 'I'm sorry. I'm sorry for many things.' When I'm here, with him, I wonder at myself. I wonder how I could ever choose my work over him – that is, if I ever had a choice. In the end, anyone with a basic knowledge of German could do my job. And what is the point of my job? What is the point of helping others when I can't be here for my David when he needs me?

There's a buzz, like an angry swarm of bees, drawing closer

and closer. David looks in the direction of the airfield and, sure enough, a speck appears on the horizon, growing, making the air tremble with the sound, breaking the quiet of the fields. The aeroplane passes right above us.

'A Spitfire,' says David, feeling his pockets for his cigarettes.

When he's up there, the warnings coming from Bletchley Park can't protect him. 'I often wonder, do you feel lonely up there?'

'Like I'm the loneliest person in the world,' he says, twisting a cigarette. 'Nothing matters up there. I mean, everything matters – section control, what my squadron is doing – but it all comes down to a single mistake. I've seen it too often.'

'I wish I could do more,' I say, and truly mean it.

Were I at Bletchley now, I could help my colleagues get into the month's codes, send the warnings out much faster. This would matter to him, though he doesn't know it.

I'm here and this is what matters to him.

I walk the thin knife edge of the blade, my feet bleeding, an abyss of emptiness opening on either side.

I think, there is no such thing as a right choice.

'You learn to live every day like it's the last,' he says.

'Do you ever forget?'

'I try,' he says. 'Drinking myself out of my senses helps, mostly. Do you know that everyone else thinks I'm an idiot and that you're leading me on? I can't even tell you what they say about what you do in London, and that's not even the half of it.'

Heavens, this small town and its glorious gossip. 'I don't even work in London.'

'Is this all you have to say for yourself?'

I've rehearsed this so much in my head. The pleading. The way I tell him how important my work is, how I can't come back home. The way I tell him that it's a secret, if only he could trust me, could he trust me? And a part of me knows that if I start gushing, if I start telling him, I don't know where I'll stop. *Not a word* – we've been told over and over again at Bletchley. The fate of this war might depend on it.

And once someone knows, someone who shouldn't, someone who is constantly grated because I'm not here, what's to say that he won't pass the secret on? When he drinks himself out of his senses. When his pride is stabbed through.

The expectation in David's eyes guts me three times over. I'm facing my own firing squadron. And yet, all I have to meet him with is silence.

He gets up on his feet, dusting off his uniform trousers. Bits of straw cling to the fabric and I go to help him sweep them off. 'It might be better if you don't, Rose. Leave it.' He turns on his heels and walks in the direction of the airfield.

'David, wait. Please.' If this is what it might cost me, what is then worth saving?

He shakes his head, without even turning to look at me. 'Just leave it.'

I sit on the ground. Who have I become now? What has this war done to us? How have we come to this? I would ask him to trust me, but I see myself as clear as morning dew: I'm not ready to do the same for him.

Evie

I pull Edmund out of the German Air Section room. 'Don't you worry about me, Evie. I'll go to my billet in a few hours.'

'No you don't,' I tell him, too tired to give a fig what everyone else in the section thinks about how close we are to each other. 'You need to rest, and eat, and then rest, because tomorrow, we're starting all over again. Or do you start at midnight?' I don't give him the chance to answer, just push the leather briefcase into his hands and take him by the arm.

Once we're outside, we walk straight by the buses that take the Bletchley-ites to their billets. One of the drivers, a powdered girl in a FANY uniform, follows us with her gaze. I wink at her.

'Where are we going?' asks Edmund, his arm soft in mine, showing no sign that he'd want to walk his own path, anyway.

'Rose asked me to take care of something before she left.' And she did, but at the time I'd waved her demand off so she could go home with peace of mind. I even had an excuse ready to explain why I hadn't done it when she returned, and then the mother of all excuses came my way when the Germans started changing the key codes again. Yet thinking about it, doing what Rose asked would probably be what my brother would like me to do. I could earn some extra points, and then make sure that he'll hear about it. Everybody wins.

'Ah, Miss Wiley. What an unfortunate time she chose to leave.'

I steer Edmund past the train station and down the road that passes under the bridge. Towards the railway cottages. 'Oh, don't. Just don't. You know bloody well it wasn't her choice.'

'She did seem quite eager to see her fiancé.'

'Wouldn't we all be? The man must be a Greek god, hearing her talk about him. But then again...' I throw Edmund a furtive gaze, gauging his reactions. He looks tired. 'She didn't want to lose him, I suppose.'

'Lose him? Why would she lose him?'

'Well. Putting aside the entire business regarding her work for the Foreign Office, in a top-secret job. The man is a pilot, Edmund. Every time he lifts off in his Spitfire, he might never come back. What do you think? That she'd want to be miles and miles away when it happens?'

Edmund chews his lip. I can tell he's never thought of this: romantic love was never a priority in his book.

I stop us on a side street, in front of a small railway cottage. The white paint is peeling off the window frames and some of the bricks are chipped, but I assume someone calls it home. I *know* who. 'Now, now. We need help. All the help we can get.' I turn to Edmund. 'She needs help, too. Remember. She needs this job.'

'Who?' says Edmund.

I ring the doorbell.

Rose

One can always guess my mother's mood by her level of chattiness. This morning, we're at the-underworld-will-freeze-three-times-over-before-I-exchange-a-word-with-you level. She plonks my toast in front of me so hard it's possible she might smash the plate.

'Thank you, Mum,' I say, forcing a smile, though I'm not hungry at all.

She sits down at the table, taking my measure as if I'm a piglet she's making ready to slaughter. My father must be able to hear the sharpening of knives because he makes himself scarce. 'You two have a nice day. I have to do something.'

Barely is he out of the kitchen and my mother starts her attacks. 'Are you proud of yourself, young lady?'

I push the plate to one side. 'I have no idea what you mean.'

'You know what I mean.' She loosens her apron. 'I can't believe it. This isn't the kind of girl I raised you to be.'

'This is precisely the kind of girl you raised me to be. You don't even know. I'm doing my duty.'

'Young woman, I will not tolerate this.' She raises her voice, something my mother never, ever does. 'I brought you up to be a decent young woman, not someone who runs off to London while her fiancé—'

'I did not run off to London!'

'Don't you dare scream at me! Don't you dare!'

First David and now, this. It would be a terrible lie if I said there weren't moments when I wished I hadn't called Aunt Mavis. But once I'd started rolling that particular snowball, I didn't have much of a way back. And even if I did, I'd probably regret it for the rest of my life. No matter what I do now, I'll regret it.

'I wish I could make you understand,' I say. 'That's all.'

My mother rubs her swollen red hands against each other. So much hard work, every day. It's not only David that I'm depriving of my presence, of my help. 'You see, Rose, I'm not unreasonable. I know you want to help. But if you wanted to help, why didn't you become a Land Girl? There's so much to be done with so many boys gone to war. And I heard on the wireless...well, it's also important war work, isn't it? With all this rationing, lending a helping hand in the fields. And you didn't even have to sign up for the Land Girls. I'm saying... You didn't have to look so far from home if you wanted to make yourself useful.'

When she's like this, the maternal mother, there's no point in arguing with her. No matter what I say, she will know best. 'Yes, Mum,' I say. 'Of course you're right.'

'And did you know, many of our local boys are exempt from the Army if they're involved in farming. The Ministry of Agriculture is very powerful.' She gives me a suggestive look. 'Why, I even asked your David why he didn't prefer to work on a farm instead of enlisting.'

I can't help myself. 'And what did he say?'

She lifts her hands in the air. 'Who will ever understand why he didn't? I always say, better safe than sorry. I hope none of you will live to be sorry. Though I should say, you should be very sorry for what you've done.'

'I am,' I say, hoping to appease her. 'You're right.' Sometimes, the larger the number of the *you're rights*, the quicker the conversation ends.

I glance out of the window, where the topography of the back of our garden has been turned topsy-turvy by the air-raid shelter. But not even the war seems to be able to defeat my mother, or her vegetable garden. Half-buried in the ground, the metal shelter has been covered by a thick layer of earth, where cabbages grow.

I don't even like cabbage. If she were growing something on the roof of the bleeding air-raid shelter, couldn't she have picked something I like, for instance carrots?

Mum pats my hand. 'Good girl. So you will do it, then?'

'What?'

'Apply for the Women's Land Army, silly.'

I will do no such thing. 'I'm not sure that's quite how it works. I'm bound to the Foreign Office for the duration of the war.'

'Didn't you listen, Rosie? The Ministry of Agriculture is very powerful. More powerful than the Army, to hold onto those boys. Don't you see? The Land Girls. It's your way out of the Foreign Office and back home.'

I don't say anything, uncertain what I've got myself into.

Evie

A long, awkward silence passes between the three of us after I ring the doorbell and Elinor opens the door. While Edmund doesn't say a word, I can feel him fidget, on the verge of running away. I claw myself harder against his arm. He's my secret weapon and he can't desert me. I won't allow it. 'Hello, Elinor. May we come in?' I say with my most charming smile.

'Hello, Miss Thompson,' says Edmund. He pushes up his tortoiseshell spectacles, as if trying to hide the lost look on his face. 'What a surprise.' He gives her his hand, shaking the tips of her fingers lightly. If I'd asked him, if I had warned him about this, he might have refused. He's so impossibly shy that I couldn't rely on him not to run away from the situation. But even if they don't know it, bringing them together is for the good of us all.

'Mrs Pike,' says Elinor. 'I go by Mrs Pike now. Please, do come in.'

'Oh,' says Edmund.

I rush him along the narrow, dark corridor, practically

running after Elinor, who has scurried into the kitchen. She puts the kettle on, her back turned to us. Yes, the element of surprise; that's what I was counting on, especially since Rose had told me that Elinor's husband wouldn't want her to have a job. If I'd been polite and announced our impending arrival, Elinor would have refused us. And why would she even want to see me? After all the harm that has been done.

'Apologies,' says Elinor. 'Where are my manners? Please, let's step into the parlour.'

'Don't bother,' I say. 'We've just come in for a quick chat.'

'But I insist.'

'We do too, don't we, Edmund,' I say, squeezing his wrist. Elinor's gaze goes where his hand meets mine and I hope she isn't thinking what I think she is. Goodness. She goes on to straighten her apron and pat her chignon. Well. At least I'm not the only one who's nervous in this room.

Elinor doesn't reply. She sets cups and saucers in front of us. The pattern is discoloured, with the golden framings erased here and there, and the cups are chipped. The fragrance of tea fails to cover the smell of oil that's permeated into the kitchen's yellow-ish walls.

'More sugar?' asks Elinor, handing Edmund a spoon. He holds it as if he's never seen one in his life. I'd have expected them to exchange at least a few polite words – I do remember having seen them speak, on more than one occasion. 'We'll cut right to the heart of the matter, then,' I say. *Or we'll never get anywhere.* 'We're both quite tired for reasons...for reasons we hope we'll soon be able to share with you.'

Elinor sits down, twisting the ring on her finger. This woman is so odd, I can never gauge her emotions.

'I've brought you two together at Rose's special request,' I continue. 'You see, Edmund, I don't know if you're aware, but Elinor speaks very good German. And Rose thought that … that Elinor would be very happy to take a job at Bletchley.'

'Is that so?' says Edmund, his eyes lighting up.

Elinor doesn't say a word. Not a single word.

'The job is so exciting,' I tell her. 'And the pay is good. Very good, I have to say. And there are so many clubs at the park, so many activities, if you have any spare time. There's a chess club, a Scottish reel club, a theatre club. I think there's even an opera club.' I realise I'm blabbering much too much. I've never been tempted to participate in any of the activities that I've strung together. Not in the least the opera club: I can't sing for the love of me, and even if I could, it would bring back too many painful memories. 'I don't know how much I'm allowed to say, so I think I should give over to Edmund.' I nudge him with my knee under the table.

'There's no need,' says Elinor. 'My husband would never accept this.'

'Your…husband?' says Edmund.

'Yes, Tom,' says Elinor. 'We… After Milton Hall, I returned to Bletchley and…we've been married for almost a year.'

'Oh. Then…congratulations,' says Edmund.

'Maybe Rose could help around the house?' I say, desperate that the conversation is going in no way like I imagined it would. I can't possibly understand why this woman is being so silly. Rose told me they need the money, and Elinor has something that Bletchley needs.

'Miss Wiley? What does she have to do with all of this?' asks Edmund.

'Rose is billeted with Elinor,' I say. 'Can we focus on the matter at hand?'

'Ah,' says Edmund. 'I'm sorry, I just find it so hard to concentrate at this hour. It all seems so complicated. I was so surprised when you and Esther left Milton Hall.'

'Ah, yes,' says Elinor. 'It's not how I wanted it to go.'

'Why didn't you say anything? Will was so shocked. He didn't understand a thing.'

Elinor looks at me, then at Edmund. 'Maybe in the first instance, before he found out what happened.'

'What did happen?' says Edmund.

Footsteps fill the hallway. Oh, no. I hope this isn't who I think it is. Though I must admit I was rather curious about the much-dreaded Tom Pike. A man appears in the kitchen, a tall, bony man with sharp features: high cheekbones, square jaw, skeletal fingers clutching a key. 'Hello?' he says.

Elinor leaps out of her chair as if her husband had caught her snogging Edmund and not having a quiet chat with an Oxford professor. 'Tom, darling, welcome home.' The man's gaze brushes on us and a fold of displeasure creases his forehead. 'Tom, this is the Honourable Evelyn Milton and Professor Edmund Walton.'

Tom's presence seems to incite quite a lot of leaping about, because Edmund jumps out of his chair, too, stretching his hand. Tom squeezes Edmund's, much harder than he probably should, but his stare is on me. 'That Milton?'

'Yes, Miss Milton's family used to employ me,' says Elinor, jiggling about as if she doesn't know what to do with her hands.

Tom's nose twitches as if he's been met with a particularly bad smell. 'Nice of you to visit.'

'I was always fond of Elinor,' I say.

And then Edmund finds his tongue in the least suitable moment. 'We're here, in fact, to offer Miss Thompson a job.'

'That will be Mrs Pike to you, mate,' says Tom. 'And Nell isn't going back to work. Not for the lot of you.' He leans with his back to the kitchen cupboard, fists closed, the key nestled between two of his fingers. I know what this means. I wonder if Edmund realises it too.

Our presence has become more than superfluous in this house – it's unwanted.

'Yes, Tom,' says Elinor in a soft voice. 'I was explaining as much to them.'

'She's not going into service again,' says Tom. 'And, in any case, not for you lot.'

'I'm afraid there's a misunderstanding,' says Edmund. He can't stop playing with those bloody spectacles. 'We'd like to offer Elinor a position at Bletchley Park. For the Foreign Office. As a clerk. The money would be nice.'

'A clerk?' Disbelief comes through Tom's voice. 'What did she ever do to be a clerk?'

'We were quite impressed with Elinor's qualifications,' I say, pasting my Hollywood-star smile on my face. I would actually like to bite the man's head off. I might not have liked Elinor much back then, but what is she doing with a bloke like him?

'It doesn't matter,' says Tom. 'Nell isn't getting a job and that's the end of it.' He grabs Elinor, his fingers clawing themselves into her soft waist. Elinor is all curves and softness; she doesn't deserve to be grabbed like that. I want to unclench his fingers from her, one by one. 'Isn't that so, Nell?'

'Yes,' she says. 'Yes, and that's the end of it.'

Chapter Twenty-Three

Rose

David is flying out today, so, after the tense breakfast with my mother, there isn't much left for me to do. Except think. I sit around in my room, avoiding my parents, and think.

About what my mother said earlier this morning. About that door she's opened, and through which I peered for a moment. I can't forget that I might have options. I throw myself on my childhood bed, my arms spread wide, staring at a dark beam crossing the ceiling. There's something moving in looking up and seeing this beam again, the beam that has been here all my life, every night when I lie in this bed, trying to sleep. I stared at this beam through my school years. I stared at it while David and I first started courting, when he first took me out to the pictures, when we shared our first timid kiss. I could come home and see the familiar beam, its dark-brown, frayed edges a lullaby in itself. Day by day, night by night.

I could have it all back.

All of it.

In the distance, not far off, there's the boom of thunder. Rain. Precisely what I needed today. Lying in my room, the drops knocking on the glass on my windows. I wonder what it is like to fly in the rain. I make a note to ask David tonight, when I see him.

If he wants to see me.

Heavens. What do I tell David tonight?

The wail of the banshee makes me jump up. I think, *shelter*. I pull the door open and find myself face to face with my mother.

'Quick, Rose, the air-raid shelter,' she shouts, grabbing my hand. Fear is written all over her face. I'm on the edge of tears myself. Never in my life, never, ever, have I seen my mother afraid. My mother has always been opinionated, hard-working, immovable. The bee which made our house hum. A rock. Fear had never been a part of the complex equation of my mother's personality.

Never before, until now.

Evie

Our work at Bletchley has become that nightmare a person keeps having, over and over again; you know it's a nightmare and you know it will not end well and yet you cannot wake up.

Or, in our case, you cannot stop showing up for work.

I can't say it's a surprise to see that at eight o'clock Edmund is already in the German Air Section room. 'Have you been here all night?' I ask him, by way of a greeting.

'I cycled round at half past five maybe,' he says, and by the way he avoids my eyes, I can tell it's a lie.

'Aha.' I take over my own traffic from Ralph. 'So please tell us you have good news for us and that the Germans kept the same keys as yesterday. Please? I have to put in a double shift today and I can't stand doing Sisyphus work until midnight again.'

Lucy barges into the room. 'Mornin'!' She makes a beeline for the blackboard. 'Bollocks. Again?'

'I'm afraid so,' says Edmund.

'No point in being afraid, Edmund. I think the worst is already happening.' I sigh and pull my lined sheets of paper towards me and uncross my legs. As I do so, my nylons catch a splinter in the leg of the table and they rip. 'Wonderful. Just what I needed today.'

Lucy drops a stack of coloured pencils. My gaze winds down to her calves, which are clad in purple stockings today. 'How do you do that?'

She follows the direction of my gaze. 'Red cabbage.'

'What?'

'Red cabbage for purple. Onion for yellow. Beetroot for pink. And always use vinegar when dying nylons.'

'I love it,' I say. Count on Lucy to brighten up the day. She's the hot pepper we definitely needed in our section.

'What are you going to do about it? Things are looking grey enough as it is.'

'Could you please make a few pairs for me too?' Just hearing Henry's comments about my stockings would be worth it.

'Sure,' says Lucy. 'You'll have to provide the nylons. With the rationing and all—'

'No problem. Can't wait.' I point at my own laddered stockings.

'I have a spare pair, if you'd like.' Without waiting for my reply, Lucy fishes in her purse and hands me a little brown package. 'Blue.'

A chair over, Edmund fingers Lucy's pencils, spinning them around and trying them on a corner of his lined sheet. 'I love purple – did you know that? But why so many colours?'

'They're for the bases,' says Lucy.

'Miss Stevens, I'm afraid I'm not following,' he says.

'If we're going to group the messages by frequency, we might as well use the same colour for bases. That might make them easier to spot.'

'Aha,' says Edmund. 'It's rather brilliant.'

'Thank you,' says Lucy and sits down to her stack of messages. There are messy piles all over the table and it's becoming increasingly hard to tell which pile belongs to whom. She lifts a few sheets of paper and puts them back. 'Where do I even begin?' It doesn't even feel like a question.

I chuckle. 'If I had all the answers—'

We start as we have for the past few days, guiding ourselves by the handful of decrypts on the blackboard. We're moving the same rock up the same hill.

It's noon by the time we've managed to move forward a bit. To inch forward, really. Edmund grows quiet and alert, as he does every time he's focused. 'What's wrong?' I can't help but ask.

'I've found something. Possible targets for today.' Lucy and I pull closer.

'Here,' says Edmund, tapping at two lines. 'Can you please

help me find these clusters? There's a fair amount of spellers, so all we need to do is crack a few letters of the alphabet.'

I write down the clusters he needs. In coloured pencils, of course. 'This is like playing hangman,' I say.

'That's what Rose also said,' says Edmund. 'Why did she have to go right now?'

'Don't start,' I say.

'Please don't tell her about HMS *Oswald*,' says Lucy. 'When she comes back.'

I have no idea what they're talking about. 'What about HMS *Oswald*?'

Lucy and Edmund exchange a look.

Lucy and Edmund never exchange looks.

Lucy and Edmund can work together but barely, because Lucy and Edmund come from two completely different planets and the only common language they have is the three-letter clusters of the Luftwaffe.

'Tell. Me.'

'All right,' says Lucy. 'Go on.'

You can tell who's the boss in this room.

Darling Edmund says, 'Miss Wiley was working on a message, two days ago, right before she left. A convoy had been spotted by the Luftwaffe.'

'Before she left.' She had been working sixteen hours, I remember. She'd wanted to stay and finish. Half an hour, she'd said. She needed another half an hour.

But she would have missed her train.

There was no way she could have missed that train. Her happiness depended so much upon it.

That's Rose for you, she wants to do everything herself.

'I couldn't finish it in time,' says Lucy. 'It was a new key sheet; the coordinates were new.'

'What precisely are you trying to say?'

'Miss Stevens, I don't think Rose could have finished in time, either,' says Edmund in a tone that manages to convey precisely the opposite. 'Too many coordinates were missing. We can't help everyone, every time. Not on the first day of the month.'

'Every day is the first day of the month,' says Lucy.

'What happened?' I ask.

Edmund opens his palms towards the sky, as if asking for mercy. 'We weren't able to warn them in time.'

'The convoy was hit,' says Lucy. 'HMS *Oswald* was lost. And people died. Lots of people died.'

'Don't start,' I say. 'Yes, the Nazis kill people. Our people. You can't blame this on Rose, and you can't blame this on yourself, Lucy. We can only do what we can do.' I pull my lined sheets closer and follow up on another of the three-letter clusters that Edmund indicated. Then I remember there was something more to say. 'And in no way will any of you mention this to Rose, all right? Good. TNM is A, by the way.' I fill it in on the blackboard.

Not much later, Lucy calls, 'PTG for L.'

'Good,' says Edmund. 'Now. Who's good at geography?' He shows us the messages he's trying to crack. I sweep my eyes over the four indicated targets, airfields that would be attacked today by the Luftwaffe. Then my heart stops for a moment.

Rose. 'Edmund. Stop. You have to call this in.'

Rose

It goes on and on and on. The buzz above our heads, the booms. Some are in the distance; some rattle our teeth. It's dark in the air-raid shelter – for once, my mother has forgotten something and that happened to be the torch. I can't see her face, but I can hear her cut-through breaths; I can hear her when she tries to pretend that she's not crying.

We don't know where my father is.

He left this morning to avoid the breakfast bickering.

'He'll be afraid, poor soul,' says my mother in a moment when even the rhythmical tack of the ack-ack guns has stopped. 'I wish he was here with us. I wish—'

I don't allow her to say that, so that the opposite might not even flicker in the world of possibilities. We will see him once we come out of here. We will see him.

'I wish you'd brought that torch, Mum. And a book or two. Or the newspaper. Even the Ministry of Food's leaflets would have done.'

'Really, Rose, all you can think of now is books?'

All I can think of now is David. And how he must be up there. I rub my palms against each other, moist as they are with sweat. He must be up there and I wonder whether he will come back and what did I do yesterday, and why didn't I tell him? How could I have not trusted him? What is this war doing to us? My mother's right; my job is turning me into someone I don't know anymore. How could I not tell him? Isn't he out there, every day, in his Spitfire, fighting to keep us all safe?

'No,' I say, 'but the newspaper might help me keep my mind off what I can't help thinking about.'

There's a boom so loud, that it shatters the shelter to its core. It wobbles, shakes and rattles. I jump into my mother's arms. She's all warmth and softness. My forehead knocks against her moist cheek and she squeezes me hard. We draw quick breaths, her chest pushing into mine. I feel like I've crawled again into childhood, wanting my mummy, wanting her to make all the bad things go away.

But no one can make it go away. No one can erase what has been happening for the past year or so.

I think, that bomb fell close. The farmhouse.

'Mother of God,' says my mother. 'I hope they didn't hit my chard.'

It doesn't stop at the boom, nor at the chard. I don't know how long we've been in the shelter. It could be midnight or it could be the next morning, as far as I'm concerned. The more time we spend in here, the less my heart races. Someone wise once told me that humans can get accustomed to anything. Or I read about it in a book. My stomach growls and I yearn for a tin of biscuits, a torch, and a newspaper. Anything instead of crawling underground like a frightened rabbit. Anything to keep me thinking of my David.

It goes on and on and on.

How long? How long can he fight them off?

Evie

I would like to say that I'm not afraid, that I can crack on with my decrypting while Rose's fate is being decided by someone else and while there's nothing I can do to help her. But I'm not that cold-blooded girl my father always wanted me to be. So I chew the end of my pencil and then gloss over the same message at least a dozen times before I decide to drop the pretence and wait for Edmund in the corridor. Lucy is behind me, arms crossed.

We stand on the threshold, attracting curious looks from the other people who are rushing past us. The most striking of all is a tall WAAF with a bunch of files under her arms, who measures us up and down.

'What are you staring at?' says Lucy in the purest Lucy style.

'The stockings,' says the WAAF, almost twisting her neck as she passes us.

'Yes. Right,' says Lucy and we resume our staring-at-the-end-of-the-corridor game.

I could make a joke about Lucy starting a business and becoming richer than Midas by the end of the war, but it withers in my throat when I see Edmund throwing out his long, skinny legs at a quick pace.

'So?' says Lucy, as Edmund ushers us back inside.

He shakes his head.

'Don't tell me,' I say. 'Too late.'

Rose

In a different world, on a different day, I'm not blinded by the sunlight when I come out of the shelter, after the all-clear sounds. I don't run past the wreckage of an aeroplane burning a few dozen feet from our farm. I don't glaze over at my father's soot-smeared face, as he tries to grasp my hand while he holds on with the other to an empty bucket. I don't place a kiss on his cheek as I wrestle my wrist free. I don't keep running, running, running towards the blazing fire. I don't stumble on cracks in the remains of asphalt that had once been a part of the airfield's runway. I don't twist my ankle in the process. I don't limp by skeletons of what had once been stingy Spitfires, calling David's name again and again and again, asking if anyone has seen him. I don't drift by men in RAF uniforms putting out fires, salvaging what they can from burning wrecks. I don't skirt around the twisted remnants of a hangar to reach a mound of new earth that has to be dug out for survivors by the firemen and ARP wardens. I don't stand rooted, even as the question about my darling's fate dies on the tip of my tongue, straining to listen for signs of life. I don't twitch when the buzz of returning aeroplanes comes closer, landing on the bits of runway that have somehow escaped the carnage unscathed. I don't squint to make out the faces of the pilots who have made it to see the wreckage of this day.

I don't turn to see what all the fuss is when a camouflaged lorry weaves its way around holes in the ground, bits of torn asphalt, and wounded grass. I don't hear when someone says my name.

I don't catch in the corner of my eye a young man with a tuft of light-brown hair leaping out of the lorry.

But it is not a different day, and it is not a different world. This broken world is ours to own. And in it, I live to hold onto David for yet another day.

Evie

Edmund's hands are shaking when he picks up one of Lucy's coloured pencils. We sit down quietly at the overloaded table. 'The Air Ministry said it was a carnage. The entire airfield has been ruined. Many aeroplanes didn't even manage to take off. The amount of damage is unspeakable.'

There's a knot in my throat. 'What about the town? The people? The farms?' Rose said her house was a few miles from the airfield. A few miles. 'What about Rose?'

'We should have issued that warning,' says Edmund. 'We should have been able to issue that warning in time but we failed. We can't go on like this. It's not enough. We need Miss Wiley here, not in the range of the cannons. We need her to be safe. And we need her to help us.'

I want to tell Edmund that he can't guarantee her safety either. That the Luftwaffe can strike just as well here as it has struck near her home. I want to tell him that it's her right to have a few days off, that we have her shifts covered.

I say none of this.

Because Rose has been in harm's way.

Because Rose belongs here.

'There's also a been a new development,' says Edmund. 'I'll need to tour the listening stations, to ensure a tighter cooperation with them without having to tell too many people about Bletchley. I'm sure you understand the need to feed back the frequencies that are most crucial, and how we explain this to the Y Stations.'

In fact, I hardly understand a word Edmund says. I try to find darling Edmund in this man who speaks. He's so anguished and upset and disappointed, that he came down from that plain of naked ideas he usually walks and started making choices grounded in reality. Choices I don't necessarily have to like.

'I've thought about this quite a lot, and I can't see any other way forward. Not while the Luftwaffe changes the key sheets daily. I'm leaving tonight for Chicksands. But Miss Wiley must be returned to us. That is, if they find her alive.'

For a moment, during all this deluge of information I can't quite swallow whole, I start to wonder if maybe I am dreaming.

And then the last bomb drops. Edmund clears his throat. 'You will all answer to Mr Thornton as the head of section while I am gone.'

I'm about to say something. Something nasty and stinging and something that would signal to Edmund that there is no way that I would allow this to happen.

But then the door to our room crashes into the wall and an RAF Squadron Leader marches inside. 'Professor Walton. They found her.'

Rose

A WAAF in her belted light-blue jacket makes the telephone call for me and then passes on the receiver. 'Professor Walton for you, Miss Wiley.'

Every second that passes between picking up the receiver and hearing the stream of Professor Walton's voice at the other end, I'm aware of David's presence behind me, the warmth of his body close to mine.

'Miss Wiley. We're glad you're alive and well,' says the professor with his usual aloofness.

I think, *I'm not well, but you'd never think to ask.*

'Professor. What happened?'

What happened to send an entire RAF squadron to my house to fetch me? What happened so urgently that I have to call you straight away from the half-bombed control tower of the airfield?

In the debris of this day, my tongue can't make out the words as fast as my mind can think them. Behind me, David shifts.

'Miss Wiley,' says the professor in a metallic voice. 'You know we have to keep our communications short. Suffice to say that since you left every day is like the first of the month.'

My mind loops and tangles itself in its thoughts. Too much is knocking for attention. I think, *Every day a first. What?* 'I beg your pardon?'

Professor Walton coughs into the telephone. 'Miss Wiley. The key sheet. It changes every day.'

What, what, what? I look to David, to the scratches on his face, the frayed sleeve, as though he's the man who will be able to give me the answers.

'I see,' I say. 'Awful.'

'You are expected at the park right away. The wing commander has received all his instructions. I look forward to seeing you soon. Do you have any questions?'

The way the Professor Walton says this, it's not a question; it's a fact. I do have questions. Many of them.

'No.' I wouldn't even know where to begin.

David seems as lost as I am.

'Ah, yes. And I'll make arrangements for you to be picked up at the airfield. Good day,' he says, and then hangs up. On the other side, my prospective questions hit a wall of busy tone. They have come to me in the meanwhile. For instance, *why?* And, *how?* And, *didn't I have one more day left of my makeshift leave?*

As if on cue, said wing commander barges into the room. 'Miss Wiley. Through here. Your aeroplane is ready.'

Evie

Edmund returns and points at me. I'm holding my breath, waiting to hear if Rose is all right, but all he says is, 'Evie, did you come here today with your Bentley?'

I nod.

'Tempsford Airfield. As fast as you can. I expect Miss Wiley will arrive in the next half hour. And ask for petrol for the journey – the Bletchley garage should be able to arrange this.'

I'm so relieved I could cry. I don't. Instead, I open my purse, check for my keys, and then, it strikes me. 'There is no airfield at Tempsford.'

Edmund is in such a state, leafing through his sheets, that he doesn't even look at me. 'Of course. If anyone asks, there is no airfield at Tempsford. But we know better than that, don't we?'

Rose

They hurry us to a bomber converted for transport, a Vickers Wellington. That's what David tells me later, on our short journey to Bletchley, after I ask the wing commander if my fiancé can come with me. The wing commander shrugs. 'Sure, it's not as if he can fly out on anything today. Maybe not even tomorrow.'

It's cold and noisy and not at all like I thought it would be.

David tells me about his own Spitfire, destroyed on the ground before he could even have a go today at the Messerschmitts, before even the first alarm was sounded. He tells me about the state of the airfield, expresses his admiration for the pilot for managing to take off despite the devastation. He tells me about landing carriages and hangars on fire and when he sees that I say nothing, squeezes my hand. And before we know it, we're preparing for landing.

'I can't believe they're flying you all the way to Bletchley. I feel like… I don't even know who you are anymore, Rose. Literally. Who are you? Why would the Foreign Office fly you back from a bombed-out airfield?'

I could say that I can't tell him, not even if I wanted to. I could say that I'm a big deal amongst the Foreign Office typists. I could say that I break German codes, if I want. I could shout it above the deafening sound of the Wellington's engines. Instead, I bury my head in his arm.

It doesn't matter anymore.

All I wanted was a bit of time with him. To seize this day and stretch it into the night, to make it a better one, to make it count. All I wanted was to take him by the hand and drag him away to a place where we could find each other, before the fear, the secrets, the distance wedged between us.

Instead, I jolt as the Wellington touches down near Bletchley Park. Or at least I think we're near Bletchley Park. Nobody bothered to tell me and I didn't bother to ask.

I should have asked. I should have asked what had happened to my leave. I should have asked why I have to go back when the girls are doing my shifts for me. I should have asked why the rules don't apply to me.

I think, when will I ever learn to behave like a woman and

not like a child, intimidated into silence? When will I finally learn to protect my own interests?

David weaves his fingers into mine. Not much longer now. A few minutes, and we'll have to part again, who knows for how long.

'I will see you soon,' I say. 'Take this as a promise.'

At first, they don't want to allow him to get out of the aeroplane with me. It's not hard to convince them – I've been teetering the entire day on the edge of tears. As we descend, guided towards the taxiways, I hold on tight to David as if he might vanish if I let him go for a moment.

Evie is waiting for us, leaning back on the polished metal door of her Bentley, fingering her cigarette. She's a modern-day Diana with her silver cigarette holder, her oversized sun shades, her blue stockings, a goddess indeed.

'Rose!' she says, opening the car door for me. 'Your carriage, mademoiselle.'

I say, 'Where are we?'

'On a secret airfield that performs secret operations and that's crawling with secret agents.' She chuckles and I have to laugh.

'Really, Evie.'

David asks, 'Yes, really, where are we?' and I realise I'm still holding on tight to him.

'RAF Tempsford,' says Evie.

'There is no airfield at Tempsford,' says David, studying her from the top of her head to her peep-toe shoes.

'Of course there isn't, if anyone asks,' says Evie. 'Seriously, though, I wouldn't tell anyone else if I were you.'

'And what do I tell the lads?'

'Nothing at all,' I say. David gives me a puzzled look and part of me wishes to tell him I could give him lessons in how to keep a secret.

'You haven't told me about your friend,' says David, and I introduce them both.

I say, 'There's a lot I haven't told you.'

David points at our calves, clad in blue and green, respectively. 'Like the fact that you're part of a secret society.'

Evie giggles. 'Yes, and we plan to take over the entire Foreign Office.'

Another wing commander appears out of nowhere. 'Flying Officer Foster, please follow me.' David's grip tightens on my waist and he twirls me towards him. We stand forehead to forehead, sharing the very air we breathe.

'I will see you soon,' he says.

I stand, rooted to the spot, watching him go, unable to do anything. Anger bubbles and rages in my stomach. It seems I'm always unable to hold onto the things I want. He waves to me one last time before he disappears again into the Wellington's belly.

'Come on, dear,' says Evie. 'Your arrival is avidly awaited at the park.'

But I refuse to budge, to move even a single inch until his aeroplane has taken off and has disappeared from sight. Only then do I step into Evie's Bentley.

She jolts the car into action, picking up speed on the airfield's runway, swallowing the asphalt underneath it. 'It's a sisterhood,' Evie says. 'I much prefer "Sisterhood" to "society". It sounds so bloody officious, don't you think?'

Chapter Twenty-Four

Evie

Today, Rose is the Queen of Sulkiness.

'David's such a handsome bloke,' I say.

She says, 'Yes.'

I switch the car into a lower gear to help her go up the hill. Rose turns her head away from me, looking towards the side of the road. Admiring the pastures?

I try again. 'How was your leave?'

'Short,' she says.

I start humming Bing Crosby's 'If I Had My Way'. 'I'm so glad to see you. Edmund will be over the moon.' Rose says nothing. Nothing at all. A few drops of water splash against the windscreen. 'I wager David was pleased to see you, too.'

There's a long pause, and then she finally says, 'You'd think.'

'Where's your luggage?' I ask.

'Home, I believe,' she says.

'Oh?'

'Evie, I honestly don't want to talk about today.' Her voice wobbles. I can't even think what she's been through – the terror of being bombed, and afterwards, being scooped up and flown halfway across England. If she wants to be snappy, I believe she's entitled to it.

'I'm sorry. I can imagine.' Edmund called today's Luftwaffe action in Rose's town 'unspeakable damage'. Perhaps the kind of damage that leaves traces. 'We're so glad to have you back. You can't imagine how bad the past three days have been within the section. With the codes changing every day. It's maddening.'

'Well, I'm about to find out, aren't I,' she says and leans her head against the car window.

'I'm sorry. But Edmund wouldn't have called you back unless it was urgent. And for a while, we knew nothing except that you were being bombed. We were so frightened for you. Especially since we should really have been in a position to warn the airfield about the incoming attack.'

By the way her eyes flicker, I can tell I have Rose's attention. 'You found the warnings?'

'We really need more people to help us with the decrypts, Rose.'

'What about Nell? I wager Nell would be a great help to us.'

I slow down the car in front of a train crossing. 'Oh, Elinor. That. Her husband was… I don't even know what to say. Strange chap. He's absolutely determined not to let Elinor work. I think that concludes the matter.'

'You think?' Her hands twitch around the hem of her skirt, squeezing. 'But that's what you always do, Evie, isn't it? You're very up and at it, until things take an ugly turn. And that's when you lift your hands in the air and say that you can't do anything more about it.'

'I honestly think you're being unfair.'

'I honestly think it's the same thing with trying to find a way to your brother.'

Her reply is a fist in my stomach. After she witnessed my conversation with Elinor, I had to tell her about Will. She'd heard most of it and, anyway, I trust her.

I trusted her.

'You had no idea what I had to do to even find my way to Bletchley and a step closer to reaching him.'

Rose says, 'No, I have no idea, but what I know is that when things become hard, you'd rather say that there's nothing you can do about it. That you've done your best. Think again, Evie. I think your personal best is still a long way off.'

I almost say she's being a little trollop. I don't. Strangely, Jasper comes into my mind. This sounds awfully like something he might say. Yet I can't bite my tongue, either, not after Rose's stab in the back. Evie Milton does not stand for this. I point at the vivid colours of our stockings. 'After all we've done for you so you could go back home.'

Rose toys with her fingernails and I count her silence as a small win. In the distance, the green roof of Bletchley's former conservatory arches above a fence of barbed wire. And as strange as it seems, it isn't even four o'clock in the afternoon.

'What happened with the warning for the Admiralty?' she asks. 'The one I was working on before I had to run off and catch my train?'

Rose

I tried to cry in the car, to mourn the distance growing between me and David. Evie wouldn't let me have even that. She tried to make small talk I didn't need, and then she ended up throwing another scoop of bad news on my plate. As I enter the German Air Section, I try to think about David again, to remember the feel of him, but his shadow on my skin is fading in front of the mess of papers on the table.

'Good to have you back, Miss Wiley,' barks the professor as he shakes my hand. 'We're in an all-hands-on-deck situation,' he says, as I acknowledge the faces of Henry and another two of our newer colleagues on the chairs. He shows me back to my seat and shoves a pile of messages in my face. 'We've rather given up on finding some warning that can be of actual use today, but any overall information we cleave can still be used for traffic analysis. And, of course, the most important point remains to find a way to decrypt faster every day, when the new key sheets come in.'

There's a dull anger directed towards the professor, pounding in my head. I was also busy finding a way – a way to my fiancé, David. And look where I am. 'If this is an all-hands-on-deck situation, wouldn't more hands on deck be rather helpful?'

The professor rearranges his spectacles with both hands. 'Yes, this is why I summoned you back, Miss Wiley.'

Couldn't you find someone new to help, like Nell?

We need more help. But even as I think it the accusations fall hollow in my mind. To train someone new would take days, even weeks, especially in this situation.

So again, I tuck my words into a hidden, hot place where I

can bake them to their full size. One day, when I am ready, I will take them out.

I prepare my sheet of paper, my messages. Lucy pushes over a bunch of coloured pencils.

I don't even ask.

I do what is expected of me in this hopeless situation.

It's about nine o'clock in the evening when I get to my feet. 'I'm sorry, I've had a long day. I think I'm bowing out for the night.'

We are making progress with the day's decrypts – the blackboard fills slowly, but steadily. Three more hours until we have to start again. Three hours, and tomorrow's messages will be here: so many warnings that, in the end, we might be able to decrypt, but probably not in time.

The three-letter clusters shiver in front of my eyes and I can't tell my RMP's from my PNB's.

Henry looks long and hard at his watch. 'You've barely been with us four hours today, Miss Wiley.'

'And I plan to be here tomorrow, too.' I look around for my purse, but remember that it's still probably at home. 'I'm rather counting on the fact that I won't be bombed tomorrow morning, so there will be a few more hours available in the day when I can take care of my work.'

Evie joins me. 'She's right. I'd rather get a good night's sleep and come in early tomorrow.'

'Farewell, everyone,' says Lucy. 'I also have plans for tonight.'

We file together towards the door.

'As your deputy head of section, I forbid you to leave,' says Henry.

Edmund stares down at the many sheets scattered in front of him, pretending not to hear anything.

'The...erm...Bletchley Park Sisterhood bids you a good night,' says Evie, as the purple, green, and blue stockings make their way out.

The Bentley, with Evie at the wheel, weaves its way through the falling night up to the door of my billet. From the outside, I can't make out any lights at the window of their bedroom; Nell respects the blackout regulations to the letter.

Evie taps her fingers on the steering wheel. It's almost as if she's about to tell me something, but then she just says, 'Good night.'

'I hope so,' I say, my body aching for the softness of my bed. Yet I will not sleep in my soft childhood bed tonight, with the wooden beam crossing above it. No. My billet is waiting for me.

The Bentley's door is open and I'm preparing to step outside, when Evie says, 'It hurt what you said about my brother, but you know, you were right. I probably should try harder.'

'Does it have to be today?' One of my feet is already on the ground; the other is itching to follow.

'No, of course not, you're right. I'm only being selfish. Good night, Rose. I'm so glad to see you again. One could almost say that I've missed you.'

I slide back into the seat and slam the door shut. I lean back into the leather seats of the car, feeling every single bone in my body sinking into the soft filling, or standing at awkward angles.

'Are you lonely, Rose?' says Evie. 'Because I am. It never occurred to me until a few days ago. I really am. I can't imagine going to a foreign country and not knowing a single soul. I've probably been lonely all my life. So I can't possibly imagine what it's been like for Esther. I never even wondered. Isn't that terribly selfish of me?'

'Yes, dear Evie, it is.' The sheen of politeness has been wiped off by the events of this day. If Evie wants an honest conversation, she's about to get much more than she bargained for. 'Esther is Nell's friend? The Austrian Jew?'

'My brother's...fiancée, I think. I'd certainly like to know. If my brother spoke to me. That would be terribly nice, you know, my brother speaking to me again? Not that I didn't deserve him turning his back on me.'

My eyes are almost closing, and yet something keeps me alert to the conversation. There's a soft, pulsing core of vulnerability to Evie tonight, as if she's finally putting aside the blackout curtains, and showing me the furnishings inside. I find this version of Evie infinitely more palatable than the one I've seen until now. 'I think we all regret the times when we could have helped, and we didn't. It happens to all of us.' I suppress a yawn, but Evie doesn't see me – she's too busy staring at the steering wheel.

'I wish there was something I could do for Esther. I mean, to help get her out of the Isle of Man. I wish there was a way of making some discreet enquiries *without* alerting my father. I've read about these things in the newspaper – I actually enjoy reading the newspaper. An A status, which is a "dangerous alien" status, can be changed to a C status, if enough proof is brought forward. And there should be more than enough proof. How could someone like Esther be put on the same level as a Nazi? She should be released. She could be released. I think so, at least. I don't know who to ask. And I can't get in touch with a lawyer without my father finding out.'

Against my will, my mind blinks back to my aunt and the Foreign Office. 'There is someone I could ask. Would you have enough money to hire a lawyer?'

She nods. 'Oh, yes, that could be arranged. But someone else has to make the discreet enquiries.'

'Count on me,' I say, against my better judgement. 'Now, if you don't mind, I'd like to go inside and sleep.'

Yet sleep becomes a distant notion again the moment I step into the kitchen. Tom is smoking with a blank look, while Nell sits at the table, holding her temples. In front of her is a creased letter with only a few words written on it.

I think, this does not bode well.

These letters are short because there isn't much more left to say.

I stop at Nell's shoulder. 'Is something wrong?'

Esther comes to mind, especially since we've just spoken about her. *Heavens, this can't happen. They can't deport her, not now, not when there's someone willing to help her.* Would the poor girl even know where she would be going? Does she know the seas are such a dangerous place, especially when it seems that the government can't even be bothered to provide an escort for these ships?

Nell shakes her head. She's never been a woman of many words – Evie has described her as cold, but I think she's wrong. I think Nell has many emotions, but she's very good at keeping them bottled up and hidden from everyone else – so very well that even when she wants to show them, she can't.

'Is it Esther?' I ask. 'Has something happened to her?'

'No, it's not Esther.' Nell's eyes are red and swollen. 'It's my brother.'

I lay my hand on her shoulder, slowly. 'Poor you,' I say. And indeed, poor her. Nell is so poor at talking about herself, that I never even knew she had a brother, despite the fact that we had started speaking to each other a little more after I found out about Esther. 'What happened?'

'His submarine was sunk,' says Nell in a trembling voice. I steal a glance at the letter. 'Missing.' Nell's brother is missing.

'HMS *Oswald*,' says Nell. 'He wasn't meant to tell me, but he did. Rob tells me everything.'

The moment I hear HMS *Oswald*, the hair on my arms stands on end. When Evie told me that the warning hadn't been issued, I asked why not. What had happened. Why we hadn't known in time.

If I had stayed, I would have saved Nell's brother. Probably. Possibly. Even a 'maybe' would have been enough.

I slip my hand from her shoulder, to a tighter grip beneath her arm. The anger glows white-hot in my belly. Anger at myself, at Tom, at the professor. We are all guilty. We have all done this. 'Let me take you outside for a moment.'

In the safety of the thickening darkness, Nell's breaths become deeper, and cut-through.

'It happened in the Atlantic,' I say. 'Far off the French coast.'

'What?'

'The sinking. Where it was sunk. I can even tell you how many German U-boats were in the pack that fell upon it.' The words gush out of my mind, unchecked.

'Rose, how? How do you know all this?'

I lean in closer. 'Three days ago, I was working on something. I didn't have enough time. I haven't done enough. Things are…harder for us now than they were last week.'

'I can't believe this,' says Nell.

'I know. Please believe me. If you were there, if you were at Bletchley, you could have helped us. You still can. Bugger what Tom says. Bugger what everyone else will say. You know German, Nell. You can help us.' The unfairness of making Nell feel guilty for what happened to her brother strikes me just as I strike her with these words. I stop, trying to gulp them back. But now they shiver in the air between us.

I think, *so what?* She will survive this. What matters is to shake off these binds of impotence, tying all of us down. What matters is to learn something from this and move forward.

Even if, today, it hurts.

And in this starless night, next to this woman who is quietly falling apart, I promise something to myself. That I will forget all of my mother's demands that I stay quiet, submit, and wait for the men to handle our problems. That I will forget how to be a nice girl and always do what I'm asked. That I will forget that being polite and not offending is more important than anything else in the world.

The time for nice girls is gone.

The times are changing and we don't know where it will toss us. All that we know is that it's time to take matters in our own manicured hands and handle them.

But not all of it necessarily this evening as the day catches up with me, making me sway on my feet. I take Nell's arm and lead her back into the house. 'Promise me you'll think about it, all right?'

And with this, there's nothing more to say. We part in the corridor and I head to my first floor cupboard. I lie down in the narrow bed, whispers and accusing tones and sobs accompanying me to sleep.

Evie

During the night, as I lie under the canopy of the four-poster bed, my head is whirring with thoughts. It will be hard, but not impossible, to free Esther. I can't think of Rose as the sort of person to make empty promises. If she said she could help me, then maybe she can. For the first time in a long time, I allow myself to imagine what might happen *after*. To dream of something good happening in my life. And not just in my life.

The greatest challenge overcome, I'll still have to reunite Esther with my brother. I can't set her free into the world, then hope she'll find Will and perhaps a job. I mean, I could, but if I want to atone for my lack of action, I should be in action now, shouldn't I? To prove to Will how much I've changed. To prove to myself how much I've changed.

And then I realise we could really use someone like her at Bletchley Park. Wait until I tell Alastair. He'd hire her on the spot. I roll over in bed, twisting the cotton sheets, gripping them between my curled legs. A brilliant idea sparks another brilliant idea. What if I didn't tell Will a word, what if I asked her, too, not to tell Will a word and find a way to bring them both here? I could use Edmund. It wouldn't be too conspicuous if his friend were to ask him to pay a visit. Especially if there was a special event. A very, very special event, one that I'll probably have to set in motion. There's something people say about things you don't do with your own hands, but I'm too tired to remember now exactly what it is.

Rose

I dream of David, calling my name. He stands in the middle of a rye field. From above, aeroplanes are throwing balls of fire, yet none of them touches him. His hair is tousled by great gusts of smoke, and yet he doesn't waver. He stretches out his hand, casting a tentacle-like shadow on the scorched earth which I try to grasp. But I can't, because the shadow is swallowed by another shadow, a more terrifying one of Luftwaffe aeroplanes circling above.

The planes grow larger and larger, a single one obstructing all of my town, all of Norfolk, as if it were glued on top of mere dots on the map that stand for towns and villages full of people, all covered by the great opening between the wings of a Messerschmitt.

I open my eyes, looking this new day full in the face, thinking, *a map. A map.* We are but nothing to the Nazis. We aren't people with everything to lose. We're clumps of tiny red dots on a map.

My head is swimming with this when I come down for breakfast – mercifully before Tom, judging by the number of plates on the table.

Guilt washes over me in waves. Nell puts down toast in front of me.

'I'm sorry,' she says, 'there isn't much to show for your coupons. But I've been thinking. I can cook separately for you, if you give me the money to buy whatever you like.'

I try to blink myself into awareness of what she's speaking about. 'I don't understand,' I say after a while.

'Tom and I sometimes can't afford to buy what's on the coupons, Rose. If you want some more nice food, an extra egg, I can buy it for you.' Today, Nell's mask is cracking and breaking in all corners. Her eyes are still swollen, but there's a soft expression in them, a hesitation when she tries to convey to me what she's saying. With a jolt I realise, *this must be so embarrassing for her.*

Guilt twists in my stomach. In the light of day, I still see that I have to become someone new, someone toughened. Hurting others in order to make a point isn't the right way, though. This isn't the Rose I want to be. I have wronged my landlady, and I don't know how to return to that moment when I was unnecessarily cruel to her, how to take my words back. I touch Nell's arm. 'Please, if there's anyone who ought to apologise, it's me. It's not your fault what happened to your brother.'

Nell looks at the door. 'About that job. I've been thinking. I'd very much like to take it.'

The edges of my heavy dream start clearing and the day seems brighter than ever before. 'That's wonderful.'

'Let's just not mention it in front of Tom yet,' she says.

I nod. 'I'll be in touch,' I say. 'Time for me to go. Evie is picking me up early today.'

Evie

As Rose climbs into my Bentley at six-thirty in the morning, I do everything in my power not to open my mouth and flood her with the fantastic ideas I've had last night. With the grandiose plans I have for the moment of the reunion between me, my brother, and Esther. Though I will probably have to remember to step back and not steal the moment from the happy couple. Jasper would probably tell me that the reunion is about them, and not about me. He'd be right. And, starting to know Rose bit by bit, this also sounds like something she might tell me. As a matter of fact, she might also tell me that I shouldn't get ahead of myself with plans involving evening gowns before we see Esther released.

But is there really any harm in thinking ahead a bit?

Thankfully, Rose stops me before I even have a chance to open my mouth. 'Good news,' she says. 'Nell would like to work with us.'

'Ah,' I say. 'This is indeed good news.'

'I can't wait to tell Professor Walton. I hope he'll call her in for an interview today.'

'Darling Edmund leaves today.' As I say this, I remember that this might get in the way of my own *personal* project.

'What? Where to?'

'Something to do with the listening stations.'

'What? Listing stations? I swear, Professor Walton, sometimes—' She rolls her eyes. Rose never rolls her eyes. She's too well-brought-up, which, come to think about it, is more than I can say about myself. 'Now, of all times.'

'What are you going to do about it?'

'Ah, yes, you see. That's it. What are we going to do about Nell? Who do we tell about her?'

A good question. We don't have so many options. I can't go to Alastair about Nell – I have other plans for him and I can only abuse his kindness so much. 'Henry, of course.'

'Then we have lost the battle already.'

Rose and I both show our passes to the Bletchley Park guards and they open the gates wide for us. Well, for my Bentley, really. We're more than an hour early for the morning shift, and the lanes are deserted. The wind rustles through the canes at the edge of the pond. Two swans are gliding on its waters. I swing by the mansion, passing the cottage, and park the car in front of the garage.

'Can't you talk to the commander? Isn't he your friend or something like that?' she asks, lowering her voice.

I was afraid of this. 'He's not *my* friend, he's my father's friend.' I don't quite know how to explain this to her, considering that the role I have for him rather heavily leans on the role Rose would have to play in Esther's liberation. Which, it strikes me this morning, isn't a given at all. What do I know about Esther's previous appearances in court? About what has been said about her, about the proof against her? And, more importantly, whether Papa would be notified or not if someone even tries to help her.

Rose says, 'My father's friends are farmers or publicans, not the people in charge of the Foreign Office's top-secret operation.'

'Ah, that was it,' I say, disappointed. 'Will you always hold against me the fact that I'm rich and well-connected?'

'What an absurd idea. How on earth did you reach the conclusion that I don't like you? That's beside the point. I just wish you would use your money and your connections to do something good in the world.'

'You have no idea how stifling my father is, how many ways he has of cutting me off from all sorts of connections.' *Jasper, Jasper, Jasper.* I raise my foot too quickly from the pedal, and the engine dies down with a thump. 'And I'm poor. I barely eat twice per week nowadays at the Bletchley Hotel, so that I can put a little something aside for Esther's lawyer.'

Rose's eyes grow as wide as saucers. 'I can't believe you said this. You barely eat twice per week at a restaurant. Why, you must be starving.'

'All right, I'm not poor; I chose my words poorly. I'm sorry. But I can't afford a lawyer for her.'

Rose opens the door and steps out of the car. 'Please, don't start telling me again you're not spoiled. Really now.'

Rose

I sit down and examine the pile of papers in front of me. My fingers tingle. On the blackboard, a few rows of codes and decodes bear testimony to the work of the night shift. A green pencil in hand, I hover. There's something lurking in a corner of my mind, something I can't quite yet grasp. As if all these coordinates were lights in a sky, waiting to be joined by hypothetical lines to form a constellation.

My vision becomes murky. The strings of three-number codes become dots, many, many dots. My mind is like a lit-up Christmas tree, glowing and sparkling, firing solutions and possible meanings of the three-number codes in the messages I have to decrypt.

I reach for the sheet at the very bottom of my pile, the one I made yesterday. I annotated my usual bases, the frequencies they transmit on, their coordinates, the trajectories of their reconnaissance flights. I begin scanning for messages from these bases.

But it takes too long to find them. They aren't indexed right. My vision jumps from line to line. How easy it would be if we could pin the coordinates on a wall, so we'd be able to recover them just by throwing a glance. That would also be useful for moving targets, like, let's say, convoys of German ships. This would be the easiest way to access and analyse the messages we decrypt. If we knew the approximate speed, and the direction the convoys were heading, how easy it would be to recover coordinates and positions then?

Dots on walls. Dots on maps. Giant planes hovering above them all. Giant. Maps.

The solution is so simple. It feels as if it came to me in a dream – and it did. Last night.

My idea is so good that it can't wait anymore, except for Henry to start his shift.

He arrives around eight o'clock and sets down his briefcase on the desk where Professor Walton usually sits. I ignore this marking of territory, despite my entire being silently calling, *get back into your place*. Instead, I head towards him with a large smile on my face.

'Hello, Henry. I hope you had a good night's sleep.'

'Not as good as yours,' says Henry and looks to my calves. He must be disappointed that I'm wearing skin-toned nylons today.

I cock my head, unable to hold my tongue. 'I made up for it by rising early today. And, as a result, I've had an idea that might help us decrypt faster.' I look back to Evie, as if looking for support. 'You know that, with Professor Walton's approval,'– and the help of a few coloured pencils I don't mention – 'we've been mapping the reconnaissance flights for a while. I was thinking, if we put together the coordinates from all these sheets, then we'll have the foundations for a set of cracks that we'd be able to access every single day when the Luftwaffe changes their key sheets.'

Henry raises his eyebrows.

I prefer to take it as a sign of interest. 'If we indexed these coordinates by using a map, we'd all have unrestrained and quick access to heaps of information. We could chart the bases, the movements of ships, both ours, and the German ones. We could see for ourselves what the range of the reconnaissance flights looks like. And we'll have a set of cracks dropping in our laps at the beginning of each day. What do you think?'

Henry rummages through his briefcase. His face doesn't betray the enthusiasm I hoped to infuse him with. 'And where might we find such a map, Miss Wiley? Do these maps grow on trees?'

'I assume Bletchley has the resources to come up with such a map. Considering the size of the entire operation. What is a single map in the greater scheme of things?'

'And how many coordinates do you suppose we might be able to fit on such a map?'

'Dozens? Maybe a few hundred? If you consider the reconnaissance flights from all the regions, and—'

He slaps his thigh with the palm of his hand. 'Hundreds! On a map! And who would be able to read them? Or shall we equip all our colleagues with magnifying lenses, too?'

'The map won't be crowded if it's as large as a wall.'

'A map as large as a wall.' Henry twists the end of his moustache.

I read it as a sign that he's considering my idea at least. I point to the wall opposite the obscured windows. 'If we clear the shelf, we could use the entire wall for the map. Nobody would have to squint to look at it.'

'Miss Wiley, I don't think you fully comprehend the amount of work needed to set up such a map. Why do you think we might have anyone to spare?' He points at the piles of unsorted, undecrypted papers crowding the trestle table. 'We don't cope with the amount of work as it is. Perhaps you've noticed. Or not. Who truly knows what goes on in the heads of women?'

I want to tell him that we could set it up in a matter of hours, since we have the sheets with all coordinates. But even I realise that it would be useless. 'Could you please forget for a moment that I'm a woman? Would that be possible? Could you please pretend that this idea came from a man?'

Henry clasps his briefcase shut. 'Yet you never allow me to forget, do you, Miss Wiley? Britain is burning and you go on leave to see your fiancé. Now, please go back to your seat. We have no more time to waste, which is exactly what you're doing instead of getting on with your job.'

'A map would help us a great deal,' I mumble.

'And who are you to tell me what you do? Insubordinate, stubborn little girls, with your coloured stockings and having an early night. And what are you, in the end? What are your qualifications, Miss Wiley?'

I've been promoted to clerk, I want to say. I could go to university, too, if I wanted. But all of this would be nothing to Henry. So, yet again, I don't say a word.

'Precisely,' he says. 'Please return to your station and get on with your work. As appointed by people who certainly know better than you.'

It's late in the evening when we leave our room, and yet there's one more stop I have to make.

'Should we have a drink?' asks Evie.

'There's something I still have to take care of,' I say, while Evie jangles her car keys. 'My aunt.'

'Ooh,' she says. 'Yes, indeed.'

I head for the Post Office with Evie following in my footsteps. 'Please,' I say. 'I need a moment alone for this.' The pressure that has been mounting these past few days is flowing, molten, through my veins. I've never asked a favour like this of my aunt and, if I fail, I don't know where else we could turn to help Esther.

'I'll wait for you outside the gates, in the car,' she says, and heads for the garages.

The red telephone box is empty, but I can't say I wouldn't have welcomed a few more minutes to gather my scattered thoughts. I think, *better to be done with it*, and pick up the receiver. Aunt Mavis isn't in her office, so I have to call again, hoping to find her at home. She answers after several rings.

'Hello?'

'Hi, Aunt Mavis, it's Rose.'

'Rose! Are you calling for the same reason your mother called? Because I'll tell you the same thing. I can't help you.' She speaks in that way she does whenever she's grated. Which is most of the time when she has to speak to my mother.

'My mother? Why did my mother call you?'

There's a long pause at the other end. 'She told me that you wanted to quit your job and go back home. Because David is coming back.'

I rub my eyes, as if this could make any sort of interference go away. 'Yes, David might be returning.' But I like what I do, and I'm becoming better and better at it. If I had to choose, really choose, of course I'd pick David. But with him so impressed by the way I was flown back to Bletchley, I'm not so sure this is an issue anymore. I'd have to speak to him about it. Me, myself. Not my mother. The pressure turns into something else, twisting in my chest. 'I can't believe she called you. I'm nineteen, for heaven's sake. Nineteen. I don't need to be constantly told what to do, like a child.'

'So you don't want to leave your job?'

'I don't know how much you know, because in here, no one is sure what the section next door is up to, but no, I don't want to leave my job.' And the moment I say it, I'm struck by how true this is. And I'm struck by the fact that my mother would, of course, say that I'm turning into my Aunt Mavis.

'Oh.'

'Yes.' My fingers ache and I realise that I've been gripping the receiver too hard.

'Well then. That's settled.' Aunt Mavis's voice wavers, as if trying to find the right tone. 'I don't think you should tell her I told you. I mean…there's no point in it. You're staying where you are and that's that.'

'Aunt Mavis, are you trying to tell me that you're afraid of my mother?' Who is this Rose? I've never heard myself speak like this.

'No, no, it's nothing like that.'

I let out an exasperated sigh.

'Look, Rose, it seems that you have a very complicated situation on your hands, and I don't think that dropping my name in would do you any favours.'

'Fair point,' I concede.

Aunt Mavis clears her throat. 'Rose. Is there something else? Because, if you don't mind—'

'Yes. Right. Getting to the heart of the matter now. Since you were talking about favours. How does one help an Austrian Jew to get released from the camps on the Isle of Man?'

When I clamber into Evie's car, my thoughts are dancing, spinning so hard in my head that I'm dizzy. I don't even know where to begin. My mother's interference? How she might be right that if I stay here, I'll kill any dream I ever had of being with David? With Esther? Evie doesn't say a word, but keeps pulling at her string of pearls. That bleeding string of pearls. She lets them go and leans forward, wiping under my eye with the tips of her fingers. 'I'm sorry. You've smudged your eyeliner.'

I rub my eyes, probably making everything much worse. Evie sits back, watching me. I drop my hands to my sides. 'Can you please take me home? I'm tired.'

She nods and starts the engine. There's worry in her eyes, but I don't know for whom.

'Don't fret about Esther,' I say. 'My aunt will arrange the lawyer. We just have to find a way to send her the money.'

Chapter Twenty-Five

Evie

L ast night, I could barely sleep from excitement. Esther
will be free. Rose has kept to her word; her aunt can help
us. I have to set the rest of my plan in motion. Mid-morning, I
try to sneak into Alastair's office. From beyond the closed
door, I detect voices. Spinning onto my heels, I turn around
and double back to the entrance hallway of the mansion. My
eyes never seem to grow accustomed to the dissonance of the
walls clad in wood, the white marble arching to my right, the
expanse of the lounge behind it, and the vaulted stained-glass
ceilings above it. It's so dissonant that it's absolutely hypnotic.

Curiosity to explore the rest of the house pushes me
forward, through the small hallway, to the room ahead of me.
It's cluttered with desks, leaving a narrow space to walk
between them. The men and women don't even bother to
look at me – it's good that I thought of snatching a few
papers before leaving the German Air Section room. I keep

going forwards and into the next room, where a terrible noise comes from. It's like stepping into another dimension. The room has a high ceiling, resting partly on carved pillars. The ceiling itself has an intricate pattern of beams of wood laced with white floral patterns jutting out of a golden background. This must have been the ballroom, before the floor was crowded with desk upon desk upon desk loaded with massive machines printing out reams and reams of paper. These must be teleprinters. I heard something about them in secretarial school. Teleprinters or not, this isn't the point. The point is that this is the perfect setting for what I have in mind.

I return to Alastair's office as two people are coming out. One of them is wearing a uniform I don't recognise at first glance, but after passing just inches by him, I realise he must be from the US Navy.

Interesting.

I step into the room. Alastair is already on the telephone, but waves me to sit down.

'Admiral, I do think that you should present us with more trust. After all, we took over some of the old structures of Room 404... Yes... No, I'm afraid that some things can't be explained, not even over a scrambler telephone.' Alastair opens and closes his fist, as if trying to hold on tight to something. 'Yes, I am aware that there are many pressing matters, but I wouldn't dismiss— Yes. Of course…Yes…Until later, then.' When he puts the receiver down, there's so much exhaustion written on his face. 'What can I do for you, Evie?'

I cross my hands in my lap, like a good girl. I rehearsed this speech over and over last night. It was all I could think about. 'Darling Edmund – I mean, Professor Walton – gave me to understand that we're all still on the lookout for good people who can speak German?'

'It depends. It's always such a complicated dance – the staff we need and the resources we have at our disposal.'

I wonder what Will would say in this situation. My brother had such a wonderful way of getting directly to the heart of the matter. 'Perhaps you've heard that we're facing unprecedented difficulties in the German Air Section?'

Alastair laces his hands on the desk. 'Yes, Professor Walton did mention this. I'm afraid this isn't the best timing.' He looks at the telephone he just put down. 'Who is this person you're putting forward?'

'Someone I'm recommending with all my heart. Two persons, in fact. They used to work for the family. I can vouch for their work ethic.' As I say this, I also say a small prayer that it would never occur to Alastair to ask Papa about the girls. I don't even want to think about the consequences. 'One of them will be no fuss for the billeting office, since she lives in Bletchley already.'

'What's her name?'

'Here, allow me.' I write Elinor's name and her address down. But when it comes to Esther, I hesitate. Alastair is a friend of Papa, ultimately. What if he starts asking questions? What will Papa do to me then? My heart thumps hard in my chest. I've been dreaming of this. And yet, I can't bring myself to write her name down, not even to speak it out loud. 'You can reach out to Elinor today; I was told she'll be available for an interview.' Panic overwhelms all the thoughts in my mind, every word of the skilful speech I'd designed to draw the conversation Esther's way. I pass on the tiny piece of paper to Alastair, hoping he won't notice.

'And the other?' he says.

This is it. The moment of truth.

And in the moment of truth, I back down. 'Mrs Pike can give you more details about her. She knows this other girl more intimately.'

'Thank you, Evie, I'll see about that. Is there anything else I can do for you?'

I clutch the armrest of my chair. I wish there was a way I could take back my words. It isn't too late, yet I'm not brave enough. I'll have to think of something else to secure a job for Esther.

But if I can't be brave enough for this, I hope I might be brave enough for the rest. I have to be. Even if what I'm about to do could backfire terribly. I shudder, gather up my remaining courage, and say, 'The opera club would like to host a little show at Bletchley.'

Rose

The day is heavy and wingless. More of the same trudging through a murk of unknown coordinates, more of the same important messages that we fall short of decoding. All harder to bear under Henry's watchful eyes that have the air of saying, *what am I to do, anyway, with a bunch of women?* We hope for a bit more help. We hope we've done something good that glitters like a gemstone in a pile of mud.

And then the commander barges in and whispers something to Henry about an interview.

'Yes, of course,' says Henry, straightening his already arrow-straight tie.

I think, *Nell*, and dash Evie a look. She gives me her proud smile and pulls at her pearls. As soon as Henry leaves, she leans in and says, 'See? I took care of it. I'll show you what Evie Milton can do.'

I say, 'I can't wait to be surprised.' I jot down a few more messages. 'Do you reckon he might bring her directly to help us today?'

Evie shrugs. 'I don't see why not.'

We go on with our work, but watch the door at the slightest sound of steps in the corridor. When Henry returns, though, he's alone. I slip Evie a look and she shrugs again. I would have thought Henry was more practical than the professor, that as soon as he had found a woman for the section he wouldn't have let her go until the end of the shift.

It is I who must wait until the end of the shift. I almost ask on two occasions, then bite my tongue. Knowing Henry, he'll resent my meddling. Better to wait until tonight. Better to wait until I get back home, to my billet.

Evie

The matter with Elinor proves to be somewhat of a disappointment, but after Ralph and Lucy take over their shifts, I have no time for prying. I have too much on my mind – first of all, finding a way to secure Esther the job she needs. When Rose asked me if I took care of it, I lied. I said I did, even if I don't see any way that I could have. I tell myself I'll sleep on it, and come back tomorrow with fresh forces, and tell Alastair about my brother's sweetheart. Or sneak into Elinor's house when Rose isn't there and ask her to take care of the problem, though that strikes even me as being over-the-top cowardly.

But I'd rather not dwell on my own failings or on what Papa might do if he uncovers my machinations. There is another task at hand. Two of them, actually. For the first one, I need Ralph's help. I circle around him and sit down next to him after Rose has given him her traffic.

'Ralph, darling, do you mind if I ask you a question?'

On the other side of the table, Lucy rummages under the scattered papers to find the ashtray and lights herself a cigarette with the speed of lightning. I could almost laugh. How dear Lucy does enjoy a good gossip.

'Yes, of course,' says Ralph. 'I mean, I don't mind.'

'If you were to reach Edmund, could you? I mean, by telephone? Do you know where he is?'

'I believe that depends on why I would want to reach him.' Ralph is unable to repress a smile. It seems that Lucy isn't the only one who enjoys a good gossip in this place. But, goodness, isn't the work oppressive enough? I enjoy a bit of intrigue, myself.

'Should we call it a family emergency?' I say.

'Family?' says Ralph.

'Yes, my family, not his family. Perhaps you know he's quite intimate with my brother Will? I have something important to communicate.'

'If it's important, then by all means.'

Ralph leads me to a side office two doors down – the same one darling Edmund invited me into when I first arrived at the park. He puts me through to Edmund then, completely unexpectedly and tactfully, leaves the room.

'Hi, Edmund, darling, how are you?' I ask.

'Evie? What a surprise. Did anything happen?'

'Well, no. I mean, yes. Elinor was interviewed by Henry today for a position.'

'Is that so? This is good news, indeed.' The enthusiasm in Edmund's voice can't possibly be understated.

'Humph. Partly. Rose tells me she only signed up for the job because her brother's submarine was sunk.'

'Oh, no. Is there— Is Rob then—'

Rob. Edmund seems to know the name of Elinor's brother. I begin to wonder how intimate they were, indeed. 'We don't know, but I think Elinor assumes the worst.'

'I'm so sorry for her. I know how fond she was of her brother.'

That is certainly something I can relate to myself. 'Speaking of brothers, I was wondering if you'd be keen to see Will again?'

'Keen? Of course I'm keen. I have no idea where to write to him, though.'

'Let's say I could give you an address. But I need you to do something for me. Do you think you could convince Will to come down to the Park for a very special occasion?'

'What occasion?'

'I'm putting together a special moment.' The opera group. I check my watch. I'm already running late. Today I've only half solved problems, and I've ended up running around after different solutions. 'He'll be very glad of it.'

'What moment?'

'I swear to you, Edmund, this isn't the time to be overly cautious. Trust me when I tell you it's for his own good.'

'I'm sorry, Evie, but he's my friend. And I'm not quite sure what's happening between the two of you, though it can't be good.'

I restrain myself from yelling down the line that this isn't the bloody time to start reading people, for once in his life. 'Edmund, I'm your friend, too. Don't you trust me?'

'Erm, I don't know how to say this to you, Evie, but… I'm queasy about this entire thing with Will. I'd rather not do it.'

I feel like banging my head against the desk the telephone sits on. After all the trouble I went through to find him. 'Fine,' I say. 'Fine. I'll find another way.' I consider whether I should tell him the entire thing, about how I plan to reunite Will with Esther. Then again, if I do, he might go ahead and blurt it all to Will – I'm so sure Edmund is completely unable to keep a personal secret, despite his job – so I think I'd much rather prefer to find another way.

'I'm sorry, Evie,' he says, and I know that he's about to put the receiver down and run away from me as fast and far as he can. 'Is there anything else I can do for you?'

Bullseye. In fact, come to think of it, there is something else he could do for me. Since he doesn't plan to contact Will, and has no means to do so, there is no risk of him compromising the other half of my plan. A part I have yet to take care of.

Have to.

'Edmund, darling, we're still much on the lookout for people for our section, right? I have the perfect candidate for you. And we're talking, again, about someone we both know. But you must not, under any circumstances, breathe a single word to anyone.'

The matter with Esther just settled minutes from five o'clock, I hurry down the stairs and towards the Assembly Hall. I literally have a few more moments before the window of opportunity closes for a week and I might miss this chance. And it isn't just about the week – this morning, I'd told Alastair that the opera club is keen on organising a show, which they don't know anything about. Not yet.

I rush to the doors of the Assembly Hall at a speed that might break a heel and…find them shut. I pull so hard at the door that I think maybe it's stuck. I curl my hand around the handle and pull again. It is not stuck. It is not. Is it locked.

As Lucy would say, bollocks.

Rose

Coming down to breakfast the next day is a flutter of me rushing down the stairs, eager to see Nell. She's placing the toast on the table, dressed like the kind of woman I imagine Henry might respect. Her chignon is perfectly set, and she's wearing a two-piece with a skirt that ends under the knee. She's out of place in this kitchen, but would fit in right away at Bletchley.

'Congratulations!' I say.

She puts a finger to her lips. 'Tom doesn't know yet. I told him I'm going to the butcher's, to stand early in a queue. I'll see you there,' she says, and beckons me to sit down at the table, while she exits through the back door.

———

There's no trace of Nell in the German Air Section as I come in, yet Henry looks terribly pleased with himself. 'Come in, do come in, ladies,' he says. 'No, we'll wait for Miss Stevens for a few more minutes, and then… Let's say I have a little announcement to make. More than one, I reckon.'

'Lucy?' says Evie, shooting me a look.

'Yes, I've reformed the shift system a bit for the next few days.' There's a smirk on Henry's face.

'What is this?' I say, pointing at a cardboard box placed in front of me. It's full of blank rectangles of paper. There are three more similar boxes on the table.

'You'll find out in good time,' says Henry, looking more smug than ever in his entire life, which is quite a feat to pull off.

Lucy comes into room, her legs clad in bright-orange stockings, and hands Evie a package. 'Red and green, just as we talked about.'

'Exciting,' says Evie, peeling away the wrapping, enough for me to peer at the glossy surface of the nylons.

'Good,' says Henry, 'Now that you're all here…' He pulls at his tie knot, tightening it. 'First of all. I have some quite pleasing news. Someone from the Admiralty is coming to visit the premises next week, to evaluate our methods and their reliability here.'

Lucy gasps and even Evie is so wide-eyed that she couldn't have known about this.

'Next week?' I say.

'Yes,' says Henry, 'and, I hope I need not say, that we must make a good impression. Or should I underline how important it is that the Admiralty thinks that we are exact and reliable?'

He glares at me and I want to say, *I know what you're implying, but in case you forget, I was right, and they were wrong about the Scharnhorst.* Instead, I say, 'The timing is quite unfortunate,' while pointing at the mess of messages on the table. 'I think all sorts of suggestions for improvement might be welcome.' I don't hope that he might take the hint about my map. At this time, I'm hoping for a miracle and that Professor Walton might walk through that door. He wouldn't turn a deaf ear to my suggestions, I'm sure of it.

'Of course. It's nice that you mention improvements,' says Henry. 'As you all know, decrypting has been moving rather slowly lately. So I have decided to implement a new device to help you with your work. On the table you'll find boxes filled with an array of cards. It is my wish that you write down the trajectories of the daily reconnaissance flights in your areas, and their bases.'

Lucy reaches into the wooden box next to her pile of messages, rifling through the cards. Some of them have notes covered in Ralph's neat handwriting, from the night shift.

'I do believe this is a device that will considerably ease your work, especially in view of the impending visit from the Admiralty. It is this kind of initiative that I'd like to see from you.'

I look to Lucy and Evie with utter disbelief, as if waiting for Henry to start laughing and declare it was all a joke, or for any of the girls to say anything. This is my idea, stripped of all its brilliancy, reduced to a stack of cards on the table. It's not much better than our sheets with trajectories, and it does nothing in the way of tracing the naval convoys.

Nonetheless, it provides some sort of improvement to our current situation.

An improvement Henry is taking credit for.

'What a pile of crap!' I mumble.

'I beg your pardon, Miss Wiley? Do you have something to say?'

Evie says, 'Didn't Rose suggest something similar yesterday?'

'I have no idea what you're talking about,' says Henry. 'If you could please get on with your work. Or do I need to stress the fact that we're under time pressure?'

'I think you know bloody well what I'm talking about,' says Evie.

Lucy lights herself a cigarette. I think, *this might go on for a while*. Henry won't concede, and Evie can be so stubborn.

I think, *is there really a point to this?*

'Let it go, Evie,' I whisper.

Lucy pulls her legs out from under the table and taps at her shins. I close my eyes to signal that I understood the message. *Later. We'll talk about it later. We might find a way.*

The girls. These girls. They're amazing.

'Ah, yes, there was something else,' says Henry. 'I think we all owe Miss Wiley a round of congratulations. Though I can't pretend I understand her reasons. Perhaps she might care to explain.'

I don't have the faintest clue what he's talking about. I think, is this about Nell, and how I persuaded her to join our section? 'Congratulations?'

'Yes, you're about to become a Land Girl. We received a letter today from the Women's Land Army. Bletchley Park is to release you of your duties as of next week.'

This strikes me so hard that I don't even know what to say. How to say this. Where to begin.

Evie says, 'What? What did you do, Rose?'

The tips of my fingers turn cold. 'Nothing at all. I didn't do anything. I have no idea what this means.'

'It means that you're leaving us, Miss Wiley,' says Henry. 'You're finally going home.'

Evie

Rose is as frozen as a bit of glacier floating off the Antarctic, so I grab her arm and pull her up. 'Let's go.'

'Where are you going?' says Henry.

'Outside,' I say.

'At this hour? You haven't even started the work.'

'Well, it's not my bloody fault that you bloody bombarded us with things we didn't care to hear, is it?' I say, shooing Rose towards the door. 'Through here.'

'This is unacceptable,' says Henry, already frothing at the corners of his mouth.

'Yes, I agree, so what are you going to do about it?' I stop on the threshold, daring him to do something. 'I thought as much,' I say, and start herding Rose down the corridor.

Rose blinks around, as if she has forgotten for a moment where she is. 'The stairs,' I tell her and place her hand on the carved wooden banister. We descend slowly, time enough for me to concoct a plan. I was intending to take Rose to the edge of the pond, forage for a cup of strong tea, let her breathe for a moment before going back inside. Or to press her into telling me what on earth is going on. But now I have a better idea. I stop us in the wide entrance corridor at the ground floor. To the left, the glass ceiling and the marble arches of the lounge. To our right, an antechamber leading to the former library, now the room of the teleprinters, and another room at the front – Alastair's office.

'Rose, what's happening?' I ask. 'You can tell me. What is this about the Land Girls?'

'I don't have the faintest idea,' she says. Her voice wobbles and I can see that she's close to tears. 'Please believe me.'

I lead her to the right and we burst into Alastair's office. He's in conversation with two men, one in a perfectly fitting tweet suit, and the other in a decrepit suit that makes me think of darling Edmund.

'Miss Milton,' says Alastair.

'I beg your pardon, gentlemen,' I say in with my most charming smile. 'We'll wait right here.'

I drag Rose outside again and we stop in the small antechamber looking into what once used to be the mansion's library. While the walls are still lined with books, the centre of the room has been taken over by tables with gigantic machines that spit paper at various intervals. They're operated by WAAFs in their neat powder-blue uniforms. The famous 'teleprincesses'.

'Next week,' mumbles Rose. 'I have to go. And the visit from the Admiralty!' She has the face of someone waking up from a bad dream.

'Don't worry, we'll sort this,' I tell her, though I don't really quite know how.

Mercifully, the two gentlemen don't take long before they exit Alastair's office. We stumble back inside. Good old Alastair stands rather stiffly behind his desk. 'How can I help?'

'I'm so sorry, dear Alastair,' I say. I know I'm rather walking on eggshells here and that I've been abusing his kindness. How long until he reports back to Papa? How long?

'I think there has been a mix-up,' I say. 'We've received an odd piece of news. It seems like Rose has been asked to present herself at home next week. I was wondering if you could enlighten us?'

'Ah, yes,' says Alastair, extracting a piece of paper from a file. 'We've received a letter from the Women's Land Army. It vexed me quite a bit, since I knew how keen Professor Walton was on Miss Wiley. I found it upsetting that she should leave us.'

'But it must be a mistake,' says Rose. 'I never applied to be a Land Girl.'

'You didn't?' says Alastair.

Rose shakes her head. 'I never asked for any of this.'

Alastair examines the piece of paper in his hands. 'Let me make some enquiries then. I'll do my best to get back to you today.'

Rose

As we return to the German Air Section room, the entire story begins to take on the mystique of a bad dream. 'It must have been a mistake,' I tell Evie, more hopeful than convinced.

'I'm sure it was a mistake,' says Evie. 'Look, Alastair is onto them and will take care of the matter, I'm sure.'

'Yes,' I say, not sure how I feel about any of this. There are other aspects that start to slip into my mind, drip by drip. If this isn't a mistake, if this is truly happening, if I'm about to become a Land Girl, I might really go home next week. Sleep again in my bed under the old beam. See David a few days per week.

I'll be able to see David.

Would that be so bad, indeed?

'Yes,' I repeat. 'Better to get back to our work. Those messages aren't about to decode themselves, are they?'

A deep quiet reigns in the German Air Section room, but no wonder, with only two people working at the table. Henry sulks, refusing to even acknowledge our presence. I feel the need to explain myself – I know what he must think about my excess of feeling. 'I'm sorry, Henry,' I say. 'The news… Well, it caught me a bit unawares.'

I sit down at the table to start my own set of decrypts. I think, *here we go once more*. For how many times have I done this in the past few days? I examine the indexing cards prepared by Ralph, the coordinates inscribed on them. My thoughts flutter back to the odd letter, to David, and what he might make of the entire story. To the fact that a nice telephone call with him is overdue.

I clench my fingers around the pen, resolve hardening in my bones. Later. I start copying coordinates onto the index cards. I know the motions, exercised so often in the past few days: find the bases, the coordinates of the flights. Try to find the spellers, look into the potential targets for the day. It's barely ten o'clock – plenty of time to issue warnings, plenty of lives that can be saved. But as I dig deeper into the work, there are fewer spellers than usual. 'Evie, do you have any plain language words? Longer messages?'

She shakes her head.

'No chatting,' says Henry.

'I'm asking about the spellers,' I say, pointing at the blackboard. 'Don't you think there are far fewer than usual?'

'I think it's too early to tell, Miss Wiley. How many messages did you actually crack today?'

I think, *of course*. Since Henry and Lucy were the only ones working while we were out in the commander's office. Today's progress isn't much progress at all.

And then it strikes me.

'Someone I know applied for a position here,' I tell Henry. For once, I'm shameless. So shameless that I almost want to giggle. I might be here next week and, on the other hand, I might not, so does it matter any longer if I vex Henry? 'How did she perform in her interview?'

Henry scrunches his nose up in disgust. 'That is none of your business, Miss Wiley.'

'I strongly disagree. It is my business, since this is our section and we need more people to help us. So why isn't she here?'

'Miss Wiley. If I were you, I'd try to look more at the traffic, and less at prying into someone else's business.'

'Listen, Henry,' says Evie. 'You can either tell us now, or I'll go to Commander Denniston again and hear it from him directly. And I will also lodge a complaint about you. So you have a choice. What will it be?'

Henry clacks his tongue. 'Mrs Elinor Pike has been assigned to a different section.'

Chapter Twenty-Six

Evie

We work in a stunned silence for the rest of the day. It's open war: on one side, there's Henry; on the other, there's us, the girls. I make an open declaration by notifying Henry that Professor Walton will find out about this without delay as soon as he's back from his tour of the listening stations. Henry shrugs, feigning that he's implacable. 'Then tell him.'

I promise him this will not end here.

And it does not end.

At some point in the afternoon, a messenger comes, summoning Rose to Commander Denniston's office. I don't even ask, simply get up to leave with her.

'Where are you going?' says Henry.

'With her,' I say, not even looking at his face.

He can't touch me.

Henry can't touch me.

Let him simmer and boil.

Ha ha.

As soon as we come into Alastair's office, I can see worry written all over his face.

'Have a seat,' he tells us both. 'Can I offer you a cup of tea?'

Rose curls her hands in her lap, probably preparing herself for what's next. 'No, thank you.'

'Alastair,' I say. 'Please, just tell us.'

'Miss Wiley, did you say that you did not apply to the Women's Land Army?'

Rose shakes her head, but I still don't know what to believe.

'And that you did not want to leave Bletchley Park?'

'It wasn't my intention, no.'

'I've made some enquiries,' says Alastair. 'The application was made four days ago, from Norfolk. Are you absolutely sure, Miss Wiley, that you weren't the one who signed it?'

'Four days ago? No, it's not possible. Four days ago… I was too busy hiding from an air raid. And then running to seek my fiancé at the airfield.' She pauses and bites her lip. 'And from there, I was flown directly into Bletchley, without even… I didn't even have a chance to take my luggage with me. I couldn't have. I didn't.'

I shoot Alastair a questioning look. We seem to ask each other, *and if she didn't submit the application, who has?*

Rose seems genuinely distressed, from the way she crumples her skirt between her fingers to the way she appears to be on the verge of tears. But who can tell anymore what is true from what isn't? She might well have tried to apply. We all know how keen she is on her fiancé David. She might be terrified of the consequences of what she's done.

What it means to us, to our section.

'This must be a mistake,' says Rose. 'Is there... How can I tell the Women's Land Army that this was a mistake? How can I withdraw the application?'

'I'm so sorry,' says Alastair. 'This is truly regrettable. I know how much Professor Walton treasured you.'

'I don't quite understand what you mean.'

Alastair examines the sheet of paper in front of him. From where I stand, I can see the WLA header. 'Miss Wiley, since you claimed that you knew nothing of such an application, I took the matter into my own hands. I tried to explain to the that this was a mistake. I do believe you know that the WLA is subordinated to the Ministry of Agriculture. Unfortunately, due to extreme food shortages, the Ministry has a certain amount of power when it comes to...requisitioning people. I don't know if you're aware that young men who work the land are exempt from being drafted into the military.'

'Yes, I know,' says Rose with shimmering eyes. 'My mother also underlined this to me when I was home.'

'It isn't in my power to extricate you. I'm sorry. You have to present yourself to the office in your home town next week.'

I can't hold my tongue any longer. 'This is impossible. What kind of world do we live in?'

'Desperate times call for desperate measures,' says Alastair. 'And the WLA does have an application signed by a Miss Rose Wiley. These are the bare facts.'

'The bare facts are that we can hardly keep afloat in the German Air Section as it is,' I say.

'And I'm working to amend this,' says Alastair quietly. I think about Elinor and if indeed Alastair is working so hard for us, how come she hasn't been assigned to our section?

Rose is quicker than me. She says, 'But this is the Foreign Office. I was told when I first signed up that I have to stay here for the duration. *For the duration.*'

'Yes, precisely. What happened to, "There is no way out of Bletchley Park",' I say, thinking that if there was a single way out of Bletchley Park, a loophole, then Rose was tossed right into it. A remarkable coincidence, considering that, since her fiancé was assigned to the local airfield, Rose has been set on finding her way home.

Alastair shakes his head. 'That is correct, Miss Wiley. Unfortunately, since we're a secret organisation, this makes it hard for me to explain why your work as a typist here is so important, without revealing too much information. I'm truly sorry. I wish there was a way I could do more for you.'

Rose pauses. Alastair glances at his watch and I understand the hint. We have taken enough of his time with what increasingly seems like a bit of petty intrigue.

'I think we should return to our section. Thank you so much, Commander,' I say. 'Your dedication to your staff is truly commendable.'

He bows his head, a weak smile on his face. 'We all do what we can.'

As she rises to her feet, Rose asks, 'Surely, if I tell them there's been some kind of mistake, they'll allow me to withdraw?'

'I'll leave you to discuss these details with the clerks on site, Miss Wiley. Unfortunately, as I have said, you'll have to report to the offices next week.'

Rose

The enormity of what is happening to me rises and falls, giving me small pinches of nausea. When Evie asks me if I want to go outside, I lead the way up the staircase, towards the German Air Section. 'We've wasted enough time.'

I lose myself in the intricate floral designs of the wooden banister and the plaster ceiling. I have never seen such an ornate, beautiful house, I think, frozen in this moment, unable to grasp what my future will look like as of next week. Evie says something, her words floating right by me and into a troubled afternoon. 'I beg your pardon?'

Evie says, 'Do you think Henry didn't hire Elinor for our section on purpose?'

'I think so,' I say, uncertain of anything.

'Are you sure you don't need a cup of tea?' she says.

I shake my head. 'No, I think we should go back to our room now.' The taint of guilt seeps through my bones. What will everyone think? I realise how it must seem to them. Someone having mysteriously submitted an application in my name. If this is possible, where will it stop? I halt in the first-floor corridor, rooted in place by the thought. If someone has done this, where is the end, indeed? Who's to say that same person won't commit some crime in my name? Who's to say I'm not to pay for something I haven't done?

'Do you think I should report this to the police?' I ask Evie.

'What?'

'This. This with the application. Are people allowed to steal someone else's identities? Is this even possible? How?'

Evie lays a hand on my arm. 'Yes, if you didn't send that application, I reckon you should go to the police. Maybe they can find out who is behind this. I mean, this must be rather frightening.'

'It is, isn't it?'

Evie gives me a long look. 'Let's get you that tea.'

I push into the German Air Section room. 'I think we've wasted enough time for today.' I've barely done any work. 'There is still so much to do.' I think, *what will Henry say?* and then realise, not without a tinge of bitterness, that I won't have to worry about this anymore as of next week.

'I'm so sorry,' I say, looking to both Henry and Lucy. 'This is all a rather frightening and terrible misunderstanding.'

Henry lifts his eyebrows. 'A very convenient misunderstanding.'

'I can't say that I've made any more sense of it than you have.' By all means, I should be offended by what Henry said, but if I were to feel offended every time Henry says something, I would spend my entire day being offended. 'And honestly, what is so convenient about this? The visit from the Admiralty is next week.'

A thought thunders through my mind: will the professor even be back by next week? That little claw scratches inside my chest. I think, what will he even make of me? Will he think, too, that I did this on purpose?

In spite of that little slip two days ago when he summoned me back to Bletchley, the professor has been absolutely wonderful to me. He has encouraged me, trusted my judgement. An Oxford professor. An Oxford professor arranged for the RAF to fly me to Bletchley because he needed me. Now that all the anger has cleared, there remains a story I hope one day I'll be able to tell my grandchildren. And then, it doesn't even matter that he flew me away from David, since I'll be with him as of next week.

I think, what if he'd never flown me away? What if I'd been able to stay my full four days of leave, and reconcile with both David and my mother?

'Miss Wiley, what are you doing?' Henry's voice shudders me out of my thoughts. 'Are you just passing time until dinner?'

I say nothing, and reach for a pile of messages instead. He's right, of course. Come what may as of next week, I still have a job to do, a duty to my country.

What may come is the visit from the Admiralty. More and more messages, that we'll all be unable to decrypt. My section stumbling through it all. I make a note to ask if I'll still be here to help for the visit. Concern surges. *What will we have to show to the man from the Admiralty except half-decrypted messages?*

My thoughts circle around their own tails and fall. I write down on the index cards a few trajectories, transcribe a few messages. *How will we ever impress the Admiralty with this tapping in the dark?*

And then a small wave of fury washes over me. *We.* But I don't even know if I'll still be a part of this *we* next week, because someone has taken the trouble of making my decisions for me. Someone who thinks he or she knows better. Or someone who has played a cruel joke on me. I should rejoice at the outcome – going home, being again with my David, sleeping again in my childhood bed and never having to see Tom Pike's weasel face again.

My heart races instead, as do my thoughts. Was it deliberate, then? Who had anything to gain from this?

I fiddle with a few pieces of paper and put them in their

place. No matter what I do, my mind won't wrap itself around the work today.

Instead, I start to wonder. David? No, this isn't something at all that David might do. And when would he have had the time? He flew with me to Bletchley.

And then, it occurs to me. On that very morning, my own mother had mentioned the Ministry of Agriculture. She'd told me how much power they had, and she had been entirely correct, as confirmed today by the commander.

My mother had known. My mother had insisted I do precisely what happened. What a terrible coincidence.

I get up and pack my belongings. 'I'm sorry, Henry, but... tomorrow, I'll come in extra early for my shift.'

Henry shakes his head. 'What did I even expect of you, Miss Wiley? And you claim you weren't the one who applied for the Land Girls. Look at you, trying to escape this place.'

'There's no point in me staying, Henry. The Germans, they aren't coming tonight. Didn't you see? No coordinates, no spellers today.' I stop, considering. I could tell Henry a thing or two. I could try to put him in his place. Or I could mind my own business, since, obviously, there is no changing Henry's opinion of me. No matter how hard I try, no matter how hard I work, he'll always choose to see the worst in me. 'I'll see you all tomorrow morning. I wish you all a lovely afternoon, considering the circumstances.'

Evie

After Rose's storm of an exit, we work in silence for a long time. There isn't much more for us to say as we trudge from cluster of three letters to cluster of three letters. By the look of Lucy, Rose's departure strikes her as hard as it strikes me. I have come to think of her as my friend, which I can't say about many people in my life. At least there will still be Lucy, with her easygoing ways and tart humour. Lucy, who attracts people around her like moths to a flame.

Oooh, Lucy. Yes. I think Lucy could be of some assistance after we finish our shift.

But until then, we must plough on. Rose had said that there were no warnings, and indeed there weren't. At least, not in the usual way. We didn't stumble upon coordinates or the names of targeted airfields. The day was quiet. Shortly after Rose left, Lucy asked, 'Is Rose right? Isn't the Luftwaffe attacking today?'

'It would be too good to be true,' I say. 'Though I haven't found any warnings, either.'

'What if someone asked the Air Ministry if today was, indeed, quiet?' says Lucy, raising her round, impeccably plucked eyebrows.

Henry pretends to ignore us, but then disappears half an hour later. He says nothing of his whereabouts until the afternoon shift, led by Ralph, comes to take over for us.

'I think today is a day when we can all go home on time,' says Henry. 'We need to rest and there have been pretty much no bombings today – just an airfield and an aeroplane factory near Birmingham.'

'Is that a change of tactics?' asks Ralph.

'No,' says Henry. 'Who knows?'

Ralph shrugs. 'All right then. Why don't you all go and enjoy your evening?'

I have big plans for this evening. After we finish our shift, I pull Lucy aside at the edge of the pond. 'Lucy, I think you know a fair amount of people at the park.'

'I wouldn't say a fair amount, but let's say I'm sociable enough.' She pulls out her mirror, checking her lipstick. I've never seen Lucy without perfectly applied lipstick. Or without rouge, for that matter, ever since I gave it to her.

'Lucy, darling, tell me, did you ever meet anyone at Bletchley who is in the opera club?'

Rose

This is certainly an emergency, as far as I'm concerned, so I call our neighbour and ask him to fetch my mother. I jingle the coins in my pocket, hoping I'll have enough for this conversation. Hoping I won't need this many for this conversation.

'Hello, Rose,' she says. Her voice has a forced brightness that snaps at the edges.

'Hello, Mum. I have some news. It seems that I'm coming home next week.'

'Are you, now? Is it certain?'

'Yes,' I say, tumbling head forward into this conversation. 'It seems someone applied in my name for the WLA.'

'So you're released of your job? At the Foreign Office?'

'Yes,' I say. 'So it seems.'

My mother exhales. 'Didn't I tell you how powerful the Ministry of Agriculture is? But you wouldn't listen. You've developed such a stubbornness, Rose. This won't serve you well in life, I tell you this. But, you see, I knew that you'd be pleased.'

I twist the telephone cord around my wrist. 'What do you mean, you knew that I'd be pleased? Mum?'

'You know very well what I mean, Rose. You have no idea what you were about to do. I've told you this again and again. Hold onto your man, especially if there's a war. Hold onto your man, especially if you find a good one. You wouldn't listen.'

'Did you fill out the application in my name?' I say, hoping at once that she'll deny and admit to this. So much for reporting the false application to the police. So much for other measures. So much for the mystery of who could do such a thing.

'Yes, Rose. Of course I did. You're still a child. Was I to sit by and watch you ruin your life?'

'I'm not ruining my life!' I scream into the telephone. 'You have no idea what you've done!'

I'm so tired of this. The way she treats me like I'm still a little girl, taking decisions in my name, depriving me of any trace of agency. Am I happy to see David? Yes, yes, yes. Do I think it was the right decision? I don't think so. In any case, it wasn't *her* decision to make.

'Young lady, don't you raise your voice at me!' she snaps.

'You have no idea what you've set in motion,' I say through my teeth. 'You have no idea how much harm you've done. You think you know everything, but what do you know?' There are so many things I could tell her: about the Luftwaffe's forces, for instance; about the convoys that supply us with food; about airfields in northern France; and about the average range of a Messerschmitt. But I know that I will say nothing. 'There's more to life than making the best recipes on rationing, than pleasing a man, Mum. Much more than that.'

'Young lady, I am so glad that you're coming home. I'll remind you to mind your manners, because you certainly aren't. Remember I was the one who washed your soiled nappies. Never did I think I'd come to raise such an ungrateful—'

One quick motion, that's all I need to sever the flow of her speech and hang up the telephone. Today, all I can give her back is anger. Perhaps one day I'll be grateful. Perhaps one day I'll see the good in what she's done. But not today. Certainly not today.

I stare at the red receiver of the telephone, blinking away my tears.

Chapter Twenty-Seven

Evie

I find Reginald precisely where Lucy told me I would: having a pint at one of the inns in Bletchley Park. An inn where most of the professors and key characters at Bletchley are billeted, as Lucy informed me. Lucy knows a lot of things about a lot of people.

'Hello, Reginald,' I say, moving closer to his table, where he sits with four more chaps. 'Just the man I was looking for.'

'Evie, darling,' he says, and kisses me on both cheeks. Reginald is an old acquaintance. It was Jasper who'd introduced me to him, back when they worked in the same company. 'We were all wondering where you'd disappeared to.'

Of course they did. One day – or rather night – we were dining at The Dorchester and dancing until the early hours in half-hidden clubs, and then the next day I'd vanished from London without saying goodbye to a single soul. There's no point in laying out the entire story in front of Reginald, who isn't famous for being able to keep a secret. Quite the opposite.

So I say, 'Well, now you know.'

'You were the last person in the world I was expecting to meet here. Though I reckon there's quite a fair share of debs around.'

'Ha!' I try to ignore the tentative slight in what he said. 'I could say the same about you. Except the part about being a deb.'

'Yes, I'm afraid my talents are wasted here.' Reginald, short and sweet-faced like a boy – I swear I never saw even a hint of stubble on his face – gives me an innocent smile. 'But what can you do? We're at war, and they don't allow us to forget, not even for a single moment.'

'Fear not,' I say. 'I have a proposition that might help your talents shine.'

Rose

As soon as I arrive in my billet, Nell asks me if I'm hungry. I am, I really am, but I also don't think I'm up for a chat.

'No, thank you,' I say, and dash upstairs. I throw myself on my bed, thinking how I might not spend so many nights in it as I believed. I think, *wasn't this what I wanted?* How often did I grumble about my narrow room, my awkward landlords? Yet Nell is such a kind woman, once you get to know her. And do I truly want to return to my childhood bed, to be wrapped in the same state of expectation as I was before Bletchley?

Nell stands on the threshold with two cups of tea. As soon as she sees me, she turns on her heel. I call after her. 'Nell?'

'I'm so sorry, Rose. I didn't mean to intrude.'

I wipe my tears with the back of my hand. 'Is that tea?'

Nell nods.

I open my hands, ready to receive what she's offering. I could do with tea. And perhaps a bit of compassion.

'Here you go,' she says.

'Please. Do sit down.'

'Really, I don't mean to—'

'No, stay. I think I don't want to be alone.' And it's true.

Nell sits down on the edge of my bed, half-turned towards me. In silence. It's as if she doesn't quite know where to grab this situation. If she'd stood by me, like this, a few weeks ago, I would have thought that she was being aloof. But the expression in her brown eyes is one of softness.

'What are you thinking about?' I say.

'Esther. She'd know what to say now. What to ask.'

'If you want, I'll tell you. You don't need to ask.'

'I wish I was better at this. Being close to people. Comforting them. I just—'

'Well, some people don't want someone coming too close. Or to be comforted. But I'd very much like to tell you what's happening.' I pause, allowing my thoughts to settle. They refuse to. 'I'm such a fool. What can I say? I'm leaving next week.'

'You're leaving us?'

'I'm leaving everyone. I have to go back home.'

'Poor mite. And you don't want to, I gather?'

What a simple question, really. What do I want? I could cry and laugh at the same time. That's how I feel. 'I don't know. See? You're not so bad at this feelings thing. You've just put your finger in it.'

'You will be so missed, Rose. Who am I to talk to about my work?'

And in the blink of an eye, I realise that I've been the unfeeling one. I can't imagine how I didn't think of this, of her day. What she has done. And *where*. 'Heavens, yes! Where were you today? I expected to see you.'

'You know, I did too.'

'They put you in a different section.' I lower my voice. 'Where are you?'

'The Naval Index.'

The Naval Index? But why? Argh, Henry. It isn't enough that he refuses a brilliant idea from my part, he has to sabotage us, too. And if he thought Nell was the chatty type, then he doesn't know people at all.

Nell says, 'The work seems quite nice. A lot of technical terms. It can be overwhelming, but I suppose I'll get the hang of it after a while.'

'I'm sure you will,' I say. What a complete debacle.

'I'm so sorry.'

'What? Why? Don't be. Will you tell Tom about it?'

'Yes,' she says. 'When the time is right. Until then—'

'Where does he think you've been today?'

'Just going about my usual business.'

I can't help but chuckle. I would never have thought Nell the contriving type, and yet she seems so good at keeping a secret. I probably shouldn't be surprised. All the secrets she kept from me, while I was living under her roof.

'Which reminds me, I should certainly get on with tea,' she says.

'Sure.' I get up and brush up the hem of my creased dress.

There's no point in sitting alone here, crying. Things will take their course. 'Do you need a hand with it?'

'I couldn't.'

'Nonsense.' By the time she's preparing to protest again, I'm already darting down the stairs. 'We'll have tea ready in a jiffy.'

'I'll really miss you, Rose,' she says, while my back is still turned to her.

I turn and wrap my hand around her shoulder, leaning my head on her arm. My heart fills with affection for this woman. 'You're so lovely, Nell, did anybody tell you that? And if Tom asks anything about my puffy face, tell him you made me chop the onions.'

Evie

I might have enjoyed my evening yesterday, but the people of London certainly didn't. When I come for my shift at eight o'clock, Henry's face is drawn and Rose looks as if she's been crying. 'What happened?' I ask as soon as I come into the room.

'We made a mistake,' says Henry, looking even grimmer than usual.

'They attacked the East End. At night.' Rose has dark circles under her eyes. No wonder, considering how her day has been. 'London is on fire. They bombed people like you and me, Evie. People, in their beds. Women and children.'

'What?' For once, I am speechless. I sit down at the table, my breakfast rolling in my belly, with the intention of coming up and out. 'Is this what it's coming to?'

Rose shakes her head. 'I dread to think where they'll strike next.'

'We need all hands on deck again,' says Henry.

'No, we need *more* hands on deck,' says Rose, determination written on her face. 'I wager you're sorry now you didn't hire Nell for our section. Nell is good and hard-working.'

'I'm the deputy head of this section and I will not have *you* questioning my decisions. I'm not a complete fool. How was I to bring another woman in this room? So you could stop working entirely to gossip and chat all day?'

'How can you even claim that?' says Rose. 'What are you even on about?'

'Oh, bloody let it go, Henry,' I say. This man always has such a talent at bringing me to the boil. 'Are you a complete idiot or do you pretend not to see how hard we work?'

'I will not allow—'

'How about trying different methods, like the one with the map, the one I suggested?' Rose cuts in.

'We *are* trying different methods, Miss Wiley. If you would stay long enough at work, you'd see that my method with the indexing cards is proving to be efficient.'

'But my idea with the map—'

Henry raises his hand, signalling Rose to stop. Always this palm in our faces, these fists in our mouths. 'Could I please ask you to return to your work instead of bickering? If you would please use the indexing cards, you'll see that we'll be able to decrypt more efficiently. We need to hurry and have enough cracks, so that by tonight when the messages with the targets start pouring in, we can decode them. Could you please do that, Miss Wiley? Miss Milton?'

Rose gives me a sideway glance, closing her eyes. If she is about to raise the white flag, I will not. My father may say what he wants to me, but my father can also blackmail me. Henry can't. 'Could you please stop insinuating that we are—'

There's a touch on my arm, a gentle squeeze. 'Let it be, Evie,' says Rose. 'This is pointless. We have enough to do without the squabbling.'

I look at this closed and determined face that seems to have aged five years since yesterday. And then I let it go. All right then. All right.

Rose

In spite of Henry's long looks, I drag Evie to lunch in what was probably once the mansion's conservatory. Six-sided bay windows dive into the lawn. They must offer a magnificent view, when they are not blacked out. Cream curtains are draped above them like fine frills on a dress. To my left, there's a tall fireplace made from sculpted wood and marble. The ceiling is covered in a geometrical flower pattern formed in plaster, with a band of arabesque leaves and flowers where it meets the wall. So much splendour. So much of what I won't see anymore, as of next week. For a moment, I wonder what I'd rather see day by day, the vexingly dark bay windows or the brown beam above my bed.

I whisper to Evie, covered by the clatter of porcelain, the chatter of voices. 'We have to do something.'

Evie pokes around in her whale meat. 'For instance?'

'I have an idea. Do you think we could talk to Lucy tonight, before she starts her night shift?'

'Sure. We can send a messenger.' Evie pouts. 'All right, I can take care of that.'

I tear apart the over-boiled potatoes on my plate, thinking how much better my mother's cooking is. I'll have enough of that as of next week. 'Did I tell you I found out who sent the application?'

'No.' There's a surge of unabashed interest in the way Evie studies my face.

'My mother. It was my mother.' I mash the potatoes with the tip of my fork, mixing them with the rather rubbery whale meat. The result looks like something babies might eat. 'I should have known from the first moment. She tried to push me to apply to the WLA on the day of the raid. She was going on about not losing my man and all that. I couldn't believe she would do this, and yet, I have to say, this is precisely something that she would do.'

Evie

'Oh, Rose,' I say. I wish I could tell her that I understand, that I know how it feels when one of your parents tries to dictate your life. I wish there was a way I could tell her about my father and what he's doing to me.

'You don't know how well I understand.'

Rose shrugs. 'Do you? I can't imagine your parents would have fiercely opposed your coming to Bletchley. And I mean, your father knows the commander. You just have to snap your fingers and you get anything you want.'

'Is that what you truly think?'

Rose stares at me blankly. I'd like to snap at her to wake up, to explain that I don't have the princess's life she accuses me of. That fairy tales are for children. But if I open that door, how far will she be able to see inside? And do I really need to squabble with someone who is going through the same thing I am?

'Oh, Rose,' I say. 'I'm sorry, but you don't know me at all.'

Rose

There are many things I can say about Bletchley Park. There are many ways in which the park has changed me. For instance, it has turned me into this creature skulking about at midnight near the wooden landing at the edge of the pond, where we wait.

There's motion at the edge of the water and a flash of light. The incandescence of red, weaving through the air.

I gasp.

Evie takes a few steps forward, then grabs my hand. 'It's just Lucy.'

The moment I found out about the bombs raining down on factories, I started concocting a plan. We can't wait for Henry to spark into action. We can't wait for Professor Walton to come back. We can't wait for a miracle. Especially not with the visit from the Admiralty next week, not with so many lives at stake. So I sent a message to Lucy that she should meet us a bit earlier by the pond, before her shift begins.

'I declare this meeting of the sisterhood open,' says Evie. 'The first point on the agenda is—'

'A secret password,' says Lucy. 'So we don't frighten the knickers off each other in the future. When we meet in the dark, that is.'

'Really?' I say.

'You read too many thrillers,' says Evie. 'Or your blokes take you to the cinema too often.'

'You'll be shocked,' says Lucy, drawing deeply from her cigarette, 'but sometimes they're disappointing kissers and I actually have to watch the picture.' She delivers her sentence in a studied tone. 'Even though I've seen it so many times already.'

We giggle.

'Nylons,' says Evie. 'How about nylons?'

'Too plain,' says Lucy. 'Besides, not much of a secret, considering it's our hallmark.'

'Opera? As in operation opera?' says Evie.

'Nah,' I say. 'I don't know. It doesn't represent us.'

'How about something tied to boats? Since we all have the issue with the Admiralty. Something like "Knot"?'

'No,' says Evie. 'Too sailor-ish.'

'I don't mind sailors,' says Lucy.

'How about "fishnet"?' I say. 'The best of both worlds. Stockings and the Admiralty.'

'It's settled,' says Evie. 'Fishnet it is.'

'Why did you summon us?' says Lucy. Her cigarette draws circles of faint light as it moves, illuminating our faces and her lips. There's the vague clop of water as it moves in the wind, slapping the wooden landing and perhaps also an unseen boat.

'We all know what a lump Henry is,' I begin.

'Agreed,' says Evie.

'Hear, hear,' says Lucy.

'And I don't need to tell you that we're in quite a pressing situation. With the nightly raids and the visit next week and all.'

'And the fact that you're leaving,' says Lucy.

'Thank you, Lucy, there's no need to remind me,' I say. 'The crux is that we're swimming against the current and we're losing. We need something to impress. A box with index cards won't knock an admiral off his feet.'

'Ah, that map of yours,' says Evie.

'Yes,' I say. 'Can you imagine all that we can do with a map? We can track not only all the bases and the trajectories of the reconnaissance flights, but also the locations of convoys in the Atlantic and the Mediterranean. The locations of U-boat packs and their movements. We might be able to predict a possible attack hours before the Kriegsmarine even spots our ships.'

'Goodness, that would be amazing,' says Evie.

'The professor might listen to you,' says Lucy. 'If you gave him this idea.'

'Yes, he might, but by the time Edmund returns…' says Evie. The end of the sentence hangs in the air. I think, I might already be gone.

I don't say this. Instead I say, 'We can't stand aside and watch everything burn down. We can't.'

'No, we shouldn't,' says Lucy. 'But what can we do?'

'We draw the map ourselves,' says Evie. 'Obviously. This is why you summoned us here, isn't it, Rose?'

I nod, and then realise the girls might not see me nod in the dark. 'Precisely. Though there are a few…logistical difficulties. The map, for instance. Where would we find a map that size?'

The girls fall quiet and I honestly hope that they're thinking. A good feeling surges within me, gives me power. I feel like I can think three times faster than usual. It is a risky plan. There are dangers. Lots of them. But I'd hoped with all my heart that the girls would be the right people to help me.

'Evie, could you ask the commander for a map?' I ask, and almost squeeze my eyes shut, half-afraid of what she might answer.

'Humph,' she says. 'I don't know. I can't push Alastair too far… Well, the situation has been rather complicated of late. He's done me quite a few favours. And if I ask for a map, he might ask questions. What do we do with the map, then?'

'We need to fill it with all that information. Bases, flights, convoys.'

'And how do we do that?' says Evie.

I take a big gulp of air and mutter under my voice. 'We'll need to steal the coordinates.' In the silence that follows, I can hear the weeds rustling on the edge of the lake. I need to go on, I need to win this battle, I need to win the girls to my side. 'We'll need to systematically take the coordinates out of the park and pin them onto the map.'

'And then bring the map to the visit from the Admiralty?' says Evie.

'Yes.'

Lucy says, 'But stealing coordinates – because that *is* stealing – that might earn us a hanging?'

I shudder, and it's not only because of the cold wind. 'Yes, Lucy. It's true. I can't deny this. We'll all be guilty of high treason.'

'What is the alternative?' says Evie. 'I mean, we stand aside and do nothing?'

'Or we stand aside and stay alive,' says Lucy.

'Since when are you the responsible one?' says Evie.

'Since my brother died at Dunkirk and I have to help my mother support my little brothers and sisters,' says Lucy.

Her answer knocks the breath out of me. So much pain and

suffering, everywhere around us. So much pain that we don't even see it anymore.

'I had no idea you lost your brother, Lucy,' says Evie. Her voice is trembling. 'I also— I almost lost my brother, at Dunkirk. I'm so sorry. It must be terrible.'

'He took care of all of us,' says Lucy, her voice changed in the midnight air. The confidence, that Lucy self-assurance is knocked out of it. 'After my father— I mean, we all know how to make do. We learned how to make do years ago. And after my brother died...let's say that I need this job, and not only for myself.'

'Lucy, I'm so terribly sorry. If I'd known, I would have never asked.' I feel so selfish and absorbed in my own little world.

'It's fine,' says Lucy, putting out her cigarette. 'It's fine. Now, if you don't mind, my shift has begun.' She brushes my shoulder as she leaves. 'Don't be sorry for telling me. I need to think about it. Because it's not only me that I'm thinking about.'

After she's gone, I find myself teetering again on the edge of tears, for what seems like the hundredth time in the past few days.

'Oh, Rose,' says Evie. 'Who knew? I wish there was something I could do for her.'

'I wish I'd known,' I say. 'I never thought Lucy was one to keep her cards so close to her chest.'

'Don't we all?' says Evie. 'Anyhow, I have an idea what to do about the map. We need atlases. If we can't find any in Bletchley, I'll ask Brown to send me a few from home. In fact, I was about to ask Brown to do something for me, anyway.'

'Who?'

'Never mind. And then, if we're missing something, I can draw the rest. At the proper scale, if not everything fits.'

'Evie, you've lost me.' These girls, these wonderful girls, they're proving to be full of surprises.

'We'll draw a patchwork, subversive map,' says Evie. 'We'll stick together maps from atlases, and I'll draw the rest. With Lucy's coloured pencils. And then, we can cut little aeroplanes and warships out of coloured paper.'

I giggle. 'I didn't even know you can draw. I'm useless with a pencil in hand.'

'Rose, you don't know the first thing about what's required of an accomplished young lady.'

Chapter Twenty-Eight

Evie

Two days later, I'm knocking at Elinor's door, early in the morning, at about the same time I would have started my shift, had I been up for the early round this week. But even if I'm not a morning person – which I have never been – and even if I'm working the afternoon today, here I am, knocking on wood at eight o'clock, my arms full of books.

Rose is the one who opens the door for me. 'Thank heavens,' she says, as she ushers me towards the first floor through a narrow corridor. This place is so dark that the stains of mould on the ceiling are barely visible.

Poor Elinor.

'Tom and Nell just left,' says Rose. 'And I'll have to pop to the butcher's later. You know, in order to maintain the illusion.' She makes a rolling move with her finger, as if she were a magician.

I chuckle. 'She still hasn't told him?'

'No, but what would you prefer her to do? I wouldn't want to tell Tom either, if I was her. And someone has to put food on the table, and Nell can't queue now, not with her working and all.'

'Good point,' I say, dropping my atlases on Rose's little table.

'You'll have to sit on the bed,' says Rose, showing me two mugs arranged on the chair.

I shrug. 'It doesn't matter.' I begin to tear pages out of the atlases – after they had been delivered to me last night, I started to earmark the pages I would use straight away.

'The sacrilege,' says Rose, covering her ears with her hands.

'What do you mean?'

'I know this is for a good cause, but I can't watch books being desecrated like this.'

'Ha! A good cause indeed,' I say. 'White paper?' Rose lifts a few sheets she had placed on the floor. 'Good.' I nod. Later, when I'll have assembled the maps that I have on hand in order to create a larger map of the world, I'll have to check what bits are missing, what I have to draw to scale. Then the real fun will begin.

Rose sits down on a cushion on the floor and begins cutting shapes from coloured paper. Blue squares for the Luftwaffe bases, as we agreed. Red dots for U-boats. Green dots for our own ships. Everything to be pinned onto our map, once it's ready. The crunch of the scissors accompanies my tearing sounds for a while, until Rose gets up and says, 'Time to go and see what can be done about those coupons.'

'The secret undercover work never ends!'

Rose giggles. 'It's for a good cause. Heaven forbid that Tom should be deprived of his ham.'

I have no idea how much time has gone by when Rose trots up the stairs, out of breath. 'Phew,' she says. 'You should have seen the size of the queue. But I think Nell will be proud of me. I managed to get two pounds of kidney, off the counter.'

I look up from my map, the zig-zagged contours of coasts still dancing before my eyes. 'What? Kidney? What for?'

'To cook, silly. Do you have any idea how hard it is to come by meat these days? No, obviously not.' Rose sniggers. 'In any case, we – the normal people – are allowed so little meat. And I asked the butcher if the animals that are being slaughtered happened to have any entrails. Innards aren't rationed, you know. So the butcher asked me to come to the back door and gave me a bit of something... Hey, listen, what do you have here?' She takes the sheet I've been working on from my hand. A detailed image of the coast of Norway that we didn't happen to have at the right scale. 'Evie, this is magnificent. Where did you learn to draw like this?'

I rub my eyes. A headache announces itself, starting from the back of my head and moving forwards. 'What, this? I'm just copying a drawing – there isn't much to it.' I take a sip from the mug Rose has left for me. It's stone-cold. 'Oh, this is some strong stuff. The food of the gods.'

'I nicked a bit from the Pikes's rations,' says Rose. 'Since it's such a special day.'

I hand her the sheet that I've already finished, a detailed outline of Corsica, and a set of pencils. 'Enjoy!'

Rose turns the pencils in her hands, making them clatter.

'It's a map,' I say. 'Time to start colouring.'

Rose

After a single day's work, the map is a beast that can't be manoeuvred anymore on my bed, so we have to divide it into two halves, and work on it separately. But there are so many missing pieces and so little time to finish it all. As quickly as I colour in and add the ships or bases, we need more of everything: hands to draw, coordinates to pin on. And Henry switches us and spins us in his rather confusing shift model as if we were paper dolls.

This morning finds us at the park, trudging through a new set of codes. It's not that Henry's system with the index cards doesn't work, it's just that it's so slow. However, for the purpose of our little team of two educated thieves, it makes our work much quicker. Who is there to check how many times we index the same piece of information? And who is there to report on us when Henry isn't in the room, and the duplicates find their way into our purses?

We grin at each other as we steal the next batch of indexes. Soon, in this rhythm, we won't have any more room to hide them. That is, if there's much more we can glean today.

When the door handle clicks, so do our purses, closing their mouths above the forbidden content. I elbow Evie, a little joke among us. But when I turn to snigger at Henry's thunderous stares, I notice he's not alone. He's joined by a young woman with a long, dark hair held back with a ribbon. She walks into the room like a doe waiting for the wolf to pounce at any moment from between the bushes – or, in our case, from between the chairs. She's wearing a soft green charmeuse dress, which catches the weak light in our room and reflects it like the surface of water.

Evie's eyes widen and she drops her pencil. 'Esther!' She leaps up and dashes over, stopping within inches of the girl, her hands making an odd move, caught between touching her shoulders and embracing her properly.

I think, so this is Esther. I'm shocked that things should have moved so quickly after contacting my aunt, but Mavis is someone who shouldn't be underestimated. I still don't quite know what she does for the Foreign Office.

I can't believe that Esther's presence in our section, of all places in the world, is a mere coincidence. Evie must have taken care of that, somehow – but she never breathed a word.

And I can't believe that the Milton machinery of relations, with its many arms and many fingers stuck in just about every pie in Britain, can reach so far.

Behind the girls, Henry pouts. 'Miss Milton, do you have any acquaintances left that you haven't tried to squeeze into this room?'

Evie takes her by the arm and guides her to the table. 'Esther, welcome to the German Air Section.'

Evie

Hours after her arrival, Rose still watches Esther, dumbstruck. She'd told me more than once, 'I can't believe it worked.' I patted her arm, stopping myself from hugging her. 'You did this, too, Rose. This is because of you.'

'Aunt Mavis,' she corrected me.

'Edmund also had a hand in it,' I told her. And then, when Esther wasn't watching, I said, 'I can see why my brother fell in love with her – she's so dignified and beautiful.'

Her features don't have the perfect symmetry of

Hollywood stars – perhaps her face is too long, and her eyes too close together. But there's something in the way she carries herself, the way she ignores Henry's attacks. I wonder if there's fear underneath all that, fear that the ground beneath her feet will start slipping again, and that nobody will help her.

'I still can't believe it,' Rose says.

'Then, darling, you should see what else I have in store for everyone.'

Lucy appears around two o'clock in the afternoon, summoned by Henry's odd machinations with the shifts. There's nothing peculiar in the way she strides in, pasture-green stockings today, or in the way she floats down into her seat. 'Lucy,' she says, extending her hand to Esther.

And if she doesn't agree with our little roguish operation, she says nothing while we copy the coordinates on the extra indexing cards.

As the day comes to its end, there are fewer and fewer coordinates for us to write. I'm wondering how much they would mean pinned on the map, how much they would lose themselves in its vastness.

That is, once it's really done.

But finally so are we, for the day. After four, when Ralph comes in, there will be no more little thieveries. And we might be better served if we head back to Rose's billet – it might be time better spent. The next time when Henry takes a warning for the Air Ministry, Rose and I slip the last few copies into our pockets.

'What is that?' says Esther, who has been watching everything we do here with enviable diligence all day long.

Rose and I glare at each other. 'Nothing,' I say.

'Nothing,' says Lucy, 'just some coordinates that the girls will bring later to the Indexing section.'

I mouth a silent thank-you and Lucy nods.

I don't think Esther would tell. No, I don't think so.

But the last thing I want is to have brought Esther all the way from the Isle of Man and then to make her crassly violate the Official Secrets Act. I have little understanding of politics or law, but I do see how that might look – a former British 'alien' involved in stealing information from the Foreign Office.

Erm.

It's one thing to try and keep her safe, and another when to throw her straight into the wolves' jaws. Esther studies our legs, clad in green, blue, and orange. 'I love this! Where can I find them, too?'

Rose

We drag Esther along to my billet, not asking her if she's tired, not asking her if she wants to settle into her new home. 'Let's take you to see Nell,' I say. 'The architect of your release.'

'Who?' says Esther, surprise written in her large, dark eyes.

'Elinor,' Evie corrects me.

If I thought Esther's eyes had been wide before, I'd had no idea. 'Elinor is here?'

'I live in her home,' I say, and for the first time it strikes me how closely connected we all are to each other.

It must have been written in the stars.

PATRICIA ADRIAN

And then I correct myself. Next week, at this time, we *will have been* connected to each other. The girls will go on with their antics, their club, their stockings.

I will be in an entirely different place altogether.

But today, I am here, and Nell can't believe it's Esther in the flesh, coming into her home. Nell, quiet Nell, stone-faced Nell, brings a hand to her mouth and muffles her screams. Today, I am here, and I refuse Nell's invitation to tea when Evie pulls my sleeve and points upwards to indicate we have more work to do.

Evie, of all people.

'Why won't you stay with us?' says Nell.

'Oh, we have to prepare a little something. It's a surprise,' says Evie, and she winks.

I am here as Evie draws more maps and then chews the ends of pencils as she considers how to proceed.

But things are slow. I can colour only so fast until my wrist begins to ache, and Evie can only draw so much without help. And we're slowly running out of coordinates.

'We should swap piles with someone tomorrow,' I say and Evie frowns. 'We only have access to the coordinates from the areas we decode. We need more.' And we have just three more days.

'Then you can have more.'

Evie and I are startled by a presence in the doorway.

'Fishnet,' says Lucy, with her green stockings, her cigarettes, and a purse full of indexing cards. She clears for herself a corner of the bed, attracting Evie's protests when she moves aside a piece of the map. 'Hey!'

'You didn't think you were going to do something subversive without me, did you now?' says Lucy.

Evie bats at the air with her hands. 'Get your cigarettes off my maps,' she says. Evie, of all people, a guardian of propriety.

I swear…some days!

'Calm down,' says Lucy. 'It's fine. Now what can I do to help?'

'Can you draw?' says Evie.

'I can draw, I can sing, I can even tell you a poem by heart. I'll do whatever you want me to.'

Evie and I exchange a look above Lucy's head. 'What about your little brothers and sisters?' I ask.

'What about them?' says Lucy.

'What if we're—'

'But we won't, will we? We won't,' says Lucy, while Nell asks, 'Is it all right if I escort Esther to her billet?'

We all jump up, half-assembled map and coloured pieces of paper flying around us.

'When did you come in?' says Evie.

'Just now,' says Nell, squinting. 'What is all this?'

Evie says, 'Trust me, you don't want to know.'

Nell crosses her arms and closes the door. 'Tell me.'

'This isn't what it looks like,' says Evie.

Fear insinuates itself, as does a tiny voice, which asks what on earth we had been thinking. We should have locked that door. Found a different place to hide. An air-raid shelter, where nobody would have thought to look for us, perhaps. I begin to doubt how well I know Nell, to doubt what she would do. Looking at the room through Nell's eyes, every single piece of paper is an accusation.

Nell closes the door. 'It appears that you're doing something forbidden under my own roof,' she hisses. 'And with Esther under it, too.'

'Listen,' I say. 'We're trying to help. We're preparing this map for Bletchley.'

'Is that so?' says Nell. 'Then why don't you prepare it *at* Bletchley? Does Edmund know about this?'

'Yes,' says Evie.

'No,' I say.

'Then perhaps someone should tell him,' says Nell.

Evie says, 'Please.'

'Please,' I say, too.

'It's for a good cause,' says Evie. 'Can't you trust me, after all I've done for Esther?'

I don't think Nell would ever trust Evie. But Nell would do the right thing for the right reasons. For the true reasons. I say, 'Do you remember what I told you when I found out about your brother? Let me tell you a story…'

The club is coming together, just as the map is, which looks like it is the brain child of Dr Frankenstein, judging by its patchwork appearance. But so are we, aren't we? If you ever looked at us, if you ever saw us on the street, who would have thought that we could ever fit together?

And yet we do, like puzzle pieces, matching the pushes and pulls and the smoothing of each other's rough spots. We steal. We draw. We pin. We stick together. Not only mock ships cut out of green paper, but we stick together. The four of us, we stick together.

Chapter Twenty-Nine

Rose

Do you know that feeling when a sonata nears its end, and it goes faster, faster, faster, and your heart races, and you can barely breathe, and you know that it will all explode in an outburst of emotions?

That's my life now. I can barely breathe from it all. The stealing of coordinates, the way we walk that knife's edge every day. The visit from the Admiralty, coming at us in big strides, wielding a knife that can cut deep. Tomorrow. And the day after that, the end, the very end. One long, deep note.

But tonight. Tonight, for a moment, the music slows down.

Evie has reserved seats for us all in the former ballroom of the mansion. The stacked desks have been pushed outwards to the walls to make room for unending rows of assorted chairs: hard chairs, sculpted chairs, folding chairs, even stools. At the front, a stage has been improvised from wooden planks.

In the middle of this makeshift madness, there are still signs of former splendour: the walls covered in wooden panels, the sculptural plaster of the ceilings, creating intricate designs on a golden background. Lush red curtains at the windows.

Bletchley, in all its resourcefulness and magnificence, waiting for an opera show. Evie, the beautiful brain behind it, shines next to me in her long lamé dress, the cut at the back so deep that it finishes where her bottom starts. A single silver chain is stretched between her shoulders, her bones and muscle rippling under the skin. She eclipses even the gorgeous woman sitting next to her, a version of Esther that dazzles an entire room of professors and former debutantes. An Esther of long, dark curls and a dress of green velvet that swishes on the polished floors like the waves of the sea.

Everyone they pass studies the girls from the corners of their eyes, but Evie navigates between them, leading us to what she called our 'reserved seats' – our places in the second row. Nobody is sitting down, except a soldier with fire-red hair and a middle-aged woman in the first row. Of all the people in the room, Evie makes a beeline for them. Lucy and I struggle to keep up – we had to leave Nell at home, since she could think of nothing plausible to tell her husband.

Evie taps the man on the shoulder and he turns. 'Surprise,' she says, and passes Esther's hand into his.

The young man's face twists and crumples, and Esther can't help her tears. She falls into his arms, almost bringing down the chairs between them. He squeezes her so tight that I think he'll knock the breath out of her for good. He whispers into her hair as tears stream down his cheeks. Esther shudders and sobs. The room grows quiet and I have no doubt, no doubt at all, that everyone is staring at us.

'Rose, Lucy,' says Evie. 'Meet my brother, Will.'

The two go outside – of course they need their privacy; they haven't seen each other in a year. I blink the tears in my eyes away. As much as Evie tries to appear impenetrable, I can tell by the way she fidgets with her purse that she's moved. 'Oh, I did hope he might have a word or two for me, first.'

'Later,' I tell her, thinking that I will be the same as Will and Esther the day after tomorrow, when I see my David again. There's a warm feeling, deep in my belly. I don't think I'd have any words to spare for anyone else.

Evie sits down next to the lady who must have arrived with Will. 'Ladies, meet Brown, my… My mother's—'

'Lady Milton's lady's maid. How do you do,' says the woman, who reminds me so much of Nell, in her dignified bearing. And with her chignon. Underneath all her powder, I could swear Evie is blushing. For all her intended unconventionality, she sometimes wants us to forget that she grew up with an army of servants catering to her every need. But that is always hovering just beneath the surface, seeping through everything she touches. Evie has had such an easy life that she doesn't even know what the opposite is.

'Rose Wiley,' I say. 'Miss Milton's partner in mischief.'

'Ha! One could say the same about Brown,' says Evie, stretching out her hand, an affectionate look on her face. 'We have plotted this little reunion between us and I daresay it was quite a success.'

'I would certainly count it as a success, Miss Milton,' says Brown. 'What better way for the two to meet than at an opera?'

'What better way, indeed?' says Evie. She is so transformed in this room, the perfect swan who is used to gliding through society. Even the way she speaks has changed.

'And I'm afraid the surprises for this evening haven't yet come to an end.'

'Oh?' says Evie. 'May I ask what kind of surprises?'

'Just you wait, Miss Milton. Not much longer now.'

We resume our seats. Lucy glances around, her eyes wider than ever before. 'Look at the gents in tailcoats, at the silk dresses. I never saw so many fancy people in one place.'

'Do you know, I arranged for a baritone and a mezzo-soprano to come all the way from London,' says Evie. 'Friends of mine.' She winks.

'From London?' says Lucy.

'How did you even manage this?' I say, pointing at the overwhelming splendour with its air of spontaneous make-do. 'The things you can do, Evie, once you set your mind to them.'

'Oh, you do know that the commander is a darling friend,' says Evie. 'And, you know, most of the people who will be up on stage today are from Bletchley's opera club. I thought, don't we all need something nice to take our minds off the war?'

'This is so nice,' says Lucy. 'So nice.'

I blink at the world around me. All of this, lurking beneath Bletchley's workaday appearance. I don't know anything about the world we live in, not even about the place where I work. I seem to have lived my entire life under a rock, hiding in my billet or behind the piles of paper on my desk.

'I can't believe that in all my time here I never went to London,' I say.

'I can't believe it, either,' says Lucy. 'How old are you, Rose? Don't even get me started on the dance clubs.'

I shrug.

The lights are dimmed and the rustle of voices also drops to silence.

A delicate music, like the flutter of angel wings, rises from the orchestra corner. I listen to classical music on the wireless, but I can't say that I'm a connoisseur. And yet, the music in this chilly hall has a particular glow to it. It touches and caresses my heart; it makes it quiver, and flutter, and flicker. A faint light, as much as it's allowed without endangering the blackout, brightens the stage. The thin curtains are drawn apart.

The voice fills the room even before I perceive all the details on the stage. There's a tall, stout, silhouette in a shimmering dress. From the long sleeves that trail on the ground, two rounded forearms emerge. The woman's voice is like the sound of hundreds of crystal glasses clinking and it rises from all around me, insinuating itself into every part of my soul, lifting me up and spinning me through the air until I'm dizzy.

The woman's hair is a mass of dark curls draped on top of her head. She has an elegant, vulture-like nose and deep-set eyes, lined in the manner of an Egyptian queen. She's a large woman – she has presence. And the voice. The voice! There's a man singing alongside her, and they glance sideways at one another, and make wide gestures with their hands. They're mesmerising. All I want to do is stare at them.

'They're dazzling,' I say. 'I never saw anyone quite like them.'

'Oh, goodness,' says Evie, the blood all drained from her face. 'Who ever asked *him* to come here?'

Evie

I rush into the foyer, unable to catch my breath. In spite of all my best efforts, I'm living through the catastrophe I was seeking to avoid. But how many people saw me and him at the same time in the same room? Perhaps there's a small chance to save this. Rose and Brown follow quickly on my heels.

'Evie, what's wrong?' says Rose.

'Calm down, Miss Milton. It's fine.'

'It's not fine!' My hands are shaking. 'It's not fine. If Papa sees this… If Papa hears of this…'

'Nobody will tell your father anything. Not if you don't make a scene,' says Brown. 'Nobody here knows.'

I grab my stomach with both hands, on the point of retching. 'Did you do this, Brown? Was it you? You know what's at stake. You know bloody well.'

There's the sound of steps from the corridor. I look up, terrified that someone might have seen and heard us. I want nothing more than to run away and hide from all of this. I can't see him. Not today. Not now.

From around the corner, Will and Esther appear, hands laced tightly. Hasn't my brother been late to every event in my life in the past year?

'Has she seen him already?' says Will.

'Will? You too?' I say. Being a Milton means that there's a certain amount of betrayal that I deal, and that I expect to be dealt to me, but I never expected any from my brother. Not from him. 'Why, Will? Was it because of Esther? Didn't I tell you that I had no idea? I had no idea!'

He grabs my shoulders in that way that is both soft and firm, stopping me from quaking. This is the closest someone has been to me since I left Milton Hall and Brown used to do my hair every morning. Perhaps with the exception of the air raid, when Rose and I trembled side by side. Why do people get so close to me lately only when I'm shaking? 'Silly you. I did this for you. All for you.'

'You have no idea,' I say. 'You have no idea what you've done. You don't know what he threatened to do. You've been away, you left me, you don't know anything.'

Brown looks to my brother. Even in my state I can tell that they've been hand in hand. 'He knew precisely what he was doing, Miss Milton. I told him.'

'Evie,' says Will, increasing the pressure on my shoulder. 'Evie. Listen to me. Don't let him ruin your life. Don't let him do to you what he did to me. And even if he tries to, run away before he can harm you all.'

'You have no idea,' I repeat, even though I begin to believe him.

Will lets me go and straightens himself up. 'Evie, Jasper is leaving for America. Two days from now. He won't be able to touch her there. Nor you.'

'You don't know him.'

'But I do,' says Will. 'He doesn't give a fig about what you do, as long as you keep well out of everyone's way. Go with him. Go to America. Take a new name.'

'I can't do that. He'll follow me everywhere. He'll harm us.'

Brown shakes her head, too. 'It won't hold there. The evidence he bought here, it won't matter there. Not even *his* arm is that long.'

'There is life beyond Milton Hall,' says Will. 'Don't be the spoiled brat you've always been. Forget you were ever a Milton. Hide. Find a job. Make a life for yourself. Let it go.' He comes nearer to me, spreads his arms, and then holds me tight. So, so tight. 'Let it all go. The car, the jewels, the expensive dresses. Do you need all that? What do you really want, Evie Milton? What do you want?'

Rose

Evie sobs and cries a bit and then lets her brother wipe her tears.

'We should return,' says Esther in a soft voice.

Evie nods. 'Agreed.'

We find our seats, weaving through the mass of people sitting in their chairs. Jasper's voice vibrates through the room when the soprano picks up a few notes. Their voices are laced in the music. As we finish knocking knees and murmuring 'I beg your pardon,' a deep rumble like the sound of a hundred thunders shakes us to the marrow. The room fills with screams.

I start quivering. Lucy grabs my hand, and pulls me under one of the desks that had been drawn to the side. She screams, 'Bomb! They're bombing!'

My limbs turn to lead. I cower underneath the desk, huddling into Lucy. Will, Brown, and Esther have upturned chairs and taken cover underneath them. All I can think is that I can't die today, how silly, and shouldn't we have known in advance? But we barely find anything anymore. If we'd been allowed to use our map, maybe we would have found the warning and been able to tell the Air Ministry to catch the Luftwaffe attackers in their net before they ruined our opera evening.

A torrent of men and women pour out of the ballroom, while the opera singers descend from the stage.

'Please calm down!' screams a flight sergeant. 'No reason to panic. There was no air-raid alarm.'

People are still streaming outside – towards the closest air-raid shelter, I assume. I have no idea where that might be. It seems much safer to crouch underneath the desk.

There's a deafening whistle. I make myself even smaller, trying to press my face against the wooden floors. The screams peak again. I glance up. Jasper stands in the middle of the room, looking around. Looking for someone. Before I manage to say another word or move a single muscle, Evie has leapt and pulled him towards her.

Lucy crawls by my side. We both tremble, shoulder to shoulder, too frightened to run towards the closest shelter. There's another thud, and the chandeliers shake, clinking. Evie and Jasper crawl under the first desk, underneath a typewriter. The air-raid alarm finally wails, and the buzz of aeroplanes is above us.

Evie

'Are you afraid?' I ask Jasper, and he squeezes my hand. Tears fill my eyes and it's not that I'm scared, but all I can feel is his intoxicating, spicy and smoky smell. I can't believe that I have lived so long without it, without his presence at my side. There's a flutter in my belly, and it has nothing to do with the Messerschmitts streaming above us, even though the next bomb might literally fall on our heads. For the first time in many, many months I have the feeling that *I* will be all right and *everything* will turn out to be all right and even if I die I know how I want to spend my last moments: the warmth of his body pressed against mine. And not just the warmth diffusing through a set of clothes, just a hint of the feel of him on my skin. I lean in and give him the slightest of kisses, the smallest, just a touch, but I know it's enough. It will be enough. This feels so good that I could cry. Then his hand is on my cheek, and we move away for just a moment, breathless, our lips not quite touching, but nearly so, his half-closed eyes taking me in, while I'm taking him in, unable to have enough of him.

Close to us, there's a boom, and everything around us clatters and trembles. It might be the end of the world, for all I care. Let it come.

Rose

Jasper and Evie kiss, while the buzz of aeroplanes stops. Around us, there's the silence of snowflakes, falling, and I doubt there's a single person left in this room, hiding, who does not see them. A handful of men in evening suits see them. Young women in silk dresses see them. Lucy, Esther, and Will see them. From the corner of the room, the commander sees them.

I watch them, too, my stomach knotting. What I wouldn't give to have my David with me now. Evie had once mentioned a beau, but she never mentioned that she was so mad about him. So mad, that even an air raid would become background noise when they met. So mad, that it wouldn't matter if a room full of people was watching – I hardly even hold hands with my David when we're in public.

I wish she's said something about how in love she was with him. I thought Evie was my friend – why would she keep this a secret from me?

We lie in the silence for a long time. Evie and Jasper whisper between themselves, and the other people in corners whisper, too. I can imagine what they're saying. You see this sort of things in movies, and I can imagine that people would have their eyes on Honourable Evelyn Milton.

A wing commander comes into our room and announces that bombs have fallen near one of the huts. The all-clear sounds, and the wing commander goes on about two bombs: a small bomb, and a much larger unexploded one. We've been lucky, apparently. If we could please evacuate the building, so that the UXB may be cleared from the site.

Nobody tells us about the woman we stream by, the one who was crushed to bits by the small bomb. About the splinters of bone, the bits of flesh, the blood-stained purse that has been blown a few yards away. About the hand that still clings to it. About how this could have been all of us, if the larger bomb had exploded.

Evie

'Come with me,' says Jasper. 'If this is what you want.'

We stand outside, before the gates of the park, shivering, even though the night is warm. Will, Esther, Jasper, and I. Beyond, the moon illuminates parts of the Bletchley mansion, a ghost house. The night is still, and everything seems to be like it was before, before the raid, before the opera. But next to one of the huts, a young woman has died. And I know that, tonight, I've crossed a threshold, and that there will be no return. And, for the first time, I feel that I'm prepared for this.

That I knew this moment would come, and now that it is here I welcome it. I know that my mind has been made up, and that I was only waiting for the opportunity.

Jasper holds my hands between his, a silent supplication. He need not beg. He need not have asked. 'Yes,' I say, unable to tear my eyes away from his. 'Though that might not be as easy as you think.' I think of Rose's struggle to go home, back when she still wanted to go home. I don't know what she wants anymore.

'Isn't there anyone who can help?' asks Will, and I could laugh.

'Everyone has helped all the time, with all sorts of things. I don't know if I have any favours left to ask.'

I try to remember whether Alastair was still in the ballroom when the raid began, but I can't. I'm so exhausted that I'd have to think hard even before putting one foot in front of the other. There is something I have yet to do: find Alastair and discover if there is, after all, a way out of Bletchley Park.

Chapter Thirty

Rose

On the day of the official visit, I put on my orange stockings – a parting gift from Evie and Lucy. Something to remind me of them when I won't be here anymore, as of tomorrow. As if I'd ever forget them.

That is, if tomorrow sees me home. There are much darker places where I could end up after today. Last night, the opera, Evie and Jasper...already it seems miles and miles away, like little cartographer's dots. We have other business to attend to – a certain map, which I wrap carefully, so as not to undo it at the stitches. I place it in a coarse cloth holdall, borrowed from my landlady.

In the kitchen, breakfast awaits me while Nell wipes Tom's plate.

'Toast and spread today,' she says, setting the dishes down in the rack.

'I'm not hungry. I'm so sorry.'

The dangers of the day dance through my head: firstly getting the map through the park's gates, but Evie promised she'd pick us up, so we can hide the map in the Bentley; then, pulling it out when the admiral comes to visit; and finally, unfolding it, hopefully away from Henry's ill-wishing eyes. If he decides to tell anyone what we've done when he discovers it… If he tells…

'Did you hear me, Rose?' says Nell, leaning forward on the table. Her legs are also clad in our famous stockings. Deep blue today.

'No, I'm sorry,' I say. I'm not quite here, my mind already racing into an uncertain future.

'I have to tell Tom tomorrow.' Nell's face crumples with concern.

'Can't you wait a few more days?'

Nell shakes her head. 'I'm up for the afternoon shift tomorrow. I can't lie to him anymore. There's no way I can explain why I won't be home until midnight.'

Poor girl. 'Did you receive your first wages, at least?'

'Yes.'

'Then make sure to show him that first.' Money might persuade my landlord, if nothing else. I feel for the itchy cloth of the holdall with my foot, under the table. 'Time to go, I think. We don't want to make Evie wait.'

But we're the ones to wait on the narrow bit of lawn in front of Nell's house.

I ask, 'Did you hear anything about your brother?'

Nell shakes her head. 'I feel it in my heart that he's alive. One of these days, they'll find him.'

The map feels heavy in its holdall, unruly in the way it wants to unfold itself. I think, *just a few more hours*. I challenge the admiral not to be swept off his feet by its magnificence. I challenge him. After Nell started stealing coordinates from the Indexing section for us, the map's significance has blossomed to mammoth proportions. 'Thank you so much for all you've done for us,' I say. 'You have no idea what difference you might have made.'

'No offence, Rose, but I didn't do it for you, as much as I like you. I did it for other women like me, who want nothing more than for their brothers or their sweethearts to come back home in one piece. I did it so that what happened to Rob will happen to no one else, ever again.'

'Nell Pike, you're one of the bravest women I've ever known.' I don't tell her that she's also the greatest rule-abider that I've ever known and that when she discovered us I was already picturing the metal gleam of the firing squad.

Or that I had imagined the three of us taking her down with sharp scissors or a pencil, to make sure she wouldn't tell anyone about what we were doing.

I almost giggle at the thought.

'What?' she says and I reply, 'Nothing,' the spot of brightness in the day dissolving into concern. 'I don't know what's with Evie, but I think we should go,' I say. 'If we hurry, we might still arrive on time for our shift.'

'Do you think something might be wrong with her?' says Nell.

'I don't know. She and Will said something about her

father, and I didn't catch much…but if I put the pieces together…You might tell me; you know the family better.'

Nell looks away. 'I think I know enough to tell you that Lord Milton would not be happy to hear about last night.'

I think about all the possibilities, about everything that Evie has said. And then I realise I don't want to think about them. Not now. 'Let's go,' I say, hoisting up the holdall with the map.

'Careful, so you don't ruin it,' says Nell.

'It will hold,' I say. 'It's made of something that doesn't break easily.' Just like us. And today is the day when we show what we're made of.

As we turn the corner, there's the loud purr of an engine, catching up with us. I pull Nell's sleeve, urging her back towards her house. And there's Evie's Bentley, all right, but with Will behind the steering wheel and Esther in the passenger seat, waving at us to stop.

'Evie left,' says Esther, breathless.

The blood drains from my cheeks. 'What do you mean, left?' *What about our plan. Sneaking the map into Bletchley?* And I had been rather relying on Evie and her iron-clad relations to be the one to get the map out at the crucial moment, hoping there will be no repercussions.

It is one thing for the Hon. Evelyn Milton to have committed high treason. It's the sort of anecdote you might read about in a newspaper twenty years from now.

It's another thing for a farmgirl to do it.

You never hear about this for good reason.

'There was no other way,' says Will. 'I'm afraid I can't say much more without compromising you or her. You'll have to trust me that she'll be safe.'

I cradle the holdall in my arms.

'Get in,' says Esther.

Will says, 'I can only take you so far.'

———————————

So far is right around the bend from the train station, at a point where the guards of Bletchley can't see us. 'Nell and I will go first,' I say, pinning Esther down in her seat with my finger.

The two lovers exchange a look.

'Trust us, Esther,' says Nell. 'I don't know how much Evie has told you, but you don't want a hand in this.'

I say, 'Not even the tip of a finger,' and drag the holdall towards Bletchley's iron gates.

At the entrance, two guards are checking everyone's passes. I prepare mine, hoping to be waved through quickly. But since we wasted so much time, the flood of people coming in for the morning shift has waned to a trickle. I nudge Nell to tackle the younger guard and I head for the older one, with a trimmed white beard that makes me think of a benevolent grandfather.

'Good morning,' I say with a huge smile, in the hope that it looks confident and not unhinged.

'How'd you do,' says the guard, his gaze moving from my pass to my face. He snaps my entrance pass shut and I exhale. As I hurry inside, he asks, 'What is that you have there?'

I think, I could outrun him. I think, but for how long? How far would I realistically get?

I think, if I've learned anything from Evie, it's that now is the time to be brazen.

I push the holdall towards him, enough to brush his uniform. As if I have nothing in the world to hide. 'I picked up a little something from London, from the Foreign Office's central headquarters. Commander Denniston's special request.' I look to the right and left, as if now I have something to hide. 'Top secret.'

He waves me through. 'Do go on, then.'

I'm so relieved that I could giggle. I put on my earnest face and hook Nell's elbow, who was waiting for me beyond the gates. 'First point on our list, checked!'

———————

I part with Nell, who heads for her Naval basement room, and hurry up the stairs towards the German Air Section. Esther catches up with me and we both go into our room. Literally almost a dozen eyes watch as we stride in, quite late – the afternoon shift is also here, in the hope that we might be able to decrypt faster and sweep the admiral off his feet.

'Miss Wiley, Miss Goldschmidt,' says Henry. 'I was wondering when you would grace us with your presence.'

'Miss Wiley!' says Professor Walton.

I'm so thrilled at the sight of his tortoiseshell spectacles, of his crumpled tweed suit, that I could jump up with joy. 'Professor! You're back!' For a moment, I think about showing him the map. Right here, right now.

But then Henry says, 'Look at them again,' pointing at my legs.

The professor frowns. 'I don't understand.'

'The stockings!' says Henry. 'Like schoolgirls.'

'Ah,' says the professor, as if unsure what is expected of him.

I think, even if the professor thinks it's a good idea, Henry could sway him. So I tuck my large package underneath the trestle table. We must bring up the map when Henry isn't watching, though I have no idea how we might make that come about.

I'm about to slip into my seat, when the professor says, 'Miss Wiley, I heard that you're leaving us. What a shame. I couldn't believe it at first. I hoped you might be the next head of shift.'

There's a knot in my throat. Me, Rose Wiley, a farmgirl who didn't even go to university, head of shift at Bletchley Park. 'I would have loved that so much. And I don't know what you've been told, Professor,' I say, looking at Henry, 'but it wasn't of my own doing and I'm endlessly sorry that things took this turn.' I speak this with all my heart, a steely conviction swathing my words.

No, my time here isn't done. And I'm less and less sure that this is the time for David and me. I try to picture my days between the moments I'd be allowed to see him, and I can't. I'm more and more certain that our dream of a life together would again be replaced by a tunnel of waiting. 'Please believe me.'

But the professor doesn't have ears for me anymore. He's all eyes, and they're directed at the woman next to me. 'Esther!' He moves towards her on his long legs. I've never seen the professor so quick on his feet. She stretches out her hand and he kisses it.

I'll never understand the complicated relationships between all these people.

'Thank you so much for the job,' says Esther in a low voice. 'Will sends his greetings. And he wants to see you. We talk later.' She winks. 'First, our big day.'

Henry has a face as if the plaster flowers on the ceiling have fallen on top of his head. There was no need for me to go to London to see the theatre; there is plenty of drama in our section.

'There's no one more anxious than me for the big day to be over,' Professor Walton says, a crease of worry cutting through the joy of seeing Esther.

'Yes, and all the better if we all do our work,' says Henry. 'Those codes aren't about to crack themselves.'

I think, but can you crack a joke? And then think twice about saying this out loud.

On the table, the piles of messages have thinned. It isn't because we've been decrypting faster these past few days thanks to Henry's 'revolutionary' system. A look at the sheets confirms what I have suspected – the older, undecrypted messages have been sorted out of our heaps, in order not to frighten the visitor from the Admiralty.

'Traffic cosmetics,' I say to Esther, reaching for my messages.

From the other side of the table, Lucy chuckles. 'Fishnet,' she says.

I get on with my job with a smile on my face. For a reason I can't possibly fathom, I have a feeling that, yes, we can do this. My hands find a familiar rhythm while copying messages. My stiff fingers begin to dance across the sheet, writing down attempts at cracks; erasing, rewriting, filling. But I can't lose myself in my work today. The atmosphere is dense. We're startled at the faintest sound of steps coming along the hallway, like gophers in a field, scouring for enemies. We hardly dare to breathe. Professor Walton forbade us to smoke in the room today, and the men are twitching their fingers. Lucy keeps sucking in air through an unlit cigarette.

At eleven o'clock, we're slowly preparing to go to lunch, when there's a knock on the door. We all look up from our sheets. The door gives way and the commander comes in. He's wearing a striped suit today. 'He's here.'

This is the professor's cue – he and Henry scurry out, tossing a 'Dr Milner, you're in charge. Nobody leaves the room,' before closing the door behind them.

The tips of my ears begin glowing. I shuffle the sheets of paper with the encoded messages on them, but the letters begin fading into each other and leapfrogging each other in front of me.

Around me, everyone is trying hard to appear as if they're doing something, while they're just as unable to concentrate. Lucy, of all people, gets up and scribbles a few more decrypts on the blackboard, then takes the seat next to me. 'When do we bring it out?' she whispers.

'I don't know.' A little fist twists in my gut. Evie isn't here anymore. Evie would know what to do. In her absence, our sisterhood is looking to me for direction. At least, the few members that are here. 'It could backfire terribly, you know that.' From the furtive looks she throws me, I can tell Esther isn't as far from the heart of the matter as we would have liked her to be. 'Maybe we don't need it at all?'

Lucy raises her eyebrows in a way that suggests she thinks that's highly improbable, but doesn't say a thing.

I keep glancing at the door, straining to listen for sounds of people approaching. The rustle of papers, the shifting, is a cacophony of whispers. I think: do or die. And then, I realise, for Bletchley, I'm as good as dead already. Or, at least, I will be, as of tomorrow.

'Lucy,' I say. 'If something goes amiss – say nothing. You never knew anything about the map. All right?'

'But, Rose—' says Esther.

'I won't even hear it. No point in all of us getting into trouble. One will be enough. It was my idea.' And I'm the one who has the least to lose, anyway. I don't have a family to feed. And I don't risk being sent to Canada, or worse.

Time ticks and passes at its own snail's pace. Soon enough, the room fills with whispers. 'How much longer?' and 'I'm hungry' and 'I wish today would be over.' I can't recall a single shift when so little work has been done so ineffectively. I stare at my rows and columns and blink three times, trying to bring it all into focus. Why is it so hard to do my best when it matters the most?

There was a time before the war, when I had dreamed of a life so different from my mother's. *I might travel, perhaps*, I told myself. After the war started, I dreamed of a higher calling, of helping with the war effort, even if it meant scrubbing a deck. Time snaps and coils within itself. Yes, the encoded message is calling to me, and only I can find its hidden language.

Did I ever even dare to dream of such work, wrestling the right answers from my own mind? I look around me, and think, *this is what I want the rest of my life to be like.*

When I set the tip of the pencil to paper, I know what I have to do. The codes click into their places, and so do the translations of my cracks. Nothing else exists.

I'm calm when the door opens and a blushing Professor Walton enters, accompanied by a tall gentleman. I say *gentleman* because this is what he looks like: tall, lean, thinning hair on a rosy scalp, and a pair of spectacles with metallic rims that rather remind me of a monocle. His Royal Navy uniform doesn't make this military man any less of a gentleman. He seems snobbish and courteous, the sort of man who would have got along just fine with Evie – or would have been impressed by her presence – had she been here.

Professor Walton and Henry accompany him through the room. They point at the piles of messages, at the lined sheets of paper, full, or half-full, of copied and translated messages. They show him the blackboard. The professor speaks quicker than I've ever heard him, and he often stutters. He talks of 'algorithms' and 'margins of error' and then proceeds to guide the gentleman onto the dais, where he shows him various tables of statistics, which he'd surely spent hours and hours preparing in advance. The gentleman nods. He squints at the professor's papers, and looks about the room, studying our faces.

This hardly feels like a coronation of our efforts. This is a massive railway accident, and it seems like there will be plenty of victims. I turn to Lucy and read the same bewilderment on her face.

While Professor Walton is making a point about the efficiency of the indexing cards, the gentleman lifts his hand in an exasperated manner, to stop the flow of words he's bombarded with.

'I see there are quite a few women in your section, Professor. Do these young women also work in night shifts alongside men?'

The professor nods. I can smell the trap in the gentleman's twitching nose as he asks. 'What provisions do you make for propriety?'

'I be-be-beg your pardon?' says Professor Walton.

The gentleman twists his droopy blonde moustache. 'Do

you compel these young women to work at night, too? Or do the night shifts consist exclusively of gentlemen?'

Professor Walton reels and places a hand on his table to steady himself. 'No, the young women, they work night shifts, too. We have to. We don't have sufficient… So many men have gone to war, or they're in reserved occupations.'

The gentleman clasps his hands around his back. 'Are we then expected to be contacted with highly classified, extremely urgent information in the middle of the night by young women, with no experience whatsoever regarding military matters? And these young women are expected to tell military men what to do, then?'

Professor Walton colours a violent red, almost purple.

Henry says, 'There's always one of us to supervise the young women. It's inconceivable that they should be left to their own devices.'

'Even at night?' says the admiral.

Lucy taps me on the shoulder.

'All our heads of shift are men,' says Professor Walton, as if this were a badge of pride. 'The information would be passed on by a man.'

'And yet, you work with so many women,' says the admiral. 'How are we to know that the information they uncover is correct? How can we trust their military judgement?'

Professor Walton draws two short puffs from his empty pipe. The admiral comes closer to the table and examines Esther from head to foot. She's wearing a gorgeous rayon dress today with a delicate golden thread running through it. 'For instance, what are these young lady's qualifications?'

'S-she came to us from an "aliens" camp on the Isle of

Man,' stammers Professor Walton. 'She knows German. She is a proficient German speaker. A native German speaker, I mean.'

'I think I've seen enough, Professor Walton,' says the admiral and turns to leave.

The unspoken insult makes Esther's eyes shine. I look to Lucy, to Professor Walton, even to Henry, watching to see whether they do anything to prevent this catastrophe from happening.

They do not. They are all standing at the foot of the dais, rooted to the spot.

It's now or never. It's laurels of victory, or the hangman's noose for me.

I dart after the not-so-gentlemanly gentleman from the Admiralty. I grab him by the coat, at the elbow. 'Sir, there is something we have yet to show you!' The wool of his jacket is soft, almost velvety. He snatches his arm free, but my fingers dig deeper into the fabric. 'Sir! I insist!'

He scowls, turning. I hurry to the trestle table and reach underneath it. I grab the holdall and take out the map. In spite of the way it has been squeezed and folded, it has withstood transport rather well, not giving way at the joints. I begin spreading it out on the table.

'Young lady, have you gone quite mad?'

I can hear him rushing to my side. The man places his hand above mine. I know this isn't the most impressive of views, this patchwork map, where the water in the oceans has at least three different shades of blue, depending on which atlas it was torn from, or whether Evie had to fill the colour in after she drew her bit.

'Young lady! What is this?'

His sour breath is in my face. I close my eyes and summon all my anger, all my fears, all my hopes from the very depths of my being. This one is for Evie. For Esther. For David, who doesn't know that what I do here helps keep him safe. So much love is pulsating within me, glimmering like splashes of colour, sprouting like blood from a severed artery.

I straighten up and move my finger across the map. 'Here, on the Atlantic coast, the Luftwaffe bases are marked in blue. The red dots in the ocean are the last known position of U-boat wolf packs. The green dots are our own ships.' I turn to look at him for the first time. His eyes are wide, and his mouth is open. 'Here,' I say, tracing the lines in dotted pencil, 'this is the "track" that the weather flights take every day.' I step back. 'Do your military analysts have anything similar in their offices? Does our data correspond with your own?'

The gentleman moves closer to the map, twisting his moustache. He begins tracing bases and lines with his fingers. Mouthing coordinates.

'Yes, yes. It's here. I recognise—' He's dazzled. 'The positions of our cruisers, of the battleships.'

I smile to myself. A gentleman of the old world would know nothing about permutations and statistics. His kind rises above numbers.

'This is just how reliable our information is,' I say. 'This is what we have access to. Information which you did not trust, not until now. I hope this will change.'

The man, whose name I still don't know, lifts an eyebrow.

I take this for as much encouragement as I will receive. 'I don't know how the Admiralty obtains their information, sir, but look at what we do here. We intercept messages *directly* from the Luftwaffe. We decode them, we translate them. It's not about trusting some doubtful sources, that reach us through second-rate channels. We analyse what people inside the Luftwaffe say to each other. Tell me, could you ever think of a source of information more reliable than that?'

The man sighs, shaking his head. I turn towards the room.

'*You* see young women here, academics, a refugee, a former teacher. A girl who grew up in the country. *I* see a dedicated team made up of men and women with extraordinary skills: they have a knack for cracking codes, they can speak German. And what an asset this is, during these troubled times, don't you agree?'

'Perhaps,' concedes the man.

I can feel Professor Walton's presence behind me – I don't know when he came to my side, and I don't want to know what he thinks about the way I have commandeered his little tour.

'More than anything,' I continue, 'these are men and women who gave up everything to come here, and work through the days, and nights, to provide you with information. Information that may save lives. Only if you allow us to.' I look him hard in the eye and try not to flinch. 'We are not the enemy. We are here to help you. The enemy is out there, and it's doing things to other human beings that make your stomach clench. And I hope we may defeat them. May the Nazis never put a single foot on our island. We are here to help you prevent that from happening.'

The silence lies like a blanket in the room, muffling all the sounds. The gentleman looks around. He really looks this time, and I hope he sees the piles of papers, our exhausted faces, how we all are a giant pulsing heart, beating for Britain, for each other, for our families, for everything we've ever cherished and loved.

The gentleman clears his throat. 'Why does this map appear to be the work of amateurs, then?'

The air wheezes out of my lungs. I think, *take the fall, Rose, take it for all of them.* For our little club. I risked. I lived. And now, I may have lost. 'I... I...'

Professor Walton steps forward and lays a hand on his arm. 'Naturally, as we explained in our reports, more funding is necessary for our operations.' He points at the map. 'We have a team of exceptionally dedicated people, and we have to make do with whatever we can find. Even if it means tearing atlases page by page.' He offers me a playful smile and I do all I can not to burst into tears. How could I have ever doubted him? Darling Professor Walton, who has always done for us as much as he could.

And then he does the most unbelievable thing in the world. He winks at me. 'But if you'd follow me, we could discuss this matter further, as well as the number of additional staff needed for our section—'

The professor leads Henry and the admiral outside. The door closes without a sound. I stand, my cheeks burning, my heart pounding. Nobody in the room knows quite what to say. When I turn, Esther and Lucy are behind me, quiet and immovable, at as much of a loss as I am.

Chapter Thirty-One

Rose

I try to work in the afternoon, but I find that I can't. Henry returns to us around two o'clock. I hold on tight to the trestle table, as if this could protect me from his fury. But there's no anger, just weariness.

'Go home, Miss Wiley,' he says.

This one short, dismissive sentence cuts deeper than a torrent of angry words. 'I—' I think, where's the professor? 'My shift isn't over yet.'

'Go home,' he says. 'Haven't you done enough today?'

Lucy pulls out her legs from under the table, enough for me to see the pink nylons. 'Fishnet,' she whispers. 'Better go now. We'll see you tonight.'

I collect my things – a purse, the empty holdall. Not much to show for my time here. All the parting words are stuck in my throat. The things I wanted to tell my colleagues. I look around the room, so I can step into it again in my mind every time I miss it: the wood-clad walls, the soft but dusty carpet. The squeaky trestle table, the piles of sheets. The strings of three-letter codes. Lucy's steely determination, Esther's delicacy. Ralph's kindness. He gets up and walks me to the door and shakes my arm again as though he wants to tear it off, just like that first time when we met. 'Jolly me, Rose, it has been such a pleasure working with you. You have no idea.'

I smile, unable to speak a word, unable to tell him how much I appreciated his kind presence those first few weeks here. 'Tell the professor I thank him,' I manage to mumble and head to the door.

I turn one last time. I say, 'Goodbye, all,' and then hurry out. I wouldn't want to make a scene, especially for Henry, though I could swear I caught him, out of the corner of my eye, waving. He's certainly pleased to see the back of me.

Nell arrives home at four in the afternoon. She finds me sitting on my bed, the few belongings I still have here scattered around me. 'What are you doing, Rose?'

'Packing.' I show her the empty holdall.

And then she does the most surprising thing in the world. She puts her arms around me and holds me tight. 'Darling Rose, I'll miss you so much. You've been such a breath of fresh air in my life.'

That's the moment when it all falls apart. That's the moment when I can't hold it all together anymore, and I start crying into her shoulder.

I'm still sobbing when the doorbell rings.

'I'll be right back up, love, all right?' says Nell.

There's a murmur downstairs, the sound of footsteps coming up the stairs. I think, heavens, I hope this isn't Tom.

But it isn't my landlord who appears in my cupboard of a room. There's no mistaking that brown tweed suit with crumpled lapels.

'Professor Walton!' I say.

'Miss Wiley,' he says, waves of indecision washing through his voice.

'Sit down,' says Nell and pulls out the only chair in the room for him. Professor Walton reaches into his pocket and hands me a handkerchief. Clean, but crumpled. I could almost laugh as pangs of guilt and fear course through my body.

'Professor. Why are you here?'

He looks at both me and at Nell. 'Elinor, if you don't mind… I know it's indelicate to throw you out of your own house, but this is truly top-secret business.'

'Yes, Nell, I think it might be better,' I say.

Nell crosses her arms and drops down onto the edge of the bad. 'Yes, it is indelicate to throw me out of the room, Rose, especially after I stole all those coordinates for you.'

Professor Walton opens and closes his mouth, like a fish on dry land. 'That was most imprudent of you, ladies, and only because I consistently lied through today, could I avoid serious consequences for both of you.'

'And we're grateful for that,' I say, tides of relief rising through my chest. 'Thank you.'

'You should also thank Mr Thornton for all the lies he told.'

'Henry?' I say. 'But he's been against the map ever since—'

Professor Walton raises his hand. 'I don't need to hear the details, Miss Wiley, thank you. Miss Stevens has been most forthcoming.' I think, *Lucy!* He rolls his eyes in an exaggerate manner and smiles at me. 'The sisterhood. Indeed.'

'We just wanted to do our best,' I say.

'And that's why you should have told me today what was coming,' says the professor with a side glance at Nell. 'In any case, I can't commend you for your work, because that would be forbidden, and as your superior, I should condemn this sort of rogue behaviour. It's illegal, to say the least. But.' He pushes his spectacles up the bridge of his nose and I can tell he's a bit nervous. 'You're a lucky young lady, Miss Wiley, because the admiral was very impressed by your map. And I used the opportunity to explain to him your...situation.'

I'm all ears, the whole of me intent on what the professor is about to say next.

'Miss Wiley, what would you make of that position as head of shift?'

'But...how? How is that even possible? I have to go back to Norfolk. I have to become a Land Girl.'

'Well, the Foreign Office may not be able to pull all the strings, but the Women's Royal Naval Service...that's an entirely different story. I've asked some questions, Miss Wiley. You can leave the Land Girls if you sign up for a different kind of war work.'

For a moment, I almost see myself in the chic blue uniform of the WRNS. The gleam of the gold buttons is almost blinding. And that fashionable cap! Me, a head of shift. An equal to Henry.

And then, David's face swims in front of my eyes. I'm not sure how kindly he would take to this. Especially since that future we both talked about is so close within our grasp. Or at least, a shadow of it.

'Thank you so much for this. All of this. For defending me when you didn't have to. For lying for us. For doing the impossible to keep me aboard.' I smile, the most genuine smile I've felt in weeks. I wonder if this kind, bohemian man even knows how much he's done for me. 'But I can't give you an answer now. And I have to return home tomorrow.'

Professor Walton's look says that he doesn't understand the first thing. Nell, the quiet presence in the room watching over me, takes him by the arm. 'Edmund, dear, thank you so much for all of this. You need to give Rose some time now. She needs to rest.'

Nell is in my room while I'm packing. 'Don't forget the pencils,' she says with a coy smile. She points at the coloured pencils on my table.

'Oh, no! I forgot to take them to work today. Can you please give them to—' Evie, I almost say, but then I remember she isn't here anymore. Esther told us she's going to America, of all the places in the world. Some of us are going back to a farm, and some are going to a different continent. 'Professor Walton,' I say.

'Of course.' She folds one of my shirts, into a perfect shape that won't crease. 'How is it to work with Edmund?'

There's the jangle of keys in the door, the thunk of heavy boots downstairs.

'Nell?' calls Tom.

'My, my, I forgot tea,' she says. 'What do I do now?'

'Well, there's no hiding anymore that something's afoot, is there? Do you reckon you should tell him?' I'm not sure what I should say – the waters of her marriage with Tom seem particularly tricky for Nell to navigate.

From the pocket of her apron, she extracts a banknote and a small pile of coins. 'Do you know, I think it might just be time. But what do I tell him?'

I wouldn't know where to start. What could she possibly tell him?

And then I think, what would Evie advise her to do? My mind is alight with ideas. An idea, to be precise. 'How about you take him out to the restaurant tonight?'

Nell's lovely features are afire. 'Do you know, Rose, that it's been more than a year since I've dined out? Could you call downstairs and tell Tom I'm getting ready?'

Nell emerges from her bedroom minutes later, dressed in a fine two-piece and a crisp white shirt. For once, she has let down her hair, and it's mesmerising: dark brown, and with the sheen of silk, falling in lovely curls over her shoulders. She's even put on some red lipstick, dark as wine. I give her the thumbs up and whisper, 'You're a sight for sore eyes.'

She smiles and bites her lip.

'Don't,' I say. 'You'll ruin your lipstick.'

After she goes down the stairs, I lean across the wooden banister to listen to their conversation. Nell says, 'Won't you put something nice on? I thought we could eat out tonight, at the Bletchley Hotel, like all the posh people.'

'Nell, have you gone out of your mind?' says Tom in his impossibly grating voice, like a nail rasping on metal. 'We barely have enough to scrape by.'

'This should be more than enough,' she says, and I think she is showing him the money. *Her* money. The money she made from her work.

'A week's wages,' she says.

There's a long pause in their conversation before I hear her voice again. 'All right, then come with me in your working clothes. If they let you in. We can talk about all this later, at the restaurant.'

Upstairs, for the first time in many days, I feel like dancing.

Chapter Thirty-Two

Evie

I ask Jasper if we could please go to one of the first-class bars and get one of those cocktails with the umbrellas stuck in them. He laughs and says that we have to take more care with our money. Buying expensive cocktails isn't something that Lucy Wiley would do during a transatlantic crossing by boat. Because Lucy Wiley is a secretary from the East End, and Lucy Wiley is careful how she spends her money.

I roll my eyes and laugh and tell him, 'Well, this is something this Lucy has yet to learn.'

Because Lucy Wiley made quite a sum of money after the sale of her Bentley. Or, better said, the sale of Evie's Bentley.

A third will go to the other Lucy, Lucy Stevens's family in Portsmouth.

A third will go into an account managed by Will, put aside

for a certain Elinor Thompson. Elinor doesn't know it yet: she will need it.

A third has gone into a secret pocket of a purse bought from a thrift store. Jasper had said, *no cheating, leave it all behind.* But Lucy turns out to be from the start a bit of a cheater. Evie Milton may have been spoiled and may never have had to worry about money in her life, but Lucy Wiley knows for a fact that money doesn't grow on trees.

When we decided to leave, that very night of the bomb and the opera, Jasper said that this is it. I have to leave my old life behind. Money, connections. Even my pearl necklace. I asked for a boon, and that was to insure my transfer to America. Where my father's connections might fail to find me, the secret services would not.

So I asked Alastair to help me and he did not, for the love of him, want to cross my father. I told him that all he had to do was to tell Papa that I'd been sent undercover for a secret operation. So secret, that I might not come up for air for all my life.

It turned out that Will had been right, and that was what Papa had always wanted to hear. The smile on Lucy Wiley's face in her new passport is genuine. Lucy is a new woman, free from everything that had been holding her back all her life.

And when Lucy roams the upper deck with Jasper in the evening, she smells the salt in the ocean breeze, and she looks to the horizon with hope. She almost never, ever thinks of the U-boats that might be lurking underneath.

Rose

We meet in the rye fields, the same place where we had our last conversation, that day when the Spitfire flew above. So little has changed – the bend of rye in the wind, the way the cap sits on David's head, the playful glow in his eyes.

So much has changed.

I touch his face, knowing what must now come. He caresses my cheek with the back of his hand. The tips of his fingers tickle my neck. The warmth of him makes my breath stop in my chest. He gives me a soft kiss that leaves my lips tingling. I wrap my arms around him. The feeling of him. So close.

So far away.

'Welcome home, Rose,' he says. His hands wander down, skirting my bosom, stopping at the waist.

For a moment, I think, why wouldn't he agree to it? Even weasel Tom had to concede to Nell, in the end, that it wasn't such a bad idea to do war work. My David, he's ten times cleverer than Tom. Why wouldn't he agree?

And then I think, because that's not what he wanted. He bargained for me, for all of me. Will just a bit, here and there, be enough?

I could once get lost in these rye fields, rolling from hill to hill to hill. But today, gaping in the distance, are the fresh wounds of asphalt and metal of the airfields. I think, I'm not the girl David bargained for. Like these fields that changed and bled and turned into something new. I think, I'm not that girl David fell in love with. I wonder if he can love me, this girl, as I am now.

And in this perfect sunset, in this stillness of late summer, I know there is no way back. I will have to tell him. I will have to show him who I am.

Epilogue

June 1941

'Do you know why you're here?' I ask the young RAF wing commander who sits across me.

I've learned to recognise their RAF and the Royal Navy's ranks in these few weeks since I've been conducting these interviews. I can tell a wing commander apart from a squadron leader from the other side of the room. Lucy keeps telling me this is truly important, indeed, whenever we make our day – or rather, evening – trips to London, we have to know who we're conniving with.

And I learned to tell more than that at a single glance. For instance, judging by the posture – back straight, shoulders pulled back and down – and the expensive watch at his wrist, this young man comes from a wealthy family. The kind of family that sent their children for a few months to Germany before the war to learn the language, and rub shoulders with other wealthy young people on the Continent.

Just like Evie, I think, and feel for the string of pearls, hidden under the pristine outer layer of my uniform. Darling Evie, who taught me so much about hiding, and about secrets, and gliding through the world. Her brother, Will, has conveyed more to me than a piece of jewellery that was meant to buy forgiveness for leaving us at such a difficult time. But forgiveness had long been granted – was not even required. I understand why she had to leave, and why she cannot write to us. We're barely at the beginning of all that is to come; our paths are bound to cross again.

And my own journey has brought me here today.

The young man shakes his head and pulls at the collar of his shirt. He might be nervous, but he might just as well be unbearably warm. The office where I'm conducting the interview is in an RAF hangar made of tin, and the improbable heat of the June sun turns it into an oven. I'd love to be able to take off my WRNS jacket and my tricorne hat underneath which my curls have surely been flattened.

I wouldn't have thought about taking off my beautiful double-breasted jacket, with its gleaming golden buttons, back when I first received it last year. I only took it off when I went to bed. After a brief stint of military training, I was transferred within Bletchley – but to another section.

A new section.

I wipe the smile off my face like a lipstick that isn't suited to the occasion, and proceed with my next question. 'Is it true that you speak German?'

The wing commander blushes and holds my gaze. 'Yes. Is that a crime? Why am I here?'

'I ask the questions for now, Wing Commander Granger.

How good would you say your German is? How did you come to learn it?'

The young man clears his throat. 'My grandmother was Austrian.'

I pretend to write something down. A bead of sweat trickles down my back. There are wounds so fresh that they still pull and smart. There are abandonments that will still hurt for a time to come. There are gambles that I lost. There are words, like 'You don't love me like you said, Rose,' and 'What will everyone else say?' and 'I can't do this,' that I will carry with me wherever I go. But while I don't forget, I'm better at keeping them hidden behind a shield of steel. And I speak from behind this shield when I ask Wing Commander Granger, 'And you speak German in the family?'

'No, my parents hired a German tutor. And I studied German literature in Heidelberg for a year, before I started helping my father with the estate.'

'What year was that?'

'1934.'

And the higher I rise, the more responsibilities I am given, and the stronger my shields become. I don't even shy away from amusing myself at the expense of people of the ilk of Wing Commander Granger here, a brilliant catch, in fact. Clever, educated. High enough in the RAF to be of actual use as an analyst. The briefing from my new head of section, Mr du Crecy, was clear enough: 'The best of the best, Rose. We can have our pick.'

And why shouldn't we? We probably do the most interesting work in Bletchley Park. All the decrypts in all the sections reach us, too, not only units in the field of battle. We're the ones who put disjointed messages together, analyse battle plans, formations, supply lines. We compile the most sophisticated and complete intelligence reports.

We're the ones who know what's happening: at home, abroad, and within the confines of the park. We're at the beating heart of this war.

The wing commander wrings his hands.

'Do you know what we do with people who know German?' I say, leaning in.

The young man shakes his head, all the blood gone from his face.

'We give them a job.'

THE END

ONE MORE CHAPTER

The author and One More Chapter would like to thank everyone who contributed to the publication of this story...

Analytics
Emma Harvey
Connor Hayes
Maria Osa

Audio
Charlotte Brown

Contracts
Olivia Bignold-Jordan
Florence Shepherd

Design
Lucy Bennett
Fiona Greenway
Holly Macdonald
Liane Payne
Dean Russell
Caroline Young

Digital Sales
Hannah Lismore
Fliss Porter
Georgina Ugen
Kelly Webster

Editorial
Charlotte Ledger
Nicky Lovick
Lydia Mason
Bethan Morgan
Jennie Rothwell
Kimberley Young

Harper360
Emily Gerbner
Jean Marie Kelly
Juliette Pasquini
emma sullivan

HarperCollins Canada
Peter Borcsok

International Sales
Hannah Avery
Alice Gomer
Phillipa Walker

Marketing & Publicity
Emma Petfield
Sara Roberts
Helena Towers

Operations
Melissa Okusanya
Hannah Stamp

Production
Denis Manson
Simon Moore
Sophie Waeland

Rights
Lana Beckwith
Samuel Birkett
Aliona Ladus
Agnes Rigou
Zoe Shine

Aisling Smyth
Emily Yolland

The HarperCollins Distribution Team

The HarperCollins Finance & Royalties Team

The HarperCollins Legal Team

The HarperCollins Technology Team

Trade Marketing
Ben Hurd

UK Sales
Yazmeen Akhtar
Laura Carpenter
Isabel Coburn
Jay Cochrane
Sarah Munro
Gemma Rayner
Erin White
Leah Woods

And every other essential link in the chain from delivery drivers to booksellers to librarians and beyond!

ONE MORE CHAPTER

One More Chapter is an
award-winning global
division of HarperCollins.

Subscribe to our newsletter to get our
latest eBook deals and stay up to date
with all our new releases!

signup.harpercollins.co.uk/
join/signup-omc

Meet the team at
www.onemorechapter.com

Follow us!
 @OneMoreChapter_
@OneMoreChapter
@onemorechapterhc
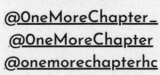

Do you write unputdownable fiction?
We love to hear from new voices.
Find out how to submit your novel at
www.onemorechapter.com/submissions